JUST ONE NIGHT

"Hold me," Alyssa said simply.

Morgan adjusted his leg more comfortably against her and pulled up the blankets. He softly kissed her temple while she absently stroked his chest, curling her fingers through the crisp hairs.

"It was a very...interesting experience," Alyssa murmured.

"Interesting!" Morgan howled, not sure he liked her description of what just happened. "A man does not appreciate his lover referring to him as interesting, my dear."

His lover! The words had such a marvelously wicked sound, they made Alyssa smile and say, "Shall I instead sing your praises, Your Grace?"

"You impudent baggage." He gave her a carefree grin. "I do believe we are acquainted well enough for you to address me by my given name. Don't you agree?"

"Of course, Morgan."

"Did you enjoy our intimacy?"

"Ummm," she murmured. "But I'm afraid there won't be another time, Morgan. I must return to my room. It shall be light soon."

Other *Leisure Books* by Adrienne Basso:
NOTORIOUS DECEPTION

INTIMATE BETRAYAL

ADRIENNE BASSO

LEISURE BOOKS   **NEW YORK CITY**

In memory of my mother,
Gloria DeStefanis Gambarani,
who would have been so proud.
And for my father, John, who is.

Leisure Entertainment Service Co., Inc. (LESCO Distribution Group)

A LESCO Edition

Published by special arrangement with Dorchester Publishing Co., Inc.

Printed in the United States of America.

Chapter One

Hampshire, England: 1813.

The sleek curricle traveled the dusty, rutted road at a clipping pace. The inferior road conditions and constant jostling did little to improve the mood of its driver and sole occupant. Morgan Edmund Harcourt Ashton, sixth Duke of Gillingham, stared gloomily ahead and concentrated on keeping his high-spirited bay geldings under control. The trip had been fraught with inconveniences from the start, and with darkness fast approaching, the duke grudgingly admitted he was lost.

"Damn Jason Cameron," the duke swore under his breath, cursing his absent secretary. "At the very least the man could have gotten accurate directions to this bloody place."

As the duke began mentally reviewing his rather limited options, he spied a young boy ahead, sprinting out of the woods on the right side of the road, a rope of impressively large fish strung carelessly over his shoulder. The duke urged his horses to an even faster pace as he keenly observed the lad's progress over the embankment and across the road. In desperation, lest he lose this one chance at finding his elusive destination before nightfall, the duke uncharacteristically let out a loud, shrill whistle.

The boy's head turned sharply at the unexpected noise. Seeing the huge horses rapidly bearing down, the boy moved swiftly off the road to avoid being trampled. His young face registered surprise when the smart-looking curricle unexpectedly pulled alongside him.

"Can you tell me"—the duke shouted to be heard above the snorting and pawing of the bays—"will this path bring me to the Hampton Gate crossroad that leads to Westgate Manor?"

"Yes, milord," the lad replied respectfully. Pointing straight ahead, he added helpfully, " 'Tis just around the next curve."

Nodding his thanks, the duke gave the horses their lead and expertly guided them into the turn. According to his secretary's rather scant directions, another four miles would bring him to Westgate Manor's front door. Allowing himself to relax a bit, the duke eased back slightly in his seat and let his mind replay the astonishing events of the past 24 hours.

Yesterday had begun badly. Morgan awoke much later than usual, hampered by a monumental hangover and only a dim recollection of the previous evening's occurrences. He distinctly remembered arriving at his club on St. James Street, but could not recall precisely when or how he returned from an evening that included overindulging in brandy, gambling until the early hours of the morning, and spending several hours in the arms of the leading lady of Covent Garden's latest production. Compounding the day's problems was the necessity of attending a private luncheon at Carlton House with the regent, an event the duke sorely wished he could beg off from, and knowing that was impossible only worsened his mood.

Arriving at Carlton House barely on time, the duke was kept waiting, clicking his heels in annoyance, until the regent, corseted in his latest and thus far most splendid field marshal's uniform, was ready to receive him. Even though the duke was too young to be a member of the raffish Carlton House set, the regent liked him and considered Morgan a special confidant.

At 35 the duke was 15 years younger than the prince, yet it was often the regent who asked for advice, especially in matters of money. The duke had a remarkable talent for making money, while the Regent was a known spendthrift, constantly in debt and living a life-style well beyond his income.

"Lady Hertford informs me you caused quite a stir at Almack's the other evening," the regent said as an elegantly garbed footman in scarlet livery served the turtle soup. "Rumors abound that you are considering marrying again."

The duke paused with his gold soup spoon in midair and, giving the regent an amused grin, replied, "Heaven save us, sire, from the matchmaking efforts of Lady Hertford and the meddling patronesses of Almack's."

"Quite right, Morgan," the regent laughingly agreed. "They spot an unattached man, titled, handsome, and rich and it sets them all aflutter. It's unavoidable, I'm afraid. Can't seem to help themselves, poor creatures. Must be in the blood." The prince slurped noisily at his soup. "Still, it can't be denied. You are an excellent catch."

"You flatter me, sire," the duke exclaimed, feeling

genuinely uncomfortable at the truthful remark. Being considered a plum marriage prize and one of the most eligible and elusive bachelors of the ton depressed Morgan. He would never marry again. His brief marriage several years earlier had been a painful, dismal failure, and under no circumstances was he willing to subject himself to a second fiasco.

"I respectfully request a change of subject, sire. I find I am fast losing my appetite for this sumptuous meal."

The regent, his own unhappy marriage to Princess Charlotte a disaster by all accounts, was glad to comply. "I must tell you about the new Dutch paintings Lady Hertford and I chose for my collection." Breathing a sigh of relief, the duke listened politely while the regent spoke enthusiastically of his latest art acquisitions.

With luncheon concluded and the new Dutch paintings seen and admired, the duke was finally able to take his leave. Waiting outside Carlton House for his carriage to be brought around, he filled his lungs deeply with the cool fresh air, attempting to clear his muddled head and vowing to never again spend another night like the last.

"I am getting too damn old for this sort of thing," Morgan muttered under his breath as he climbed into the waiting coach. However, he quickly pulled up short when he saw the carriage was already occupied.

"What the hell!" he exclaimed in annoyance. He felt two strong hands forcibly shove him inside the coach. Morgan instinctively thrust out his arms to keep himself from sprawling onto the carriage floor. The door was quickly latched behind him, leaving the duke only a few seconds to straighten himself before the vehicle began moving.

"Please excuse these rather unorthodox circumstances, Your Grace." A man seated in the far corner of the coach spoke quietly, his features indistinguishable in the shadows. "It is imperative that our meeting be kept confidential."

"Lord Castlereagh?" the duke queried in an amazed tone, thinking he recognized the stranger's voice, yet finding it almost impossible to believe a government official as important as the foreign secretary would act in such a ridiculous manner.

"I am impressed," came the reply. Lord Castlereagh leaned forward into the small band of light coming through the partially drawn shade. "Again I apologize for my rudeness, but we have been unsuccessful for the past few days in arranging a chance meeting."

The duke shook his head in puzzlement. "I saw you at White's last evening, did I not?"

"Ah, so you do recall. I thought you looked none the worse for wear, but my man informed me you were drinking for several hours before I arrived."

"Things did get a bit out of hand," the duke admitted ruefully. "It was a celebratory evening. My brother Tristan has recently become engaged."

"Congratulations."

Lord Castlereagh paused a moment before continuing. "First I must inform you I am here under the direct orders of the prime minister. Lord Liverpool and I have discussed this matter at length and have both determined you not only have the right to know, but ultimately may be able to assist us in discovering the truth."

Pausing dramatically for effect, Lord Castlereagh announced somberly, "It appears, sir, according to our latest intelligence reports, you are using your considerable power to aid the emperor Napoleon."

"What! I know the country has gone mad over this damnable war with France, but that is a totally ludicrous accusation."

Pleased with the duke's reaction, Lord Castlereagh

held up his hand to stop Morgan's tirade. "We have uncovered enough inconsistencies to know you are being deliberately incriminated, Your Grace. Yet the evidence against you is considerable and warrants an investigation. This situation is rapidly escalating into a major concern for the war department. For nearly two months, vital information has been moving both in and out of England through a network of French spies who are routinely receiving and sending couriers along a stretch of secluded private beach in Portsmouth, near Ramsgate Castle."

"My private beach?"

"Precisely."

The duke grimaced. "I find it difficult to believe my people are involved with French spies, Lord Castlereagh. Nearly everyone who lives at Ramsgate Castle has been with my family for generations."

"At this point we have no concrete proof anyone from the estate is directly involved, except for the manufactured evidence against you personally. It is clear, however, someone who is very knowledgeable about the activities on your property is aiding these spies. And implicating you."

The duke leaned back in his seat, unconsciously drumming his fingertips on the armrest. "I can't think of anyone, but apparently no one is above suspicion."

"The war department agrees, and therein lies the dilemma. All we know for certain is the person directing these activities is called the Falcon. We thought the inner circle of this organization was successfully infiltrated. Regretfully our informant's body was found in a London brothel three days ago."

The duke sat up abruptly. "My grandmother, the dowager duchess, is currently in residence at Ramsgate. Is she in any immediate danger?"

"I don't believe the dowager is in any personal danger, but it might be prudent to move her elsewhere until this mess is resolved."

"Clearly you are not acquainted with my grand-mother," the duke remarked dryly. The dowager duchess was not a woman to be "moved elsewhere." Morgan seriously doubted there ever was a time when others told the dowager duchess what to do.

Addressing the current problem, Morgan asked simply, "What is to be done, Lord Castlereagh?"

The foreign secretary took a moment to scrutinize the man sitting opposite him. He was not personally acquainted with the duke, but the prime minister expressed complete confidence and trust in the duke's abilities. "A plan has been devised to unmask the Falcon. Will you assist us?"

Morgan did not hesitate for an instant. "When do we begin?"

A sudden jolting of the curricle as it hit a deep rut jarred the duke back to the present. He was relieved to discover he had successfully reached the drive to Westgate Manor. All was quiet as he drove up the gravel drive. Halting the energetic bays in front of the stone portico, the duke waited expectantly for a servant to emerge from the house and offer assistance. He was traveling without the benefit of servants because his secretary, Jason Cameron, had taken ill that morning, and Morgan wanted no one in his household aware of his comings and goings.

An unusual set of circumstances brought Morgan to Westgate Manor on this brisk February afternoon. Early last week, Lord Jeremy Carrington, the Viscount Mulgrave, created quite a stir as he stood atop a table in the middle of White's dining hall.

"Your attention, gentlemen," Lord Carrington shouted. "It is my intention to sell off, this very instant, to the highest bidder, my country estate known as Westgate Manor. 'Tis a fine property, located in the county of Hampshire. The sale I now propose shall include the manor house, its furnishings, and all surrounding properties. Who will be so bold as to give the opening bid?"

After deciding Lord Carrington was not in his cups and was perfectly serious, Morgan entered the impromptu auction and at the conclusion of the heated bidding found himself the new owner of Westgate Manor. Viscount Mulgrave accepted Morgan's chit with a distracted air and enthusiastically returned to the gaming tables.

Morgan gave no further thought to the estate until several days ago when his secretary produced the deed of ownership. Acting on impulse, Morgan decided to stop at Westgate Manor before continuing on to Ramsgate Castle in Portsmouth. Sitting alone in the biting wind, the duke was now regretting that impulse.

He stomped his feet vigorously on the carriage floorboards to stay warm and took a good look at his new property. It was a pretty house, large in size, yet not overbearing. There were symmetrical leaded glass bay windows, carved corner posts, and high gables proclaiming its Elizabethan origins. At one time it had been an impressive property, but the peeling paint and falling brickwork attested to the fact it had been neglected for some time.

Morgan was not surprised. Jeremy Carrington did not strike him as a man who would spend his money on the upkeep of a country estate. Overall, the house appeared to be in better condition than Morgan had anticipated.

"Damn inconvenient," Morgan muttered, his impatience growing over the lack of servants.

Before he was able to give a rather undignified yell to gain some attention, the heavy oak door slowly creaked open. A man Morgan could only classify as well advanced in years descended the three stone front steps in a measured, dignified manner. Looking at his formal attire and stiff demeanor, the duke correctly surmised he was the butler.

"Can I be of assistance, my lord?" the older man asked tonelessly.

The duke favored him with a chilling stare, but the stouthearted butler stood his ground. With a grunt of admiration, the duke jumped gracefully down from the curricle, tossing the stone-faced butler the reins.

"Kindly inform Viscount Mulgrave the Duke of Gillingham has arrived," Morgan instructed. "And have someone fetched to see to my horses."

The butler nodded his snow-white head in understanding, expertly transferred the reins to one hand, and raised his unencumbered white-gloved hand slightly. Almost magically, a thin young man appeared from behind a tall hedge to lead the horses and carriage away. Relieved of the burden of the reins, the butler walked slowly up the steps and expectantly held the door for the duke.

Morgan paused momentarily in the entrance hall as the butler divested him of his hat, gloves, and greatcoat. He was then silently led to the front salon, poured an excellent glass of brandy, and left to his own thoughts.

Alyssa Carrington sat back in the tall wooden chair clasping a lukewarm cup of tea in her hand. She had been trying to enjoy the fragrant brew for the past half hour, but thus far had been interrupted twice to attend to estate business. Listening with half an ear as the cook, Mrs. Stratton, repeated various pieces of local gossip, Alyssa now absently sipped the beverage, hoping for a few quiet moments.

"Lady Alyssa," Mrs. Stratton admonished in a stern voice, "you have barely touched my apple tart. I made

15

it especially the way you prefer, with extra cinnamon."

"It looks wonderful," Alyssa instantly replied. Hoping to avoid a long discourse on how she must eat more because she was too thin, Alyssa broke off a small portion of the tart and began vigorously chewing.

Satisfied that her mistress would comply with her wishes, Mrs. Stratton returned to the large stockpot simmering on the stove. Deftly she chopped onions and carrots, adding them to the broth. The pungent aroma drifted through the air, giving the kitchen a feeling of comfort and warmth completely separate from the heat radiating from the iron stove.

Alyssa closed her eyes and savored the warmth of the cluttered kitchen. She always tried spending at least an hour of her busy day here; partially to escape the endless flood of difficulties encountered in running Westgate Manor, but mostly because she enjoyed the friendly atmosphere.

Mrs. Stratton could always be counted upon to know the very latest gossip from the neighboring estates, and even though Alyssa knew she shouldn't encourage it, she was frankly curious about this strange world of the aristocracy that was virtually cut off to her. For years Alyssa was concerned about her neighbors' impressions of her unorthodox life, but after hearing about the local gentry's reckless and occasionally shocking behavior, she doubted her eccentricities would be of much interest to them.

Her father, Viscount Mulgrave, was a man who detested country life and spent the majority of his time in the clubs and gambling dens of London, leaving his young motherless daughter to be raised by servants and a succession of governesses. It was an unconventional and oftentimes lonely upbringing, but not an unhappy one. The servants at the manor soon adopted the somber little girl into their hearts and Alyssa grew to maturity surrounded by love.

By the time she reached an age to be introduced into society, her father was too far in debt to consider wasting money on a lavish coming-out season in London. Consequently, at 24 Alyssa was unmarried, with no prospects and a realistic acceptance of her life as a spinster. She never let on if this upset her, because she had taken on a far more formidable task than marriage—the running of the estate.

It was an unlikely occupation for a young woman, but Alyssa embraced her role in her usual forthright manner. She did not hesitate to ask for help from those she trusted, the men who worked and lived on the tenant farms for generations. Her knowledge increased steadily over the years and in some instances surpassed those men who taught her. The estate flourished under her guidance, and her tenants, skeptical at first, embraced her heartily for her fairness and genuine feeling for the land and its people.

Alyssa was pleased with her success, and although the burdens became almost overwhelming at times, she felt useful and accomplished. The only dark clouds appeared when her father would make an unexpected visit. Lord Carrington was constantly looking for funds, indulging in too much drink, insulting the servants, and generally making a nuisance of himself. Thankfully his visits were short and well spaced.

Alyssa was taking another bite of the scrumptious apple tart when the butler, Perkins, suddenly appeared in the doorway. She immediately noticed he was wearing his coat and gloves. The piece of pastry fell to her stomach like a stone. Perkins only wore formal attire when there was a stranger at the manor. And strangers only came to collect on gambling debts.

"He is in the front salon, Lady Alyssa," Perkins informed her quietly, reading the stricken look on her face.

17

At the butler's announcement Mrs. Stratton turned sharply, watching Alyssa with anxious eyes. It is always the same, Alyssa thought miserably, feeling the tension building in the room.

"Did this gentleman give his name?" she questioned, slowly rising to her feet.

"He claims to be the Duke of Gillingham."

A duke! Alyssa was momentarily stunned. This was very unusual. Only the truly desperate men came themselves; most sent a secretary or lawyer to collect on the markers Jeremy Carrington wagered when he ran short of funds but refused to leave the gaming tables. She silently prayed there was another, less costly reason for this man's appearance.

"Do you think he really is a duke?" Alyssa asked, trusting Perkins's opinion.

Perkins thoughtfully considered the question before responding. "He is expensively dressed and carries himself with a duke's arrogance. He gave the impression we were expecting him, yet he arrived alone, without servants."

This was odd, Alyssa thought. "Thank you, Perkins. I shall attend our duke at once."

Alyssa quietly followed the butler through the kitchen and up to the main entrance hall. Pausing a brief moment outside the salon door, she successfully conquered an almost uncontrollable urge to turn and flee. Taking several deep breaths to steady her nerves, Alyssa finally nodded slightly, and Perkins opened the door.

She entered the room soundlessly and stood in the doorway. She remained unobserved until the door closed behind her. At the sound, the duke turned expectantly. She saw surprise register briefly in his face before his features took on a questioning look.

Alyssa nearly gasped aloud as she got her first good look at him. The elegant man standing before her was unlike anyone she had ever seen, or even imagined. His hard masculine presence seemed to fill the room, and Alyssa found herself unwittingly staring at his bronzed face, admiring the finely chiseled features.

The duke was a tall man, powerfully built, with broad shoulders and muscular legs. He was dressed impeccably in a slate-blue double-breasted coat, fitted snugly over a high-collared white waistcoat and accented with a faultlessly tied cravat. His fawn-colored leather breeches clung tightly to his legs and fitted expertly into his polished black knee-high Hessian boots. His hair was jet black in color, cut close to his head and curling slightly at the ends. He took several steps closer and Alyssa became captivated by his hypnotic silver-gray eyes.

Beautiful. The word echoed through Alyssa's mind. He was positively beautiful. This stranger was such a cut above the usual men her father associated with, Alyssa felt certain she misjudged his reason for visiting Westgate Manor.

Forcefully shaking herself out of her admiring stupor, Alyssa spoke. "Good afternoon, Your Grace. I see Perkins has provided you with some refreshment." She gracefully inclined her head toward the half-empty glass of brandy he held. "Is there anything further we may bring you?"

"I was expecting Viscount Mulgrave," the duke replied in confusion. "Or if he is unavailable, perhaps the estate agent can be summoned."

Alyssa's heart sank at his words. If this beautiful stranger wanted to see the estate agent, he wanted a gambling debt settled. Unconsciously she let out a sigh of disappointment, but regained her composure quickly when she noticed the duke watching her closely.

"Please follow me." Alyssa turned on her heel and swept out of the room with regal disdain, wanting very much to conclude this unpleasant task. The duke barely had time to catch his breath before she disappeared.

"What the devil is going on?" he shouted. Temper rising, the duke slammed his brandy glass down on the mantel and raced after Alyssa's retreating figure.

He crossed the vast entrance hall in several long strides, catching up with Alyssa as she reached the heavy paneled doors of the drawing room. She swung the doors open in a dramatic manner and strode purposefully into the room, never once glancing back to see if the duke was following.

Alyssa headed directly for a mahogany leather-topped desk from which she produced an account ledger and a pair of small, round, gold-rimmed reading glasses. Perching the glasses on the edge of her nose, she spoke to Morgan in a cool tone. "Shall we conclude your business as swiftly as possible, Your Grace?"

The duke stood in the doorway carefully scrutinizing the room, not quite sure if his eyes were deceiving him. The last remaining rays of sunlight streamed through the open drapes, casting a golden hue on the room's contents. It was an amazing sight. Long wooden tables joined together against the wall were filled with gold, silver, and bronze plate. Running through the center of the room were six rows of additional tables that held magnificent objects of beauty and art collected from previous centuries and various parts of the world. Unusual Chinese vases stood on one table, a set of early Byzantine chalices on another.

Venetian glass sculptures stood side by side with crystal goblets and porcelain figurines. A spectacular jade collection filled a large glass curio cabinet in the corner, and the walls were hung with countless paintings, from the Italian Renaissance to seventeenth-century Dutch. Even the regent's most lavish rooms in Carlton House paled in comparison to the treasures housed in this room.

Alyssa observed the duke's reaction carefully. Finally he sent a questioning glance her way, surprising her. There were always different reactions upon first entering this room, but in Alyssa's experience a face struck with awe eventually turned to one of greed. Puzzled, Alyssa questioned the duke.

"Am I not correct in thinking you have come to Westgate Manor to collect on a debt owed you by Viscount Mulgrave?"

Morgan favored Alyssa with a long stare, his patience giving out.

"Madam, if you harbor any hope of retaining your position in this household you shall immediately produce the viscount, or his agent, or some person in authority so I may conduct my business," Morgan declared in a tight voice.

"I run the estate, Your Grace," Alyssa replied, matching the curtness of his tone.

"And who the devil are you?" he shouted.

"Alyssa Carrington," she answered, her voice also rising in volume.

"His wife?"

"His daughter," she corrected.

Her answer stunned him. She was dressed like a servant. Nay, worse than a servant. The duke's eyes raked her in puzzled appraisal, taking in every aspect of her appearance with a critical eye. She was tall, taller than most women he was acquainted with, and she held herself erect, almost rigid. Her face was angular, with high cheekbones, a straight, defined nose, and a full, wide mouth. Her complexion was fair, with just a hint of color in her cheeks. It was, however, her eyes that drew him. Even behind the lenses of her glasses he could see they were almond shaped, deep green in color, accented by lashes that were long, dark, and full. They gave her an exotic, almost mysterious look.

Her hair was pulled back in a most unbecoming manner, making it difficult to determine the color. Her gown was a drab-brown garment, very plain and hopelessly out of fashion. It was too loose and too short and completely hid her figure. Still, her lovely face held Morgan's attention against his will. She was not beautiful in the conventional sense, but her features were classic and she radiated an aura of confidence and refinement he found utterly intriguing.

"I was unaware Jeremy Carrington had any family living at Westgate Manor."

"Well, he does." Alyssa directed a withering look at the duke. He ignored it.

"You run the estate, Lady Carrington?"

"Miss Carrington," she corrected in a tight voice.

"I beg your pardon?"

"Lady Carrington was my mother. I prefer to be addressed as Miss Carrington."

"Very well, Miss Carrington," the duke replied in a deep voice, punctuating each syllable. "Do you run the estate?"

"Yes, I am in charge."

"What then, may I ask, is all of this?" Morgan queried sarcastically, sweeping his arm about the room. "Your private study where you conduct estate business?"

"Not exactly." Alyssa responded with a distinctly challenging note in her voice and a decidedly stubborn look in her rich green eyes.

She could see he was having difficulty controlling his anger, yet she refused to volunteer any additional information. She knew she was being rude, but she honestly did not care. After all, the duke had not explained the purpose of his sudden unannounced appearance even though she understood all too well why he was at the manor. Feeling completely justified, Alyssa stood her ground.

"Start at the beginning, Miss Carrington," he commanded softly.

"Beginning of what, Your Grace?"

That remark brought Morgan swiftly into the room and up to the edge of the desk. The dark scowl on his handsome face told Alyssa she had pushed him too far.

"Do not play games with me, Miss Carrington. I warn you, I am in no mood for them," he threatened softly.

Alyssa's composure slipped slightly as the duke leaned menacingly across the desk to emphasize his point. He was so close she could feel his warm breath on her face. Her heart thumped wildly. Wisely, she decided to comply with his demands for answers.

"Lord Carrington, as you have already discovered, is not in residence at the moment. In his absence I take responsibility for these ... umm ... matters of business. I assume he owes you a sum of money?"

The duke's scowl darkened and Alyssa hurriedly continued.

"I have inventoried and cataloged the various items in this room. As you can plainly see, all are of great value: some are considered priceless. You may select any item or items that are equal in value to the sum owed you by Lord Carrington. If you prefer your debt to be settled in coin, I respectfully request you grant me 24 hours to procure the necessary funds. May I inquire how much you are owed?"

"A well-rehearsed speech. I can only surmise you have done this before."

Alyssa glanced at Morgan sternly but refused to answer his taunt. "May I have the marker, Your Grace?" she asked, extending her hand gracefully.

For a split second Morgan was tempted to give her

the deed of ownership in his possession, but even he could not be so cruel. Clearly Alyssa Carrington did not have any idea what her father had done. Glancing at her thoughtfully, it struck him suddenly what an absurd picture she made, standing amid the glitter and splendor of this room in her drab gown.

"Is there something you do not understand, Your Grace?"

No, he thought, it is all perfectly clear. Characteristically deciding that straight-out was the only way both to dispense and receive bad news, Morgan spoke.

"I regret having to be the one to inform you, Miss Carrington, but I am now the owner of Westgate Manor."

Chapter Two

Alyssa stared at Morgan in shock, her face void of color. A lump formed in her throat and she swallowed hard, attempting to dislodge it.

"May I see the marker?" she repeated in a quiet voice.

Morgan reached into his breast pocket and withdrew the property deed. Wordlessly he handed it to her. He watched her carefully, not really certain what to expect. His vast experience with women had taught him they were emotional creatures. In times of crisis they usually fainted or became hysterical.

Alyssa Carrington did neither. She accepted the paper with steady hands and read it thoroughly. The entire estate, the manor house and its furnishings, the stables, the tenant farms, and all surrounding properties.

Raising confused eyes to the duke, Alyssa again stated her request. "I want to see Lord Carrington's marker, Your Grace. Not the property deed."

Morgan understood. "I did not win the estate in a

card game, Miss Carrington. I purchased the property at auction."

"Auction? I read no notice in the newspaper."

The duke shifted uncomfortably on his feet. Her quiet pain stirred strong feelings of guilt. "I don't believe a notice was printed."

"I see," Alyssa replied vaguely. "May I be so bold as to inquire the price you paid?"

The duke reluctantly named a figure Alyssa knew was more than fair. She nodded her head slowly, trying desperately to assimilate the information. Deep within her heart she always knew this day would arrive, but that did not lesson the shock. She felt a warm numbness engulf her body and allowed herself to succumb to it. Off in the distance she heard a deep, rich voice.

"Are you all right, Miss Carrington?"

She looked up at the duke and saw the concerned expression on his handsome features.

"I am perfectly fine," Alyssa responded slowly, her voice sounding strangely far away to her ears. She gave a small, high-pitched laugh. "I guess this means you will be staying for dinner. I must inform Mrs. Stratton."

Alyssa methodically removed her glasses and arranged the papers on her desk before walking toward the drawing room doors. Upon reaching her destination, she straightened her back, squared her shoulders, and turned to face the duke.

"Perkins will show you to your rooms and offer any assistance you need." Alyssa stumbled slightly over the word *your* but retained her composure. "If you will please excuse me, I must speak with the cook. I shall see you at dinner." She offered him a deep curtsy and quit the room.

Perkins appeared immediately, leaving Morgan to wonder if he was eavesdropping. One look at the butler's distressed expression confirmed that he had been.

Lead on, Perkins," Morgan drawled. "And be sure to bring a full decanter of brandy along." Morgan had a feeling he was going to need it before the night was over.

Alyssa headed directly for the kitchen to speak with Mrs. Stratton. Dinner arrangements had to be made, but more important, the staff had to be told the devastating news.

When she arrived, the small staff was beginning the evening meal. Hawkins, the groundskeeper, was slicing a large loaf of bread while the maids, Lucy and Molly, filled the glasses and brought the rest of the meal to the table. Young Ned, who took care of the horses, was flirting outrageously with the maids, causing them to simper and giggle. Mavis, the old nanny who raised Alyssa and her mother before her, was scolding Ned to stop pestering the girls, which only increased his efforts to gain their attention. Mrs. Stratton was serving soup from a large tureen as she supervised the group, calling her commands loudly over the cheerful chatter.

Alyssa paused, drinking in all the sights, sounds, and smells that were so familiar. These people represented the only family she had ever known, and now they would be separated. Her eyes filled suddenly with tears, and her body was held motionless by the enormity of what her father had done. Her heart was beating with such force she felt it rising into her throat, and she was overcome with a feeling of total helplessness.

I will be strong, Alyssa admonished herself. Swallowing her tears, she cleared her throat loudly to gain everyone's attention. Weighing her words carefully she spoke.

"The Duke of Gillingham has informed me that he is now the owner of Westgate Manor." Mrs. Stratton gasped and nearly dropped the hot soup in Ned's lap. Molly began to whimper. The others remained silent.

"I know this is a terrible blow for us all, but the duke seems a fair man, and I shall do everything in my power to secure your positions at the manor before I take my leave. Can you serve dinner in an hour, Mrs. Stratton?"

Mrs. Stratton, speechless with emotion, nodded her head.

"I shall tell Perkins to set the table in the main dining room. Ned can help him serve."

Alyssa anxiously searched the servants' grave faces. So many thoughts and emotions rushed through her mind, but she could barely formulate a coherent sentence. "I shall miss you so very much," she finally uttered in a soft whisper.

With that said, Alyssa quickly withdrew, leaving the stunned group to stare at each other in shocked silence.

Alyssa was waiting in the dining room when the duke arrived. Upon his arrival they were seated and dinner began. Morgan felt strange sitting at the head of the table, but he made no comment. Alyssa sat on his right, and he was curious but not displeased by the intimate arrangement.

He noticed she was wearing a different gown, and although the soft gray color was a slight improvement over the hideous brown, it fit just as poorly. He caught himself wondering what her figure was like beneath the loose garment, and was amazed at the direction of his thoughts.

His relationships with women since the death of his wife had been limited to brief, mutually satisfactory liaisons that seldom lasted more than a few months.

Morgan was a handsome, titled, wealthy man with a reputation for being a generous lover, and he attracted more than his share of female admiration.

Some women were intimidated by his haughty demeanor, but most found him a fascinating challenge and went to great lengths to capture his attention. He found their efforts flattering and occasionally amusing. Yet he never felt any interest in a female until she had made it abundantly clear she would welcome his advances. Until now.

Morgan glanced speculatively around the dining room as Perkins served the soup. The evening shadows were reflected in the soft glow of the numerous candles strategically placed on the mahogany dining table and sideboard. He surmised the candlelight hid a multitude of sins, yet even in the dim light Morgan could see the faded wallpaper was sporadically brighter in spots where a painting or wall adornment had obviously been removed.

The starkness of the room seemed to emphasize the grandeur of the table setting of cream-colored porcelain dishes, delicate gold-and-silver filigree flatware, and fine diamond-cut crystal goblets. The duke grinned as he pictured the very proper Perkins raiding the drawing room in order to produce the lovely tableware. He doubted Alyssa often dined this way.

Perkins majestically served dinner, hesitantly assisted by a young man. The meal was simple, yet surprisingly good. It included a tangy mulligatawny soup, followed by glazed duck, buttery new potatoes, fresh greens, and pear torte for dessert. Morgan ate heartily while noticing Alyssa pushing her food around on the plate.

The dinner conversation was limited to safe, mundane topics such as the excellently prepared food and the weather. As the table was being cleared of the final course, Perkins placed several bottles of spirits on the table within easy reach. "Do you require anything else, Your Grace?"

"No, Perkins. Please convey my compliments to the cook," the duke replied, dismissing the butler. He saw Perkins hesitate momentarily, but at a nod from Alyssa he left the room.

"Sherry, Miss Carrington?" the duke asked politely, filling her glass when she agreed. It felt strange sharing a drink after dinner with a lady. Custom always dictated the women withdraw after the meal, leaving the men alone with their brandy and cigars. A small smile tugged his lips. Nothing about Alyssa Carrington or Westgate Manor remotely resembled the rigid order of society to which Morgan was accustomed.

"I'm glad you enjoyed the meal, Your Grace," Alyssa said. "Mrs. Stratton was rather nervous about dinner, since she had little time to prepare. You will find she is excellent at her job, as are all those who work here."

A dark eyebrow lifted over a silver-gray eye. Morgan heard the anxiety in her voice and was instantly on his guard. Thus far Alyssa had impressively retained control of her emotions, but Morgan was convinced she would eventually loose her iron grip.

"Can you tell me, Miss Carrington, why your father is not here?" Morgan asked, deliberately shifting the subject.

Alyssa eyed him cautiously. "Lord Carrington is very seldom at the estate. He has never liked the country, and much prefers the many diversions of London."

"You were not informed of my impending visit?"

"Hardly," Alyssa replied with a taut smile. "I imagine there wasn't sufficient time."

"Nonsense." The duke shook his head. "It has been nearly a week since Lord Carrington signed the deed over to me."

"That long," she remarked dryly. "You certainly exhibited great restraint by allowing so much time to pass, Your Grace."

Morgan slanted her a cool glance but held his tongue. Few people, especially women, possessed the audacity to display their irritation with him. The majority of them were too impressed by his title and wealth. Clearly Alyssa Carrington was made of sterner stuff.

"Do you also prefer the diversions of London, Miss Carrington?"

Alyssa turned sharply toward the duke, fearing he was mocking her, but his handsome face appeared sincere.

Her chin jutted out defiantly. "I have never been to London."

His gray eyes narrowed in surprise. Suddenly she looked very vulnerable and alone to him. For the first time Morgan wondered what kind of life she had led.

"You have no cause to repine," the duke replied solicitously. "I often find the social crush in London a great bore, and the majority of individuals unworthy of acquaintance."

Alyssa flashed him a wan smile. "I can assure you, sir, I am hardly the sort of woman who would repine over anything as inconsequential as the activities of London society," she retorted with a tinge of sarcasm.

Her lack of pretense was a refreshing change. Feeling himself inexplicably drawn to the fire burning in her deep green eyes, Morgan inquired softly, "What activities do you prefer, Miss Carrington?"

"Riding," she answered readily. "I greatly enjoy being out-of-doors. Needlework can be relaxing in the evenings, and reading for pleasure is always a treat, though I seldom have time to pursue any avenues of personal interest."

"Do you manage the estate entirely on your own?"

"I employ few retainers," Alyssa admitted. "I work

better alone, and Lord Carrington has no objections."

"Lord Carrington? Why are you always so formal when referring to your father?"

Alyssa stared at the duke with a lack of comprehension. "I never think of him in any other context. He has always been Lord Carrington, even when I was a small child."

Morgan wondered at the strangeness of a father insisting on such formality from a young girl. "He seems to have provided a genteel upbringing. You are hardly lacking in the social graces."

"Well, I don't slurp my soup or eat with my hands," Alyssa responded with a laugh. "My nurse, Mavis, has been a steadying influence. And a succession of governesses managed to polish most of my rough edges."

"A succession? Were you a difficult child?" Morgan could just imagine her as a willful little girl, bright, inquisitive, and opinionated.

"High-spirited is the polite term, Your Grace," Alyssa responded. "Truthfully, I was usually well behaved. An intense desire to please my many different governesses moderated my behavior."

"Then why were there so many of them?"

"Lord Carrington had an annoying habit of neglecting to pay their salaries. Eventually each was forced to move on to a more stable position. Some left more quickly than others."

Morgan refilled his glass and gave her an inquisitive appraisal. The more he learned about Alyssa, the more enticing she became to him. She appeared to be an uncomplicated woman. A country-bred girl, possessing honesty and intelligence. And the prettiest green eyes he had ever seen.

"So you enjoy the quaint society of country life, Miss Carrington?"

"I do not participate in the social gatherings of this small community, Your Grace. Lord Carrington's repıtation as a spendthrift and a gambler placed me in a enuous position among the local gentry years ago. Unfortunately I have gone far beyond the traditional ole of spinster by running the estate. I am not received by the noble households of the county."

"It is not so unusual for a woman to be involved vith her own finances," the duke insisted, his handome expression growing conciliatory. "My grandmother, the dowager duchess, takes an active interest n all her affairs."

"Your grandmother is a widow. Greater latitude in behavior is always afforded to widows. Besides, taking an interest in financial matters is a far cry from being in control."

"People are often suspicious of matters they don't ully understand," Morgan said.

"Perhaps," Alyssa conceded. "However, in this case ny unacceptability is not solely based on the fact that am an unmarried woman working at a man's job. Alas, my unpardonable sin is that I am competent and uccessful." Alyssa got to her feet. "Perkins has lit a ire in the front salon. Shall we adjourn?"

Alyssa felt uncomfortable with so much of the conversation focused on her and was glad for the opportunity to shift the duke's attention. As they crossed the vast hallway, she studied the tall man who walked beside her, trying to determine the best way to broach he subject of retaining the staff. She had told her servants he was a fair man, but that was merely a hopeful assumption.

"Do you play, Miss Carrington?" the duke inquired vhen they entered the room.

"No, Your Grace, I do not play the pianoforte. Miss Gibbons, the one governess who possessed a small nusical talent, was employed only long enough to each me the basic piano scales. I cannot even properly read the notes."

33

"She was forced away by lack of salary payment?"

"No. Lord Carrington frightened her off," Alyssa replied with a faint flush of embarrassment. "Miss Gibbons was considerably younger than most of my other governesses and fairly pretty. I am afraid Lord Carrington overindulged in his port and attempted to physically abuse her one evening. Miss Gibbons left rather quickly as I recall."

The duke made no comment and Alyssa briefly regretted the indelicacy and bluntness of her response. She wondered if she had shocked the duke by having the gall to speak of an incident where Lord Carrington had gotten drunk and tried to take advantage of a woman under his protection. Alyssa knew this was an event she should not have understood, much less spoken about. Rules of polite discourse were rather stringent; honesty had a limited place.

Determined to draw the duke into conversation so she might better understand him, Alyssa settled herself in a small chair near the fire. Her expressive green eyes never left the duke's broad shoulders as he paced the room aimlessly.

She could not help but admire the elegant cut of his evening clothes and the carelessly artful way he wore them. There was an unmistakable aura of controlled power and command about the duke. Clearly he was a man used to getting what he wanted. It was imperative that she tread cautiously and avoid antagonizing him if she harbored any hopes of placing her small staff in his household.

The duke ceased his pacing and turned to face her. The smile he flashed her was utterly disarming, and Alyssa felt herself drawn by the magnetism of his silver-gray eyes. For a long moment they contemplated each other.

Feeling totally flustered Alyssa blurted out, "What are you going to do with the estate?"

The duke shifted his feet uncomfortably under her open gaze.

"My younger brother, Tristan, will be married later this year. I've decided to give the estate to him. Tristan has always enjoyed the country. I believe he will be happy living here."

Feeling slightly calmer, Alyssa took a moment to ponder this new information, trying to decide if it could work to her advantage.

"Your brother will be in charge of the estate?"

"Of course," he answered.

"He will decide who shall stay on and who shall leave?"

"Does it really matter who is in charge, Miss Carrington?" Morgan inquired. "Were you planning on working here?"

"Do you think your brother would consider it?" Alyssa replied, her eyes bright with hope. "I know it is unusual, but I am eminently qualified to be an agent, and I have amply demonstrated I can make the estate turn a healthy profit."

It took Morgan a few moments to realize she was serious. When he finally replied, his skepticism was evident. "It is one thing for you to manage your family estate and quite another for you to be employed by someone else in that position. I'm afraid the idea of a female estate agent is far too avant-garde for Tristan. He believes, as I do, that women should remain within their proper place in society."

"A woman's proper place," Alyssa repeated softly, taking offense at the duke's arrogant tone. "Where precisely is that?"

The duke's lip curled in amusement at her indignant manner. "A woman's proper place?" He leaned back in his chair, stretching his long legs out and crossing his ankles. "A woman must be shielded and protected from the harshness of the world so she can devote all her energy toward the comforts and pleasures of the man who is responsible for her. By day she should be at his side, beautiful and adoring. By night, she must be loving and submissive in his bed."

"Stand by his side, Your Grace? Not under his foot?" Alyssa snorted in disgust.

"Only if absolutely necessary," he quipped. Morgan smiled cynically. "Do you not agree, Miss Carrington?"

She thrust her chin up defiantly. "I have never been sheltered or protected in my life, Your Grace. And I find your opinion of my gender rude and unenlightened. I believe men have a need to cosset and protect a woman only because it makes them feel superior."

He smiled cagily and Alyssa struggled to remain composed under his smug grin. She had the distinct feeling he was deliberately taunting her, yet she found their conversation oddly stimulating. With each passing moment Alyssa was becoming more aware of the duke as a man, and in turn, herself as a woman. His handsome face, alluring smile, and sensuous eyes that gazed so boldly into her own were affecting her in a most peculiar way. Alyssa felt a definite sense of intoxication she instinctively knew was dangerous. And nearly irresistible.

Deciding it would be safest to conclude the evening as quickly as possible, Alyssa steered the conversation back to the new estate owner.

"Since your brother would be mortified to consider a position for me in his household, do I dare ask if he would allow the others to retain their positions? As you can judge for yourself, I alone am the oddity."

"Despite what I may have led you to believe, I can assure you, Miss Carrington, Tristan is not a tyrant. I'm certain as long as the individual in question is well suited for his position, he will be asked to remain. Beyond that I cannot say."

It was a fair answer and Alyssa nodded her head in acceptance. "I can only hope, Your Grace, that your esteemed brother is as progressive and open-minded as yourself." Inclining her head slightly in farewell, Alyssa rose quietly and left the room.

Morgan grinned broadly at her retreating back, unsure if she meant to amuse or insult him. Alyssa Carrington was unlike any other woman he had ever encountered, and he found her fascinating. French spies at Ramsgate Castle and the inciting Miss Carrington. It was turning out to be a far from ordinary week, Morgan decided. The innocent, plainspoken Alyssa stimulated and aroused him infinitely more than a roomful of beautiful, sophisticated courtesans.

Shaking his head at the irony, Morgan slowly climbed the staircase, wondering where in the vast hallways on the second floor her bedchamber was located.

Alyssa awoke earlier than usual the next morning, and for a brief moment thought the earth-shattering events of the previous day had all been a horrible dream. The realization it was not a dream brought forth the urge to bury herself under the covers for the rest of the day. Instead, Alyssa trudged bleary eyed to the bedroom window and gazed despondently at the early morning mist.

Her eyes filled with tears, but she refused to allow herself the luxury of tears, believing it would be impossible to stop crying once she started.

Closing the drapes, Alyssa crossed the room and repeatedly splashed cold water on her face in an effort to erase the telltale signs of a fitful sleep. She dressed rapidly, securing her long hair in a severe chignon at the nape of her neck. Her toilette complete, she left her room to join the staff for breakfast in the kitchen.

Alyssa raced swiftly down the hall, rounding the corner at a quick gait, and collided headlong with the duke. He instinctively grabbed her shoulders to steady her as they were thrown off balance.

"Hellfire and damnation!" Alyssa swore under her breath, trying to regain her footing.

"A pleasant good morning to you also."

Alyssa drew in her breath sharply and looked up into the duke's silver-gray eyes.

"I beg your pardon, Your Grace," Alyssa replied breathlessly. She felt herself flushing and brought a cool hand up to her warm cheek.

He gave her a roguish grin. "For what, Miss Carrington? Nearly knocking me down or cursing at me so charmingly?"

"If you are going to be rude, I shall withdraw my apology," she retorted.

The duke cocked his head to one side. Seeing her indignant expression struck his humor and Morgan laughed heartily. His laughter was the most infectious thing Alyssa had ever heard, and she unwittingly found herself smiling.

As the laughter ended, Alyssa noted the duke was dressed for riding. His exquisitely tailored clothes emphasized the hard, muscular lines of his body, and her pulse quickened.

Her hand lay on his strong shoulder. Unconsciously, she ran her fingertips caressingly along his broad chest and shoulder, marveling at the contrast between the smooth velvet of his riding coat and his lean, muscular body.

The duke felt a powerful surge of lust at her gentle exploration. Reaching down, Morgan gently lifted her chin. His silver-gray eyes took in the open curiosity and tentative passion on Alyssa's sweet face. Her expression quickly turned to horror when their eyes met and she became aware of what she was doing.

Alyssa snatched her hand away in mortification. For the barest instant she thought her heart would stop beating. She bit her lip hard to master her reeling senses. Her face flushed red with embarrassment, and she refused to meet his gaze.

Morgan saw her distress and, taking pity on her, spoke softly. "I was hoping you would conduct me on a tour of the estate this morning. Perhaps after breakfast?"

Still too overcome with embarrassment to reply, Alyssa merely nodded her head.

"Excellent. Let's go see what culinary delights Mrs. Stratton has prepared for us this morning." Morgan clasped Alyssa's arm firmly, and before she had a chance to protest, propelled her down the stairs and into the dining room.

Mrs. Stratton had indeed been busy. Perkins poured the coffee while Molly and Lucy carried numerous silver trays of steaming hot food into the room and carefully set them down on the sideboard.

"Shall I fix you a plate, Your Grace?" Perkins inquired.

"Yes, Perkins, and one for Lady Alyssa also."

Alyssa noted with pride the freshly ironed linen tablecloth and matching napkins, the polished silver cutlery, and the simple but elegant flower arrangement. Perkins had even managed to scare up a copy of the *Morning Post*. She fervently hoped the duke would appreciate all the staff's efforts to see to his comfort.

Alyssa smiled her thanks as Perkins set her plate before her, but nearly dropped her china coffee cup when she saw its contents. A quick glance over at the duke's plate revealed the same: a plate piled high with kidneys, poached eggs, fried potatoes, a thick slice of sirloin, and several thin slices of baked ham. This was more food than she ate in a month! My food budget, she thought in dismay, but then caught herself. The duke was providing breakfast this morning.

This fact did little to enhance Alyssa's appetite. Absently she picked up a piece of toast and nibbled at it, not even bothering to add butter.

"I was wondering, Miss Carrington, if I might be so bold as to inquire about your future plans," the duke asked politely.

"Plans? I thought you wanted me to give you a tour of the estate," she replied blankly.

"I didn't mean just for today," he said pointedly.

"Oh," she replied, understanding. "You'd like to know what I'm going to do after I ... umm ... leave ... Westgate Manor? The arrangements have already been made."

The duke blinked in astonishment. "So soon?" His cool gray eyes narrowed. "You told me you knew nothing of my arrival until yesterday afternoon."

"You misunderstand, Your Grace," she replied soothingly. "My plans were made long before you arrived."

As he scowled at her, Alyssa hastily explained. "Despite your exalted opinion of womankind, we are not all weak brained, helpless, and incompetent. A few of the fairer sex are eminently capable of fending for ourselves. It became glaringly obvious the first time I read the estate account ledgers that Lord Carrington's greatest talent is spending money. I knew eventually he would lose the manor. Two years ago I purchased a small cottage on the outskirts of the village from a retired professor who had decided to live abroad. At the same time I invested a small sum of money I managed to save. 'Tis not a large sum, but if I am frugal, I shall be able to live on the income it provides. Lord Carrington spent the dowry left to me by my mother. I therefore felt I was entitled to some compensation for my work on the estate," she finished defensively.

Morgan looked at her in fascination. "In the short time since I have made your acquaintance, Miss Carrington, you have never ceased amazing me."

She smiled up at him. "I shall take that as a compliment, though I'm not certain it was intended as such."

Perkins entered carrying a letter on a silver tray. Pausing by Alyssa's chair, he formally presented the contents to her.

"The post has arrived at this hour?" she inquired, surprised.

"The letter came from London by special messenger, Lady Alyssa."

Curious, Alyssa picked up the heavy cream-colored envelope and at once recognized the distinctive stationery.

"It is from Lord Carrington's solicitors," she told the duke. Her lips twisted ironically. "It is probably a message informing me of your arrival."

Her smile quickly faded, however, as she began reading the letter. Her green eyes became very round and her entire body stiffened with tension. Lifting a pale, drawn face to the duke, Alyssa softly whispered, "Lord Carrington is dead. He was found in his rooms last night with a bullet in his head."

Chapter Three

An eerie silence filled the room as the two men waited anxiously for Alyssa to continue. Becoming impatient, the duke reached for the letter.

"May I?" he inquired, snatching the letter away. "It appears your solicitor, Mr. Bartlett, has been successful in dissuading the authorities from making a formal inquiry into the matter. Lord Carrington's death was deemed an accident."

"An accident?" Alyssa repeated dully.

"Perkins, bring the brandy," Morgan ordered when he saw her wretched state. As Perkins shakily complied, the duke clasped Alyssa's cold hands tightly. Instantly she felt comforted by the warmth and strength of his touch.

"Drink this," Morgan commanded, placing a glass filled with a generous portion of brandy in her left hand. "It will help to steady your nerves."

Ignoring his order, she repeated her question. "How can it be ruled an accident?" A trace of desperation entered her voice. "Shouldn't there be an inquiry to determine if there was any foul play?"

"That will be all, Perkins," the duke said, dismissing the butler. As soon as they were alone, he once again took Alyssa's hand. Morgan was touched by the haggard look in her eyes, but it did not deter him. Choosing his words carefully, he attempted to explain.

"Mr. Bartlett has done you a tremendous service, Miss Carrington," he said in a placid voice. "It is best for all concerned, especially you, if the matter is not examined too closely."

The air was charged with tension as Alyssa voiced her most dreaded suspicion.

"Suicide?" she whispered, her voice choked with emotion. "Are you implying it was suicide?"

"It would seem likely," Morgan said gently, hating to confirm this loathsome notion.

"You think I should let the matter drop," she said woodenly.

"It would probably be wise," he answered.

"What am I supposed to do next?" She asked distractedly. "Must I go to London to . . . to . . ." She could not say the words.

"Mr. Bartlett will make all the necessary arrangements. Instruct him to bring Lord Carrington's body here."

"Here? But why? Westgate Manor no longer belongs to the Carrington family."

"I am not such a monster that I would deny a man his final resting place. Of course he will be buried here." Morgan insisted, his feelings of guilt causing him to respond more harshly than he intended.

"Thank you," Alyssa said in a toneless voice. "I shall send word to Mr. Bartlett directly."

Alyssa sat motionless in her chair, the glass of untouched brandy forgotten in her hand. *Suicide, suicide.* The word reverberated through her mind. She let the shock and pain wash over her as she tried desperately to recall some happy memories of her father.

It saddened her even more to realize she had none. Jeremy Carrington had been a selfish man and a cold, indifferent father. And now he had killed himself, leaving his daughter behind to make amends.

The duke was speaking to her. Alyssa looked up at him, unseeing. She tried to collect herself and become unfrozen. The duke repeated himself.

"Is there anything you want me to do, Miss Carrington?"

Yes, she wanted to shout. Make this all go away. Let everything be as it was before you walked into this house. She closed her eyes in an effort to chase away the screams in her head. I want to worry about the price of grain and how the weather will affect our crops this year, instead of being thrown out of my home and burying a father who has just killed himself.

Defeated, Alyssa drained the brandy glass she held so tightly.

"You've done quite enough already, Your Grace," she said in a cold voice, knowing full well she did not have the right to place any of the blame on the duke, but needing to direct her suffering somewhere. "You will forgive me if I don't spend the morning touring the grounds with you. I have some correspondence that needs my immediate attention."

For several minutes after she left, Morgan stared at the closed door, debating whether or not to follow her. He was surprised how deeply her misery affected him and wished there was something, anything, he could do or say to make it easier for her—but there wasn't.

Morgan felt intense and unexplained rage toward Jeremy Carrington. How could a man be so uncaring and cruel to his own child? It was unthinkable.

The duke delayed his departure as long as possible, hoping Alyssa would seek him out. Eventually realizing he would have to approach her, Morgan proceeded to the drawing room, where he discovered Alyssa absently staring out a leaded-glass window.

She heard him enter and turned, and he saw a brief but unmistakable flicker of pain in her eyes before she conquered it.

"Are you ready to leave, Your Grace?" Alyssa inquired in a steady voice.

"If I can be of no further assistance . . . ?"

Alyssa shook her head. Impulsively she advanced toward him, extending her hand in farewell, hoping to convey her apology for her earlier rudeness. The duke did not mistake her meaning, and clasped her hand firmly as he brought it to his lips and gently kissed the top of her wrist.

Above her hands, their eyes met. And held. And for a brief moment they stared at each other as if they were bound together on a deep, soulful level. Soon the intensity became too great and Morgan succumbed to his need to hold her. He gently yet forcefully pulled Alyssa into the circle of his arms and held her close, comforting her with his strong masculine presence.

His action caught her by surprise, but Alyssa relaxed her rigid control, gratefully accepting the safety the duke's embrace offered. His greater physical and emotional strength gave her a wonderful sense of security. Marveling at how perfectly their bodies fit together, Alyssa lifted her face to offer silent thanks for his compassion.

Powerful, unfamiliar emotions pulsed through Morgan as their eyes locked again, and without thinking he claimed her lips in a sensuous kiss. He kissed her long and searchingly, succumbing to the emotion and passion she inspired. Morgan felt Alyssa's astonishment and her tentative response just as he realized what he was doing. Feeling confused, he ended the kiss as abruptly as he had begun it, and stepped away from her, dismayed by his lack of control.

Alyssa stared at him with startled eyes, breathlessly trying to concentrate. She swayed slightly, wondering giddily whether if she landed in his arms, he would kiss her again. His kiss was the most remarkable thing she had ever experienced: strong, yet gentle; hard, yet tender. She was sorry he stopped.

Morgan scowled at Alyssa's dreamlike expression. He swallowed against the sudden, intense emotions that filled his throat and moved further away, deciding it was time to beat a hasty retreat.

"Good-bye, Miss Carrington."

"Your Grace," she answered, confused by the harshness of his voice. She watched him unwaveringly as he exited the room, obviously in a hurry to be gone. Shaking her head sharply, she tried, without success, to force the entire incident from her mind as she returned to the unfinished correspondence on her writing desk.

The duke climbed into the waiting curricle, but paused to give Perkins some parting instructions.

"Tell Miss Carrington she may contact me at Ramsgate Castle near Portsmouth. I will be there until Thursday of this week. After that, she can reach me at my London residence." He handed the butler a paper with the information.

"Keep a close eye on her, Perkins," Morgan requested, astonishing both himself and the butler. Then at a light tap to their reins, the fiesty bays took off at a brisk pace down the drive.

Morgan was distracted during the drive to Ramsgate Castle. His mind continually wandered to Alyssa, and he was unable to explain why she so strongly affected him. The kiss they had exchanged had been passionate and wildly delightful, despite her obvious inexperience. He had enjoyed it immeasurably and so, apparently, had Alyssa.

Yet his fascination went far beyond the physical. He admired her spirit and intelligence, her ability to adapt gracefully, even triumphantly, to circumstances that would have defeated many men and over-whelmed most women. She repeatedly demonstrated her inner strength and courage, winning his respect during the short duration of his visit.

And still there was something else that drew Morgan to Alyssa, something he couldn't define. And he didn't like it. He didn't like it at all.

He had also been inexplicably drawn to his wife Valerie many years ago. Not in quite the same manner, of course, but he had felt a spark of excitement when in her company. Unfortunately, the spark had sputtered and died soon after their marriage, leaving Morgan feeling trapped, permanently tied to a woman he neither loved nor liked, who constantly reminded him what an ordeal it was to be his wife.

Valerie had wept passionately while telling him how he offended her tender sensibilities with his physical demands on her person. She was horrified by his touch and accused him of using her solely for the purpose of sowing his seed to breed an heir. Upon reflection, Morgan had been ashamed to realize she spoke the truth, and as a concession stayed out of his wife's bed.

Consequently Valerie died without producing an heir, but Morgan was no longer concerned about the succession of his title. His younger brother, Tristan, had recently returned from the fighting on the peninsula, wounded yet mercifully whole. Morgan promptly named his brother the heir to the dukedom, effectively passing on his responsibility and sparing himself the distasteful notion of entering into another marriage. It was now up to Tristan to continue the Ashton line and produce the next generation that would inherit the vast family holdings.

Morgan's gloomy memories faded as he spied Ramsgate Castle in the distance. Though not his primary residence, the castle held many fond memories of carefree, boyhood summers. It stood majestically on a hilltop, surveying everything below. The sun glistened off the gray stone walls, softening the vastness and grandeur of the castle. It had originally been built by Henry VIII as one of a chain of coastal forts for protection against French raids, but was reborn when the fourth duke, Morgan's grandfather, had decided to renovate the castle after returning from his European grand tour.

The renovation had taken almost twenty years, but the result was an incomparable showcase of fine craftsmanship, wealth, and imagination. Rebuilt in the Gothic style, the original structure had been transformed into a work of art, with tall stone spires encased in florid ornamental detail, endless arched windows with both clear and stained glass, and intriguing stone carvings on the exterior.

The interior was equally impressive, with marble floors, patterned in black, red, and white, sunken ceiling panels enriched with gold, and high relief carvings.

Morgan's unexpected arrival put the place in an uproar. Burke, the castle butler, was practically wringing his hands as he followed Morgan into the grand entrance hall and assisted the duke out of his greatcoat and gloves.

"We were not properly notified of your arrival, Your Grace," Burke said, the panic evident in his voice. "Cook will barely have time to prepare a proper evening meal."

"Don't go all to pieces on me, Burke," the duke replied lightly. "I had business to attend to nearby and could not return to town without visiting my grandmother. How is she?"

"The dowager duchess is in perfect health as always, Your Grace. I believe she and Mrs. Glyndon are in the morning room working on Her Grace's correspondence."

That brought a smile to Morgan's face. His grandmother was always working on her correspondence. He once told her she sent more letters to her friends than Napoleon did to his generals.

"Fine. I shall go there directly after I have cleaned up." The duke began climbing the long winding staircase at a nimble pace, with a puffing Burke trying to keep up. "Oh, and Burke, I should like tea served in the morning room in one hour."

With a dismissive wave of his hand, Morgan took the last steps two at a time. The exhausted Burke remained on the staircase, clutching the wrought-iron balustrade tightly while trying to catch his breath, hoping he would be able to comply with the duke's orders in a timely manner.

Feeling infinitely better after washing and changing into fresh garments, the duke proceeded to the morning room to greet his grandmother. He arrived just as tea was being brought in.

"Morgan," the dowager duchess exclaimed with delight. "What a wonderful surprise."

Morgan crossed the room and leaned down to kiss his grandmother's cheek in greeting. "You are looking well, madam."

The dowager duchess patted the seat beside her, and Morgan sat down. "Imogene and I are just finishing."

Morgan inclined his head toward the duchess's companion. "How are you today, Mrs. Glyndon?"

"Just fine, Your Grace," Mrs. Glyndon replied breathlessly.

"Will you join us for tea, Imogene?" the dowager duchess asked politely.

Mrs. Glyndon wisely declined. Although a woman well into middle age, she always became a bit flustered in the presence of her employer's handsome grandson. Besides, she knew the dowager duchess preferred spending time alone with the duke.

"Then we will see you at dinner," the dowager duchess said in a dismissive tone.

"So tell me, my dear boy," she said after Mrs. Glyndon left the room, "to what do I owe this delightful surprise? It isn't like you to come out here without letting me know first." The dowager duchess felt a sudden stab of fear. "Has something happened? Is Tristan all right?"

"Tris is fine," Morgan replied reassuringly. "What is wrong with everyone today? Can't a man arrive at his own home without everybody going into a frenzy? First Burke and now you."

"Don't pout, Morgan," the dowager duchess admonished, regarding her grandson thoughtfully. Morgan was not known for his even temper, but she could see beyond the agitation that something was upsetting him. Biding her time, she served the tea.

The dowager duchess elegantly lifted the Spode teapot, filling the thin porcelain cups. She added sugar and cream, then handed Morgan his cup. While he balanced the delicate vessel in his large hand, she filled a plate with biscuits, cucumber sandwiches, scones, and Morgan's favorite cream pastries. She placed the plate on the low table in front of him and watched as he dove into it with relish.

Absently she sipped her own tea while continuing to observe her beloved grandson. She noticed his tired eyes and the grim set to his mouth. Yes, something was definitely bothering him, but experience taught her Morgan would tell her in his own good time.

Although the dowager duchess loved both her grandsons, it was Morgan who held a special place in her heart. She was not blind to his faults; he was quick-tempered and demanding and at times could be positively dictatorial. But his often gruff exterior hid a generous and loyal heart, and a sensitive soul.

Few people ever saw the sensitive side of Morgan, but the dowager duchess did. She knew his marriage had been an unhappy one and she in part blamed herself because she had encouraged the match. Only the dowager duchess knew the pain and guilt Morgan suffered when Valerie had died.

She had seen him turn inward more over the three years since Valerie's death. The duke was a complex man; well liked and well respected among his peers, yet there were few in society who could claim his friendship. Morgan was a man who kept his own counsel. As for women, the dowager duchess was well aware of Morgan's less than sterling reputation. She was not naive; she knew he kept mistresses as well as indulging in affairs with married women of the ton. She had long since given up trying to introduce him to respectable, eligible young women. He had expressed his refusal to consider marriage again in no uncertain terms and the dowager duchess tactfully respected his desires. It was an unspoken agreement between them.

After deciding Morgan had eaten his fill of pastries, the dowager duchess began her inquires.

"How are Tris and dear Caroline progressing with the wedding plans? Has Caroline's scatterbrained mother been able to set a definite date yet?"

"Grandmother," Morgan warned, "you must not refer to Lady Grantham as a scatterbrain all the time."

"Why ever not? It is the truth. Thank goodness Caroline has only inherited her sweet nature and not her lack of sense. You know I can't tolerate stupidity in anyone, especially women. But what about the wedding plans?"

Morgan gave her a quelling look. "Really, madam, if you insist on discussing wedding plans, I shall have to leave."

"Oh, do stop being so grumpy, Morgan, or I shall take back my delight in seeing you."

"I am sorry. I've had a very troublesome week." Morgan ate two more small sandwiches. "Grandmother, have you ever made the acquaintance of Jeremy Carrington, Viscount Mulgrave?"

The dowager duchess paused a moment to think. "I do recall meeting an Eleanor Carrington many years ago. She died young, poor creature; it was rather sad. I am not sure if she was his wife or sister. No, wait, Eleanor was his wife. I remember they had a child, a little girl."

"Alyssa," Morgan murmured.

"They had a lovely home in Hampshire. Westgate Manor, I believe it was called."

For once Morgan wished his grandmother didn't possess such an excellent memory. She knew more about the Carrington family than he did.

"I now own Westgate Manor," Morgan informed the dowager.

"I wasn't aware that you had purchased another estate."

"Actually, I bought it at auction," Morgan hedged.

"An auction? At this time of year?"

"This particular sale was a tad unusual. It was held in the club room at White's," Morgan reluctantly admitted.

"Gracious! What sort of fool would sell a prime piece of property in such a ridiculous manner?" The dowager duchess's eyes narrowed in suspicion. "Was Lord Carrington drunk?"

"Certainly not," Morgan replied indignantly. "I can assure you, Grandmother, I paid Carrington a fair price. More than fair, judging by what I saw of the estate yesterday."

The dowager duchess pursed her lips in a thin line. "I still find the entire incident extreme, even for you, Morgan."

The duke lifted an eyebrow. "Are you implying my actions were inappropriate, madam?"

"No," she responded slowly. "I am telling you that your actions were inappropriate."

"Touché, madam." Morgan knew when to retreat. He prudently decided to wait a few days before telling his grandmother about Lord Carrington's untimely death. "I thought Tris might like to have the estate after he marries."

The dowager duchess considered the idea. "I'm sure he will be pleased. Deep down, I think Tris has always fancied himself a bit of a country squire. It would also be prudent to keep Caroline out of London and away from her mother's influence. One can never be too careful, my boy."

"You are awful, Grandmother," Morgan joked.

"Yes, I am," she agreed, with a sparkle in her eye.

Dinner began that evening on a congenial note. Morgan gallantly seated the ladies before taking his place at the head of the table. The formally attired footmen, one for each of the three diners, served the first course.

Morgan ate routinely, not really tasting his food. His mind was occupied by the upcoming interview he had scheduled with his estate agent, Vickers, for the following morning. Morgan was also feeling a bit foolish over the idea of setting a trap in his own home.

Lord Castlereagh's information must be wrong, the duke decided while downing his third glass of wine. It is not possible for someone at the castle to be working for the French.

The dowager duchess caught his eye and frowned disapprovingly at his now empty wine goblet. Morgan gave her a boyish grin calculated to melt her ire. Holding out for only a moment, the dowager duchess was unable to resist his charm and returned the grin.

"Did I tell you yet, madam, how ravishing you look this evening?" Morgan said to his grandmother as he took a bite of the tender pheasant.

The dowager duchess preened under his compliment. "You did not, sir," she retorted. " 'Tis about time you noticed."

The dowager did look splendid. She was dressed in a simple gray satin gown with a square-cut neckline that effectively showcased the large sapphire-and-diamond necklace she wore. Her hair was wrapped in a turban, which added height to her small frame. Compared to the short and plump Mrs. Glyndon, the dowager duchess barely looked her sixty years.

Mrs. Glyndon. Morgan's eyes narrowed on his grandmother's companion of the past two years. He vaguely recalled hearing about her relative in France. Could there be a connection?

"Tell me, Mrs. Glyndon, do you still have family living in France?" he asked the older woman.

"Why yes, Your Grace," she answered, flattered the duke would remember something so personal. "My widowed sister and her three sons live outside Paris."

"Do you correspond with them often?"

"Not anymore." She sighed regretfully. "It has been difficult getting letters through these last few years."

"But there are ways," Morgan insisted.

"Well, I suppose," Mrs. Glyndon answered hesitantly, not understanding exactly what the duke meant.

"Are your nephews in the French army?" Morgan pressed on.

"Oh, my, no, Your Grace," Mrs. Glyndon responded.

"They are still young boys. Phillip, the oldest, has just turned thirteen."

"What of your sister, Mrs. Glyndon? Does she sympathize with the French cause?"

"I . . . am . . . ah . . . not sure what you mean," Mrs. Glyndon stuttered.

"It is a very simple question. Does your sister support Napoleon?" Morgan said accusingly.

"Morgan, really!" the duchess intervened. "Whatever do you think you are doing talking to Imogene in such a manner?"

Morgan looked at the two women. Mrs. Glyndon was near tears and his grandmother looked angry enough to throw her wine goblet at him.

Morgan rubbed the back of his neck. *What is wrong with me? I am acting like the woman is on trial for murder.*

"Ladies, I beg your pardon. Madam, Mrs. Glyndon, you must excuse me. I fear I'm not fit company this evening." He rose purposefully from the table and inclined his head graciously in farewell before leaving the room.

Later the next morning, Morgan stared gloomily out of the library windows at the magnificent gardens. The interview with his estate agent had yielded no pertinent information. No new people had been hired to work on the estate in over a year. Morgan was completely frustrated, and it was a feeling he did not enjoy.

Crossing the room soundlessly on the thick oriental carpet he locked the library doors with some misgivings.

Laying the trap for the Falcon was fairly simple. Morgan was given three sets of documents, each containing important but different information on troop and supply movements on the peninsula.

Morgan was instructed to lock the first set of documents in his desk at Ramsgate Castle, the second set in a more unusual place in the same room, and the third set in the safe of the private study of his London residence.

Lord Castlereagh intended to selectively circulate the news that Morgan was taking an active role in the War Ministry, thus letting the Falcon know there was valuable information to be obtained from the duke. It was fully expected the Falcon would then activate his contact at Ramsgate Castle to obtain the information.

British agents working in France would relay back to Lord Castlereagh what information had been received by the French.

Anyone who knew the workings of the estate and had access to Ramsgate Castle would be able to discover the first set of papers locked in the desk. The second set would be more difficult to locate and retrieve. If they were discovered, it could be concluded the informer was someone who was personally known to the duke. And if the final set of papers were uncovered in London, Lord Castlereagh's suspicions would be confirmed—a member of British society was selling military secrets to the French.

With the door securely locked, Morgan took stock of the room. Quickly he removed two sets of documents from his inside breast coat pocket. He placed the first set in the top left drawer of his desk and locked the drawer. The second set of papers were hidden inside a strongbox which was locked inside a Sheraton satinwood cabinet.

Once the documents were in place, Morgan left the library. The trap was set at Ramsgate Castle. There was nothing left to do but wait.

Three days later, Jeremy Carrington was laid to rest next to his wife in a simple service in the family graveyard. Alyssa sold her only piece of jewelry, a garnet-and-pearl brooch of her grandmother's, to pay for the funeral. She remained dry-eyed throughout the service, standing alone in the cold February mist. Composed, Alyssa watched with a detached air as the heavy oak coffin was placed into the ground.

Alyssa knew she appeared coldhearted, but felt no obligation to display false tears for the benefit of those few who attended the service. Some of the local gentry were present, but they came more out of curiosity than grief or friendship. To Alyssa, they were all virtual strangers.

Mr. Bartlett, Lord Carrington's London solicitor, attended the service, and when it was concluded, he and Alyssa met briefly to finalize Lord Carrington's estate. The news was not good.

Once they were seated comfortably in the library, Mr. Bartlett began. "Westgate Manor, as you already know, Lady Alyssa, is now owned by Morgan Ashton, the Duke of Gillingham."

The Duke of Gillingham's impressive likeness came to life in her mind and her heart beat a little faster.

Mr. Bartlett continued. "It is my understanding that the new Viscount Mulgrave is your uncle, Mr. Richard Carrington."

"My uncle?" Alyssa said blankly. She had totally forgotten about the existence of her father's younger brother. "I've never met him. He emigrated to the colonies long before I was born. I believe there was a quarrel of some kind between the two brothers. As far as I know, there was no contact for over thirty years. I know nothing about Richard, yet I imagine an English title is a rather useless commodity to an American, especially since there is no property to inherit."

Alyssa looked to Mr. Bartlett for his opinion. Mr. Bartlett, a short, stocky man, squirmed uncomfortably under her open gaze. He cleared his throat.

"Unfortunately, Lady Alyssa, it is of extreme importance that the new Viscount Mulgrave be located. I have thus far been unable to learn anything of the whereabouts of Richard Carrington or any of his heirs. I was hoping you would be able to assist me in the search."

"Why is it so important that my uncle be found, Mr. Bartlett?" Alyssa asked with a sinking feeling.

"At the time of his death, Lord Carrington had a substantial number of unpaid bills." Mr. Bartlett removed a stack of papers from the leather pouch he held in his lap.

Alyssa turned stricken eyes to him. "It is not possible. Lord Carrington sold Westgate Manor at auction," Alyssa insisted. "Surely there are sufficient funds to settle his gambling debts."

"The profits from the sale of the manor were spent before Lord Carrington died." Mr. Bartlett held up the thick pile of papers. "These are not gaming debts, Lady Alyssa. They are merchants' bills: his tailor, bootmaker, rent for his lodgings, and so forth. These bills are now the responsibility of the new heir, and if we cannot locate him, you will be held accountable for these debts."

"How much?" Alyssa asked shakily, her face ashen.

"The total is almost six thousand pounds."

Six thousand pounds! Alyssa slowly exhaled the breath she had been holding. Her stomach churned with fear, and she put a trembling hand to her mouth. *God help me, this must be some sort of cruel mistake.* But one look at Mr. Bartlett's face confirmed it was not.

"What if I cannot pay, Mr. Bartlett?"

Mr. Bartlett chewed furiously on his lower lip.

"Debtors who do not pay their bills eventually wind up in Newgate Prison," he said as gently as possible.

"I feared so, Mr. Bartlett." Alyssa crossed the room

and withdrew two papers from her writing desk. She felt a tightening in her throat and a moment of pure terror as she realized what she was doing. Silently she handed the solicitor the documents.

"I have a small amount of capital invested and I own a modest cottage on the outskirts of the village. If the cottage is sold and the investments liquidated, do you think there will be enough money to cover these debts?"

She spoke calmly, but Mr. Bartlett could see the fear and uncertainty in her eyes. He looked briefly down at the papers she gave him, resolving to make up the difference from his own meager funds if necessary.

"I am sure this will be adequate. I do hope you will allow me to handle this matter for you."

"I would be most grateful, Mr. Bartlett," Alyssa replied softly, walking him to the library door. "I sincerely thank you for your kindness today."

Mr. Bartlett stared into her lovely face, feeling deeply the sadness reflected in her green eyes. Giving her an encouraging smile, he left.

As the door closed behind him, Alyssa sank slowly to the floor, her hands covering her face. Her mind refused to function, concentrating instead on one indisputable fact—she was now totally without funds or property.

Chapter Four

"Do you think Rev. Jameson will be able to help me secure a position, Mavis?" Alyssa asked her former nurse.

In the week that had passed since her disastrous meeting with Mr. Bartlett, Alyssa had searched in vain for employment. In an act of pure desperation, she sought help from the local vicar, hoping he could at least supply her with a character reference. To her surprise, he offered to contact his sister in Cornwall, a lady of affluent means, believing she might know of a family in need of a governess or companion.

"I'm sure Rev. Jameson will do all that he can." Mavis sniffed. "He's a good sort, even if he is a man of the cloth." She held little regard for the men of the clergy and used every opportunity to express her opinion.

The two women were in the master bedroom suite sorting through Lord Carrington's belongings in an effort to clear the house of the few remaining personal items.

"Well, even if you don't completely approve of Rev. Jameson, I admit I am most grateful for his help."

Mavis paused in her work, turning her face away from Alyssa. Her voice was choked with emotion as she tried to speak.

"How I wish I could take care of you, just as I did when you were a tiny babe. It breaks my heart to think of you locked away in some dreary nursery with a parcel of brats, wasting away all your youth and beauty." Mavis pulled a handkerchief from her apron pocket and blew her nose loudly.

"Oh, Mavis." Alyssa rushed over and gave the plump woman a reassuring hug. "I'm a far cry from a beauty and long since past my youth. And I would like to believe I have the intelligence and fortitude to make my own way in the world."

" 'Tis not proper," Mavis retorted. "You are a lady born and bred. You should be married, with children of your own to love and a husband to look after and protect you. Not worrying about earning your keep."

"Mavis, you must not upset yourself. I shall be perfectly fine. I'm sure if I cannot find a position as a governess, I'll be hired as a companion."

"That sounds dreadful."

"There really are no other options for a woman in my circumstances." Striking a saucy pose, Alyssa quipped, "Of course, I could always try going on the stage."

"Lady Alyssa!" Mavis's mouth opened in shock.

Alyssa laughed heartily. "Good. Now I've stopped your crying. No more gloomy thoughts. We've too much work to finish and I want to be done with all this before the duke takes possession of the house."

"Still no word on when that will be?" Mavis inquired as she pulled out a moth-eaten pair of breeches from the wardrobe.

Alyssa shook her head. "I'm sure we shall hear all too soon."

Alyssa's only contact with the duke had been a short note she received four days after he departed Westgate Manor. The simple note stated she was to take as much time as necessary before vacating the property. It was a brief message, but the duke penned it himself instead of delegating the job to his secretary. He signed it informally, and the intimacy of seeing Morgan Ashton signed so boldly at the bottom of the parchment had captivated Alyssa's attention for the entire afternoon.

Alyssa knew she was being foolish, but she was unable to exorcise the duke's parting embrace and kiss. She was a woman not used to being touched, much less kissed, by a man, and it was an incident not easily forgotten.

Alyssa opened a large traveling trunk, piling clothes on the floor as she sorted through them. The majority of clothing was worn and stained with wine and food. It was an awful mess; several of the trunks hadn't been opened for years. The room depressed Alyssa, the decay, the dreariness. Mavis's worries about her uncertain future had shaken her too, more than she wanted to admit. Alyssa didn't relish the idea of spending the rest of her life with strangers, hardly more than a servant.

"There's a carriage coming up the drive," Mavis announced, looking out the bedroom window. "Were you expecting anyone?"

"No. I don't recognize the crest on the door. Do you?" Alyssa craned her neck out the open window to catch a glimpse of the vehicle as it proceeded up the drive.

"I can't make it out from up here," Mavis remarked. "These old eyes don't see as well as they used to, but it must be someone important. It's been a long time since I've seen a coach that grand around these parts."

Both women watched from their vantage point as the large vehicle came around the drive and drew to a halt in front of the main entrance to the house. A lanky footman jumped down from the back of the coach and opened the carriage door.

The first person to alight from the impressive vehicle was a man, followed quickly by two women. Even at that distance, Alyssa could see they were fashionably and expensively dressed. They could be neighbors coming to pay a condolence call, she thought, but it seemed unlikely.

Suddenly a rider entered her vision, thundering down the drive. He was mounted on the largest black stallion Alyssa had ever seen. He reined up alongside the coach and spoke to the three who had just descended.

Alyssa leaned farther out the window in hopes of hearing their conversation. As she leaned forward, part of the wooden window casing, rotted from age and neglect, gave way and she began falling. She cried out in alarm as she felt herself helplessly pitching forward. Alyssa flayed her arms wildly in an attempt to regain her balance, her voice rising in panic. Mavis heard her cries and managed to pull Alyssa back to safety by placing two large hands on the younger girl's waist.

At the sound of Alyssa's cry, all four heads below turned up to the window. Mavis stood Alyssa upright, and she swayed dizzily for a few seconds. Alyssa smoothed down her tumbling hair and glanced out the window. Four pairs of inquisitive eyes stared back. She immediately recognized the Duke of Gillingham as the mounted rider.

He gave her a jaunty salute in greeting, and Alyssa felt her cheeks flush with humiliation. How utterly mortifying to be caught hanging out the window like a disobedient child.

"Why, look here, the wood is rotted right through," Mavis exclaimed as she examined the splintered windowsill. "This whole place is falling to ruin. You could have tumbled right out onto the drive and broken your neck."

"I am fine, Mavis. Nothing wounded except my dignity." Alyssa took a deep breath. "How awful for them to have seen me." She groaned. "The duke certainly has a talent for catching me at my worst."

"It is the duke then?"

"Yes. I'd best be getting downstairs. Perkins is helping Mrs. Stratton inventory the storeroom. I'm not sure he can hear the front door from back there."

When she entered the front hall it was empty. Alyssa was about to start searching for the unexpected guests when Perkins emerged from the front parlor.

"The duke wished to be shown to the front parlor," Perkins explained. "He has instructed me to bring refreshment."

Alyssa sighed in vexation. They were hardly prepared for visitors. "I'm sure Mrs. Stratton will be able to create something appropriate. Tell her to make tea and sandwiches, and bring wine for the gentlemen." She touched the older man's arm in reassurance. "It will be fine."

"Ahhhh, now that is quick service," a male voice spoke as Alyssa entered the room.

She turned toward the young man who had spoken, and favored him with a chilling stare. He wasn't the least bit affected by her coldness, and returned her stare with a heart-melting smile. Alyssa instantly realized her mistake. His strong resemblance to the duke proclaimed him a relative, most likely his younger brother, Tristan. This was the one person Alyssa could ill afford to offend if she harbored any hope of placing her small staff in Tristan's household.

"Miss Carrington, how pleasant to see you again," the duke said, walking forward to rescue her from the awkward silence. "I trust you are uninjured from your little mishap?"

"Oh, quite unharmed, I assure you, Your Grace," she answered him tersely. "How very kind of you to be so concerned."

Her comment, meant to chastise, instead amused him. She looked thinner, and rather pale in her black crepe mourning gown that was customarily ill-fitting. But her spirit had not suffered. Morgan was inordinately pleased to see her.

"Miss Carrington, may I present my brother, Lord Tristan Ashton; his betrothed, Miss Caroline Grantham; and Caroline's sister, Lady Priscilla Ogden."

Alyssa dipped a curtsy in greeting. They certainly were an impressive party. Tristan was not as tall as the duke, but he was comparably built, with broad, powerful shoulders. He was exceedingly handsome in his dark-blue velvet double-breasted coat that matched his sapphire-blue eyes.

He did not possess the air of authority and command his older brother carried so naturally but he was clearly a man to be reckoned with. His fiancee, Caroline, was pretty and petite, all blond curls and rosy cheeks. She was dressed flatteringly in a pink satin traveling costume, complete with a large straw hat trimmed with a matching pink satin band and curtain veil of white lace. She was the very picture of feminine gentility. Alyssa felt perfectly dowdy beside her.

Alyssa could see little family resemblance between the two sisters. Lady Ogden was as dark as her sister was fair, and while not as pretty as Caroline, she was nevertheless a handsome woman. She was dressed entirely in mourning black.

"We were not informed of your impending arrival,

Your Grace," Alyssa said keenly. "Had we known, we would have been able to prepare a more comfortable greeting for you and your guests."

"I'm afraid that's my fault, Lady Alyssa," Caroline said in a soft, sweet voice. "When Morgan told us of his wonderful wedding gift, I insisted to Tris we come at once to see the estate. I do hope we have not inconvenienced you?"

Alyssa was unsure how to respond. She certainly had no right to be annoyed; the house now belonged to the duke. By rights, it was Alyssa who was intruding.

"The staff wanted very much to make a good impression," Alyssa said slowly, her manner less sharp. "I do hope you will not judge them too harshly."

"Goodness no," Caroline assured her. "Morgan has already told us of the efficient staff. We shall only be here a few short hours. The duchess is expecting us at Ramsgate Castle this evening."

The duchess? The duke's wife? A strong rush of regret curled through Alyssa, and it annoyed her to feel a sharp pang of disappointment deep within her heart. Naturally a man of the duke's stature would be married. She wondered how many children he had. Alyssa stole a quick glance at the duke, but his expression was unreadable.

"Will you show us around the house later?" Lady Ogden formally requested.

Alyssa stared at her, tongue-tied. What could she possibly say? How could she refuse without looking churlish? Yet how could she comply without feeling degraded, taking these strangers through a home that was no longer hers?

Alyssa nervously clutched at the black fabric of her gown, balling it up in her fists. She eyed the duke warily, but his expression remained unchanged. There would be no help from that quarter.

The occupants of the room waited expectantly for her to agree. Seeing no graceful way out, Alyssa conceded defeat. She forced her features into a bright smile. "I shall be pleased to attend you after tea. If you will excuse me, I must see what is keeping Perkins. Just ring when you are ready."

Alyssa gave a hasty curtsy to no one in particular and bolted out the door before anyone had a chance to stop her.

Escorting everyone through the manor house proved to be a more depressing, rather than embarrassing, task for Alyssa. They started the tour on the very top floor, first inspecting the attic rooms normally used as servants' quarters. Alyssa could not ever remember any servants actually living there and the many years of disuse were obvious.

They encountered loose floorboards, cracked windowpanes, broken furniture, and endless clouds of dust. In the corner of one room a small family of mice was discovered, which gave Caroline a mild case of hysterics. She actually squealed when the rodents ran across the room, and she clung to Tristan as if she were in danger of being eaten alive. Tristan seemed to think it was all great fun, and received tremendous satisfaction from "spotting" mice in nearly every room they entered.

Lady Ogden, a woman apparently unaffected by mice, reprimanded her sister.

"Caroline, will you please stop acting like such a ninny," Lady Ogden scolded. "And you are no better, Tristan, encouraging her like that."

"I'm merely protecting my beloved," Tristan replied easily, clearly not the least bit offended by his future sister-in-law's remarks.

"Nonsense, Tris," the duke interjected with a grin. "You are enjoying having Caroline leap into your arms each time you discover a mouse." Morgan gave Caroline a broad wink. She responded with a pretty blush and a shy smile.

Alyssa was tired and felt a headache coming on when they finally reached the main floor. She paused hesitantly in front of the drawing room doors, mentally berating herself for not dismantling the "treasure room." The house would have appeared less shabby and run-down if some of the beautiful items stored in the drawing room had been restored to their original locations in the house. She simply could not fathom Caroline's and Lady Ogden's reactions when they saw the collection housed in the room. Reluctantly Alyssa swung open the doors.

"My goodness," Caroline exclaimed, her blue eyes round with wonder.

"What in the world is all this?" Lady Ogden cried in amazement. Both women turned toward Alyssa.

Alyssa stared stonily ahead, refusing to give an explanation. What can I tell them? she thought peevishly. Here is the room where I settled Lord Carrington's gambling debts? Of course, that was before he shot himself.

"Morgan informed me you were going to inventory the estate for us," Tristan said in a casual voice, breaking the awkward silence. "I must commend you on an excellent job, Lady Alyssa."

Alyssa gazed at the duke with some surprise, but he was looking at his brother with equal astonishment.

"This is for us?" Caroline gasped in disbelief. "All of it?"

Everyone turned to the duke for confirmation. He cleared his throat. "Nothing but the best for my brother and his lovely bride," he remarked in an offhand manner.

There were a few seconds of complete silence, and then the room erupted with chatter as everyone began talking at once. Alyssa's eyes met Tristan's and he gave her a conspiratorial wink. She felt a warm flush of gratitude at his kindness and favored him with a small smile.

Alyssa led the group outside to the rose garden, the only garden on the entire grounds that was properly maintained. The sky was ominously dark as they headed for the overgrown boxwood maze. The wind gusted mightily, and suddenly, without warning, the storm clouds burst. Everyone gave a mad dash for the terrace and rushed through the French doors into the morning room trying to avoid a soaking.

The duke latched the doors securely against the torrential rain and swirling winds. "I'm afraid if this storm doesn't let up soon, we shall be forced to stay the night."

Alyssa rubbed her temples absently as the pounding increased in her head. What next? she thought wearily. What next.

The rain continued with a vengeance, and Alyssa spent the next three hours with the maids, Molly and Lucy, trying to prepare suitable bedchambers for everyone. Caroline graciously insisted she and her sister would be perfectly fine sharing a room. Alyssa decided to give them her bedchamber. She would move a small bed into Mavis's room for herself, remove her few personal belongings, and have fresh linens put on the bed. The room would be acceptable.

The duke could stay in the master suite, as he had on his first visit. With some basic housekeeping and fresh sheets, the room could be made ready for him. That left Tristan. The remaining four bedrooms in the east wing were a sorry lot at best. They were all in various stages of disrepair. In one room the fireplace smoked badly; in another there was no bed. The third room contained the best furniture—it even had a rug—but the mattress was a disgrace and the drapes smelled of mildew. The fourth room was the barest, but had the basics and boasted a comfortable bed. Alyssa decided on the fourth room for Tristan, choosing comfort over furnishings. Tristan had admirably demonstrated his good humor and easygoing charm. She doubted he would complain about his less than luxurious bedchamber.

After the rooms were finally prepared, Alyssa instructed Perkins to show everyone to their respective rooms so they could change for dinner. Next she went to the small servants' wing off the kitchen to make arrangements for the duke's coachman and footman. She took Lucy with her and left Molly with Caroline and Lady Ogden to assist the two gentlewomen as best she was able.

In the kitchen, Alyssa consulted with Mrs. Stratton about the dinner menu before proceeding to Mavis's bedchamber to freshen up before the evening meal. The duke had insisted she join them for dinner, and Alyssa had been unable to refuse.

Alyssa met Morgan accidentally outside the salon doors. Morgan skillfully smoothed over the awkward moment with a gracious greeting, and her heart began pounding erratically at the sight of him in his formal black silk evening clothes. They entered the room together, but Alyssa was no longer listening to the duke's comments about the weather. She was staring openmouthed at Tristan and Caroline. They were standing in front of the fireplace, locked in a heated, passionate embrace.

Tristan was holding Caroline tightly against his body while nibbling down the side of her neck to the hollow of her throat. Caroline's arms were wrapped tightly around Tristan's shoulders, and she was standing up on her toes to give him easier access to her body.

Tristan's hands delicately cupped her breasts, rubbing against the soft curves as he moved up to take her lips in a seductive kiss. Caroline responded with a soft moan and pressed herself even closer to him.

Alyssa felt herself flush with a yearning she couldn't name. A tightness gripped her throat as she envisioned herself locked in a similar embrace with Morgan.

The duke gave a loud cough, bringing Tristan's head up. Still holding Caroline tightly against his lean body, Tristan turned his eyes toward the sound. "Morgan, Lady Alyssa, good evening," he said in a cursory voice.

"Good evening, Tristan," Morgan answered casually, clearly implying he was taking no notice of the ardent scene he and Alyssa had just interrupted. "Would you and Caroline care for a glass of sherry before dinner?" Morgan walked to the satinwood table where the wine stood and began filling glasses.

"Sherry would be just the thing," Tristan said. "I'm sure Caroline would enjoy some." He answered for his fiancee, who had her face hidden in his shoulder and apparently was trying to compose herself.

At first embarrassed to be caught in such a compromising position, Caroline had tried to pull away from her betrothed. Tristan had held on to her, his strong arms never relaxing their grip. So she waited, knowing Tris would release her when he was ready. Not that she wanted him to let her go. She loved him with a passion that frightened her sometimes with its intensity.

"Sherry?" Morgan held a glass up to Caroline's ear. She choked back a laugh, then pushed gently against Tristan's shoulder to free herself.

"Thank you, Morgan," she said, maintaining a calm facade. Morgan gave her a wicked grin, so like Tristan's she felt her embarrassment begin to fade.

"I think you shall make a wonderful addition to our

71

family," he said with a twinkle in his silver-gray eyes. "And I am deeply gratified knowing that left in your capable . . . um . . . hands, the succession to our family title will be secured. I fully expect to become a doting uncle sometime next year."

Caroline was saved from further teasing by the arrival of Lady Ogden, who declined a drink and sat primly near the fireplace in a small rosewood armchair until Perkins announced dinner. Morgan instinctively offered his arm to Lady Ogden, before realizing Alyssa would also require an escort. Belatedly he turned to offer Alyssa his other arm, but she was already leaving the room, conversing quietly with Perkins.

There were a few awkward moments in the dining room as everyone was seated. Morgan assumed Tristan and Caroline would sit in the customary host and hostess positions at the opposite ends of the large mahogany table, leaving him free to sit where he wished. Tristan apparently had other ideas.

Tristan seated Lady Ogden and Caroline and then settled himself comfortably between the two ladies, flashing Morgan a satisfied grin. The duke had no choice but to occupy the head of the table, and Alyssa quickly sat in the remaining chair to the duke's left.

Perkins and Ned served the turtle soup while Caroline maintained a lively flow of chatter. Alyssa learned over the fricandeau of veal and carrot pudding that Lady Ogden was a widow; her husband had been killed during the fighting on the peninsula early last year. He and Tristan had served together in the same regiment, which explained how Caroline and Tristan had met. Tristan had resigned his commission after being badly wounded in the same battle that claimed Lord Ogden's life.

Caroline skillfully directed the dinner conversation, and during the roasted beef, broiled mutton, parsnips in butter, and boiled potatoes with mint sauce, Alyssa caught a glimpse of the raffish high society of London. It was an endless social whirl of balls, soirees, parties, and afternoon teas. The gaming clubs and prizefights, the theater and the opera, the circus and Vauxhall Gardens: it was pure fascination to Alyssa.

Alyssa studied her dinner companions during the meal, saying little. Lady Ogden maintained a very proper air, as did the duke, although he seemed to be enjoying himself. Caroline was in her glory with the majority of attention focused on her, although Alyssa saw she often glanced at Tristan. He in turn could not keep his eyes off her. *He loves her,* Alyssa realized with amazement. She had witnessed their passion firsthand, but it surprised her to discover their love for each other. Marriages for love were a rarity among the ton. Tristan and Caroline appeared to be among the lucky few.

As the talk turned to gossip, it was obvious Caroline held certain people in particular fascination. The first was a gentleman named George Brummell, who she constantly referred to as "Beau."

"Well, I don't care if Beau is no longer on good terms with the regent," Caroline said flippantly. "I find Beau absolutely charming. His constant aim is toward a sober but exquisite perfection, and you cannot deny he has genuine good taste in everything. Beau's clothes, house, furniture, library, all his possessions are much admired."

"As are his eccentricities, Caroline," the duke responded to her glowing recitation of Brummell's character. "I've heard tell that he sends his washing nearly twenty miles outside of London because that is the only place it can be done properly, his boots have to be cleaned in champagne, and it takes three people to make his gloves."

"He is an original, Morgan," Caroline stated firmly, defending her Beau.

"Henry Cope has also been labeled an original, my dear," Tristan said laughingly. "He is known as 'the green man' because everything he wears is green, his rooms and all his possessions are green, and it is said he eats nothing but green fruits and vegetables."

"How very odd," Alyssa slipped in.

"They are both eccentric fops," Lady Ogden said, her tone sour.

"Honestly, Priscilla, you say that about every man who isn't the Duke of Wellington," Caroline replied.

"Arthur Wellesley might not be a romantic, Caroline, but he is a genius, and the best hope this country has in defeating that Corsican monster and his French marshals," Lady Ogden said primly.

"I still prefer a true romantic," Caroline said with good humor. She stroked Tristan's hand. "Like my darling Tris, or that lovely Lord Byron. His poetry is sheer magic."

"I didn't know you were writing poetry these days, Tris," Morgan drawled mockingly.

"You heard Caroline's critique yourself, Morgan." Tristan chuckled. "Sheer magic."

"Oh, you." Caroline wagged her fork at Tristan. "I'm not the only woman in London who finds Lord Byron fascinating. I've heard tell of a very married lady who is wildly indiscreet where Byron is concerned. They are seen everywhere together, and after late-night parties she always leaves in his carriage."

"Poor Lord Melbourne," Lady Ogden sympathized. "How perfectly dreadful to be unable to control your own wife."

"Anyone who would allow an impulsive woman like Caroline Lamb loose in London deserves the scandal she causes," the duke sneered.

"But she does have marvelous legs," Tristan quipped. "I saw her at Lady Holland's ball last week. She hadn't been invited, so she turned up in her favorite masquerade: a page boy."

"Tristan!" Lady Ogden admonished. "That is quite enough about Caroline Lamb's physical attributes. I hardly think that is fit conversation for our dinner table." She looked to the duke for his support.

"Tell us the latest news from the War Ministry, Tris," Morgan requested mildly.

Tristan nodded his head and repeated the latest war news. Alyssa noticed it seemed to appease Lady Ogden. She became more attentive and relaxed. Alyssa supposed listening to news about the war made her feel closer to her dead husband.

The gentlemen did not linger over their port, but instead joined the ladies in the front salon. Tristan persuaded Lady Ogden to play the pianoforte, while he and Caroline sat very close together on a nearby settee.

Alyssa retreated to a faded, overstuffed chair in the corner of the room, hoping to remain unobtrusive until she could excuse herself. She was no sooner seated than Morgan materialized at her side, dragging a rosewood armchair with him so he could sit near her.

"You were very quiet during dinner this evening, Miss Carrington," the duke said.

"Was I?"

"I hope you did not find our talk of London boring."

"Quite the contrary, Your Grace," Alyssa replied. "I found it very . . . enlightening. It made me realize how very little I know of society."

"Do you wish to know more? Firsthand perhaps?"

She shook her head. "I learned a long time ago it is fruitless to want what can never be," she said simply.

"You will be content to pass the rest of your days alone, in your tiny cottage, Miss Carrington? Funny,

I thought you a woman of more spirit," Morgan said provocatively.

She did not disappoint him. Morgan saw her spirit emerge with a flash of fire in her green eyes.

"I will not be in my 'tiny' cottage, Your Grace. I plan on going to Cornwall as soon as all the arrangements are made," she informed him icily.

"To be with family?"

"To be employed."

"Employed! Doing what? A governess? Or better still, a companion?" Morgan asked incredulously. Unwittingly a picture of Mrs. Glyndon, his grandmother's companion, came to mind.

"Those are the positions I am currently seeking," Alyssa responded briskly. "Since all the estate agent jobs were filled, I have little choice." Alyssa's attempt at lightness fell on deaf ears.

Morgan gazed at her profile sharply. "Why this sudden change of plans?"

Alyssa turned to him, fully intending to tell him to mind his own business, but his questioning eyes stopped her. Does it really matter if he knows? she thought wearily. Not fully understanding why the duke would be remotely interested, Alyssa nevertheless explained.

"Additional expenses from Lord Carrington's estate have forced me to alter my plans," she said quietly.

"What of the new Viscount Mulgrave? Or your family?"

"There is no family. The new viscount is Lord Carrington's brother, an American," she replied. "He cannot be located, so the responsibility has fallen to me."

"As always," he countered, his eyes filling with sympathy.

Alyssa saw it, and for once was not moved by it. It wounded her pride to be constantly viewed by the duke as an object of pity.

"I shall manage, Your Grace," she replied briskly, thrusting her chin up. "I always have. I know I will be able to secure a position eventually. My primary concern is for my former nurse, Mavis."

"What is wrong with Mavis?"

"Nothing is wrong with her. Your brother has indicated he is willing to keep the servants on, but Mavis is too old to start over. Lord Carrington made no provisions for any of the servants and I have nothing left to give." Alyssa sighed softly and turned her head away.

"Then I will provide a pension for her."

"But why? Mavis is not your concern." She looked up into his face, testing his sincerity.

"I will provide for her," Morgan insisted. "Unless you object?"

"Quite the contrary. I find myself in your debt, sir. Thank you."

"Is there anything else I can do to assist you, Miss Carrington?" Morgan pressed on. Alyssa gazed into his mesmerizing gray eyes, enthralled by the way they suddenly glowed with an inner light. A strong, almost primitive need to plead for his protection coursed through her veins, but she suppressed it. Flustered by these feelings, Alyssa fought hard to preserve her countenance and managed to answer in a calm voice.

"No, thank you, Your Grace. You are already doing more than propriety allows. If you will excuse me, however, I find I am extremely tired. I bid you good night."

Alyssa rose quickly from her chair and, after bidding the others good night, left the room. Morgan filled a glass with a large portion of brandy and settled himself into a chair closer to the pianoforte, staring stonily at the door long after she was gone.

Chapter Five

Morgan awoke with a start at a loud clap of thunder outside his bedroom window. He had not closed the bedcurtains, and the full moon cast eerie shadows across the carpeted floor. Fumbling in the dark, he found the flint on the small table by his bed and lit the candle there. He shivered slightly. There was a chill in the room. The fire had gone cold.

Morgan sat up in the bed, listening to the howling wind and pelting rain. Casting his eyes skyward he quickly inspected the ceiling, knowing he wouldn't be surprised to feel raindrops on his face.

Why shouldn't the roof leak? The majority of the house was in disrepair. Good thing Tristan is rich, he laughed to himself. It is going to cost him a bloody fortune to repair and renovate this mausoleum.

Morgan sat back against the feather pillows thinking about Alyssa. She had kept the estate productive only by foregoing her own creature comforts. He doubted her wardrobe contained a single presentable gown, yet she always carried herself with grace and dignity. Morgan would never understand how she had managed to live that way for so long.

The restless passion Morgan felt each time he thought about Alyssa returned. Knowing he would be unable to fall back to sleep, Morgan debated his options. He could get a boring volume from the library downstairs—that would certainly put him straight to sleep. Or perhaps a snifter of brandy would do the job nicely.

Rising naked from the bed, Morgan donned the brocade dressing gown Perkins had left on the chair. Grabbing his bedside candle, the duke padded barefoot from his room soundlessly down the corridor to the staircase.

He paused a moment in the large entrance hall, getting his bearings. He headed for the front salon, remembering the large decanter of brandy he and Tristan shared but had not emptied after dinner.

Morgan raised the candle he carried high in front of himself to illuminate the dark entrance hall. He was approaching the front salon when a strange noise brought him up short.

Was it the wind? It sounded like crying—no, whining perhaps? He cocked his head to one side and listened intently. He moved slowly down the hall, following the sound. When Morgan reached the end of the hallway, he saw light emerging from the partially closed library doors.

Again he heard the unusual sound. It wasn't crying. It was singing. Someone was singing. Loudly and off-key. Morgan gently pushed open the door and stepped into the room.

A roaring fire bathed the room in soft light, making it warm and inviting. Directly in front of the large fireplace, sprawled out in a high-backed wing chair, sat Alyssa. Her legs were dangling over the side arm of the chair. A half-empty glass in one hand was raised comfortably across the top of her chair, while the other arm dangled down onto the carpeted floor.

Not wanting to startle her, Morgan spoke softly. "Miss Carrington?"

Her head whipped up, and she grinned crookedly at him. "Your Grace! What a lovely surprise. Please come in."

She indicated the matching wing-back chair. "Do sit down. I was just enjoying a spot of brandy. I insist you join me."

She struggled a bit to get up from the chair and was successful on her third attempt. "Whatever are you doing awake at this ungodly hour?" she asked, rising awkwardly to her feet. When she stood up, Morgan saw she was in her nightclothes.

She turned and walked in front of the fireplace, and Morgan sucked in his breath sharply. The glow of the firelight illuminated her simple cotton nightgown, allowing him to view her as if she were naked. He wondered how he ever could have thought she was thin. Her body was all sensuous curves: long legs, lean thighs, narrow waist, smooth buttocks, and lush, full breasts. Her hair, revealed to him for the first time, was long and thick, a rich, vibrant copper color. She looked different, so free and wild and beautiful. He felt the blood rush to his head at Alyssa's incredible transformation.

Blissfully unaware of his scrutiny, Alyssa absently ran a hand through her disheveled hair as she searched the Pembroke table for the brandy decanter and a clean glass.

"Ahh, here we are, Your Grace." She handed him his drink before settling back into her chair. "Would you also care for something to eat?"

"What? Something to eat? No. No, thank you."

"Are you sure? You look rather hungry." She took a small sip of her drink and grimaced at the strong taste.

"You still haven't told me what brings you down here so late."

"The storm woke me. I thought a glass of brandy might help me sleep. When I came downstairs, I heard a noise, so I came to investigate."

"Ha!" she exclaimed loudly. "My singing." Alyssa giggled. "I hope it didn't frighten you. Lord Carrington always told me my singing sounded like a cat being tortured."

"Why are you here at this hour, Miss Carrington?"

"I am visiting my brave captain," she told him in a serious voice. She raised her glass, toasting the portrait over the fireplace of a rakish man, elegantly dressed in Elizabethan costume.

"My noble ancestor, Sir Thomas Carrington. A sea captain and privateer, though I'm sure he was more a pirate. He does have that look about him." She turned to Morgan for confirmation, but continued before he could respond.

"He was knighted by good Queen Bess herself for services to the Crown. God only knows what that entailed." Grinning broadly, she winked at Morgan.

"Good God, woman, are you foxed?"

"I should say not," she bristled. "I've only had this one drink." She held up her nearly empty glass.

"One drink can do the trick when you are not used to strong spirits."

"I bow to your authority on the matter, Your Grace. But I still must insist that I am not drunk."

Morgan took a sip of his brandy, and for a moment simply stared at her. "What has upset you so much that you seek comfort here alone with a bottle?"

"Do you mean in addition to my being destitute, not yet employed, and in immediate danger of losing the very roof over my head?" She laughed again, but it had a hollow sound.

"A difficult situation, but is that truly the reason?"

"Not entirely," she confessed. "I rediscovered some long-forgotten emotions tonight."

"What?"

She squirmed uncomfortably in her chair. "Not since I was a young girl have I felt this intense jealousy. And envy. I don't like it."

"Jealous of whom?"

"Caroline," she whispered softly.

"You have no need to be jealous. You are every bit as lovely as Caroline, in fact more so."

She looked puzzled for a moment. "Why do you assume I wish to look like Caroline?"

"Am I wrong?"

"Yes. It is not Caroline's looks that I envy. It is her relationship with Tristan."

"You want Tristan?" Morgan barked, feeling a bit of jealousy himself.

Alyssa shook her head. "That is not what I mean. Tristan is a fascinating man, to be sure, but it is obvious his emotions are already engaged. What I want is someone . . . someone to look at me the way Tristan looks at Caroline."

"And how exactly does Tris look at Caroline?"

"With delight . . . and happiness . . . and wonder, even when she says the silliest things." Alyssa spoke very softly. Morgan leaned closer to catch her words. "He looks at her . . . with love."

"Love?" Morgan asked, not sure he understood. "Don't you mean lust?"

Alyssa shook her head. "Oh, no. I thought it was lust too at first, when we interrupted them before dinner. But it is more than that. I saw the way he soulfully gazes at her. During dinner and afterward when Lady Ogden was playing the pianoforte. Tristan is very much in love with Caroline."

She said it with such assurance Morgan was almost convinced. He had not thought much about it before, but he supposed it was possible. Cynic that he was, Morgan doubted it would last.

"You seem so surprised. Don't you love your wife, Your Grace?" Alyssa asked in a small voice.

"What? What did you say?"

"I asked if you loved your wife," Alyssa repeated, needing very much to know.

"My wife is dead," Morgan said in a flat voice. Her question made him think of Valerie. At one time he did believe he could learn to love his wife. Valerie had always claimed to be madly in love with him, at least in the beginning of their marriage. No, he did not ever truly love his wife. All he could remember now was the misery they had shared.

"I'm so sorry. I did not know. Caroline spoke earlier of the duchess waiting for all of you at Ramsgate Castle. I assumed she meant your wife." Alyssa reached over and closed her fingers tentatively around his arm. "I did not wish to cause you any pain."

Morgan looked into her clear green eyes and saw her concern. She wasn't intoxicated, he determined, perhaps a little less inhibited, but not foxed. He reached out with his hand and gently stroked Alyssa's soft cheek. She accepted his warm touch, closing her eyes and moving her face against his hand. It felt wonderful.

"Is love such a rare thing? I was hoping to understand it a bit better," she said, reaching up to hold his hand.

Morgan stared at her, mute. His throat tightened with desire, and the sudden passion he felt was strong enough to drive any sane man past reason.

Fate, so often cruel in the past, had suddenly smiled upon him. This remarkable chance encounter with the openly curious Alyssa provided an opportunity to explore a physical relationship with a woman he admired. He would be a fool to toss this extraordinary opportunity aside. The temptation was simply impossible to resist.

"Open your eyes, Alyssa," he finally murmured in a thick voice.

She obeyed. Silently they surveyed each other as if they were kindred souls mesmerized by emotions they couldn't identify. Without warning, Morgan pulled Alyssa toward him and kissed her fiercely, his lips pressing firmly, commandingly, against her soft mouth. Instinctively she responded to his passion, parting her lips, allowing him to deepen his kiss.

A violent shudder shook him at her response and he pulled her out of her chair and onto his lap. She clasped her hands on his shoulders, drawing closer to him. Morgan's probing tongue moved in and out of her mouth, making her feel dizzy and creating tremors of unexpected pleasure.

His lips wandered freely, gently kissing her face, nuzzling her ears. Morgan buried his face in her hair, breathing in the sweet, clean smell. Alyssa could feel the violent pounding of his heart against her chest and the hardness of his growing desire against her thigh. It was a new and exhilarating experience. Her body, her whole being, felt strangely alive.

"Oh, sweet," he murmured passionately. "There's a fire in you I never dreamt of."

His words penetrated her passionate haze. She pulled away, her breath coming in loud gasps as she fought to still her pounding heart.

"Is there really a fire within me?" she whispered with amazement. The gentle wonder in her voice nearly did him in. Morgan glared hotly at her, his face flushed with desire, his lean body taut with barely controllable passion.

"God, yes," he murmured, pulling her close against his broad chest. His mouth was warm and hungry as he kissed her with an urgency that left her moaning small sounds of ecstasy.

His mouth felt so good, so right. The touch of his tongue sent steamy liquid waves of feeling throughout her body, deep into her belly. Alyssa's arms twisted around his neck, ardently encouraging his explorations.

"Darling," she heard him mutter, his breath jagged and warm on her neck. She tried to answer, but was unable to speak, beyond anything but the urgency to kiss him, caress him, feel him.

He lifted his head and looked directly into her eyes. "I want you."

Her green eyes darkened with unleashed passion at his simple statement. Good lord, he wants me, she thought. He desires me; he has a need, nay, an ache for me. Me. This beautiful, wonderful, glorious man, who can have any woman he desires, wants me.

It was a heady feeling to be the object of Morgan's intense passion. Yet it was more than mere desire that drew Alyssa to him. There was a connection, an invisible bond that existed between them. It frightened and fascinated her.

Feeling too overwhelmed to respond, Alyssa merely pressed herself closer into his arms, burying her head in his neck. As she nuzzled closer to him, Morgan's hand began to roam her back and buttocks.

"Shall I take you now, love?" he whispered hypnotically in her ear. "Shall we lie down on the rug before the fire together?"

Gently he tugged on her nightgown. She felt the warmth from the crackling fire on her bare legs as his fingers moved slowly, ever so slowly, up the bare flesh of her thigh. His hand slid softly between her thighs, and he kissed her lips with an almost desperate need. She sprawled wantonly in his lap, offering herself to him, arching her back as he rhythmically stroked his

85

hand back and forth between her thighs.

What is he doing to me? Alyssa thought wildly, feeling the heat and dampness on his hand and realizing it came from her.

Morgan broke their kiss and gazed into her upturned face. Her lower lip was held tightly between her teeth, her eyes were half closed, her breathing was ragged. He thought she looked magnificent. So warm, so soft, so giving. Her passionate response touched a deep chord within his soul. Feeling a surge of tenderness, he hugged her tightly.

Alyssa felt warm and safe within the circle of Morgan's strong arms. She adjusted her body, tightening her grip around his neck.

She could feel the pulsating hardness of his manhood pressing against the soft flesh of her belly, and it made her tremble. Curious, she slid her hand down to his lap and touched him. She ran her fingers over his tightly pulled dressing gown, exploring up and down the hard bulge. Morgan sucked in his breath sharply. Yanking her hand away, Alyssa froze.

"Am I hurting you?" she whispered in concern.

Morgan gave a harsh laugh that sounded more like a groan. "If you hurt me any more, love, I shall disgrace myself."

She smiled, not really understanding.

"Teach me," she pleaded, surprising them both with her request.

He looked into her innocent, trusting face and felt his heart constrict. He ached with wanting her. Yet he hesitated. Despite her sensual response, Morgan felt certain Alyssa was a virgin. He was not sure she fully understood what she was asking.

He was not, although his reputation with women might indicate otherwise, a despoiler of innocent ladies. Gently he disengaged himself from her arms. Clasping her small hands between his large ones, Morgan gazed deeply into her eyes.

"Do you know what you are asking?"

She nodded.

"We will only be together this one night, Alyssa, but I will try to make it a magical one for us both. Do you understand?"

She nodded again, not trusting her voice.

"Then will you come upstairs with me now, Alyssa? Upstairs and into my bed?" Morgan asked in a solemn voice.

She gazed up into his handsome face and felt her throat tighten with emotion. *It is wrong*, a voice sounded in her head. *How can you even consider such an indecent proposal?* What he was saying went against every moral principle she had ever been taught. But she didn't care.

"Yes . . . yes, I will come with you." Her voice was barely audible, but Morgan saw her eyes glisten with determination.

"Come, then," Morgan replied, letting out the breath he had unconsciously been holding. They rose from the chair simultaneously. Morgan grabbed his nearly extinguished candle in one hand, Alyssa with the other, and led her from the library.

As they climbed the stairs side by side, Alyssa leaned closer against him, resting her head on his upper arm. She hesitated briefly outside his bedchamber, but he still clutched her hand in an iron grip. Pulling her inside, Morgan slammed the door.

He left Alyssa momentarily to place his candle by the bed and bank the unlit fireplace.

"It is cold," he muttered, rubbing his hands together as he set about starting a new blaze.

He is giving me a chance to change my mind, Alyssa realized, but she stayed rooted to the spot. *Leave*, her conscience shouted, *leave quickly*. Yet Alyssa could not move.

One night, another voice inside her called. *Here at last is a chance to experience love, to experience life. Is it so terribly wrong to share one night of passion with this man? This one special memory can warm you on all those cold, lonely nights that will follow.* Alyssa felt as though she were outside her own body, looking down at herself and merely observing, not participating in the moral debate in her mind.

Closing her eyes to shut out the voices, she was startled when Morgan drew her into his arms.

"No regrets?" he queried, giving her a final opportunity. She started to speak, but instead pressed herself hard against him, raising her lips for his kiss.

He attacked her mouth as if he were starving for her, his tongue boldly demanding entrance. Expertly he undid the tiny buttons down the front of her nightgown and placed a warm hand on her bare breast. Softly, gently, Morgan brushed a fingertip lightly from one side to the other over the swelling peak. The nipple stiffened, sending shudders through Alyssa's body. She felt a dampness between her legs as her breasts swelled, the nipples rising to meet his questing hands.

Morgan pulled the nightgown off Alyssa's shoulders, and it dropped to her feet. He kissed her neck with tiny sweet kisses, and whispered to her as his lips followed his hands down her silky body to caress her breasts.

"You are beyond beautiful, Alyssa. Your body is perfect: creamy, firm, smooth. 'Tis a crime the way you hide yourself beneath those ugly dresses." Morgan's tongue gently stroked her sweet flesh and pert, rosebud nipples.

"Come over to the bed, love, so I may see you better. I want to see your face when I take you. I want to feel you move beneath me. I want to hear you moan with pleasure when I make you mine."

Morgan was almost out of control as his hands sensually caressed her body. He couldn't remember ever wanting, needing a woman so intensely. He pushed Alyssa down onto the bed and loomed enticingly above her. His tongue came down and circled her nipple hungrily, suckling at her breast like a babe.

Dropping to his knees he began kissing her mouth again, deeply. While he kissed her, he shrugged out of his dressing gown. Gloriously naked, Morgan lowered his body to hers.

"Touch me," he breathed against her neck.

Her hand boldly explored the hard muscles of his chest, and she delighted in the springy pelt of hair curling around her fingers. She discovered his nipples, so different from her own. Yet as she pinched them between her fingers, they reacted as hers did, hardening with desire.

"Oh, lord!" he swore huskily, reaching down until he was lightly cupping his palm over her. He stared into her passion-darkened eyes, watching every expression as his knowing fingers caressed the aching core of her womanhood.

"Oh, love, you've set me afire," Morgan whispered into her ear.

Suddenly his finger slipped inside her and Alyssa felt her breath catch in her throat.

"Good lord," she gasped. He felt her nails dig into his arms, her body tensing under his invasion.

"Follow your feelings, love," Morgan encouraged, probing further into her slick warmth. He was determined to bring her to fulfillment before claiming her, but she was driving him to distraction with her passionate, giving response.

"Move your hips, Alyssa. Feel the rhythm of your body."

Alyssa arched her back, making her hips brush against his fingers. She moaned breathlessly, whimpering as the tension began to build.

"What are you doing to me?" she cried, looking into his eyes. Her mind and her body were captivated by this wondrous man, and she continued to stare hypnotically into his silver-gray eyes as his strong, sensual fingers worked their magic. She felt the pressure building and she moved her hips faster and faster, concentrating on his mesmerizing eyes, his masterful mouth, his beautiful face. As she reached the crest of excitement, the pressure broke and the pleasure washed over her entire being.

Morgan experienced endless delight watching the wonder and enchantment on her face as her body exploded in ecstasy. His own body was hard, throbbing, and aching for release. Wild, rippling feelings pulsed through him, and Morgan knew he could wait no longer.

"Spread your legs," he said hoarsely.

Alyssa did as he commanded, not fully comprehending, still too caught up in the enjoyment of the experience to much care. Morgan positioned himself and, reaching down, parted her softness. Kissing her deeply, he sheathed himself within her silky warmth.

He thrust forward and felt her body recoil from the assault as he broke through her maidenhead. He realized instantly he had taken her too roughly, but her uninhibited passion had pushed him beyond control.

Alyssa cried out at the unexpected pain, pressing frantically on his chest to remove him. She felt as though she were being torn in half. Morgan withdrew slightly and she tried to squirm out from under him.

He was instantly still.

"I'm sorry, love," he murmured, resting up on his elbows, his breath coming in gasps. "Lord, you are so sweet, so tight, 'tis driving me wild. Try to relax; the pain shall pass."

Alyssa forced her body to go limp. Slowly Morgan started to move, but she immediately tensed again.

"It hurts," she whispered.

"Oh, hell," he cursed loudly, knowing he was causing her pain, but unable to stop himself. Grabbing her buttocks, he lifted her toward him and thrust. She groaned at the burning sensation as he moved against her, but did not try to pull away.

Slowly, gradually, the pain subsided, and Alyssa felt herself becoming caught up in the rhythm of his lovemaking. She clung to Morgan, moving her hips tentatively in response. She could feel his body change, become tense as his movements became more urgent, harder, deeper, faster. He grew even larger inside her, and then suddenly Morgan stopped and cried out, spilling his seed. Spent, he collapsed on top of her.

After a few moments, Morgan came up on his elbows, trying to regain control of his breathing. Lightly he caressed her damp face and hair. Alyssa thought he had never looked more handsome. His hair was in wild disarray, his face covered with a thin layer of sweat. She touched the wetness near his brow, and he grabbed her finger in his mouth playfully.

"Forgive me, sweetheart."

She winced slightly as he withdrew from her and rolled to his back. Turning to face him, Alyssa got her first frontal view of Morgan's body. She gasped loudly.

"My God, you're bleeding," she cried in alarm, pointing to his semierect manhood.

Before Morgan could explain, Alyssa jumped from the bed. She returned quickly with a clean cloth and a basin of water. Gently and naturally she bathed him, showing no embarrassment at performing such an intimate act for him. He watched her sweet face closely as she ministered to him, and he felt himself begin to stiffen again.

After she rinsed the cloth clean, he sat up and took it from her, pushing her down onto the bed.

"I'm sorry I took you so roughly," he said. "The

blood is from your maidenhead, love, not from me."
As he spoke, Morgan placed the damp cloth between
her thighs, washing off the blood. The cool cloth felt
good against her tender skin. She took the cloth from
him when he was finished, and placed it in the basin
on the small table near the bed.

Then she expertly fluffed three pillows against the
headboard for Morgan to recline on. When he was
comfortably situated, she snuggled up to his naked
chest, resting her head on his shoulder.

"Hold me," she said simply. And he did.

Morgan adjusted his leg more comfortably against
her and pulled up the blankets. It felt oddly natural,
holding her thus. He softly kissed her temple while
she absently stroked his chest, curling her fingers
through the crisp hairs.

"It was a very . . . interesting experience," Alyssa
murmured.

"Interesting!" Morgan howled, not sure he liked her
description of what had just transpired. "A man does
not appreciate his lover referring to him as interesting, my dear."

His lover! The words had such a marvelously
wicked sound, they made Alyssa smile and say, "Shall
I instead sing your praises, Your Grace?"

"You impudent baggage." He gave her a carefree
grin. "I do believe we are acquainted well enough for
you to address me by my given name. Don't you
agree?"

"Of course, Morgan." She blushed. "It is a strange
occurrence—this intimacy between men and
women."

"Did you enjoy our intimacy?"

Alyssa considered his question. "Yes." She burrowed her face in his muscular chest. "Especially the
beginning. Is it always so . . . so earth-shattering?"

"Only if you are very lucky," he answered, trying to

recall such complete contentment after making love with a woman. "I am sorry I was so rough. Do you still hurt?"

"Just a bit," she lied, not really caring about the pain. It had been a wondrous experience for Alyssa, and she had no regrets, at least not now.

Morgan lifted his head to look down at her. "Next time will be better, sweet, I promise," he said, stroking her hair. "No maidenhead, no pain, just wild, rampant pleasure. Would you like that?"

"Ummm," she murmured, her mind filling with erotic images. "But I'm afraid there won't be another time, Morgan. I must return to my room. It shall be light soon, and Mavis will wonder what has become of me."

Morgan abruptly sat up, realizing it was nearly dawn. He also realized their magical night had come to an end, and his mood turned from contentment to melancholy. Only this one night together, he had told her, but now he deeply regretted those words. He wanted more from her, much more. Yet he must tread carefully.

"Are you determined to go to Cornwall, Alyssa? Is there nothing I can do to persuade you to stay?"

She gave a small laugh, thinking he was jesting with her. "How can I stay here without a position? Do you know of one for me?"

"I might."

"You are speaking in riddles," she said, looking at him strangely.

Morgan was momentarily stymied. For all her wild abandon tonight, he knew Alyssa was not an amoral woman. And she was proud, very proud. He did not want to risk offending and then losing her. Not yet. Not after he had decided to keep her.

"You don't need to find employment, Alyssa. I would be honored to take care of you. If you will allow me,"

Morgan declared in his most charming voice.

"Aren't you a bit old to be a governess?" she said.

He smiled. "With the protection of my name, Alyssa, you will never want for anything. I give you my word."

His name! Alyssa felt her heart turn over in her breast. He was serious. *He really does want me, and not for just one night.* Her pulses quickened at the thought of being with him, belonging to him.

"Are you sure this is what you want?" she asked shakily. "Even though I am twenty-four years old, I have very little worldly experience."

Morgan laughed with relief that she had not refused him outright. He leered seductively at her. "I will teach you everything you need to know, love."

"Are you sure?" she asked again, still not believing it was possible.

"I've never been more certain of anything. We shall deal very well together, you and I. Say yes."

"All right then—yes," she agreed breathlessly.

Morgan hugged her tightly, inordinately pleased. He saw the first rays of sunlight beginning to creep through the window and knew dawn was indeed fast approaching. It was time for Alyssa to leave.

"Come, Alyssa," Morgan said, searching about the room for her nightgown. "You must return to your bed before the rest of the house awakens."

Alyssa's head turned sharply to the window and, seeing the telltale signs of the coming dawn, rushed to comply. She donned her bedclothes quickly, feeling strange as they stood together at the door, Morgan naked in all his male splendor while she was clothed.

"We will discuss our future plans after breakfast," he assured her. With a quick, hard kiss, Morgan propelled Alyssa out the door.

Once alone, he stretched contentedly and padded back to the bed, fully intending to grab a few hours of much needed sleep before the new day officially began. For the first time in many years Morgan felt a true sense of peace and contentment. What a marvelous stroke of good fortune. The charming Alyssa Carrington had just agreed to become his mistress.

Alyssa walked soundlessly down the hallway, conscious of a faint soreness between her thighs. She flushed, remembering the cause. It was not, however, going to affect what was certain to be a glorious day. For the first time in many years, Alyssa felt her heart fill with pure joy. She had just agreed to become Morgan's wife.

Chapter Six

Morgan drifted slowly awake, the strong aroma of coffee assaulting his senses. Disoriented by his unfamiliar surroundings, he didn't immediately remember he was at Westgate Manor. Morgan sat up in bed and spied Tristan casually leaning against the fireplace mantel, sipping a cup of coffee.

"Morning, Tris." Morgan yawned. "To what do I owe this unexpected pleasure?"

"Finally," Tristan exclaimed. "You wouldn't have survived long in the army, sleeping so soundly. I've already been here fifteen minutes. I swear, Morgan, you sleep like the dead."

Morgan grinned sheepishly. "The rain woke me last night. I guess I didn't fall asleep until early morning."

Morgan alighted from the bed and shrugged into his robe. He poured fresh water from the large pitcher into the porcelain basin and began to wash. "Is there any coffee for me?" he asked his younger brother.

Tristan produced another cup for Morgan, filled it from a large silver pot, and handed it to the duke. "The women were getting a bit anxious about leaving for Ramsgate Castle, so I volunteered to brave the lion in his den."

"Honestly, Tris, it cannot be that late," Morgan protested.

" 'Tis nearly noon."

"What!" Morgan exclaimed in surprise. "That's impossible."

"Look for yourself," Tristan insisted, pulling back the heavy drapes, instantly flooding the room with brilliant sunshine.

"We should have left long before now. Why didn't you wake me?"

"I was having too much fun," Tristan replied glumly. He sat down in a faded velvet chair and lazily stretched out his legs, crossing his ankles. His clear blue eyes studied Morgan openly in the mirror while he shaved.

"I managed to get lost in the boxwood maze with Caroline and was having a charming dalliance before Priscilla descended upon us." Tristan sighed heavily. "I swear that woman has eyes in the back of her head."

"Maybe you should consider moving your wedding date closer," Morgan remarked dryly. "At this rate you won't last till your wedding night before bedding Caroline."

"Who said anything about waiting?" Tristan responded in an offhand manner.

"Tristan." Morgan's voice was stern. "Need I remind you, little brother, this is not a matter to be taken lightly." Morgan was about to launch into a rather stuffy lecture on propriety, but caught himself. What right do I have to reprimand Tristan, Morgan thought, after what took place in this room with Alyssa last night?

Tristan held up his hand to stop any additional comments from his older brother. "Enough said, Morgan.

For God's sake, give me some credit. I would never compromise Caroline before our marriage. I have far too much respect and affection for her."

Tristan's innocent words struck a chord in the duke, but he swiftly trampled his feelings of guilt. Turning away from the mirror Morgan wiped his face clean of soap and took a long sip of lukewarm coffee.

"What else have you been doing this morning besides chasing Caroline?"

"You mean while you've been sleeping the day away?" Tristan said teasingly, unable to resist the urge to needle Morgan. "Actually, we've had a delightful time surveying the grounds. Lady Alyssa has been very informative, as always."

At the mention of Alyssa, Morgan ceased dressing, his mind filling with erotic images. Alyssa naked in his arms, her breathing ragged and shallow, her body clasped tightly around his, clinging to him as he deeply entered her softness.

"She is a unique woman." Tristan's comment brought Morgan out of his passionate remembrances. "I don't understand, however, why she is living here." He looked at Morgan for an explanation.

"It's very simple," Morgan replied as he sat on the edge of the bed and struggled with his black Hessians. "Alyssa has nowhere else to go. I recently discovered her father left her penniless, and her only relatives live in America."

Tristan whistled in shock. Kneeling down he assisted Morgan with his boots. "What is she planning to do?"

Tristan's inquiry presented Morgan with the perfect opening, and he seized it. "I was rather hoping you would keep her here for a time."

"Here? Doing what?"

"This and that," Morgan hedged. "It's obvious the manor house needs considerable renovations before it's fit to occupy. Miss Carrington can provide invaluable assistance in selecting and supervising the workmen. She is well acquainted with all the locals and appears to be a highly capable woman. From what I have seen of the estate, she has managed remarkably well without the benefit of formal training."

Tristan rubbed his chin thoughtfully. "It would be very helpful having someone familiar with the area working with us." Smiling, Tristan added, "And if I am very lucky, Priscilla will not always be able to accompany Caroline during our visits to the manor. Miss Carrington could serve as chaperon."

"She could," Morgan replied slowly, unsure about Alyssa's qualifications as a chaperon.

"Do you think she would be interested in the position?" Tristan asked.

"I'm sure she would be. I'd be glad to talk to her about it for you."

"Splendid."

Morgan smiled brightly at Tristan's agreement. It had been much simpler than he expected. Alyssa would be safely installed at Westgate Manor, easily accessible to him until he could make more permanent arrangements. He was prepared to be generous with her: expensive clothes and jewels, a new carriage, a modest house. Morgan felt she deserved a life of comfort and ease after struggling valiantly in an environment of financial uncertainty for so long. He was going to enjoy enriching her life.

Making a final adjustment to his cravat, Morgan turned to his brother. "Shall we join the ladies?"

The ladies were seated in silence in the morning room, taking refreshments after their garden tour. Caroline paced the room impatiently, her agitation over Tristan's long absence evident. Lady Ogden stared quietly out the large window, ignoring her sister's mood. Alyssa also sat silently, nervously picking off the small pieces of lint on her skirt.

Alyssa had lain awake in the early dawn hours reliving every moment of her night in Morgan's bed. Exhausted, but still too wound up to sleep, she recalled with stunning clarity the gentle caress of his hand, the warmth of his kisses, the strength of his embrace. It all happened so quickly, and yet Alyssa had instinctively known it was right. Fate had intervened to intertwine their lives permanently. Perhaps even for eternity.

Alyssa dressed quickly but carefully that morning, anxious to see Morgan again, yet still uncertain of the unbelievable change their relationship had undergone. When he had not appeared at breakfast, she had smiled secretly to herself as the others speculated on what kept him abed. As the morning wore on, however, she became increasingly nervous about his absence.

Is he trying to avoid me? Does he regret last night so much that he cannot face me? The questions raged in her mind, giving way to slow panic as the morning drew to a close without Morgan making an appearance. Finally Tristan announced his intention to rouse the duke, and Alyssa breathed a sigh of relief.

"I cannot imagine what is taking Tristan so long." Caroline sighed in exasperation. "Perhaps I should go upstairs and see if he needs any help?"

"Stop being so ridiculous, Caroline," Lady Ogden admonished in a sour voice. "You are behaving as if Tristan has been gone for a year instead of an hour. I'm sure if your assistance is needed, you shall be summoned."

Alyssa could tell by the toss of Caroline's head she was not pleased with her sister's response. Caroline finally ceased her endless pacing and began tapping her fingers rapidly on the windowpane. Alyssa took a moment to admire her. She looked very pretty in her white muslin gown. The high waistline accented Caroline's small bust, and the long flow of the skirt, with its flounces of pink at the hem, gave her the illusion of height, even though she was no taller than five feet. The open neckline of the dress was modestly filled with matching pink muslin, with a small ruffle high at the throat, gracefully displaying Caroline's neck. Even her shoes were pink, decorated with small white satin bows.

Caroline is so dainty and feminine, Alyssa marveled. No wonder Tristan loves her. After inventorying Caroline's many attributes, Alyssa felt clumsy and awkward, worrying how Morgan would possibly find her attractive in the light of day. For the first time in her life Alyssa wished she were tiny and petite, instead of tall and lanky. She longed to possess a gown made especially for her instead of an altered dress from her mother's trousseau. Her lack of a decent wardrobe had never bothered Alyssa, but suddenly all her insecurities were brought into focus and she desperately wanted to possess a beauty and presence that would dazzle Morgan.

Tristan and Morgan entered the room unannounced, and Caroline gave a small squeal of delight at their sudden appearance. Lady Ogden huffed her disapproval of Caroline's behavior, but held her tongue. Alyssa felt her heart begin to thud loudly as the duke approached. She rose quickly, searching his handsome face anxiously for an indication of his mood. His expression was unreadable, but he reached out and gently caressed her hand in greeting.

"I must apologize for being so tardy this morning. Tristan informs me that I have missed a delightful morning tour of the grounds. Perhaps I can persuade you to give me a private tour at a later time?"

Alyssa felt the color rise to her cheeks at his comment. To her ears, his every word held a double meaning. She was certain everyone in the room was staring at them. A quick glance at Tristan and Caroline revealed they only had eyes for each other, and Lady Ogden was too busy watching them to be the least bit interested in Alyssa and Morgan.

"We really must leave for Ramsgate Castle as soon as possible, Morgan," Lady Ogden insisted. "I'm sure the duchess is wondering what has become of us."

"We will depart after I have eaten," Morgan replied, disappointed his chance for a private meeting with Alyssa would be missed.

"I shall inform Mrs. Stratton you are ready for your breakfast, Your Grace," Alyssa volunteered.

Morgan made a hasty excuse and immediately hurried after Alyssa.

He caught her in front of the kitchen doors and, grabbing her hand, swung her around and into his arms.

"You haven't given me a proper greeting yet this morning, my dear," he said huskily, his lips claiming hers in a passionate kiss.

Alyssa felt herself melting as his lips touched hers, and she hugged him tightly to her body in response. He is glad to see me, she thought with elation. Last night was not just a dream.

"I like the way you say good morning," she said pertly, her face shining with delight. Alyssa felt young and alive and carefree knowing Morgan still desired her.

"If we were alone in my bedchamber, I could give you a proper morning greeting," Morgan drawled with a sensual leer.

"Then I shall look forward to the next time we wake up together," Alyssa said, raising her face, her lips wantonly parting.

"Oh, you do tempt me, wench," Morgan answered

with a laugh. "If you keep looking at me like that, I shall have to drag you upstairs and keep everyone waiting another several hours."

"Your Grace!" Alyssa exclaimed, suddenly feeling out of her element with his sexual banter.

"So formal, my love. I thought you were going to call me Morgan from now on." He began to nuzzle her neck.

"Morgan, please," she whispered breathlessly. "Someone could pass by at any moment."

Knowing she was right, Morgan gave her one last kiss and reluctantly stepped away.

"Unfortunately we don't have time for a proper conversation either. Priscilla was correct: we should have left hours ago."

"I'll speak with Mrs. Stratton and have your breakfast brought to the dining room straightaway." Impulsively she gave him a quick kiss on the cheek before leaving.

A smiling Morgan waited patiently in the dining room until Alyssa appeared with a large tray of food. She fussed a few minutes, arranging everything to her satisfaction, and then sat close to Morgan as he devoured his breakfast.

She was pleased when he informed her of Tristan's request for her services at Westgate Manor.

"Tristan will allow me to work for him?" Alyssa asked incredulously.

"Only if that is what you want, Alyssa," Morgan assured her. "I promised to take care of you last night and I have every intention of fulfilling my promise."

"I want very much to stay here," Alyssa said, looking down at her hands. The warmth and concern in his voice made her feel shy. "And I intend to hold you to your promise, Morgan."

Tristan and Caroline entered the room, preventing any further comment from the duke.

"Here you are," Tristan declared in mock frustration. "We have been searching everywhere for you, Morgan. Priscilla thought you might have left without us."

"Tris," Caroline chastised. Arms akimbo, she directed an irritated frown at her fiance. "Don't listen to a word he says, Morgan. Tristan has been positively impossible all morning."

"You may inform Priscilla we will leave within the hour," Morgan told Caroline in a dismissive tone. Taking the hint, she left. Tristan, however, sat down at the table and prepared himself a plate of food.

"Miss Carrington has agreed to accept your offer of employment, Tristan."

"I'm very pleased, Miss Carrington. I'm sure you will be of invaluable help to us. I shall make a list of the various items that require immediate attention before we depart and also give you the address of our residence in London so you may contact me as needed."

"Fine," Alyssa replied. "If you will excuse me, gentlemen, I must attend to the ladies."

"I think I have made the correct decision concerning Miss Carrington," Tristan said to Morgan as soon as they were alone. "She might prove to be a steadying influence on Caroline."

Tristan continued eating heartily while Morgan sat engrossed in his own thoughts. *Enjoy her assistance while you can, little brother. As soon as I can make other arrangements, she will soon be out of your employment and established in her own house.*

As they waited for the traveling coach to be brought around, Caroline spoke to Alyssa.

"Tristan has informed me that you have agreed to assist us in renovating the manor house. I am so pleased."

"I must confess, Miss Grantham, I am looking forward to restoring the manor to its former grandeur," Alyssa responded honestly.

"I am certain you will do a commendable job," Lady Ogden interjected. "It is far too difficult a task for Caroline to undertake on her own. Your guidance should prove invaluable."

"Thank you, Lady Ogden," Alyssa said, surprised at her enthusiastic support.

"We must be off now, ladies," Tristan announced. With strong arms he handed Caroline and Lady Ogden into the carriage. Turning to Alyssa he said, "I shall contact you the moment I have secured the services of a reputable architect. Good day, Lady Alyssa." He gave her a stunning smile before jumping lithely into the coach.

"Enjoy the ride, Tris," Morgan teased from his vantage point high atop his stallion. He knew full well his brother would have preferred riding a mount, instead of being cooped up inside the coach with his two female companions.

As soon as the coach pulled out of the drive, Morgan leaned down. "I will try to get away from Ramsgate as soon as I can, love," he promised Alyssa. "We need to spend some time alone."

Alyssa nodded in understanding, suddenly feeling overcome with emotion. As she watched everyone prepare for the journey, a feeling of loneliness had engulfed her. She hated standing alone on the front steps, left behind. Most of all she feared being separated from Morgan.

"Don't forget about me, Morgan," she whispered brokenly. The duke gave a farewell salute before thundering down the drive and out of sight. "Please don't forget."

When a young seamstress appeared unexpectedly at the front door several days later, Alyssa discovered

Morgan had not forgotten her.

"The duke was very specific in his instructions," the young woman explained to Alyssa. "I am to take all the appropriate measurements for my mistress, Mrs. White. She owns a dress shop in London, and a very good one, if I might be so bold as to say. We were commissioned to produce a complete wardrobe for you as soon as possible."

Overcome by Morgan's generosity, Alyssa stood patiently as the young woman completed her task. Within the week the trunks began arriving, filled with a stunning array of garments.

With trembling hands Alyssa unpacked the first trunk, uncertain of what she would find. She knew Morgan had excellent taste in his own clothing, but was unsure how his taste ran in feminine attire. Instinctively she knew she could not carry herself dressed in the frilly style of Caroline nor the somber decor of Lady Ogden.

As she lifted the first dress from the trunk, she knew at once her fears had been groundless. The gown was simple in style, allowing the richness of the green silk to carry the elegance of the dress lines. Alyssa stood in front of the mirror dressed in her new finery, amazed by the transformation. Her confidence soared and she finally allowed herself to believe she had the makings of a duchess. Properly gowned, she felt she could compete with anyone.

Each day brought the arrival of more clothes. Morning, walking, and carriage attire, as well as evening dresses, were carefully unpacked, pressed, and hung in the armoire. The fabrics were as varied as the clothes: silks and satins, cambric, crepes and heavier muslins, in addition to gossamer nets, gauzes, and Indian muslins. The colors were gorgeous: rose, amber, sea green, lilac, and sapphire blue, with white for formal wear.

There were also delicate underthings: silk stockings, garters, lacy underdrawers, as well as a corset with straps cinched in front to hold the breasts high. There were shoes in a variety of colors to match the various outfits. Alyssa's favorite outfit was a beautiful forest green velvet riding habit, with a jaunty silk hat trimmed with a small feather, and sturdy black leather riding boots.

The sudden arrival of an extensive and costly wardrobe did not go unnoticed by the servants of Westgate Manor. Mrs. Stratton first questioned Mavis, who knew nothing about it, and then both women confronted Perkins. The older man was flabbergasted at being asked to gossip with the women, but he was also unable to shed any light on the situation. Finally Mavis asked Alyssa outright.

"Where in heaven's name are all these lovely and very expensive clothes coming from?" Mavis asked when she caught Alyssa working alone in the estate room one afternoon.

Alyssa shifted uncomfortably under her former nurse's gaze. She was reluctant to mention anything about her relationship with the duke before arrangements had been formalized. Deep within her heart Alyssa feared Morgan might just decide he no longer wanted to marry her, and Alyssa desperately wanted to spare herself the humiliation of explaining a broken engagement to the staff. Yet she realized how foolish she was being. Of course the servants would notice an entirely new wardrobe. Naturally they were curious.

"The clothes are a gift from the duke," Alyssa explained lamely.

Mavis grunted in disapproval. "Since when do you accept such elaborate gifts from a man you hardly know?"

"Since he asked me to become his wife."

"God's blood!" Mavis sat down in shock. "When?

When was all this decided? When are you going to be married?" The old woman's eyes danced with delight, then suddenly narrowed. "And just when were you planning on telling me?"

"I am sorry, Mavis," Alyssa apologized. "It happened so quickly I've hardly had time to get used to the notion myself. Imagine. Me, a duchess." She shuddered at the thought.

"Why not you?" Mavis insisted. "You will make a lovely duchess." Alyssa's reluctance made the old nurse suspicious. "Do you want to marry this man?"

"I confess there have been many times I longed to lay aside the burdens of managing the estate and caring for our tenants," Alyssa admitted honestly. "I believe the duke is a good man, and I think we shall deal well together. Yet I am reluctant to surrender my independence."

"You lost your chance for an independent life the day you sold your little house to pay off Lord Carrington's gambling debts," Mavis observed. "Far better for you to be a wife than a governess or companion. In my opinion, the duke is lucky to get you."

" 'Tis I who am the lucky one, Mavis," Alyssa answered. "It is almost inconceivable that a man like the duke would want someone like me."

"Someone like you," Mavis huffed. "You are not a mongrel dog, girl, so stop acting like one. Just because your daft father could never see the good in you is no reason to berate yourself."

Alyssa silently considered Mavis's words. "You are right, Mavis. I am being silly. I will announce my marriage plans to the entire staff as soon as the wedding date is set."

Mavis left the room with a happy smile, and Alyssa returned to her papers. Yet she had a difficult time concentrating. She shifted restlessly in her chair, knowing she had managed to chase away some of the demons of doubt, but not all of them.

Alyssa had little time for her doubts over the next few days. She was kept busy hiring men to work on the renovations for the manor house. Tristan had located an architect, Mr. Henry Walsh, who after much tongue-clicking and raising eyebrows had pronounced the house a disaster but vowed he could save it. Alyssa did not much care for his flamboyant mannerisms, but when he began to produce blueprint drawings of each room, complete with color schemes and suggestions for furnishings, Alyssa was forced to acknowledge his talent. His attitude aside, Mr. Walsh proved to be a competent craftsman, and she shared both his desire for perfection and his visions of grandeur for Westgate Manor. Even though she would no longer have a claim to it, she wanted the manor to shine.

Another point in his favor was Mr. Walsh's behavior toward her. If he was at all shocked at her unusual position in the household, he gave no sign of it and always treated her with respect. It quickly became obvious to Alyssa he possessed the power to make her job easier and exhibit her abilities to their best advantage. She hoped Tristan and Caroline would be pleased and Morgan impressed by her accomplishments.

The manor house soon hummed with the activity of bustling workmen in all corners of the house. Each day brought a new set of blueprints from Mr. Walsh and a new set of difficulties for Alyssa. One of her primary problems was finding a place to work in relative peace and quiet where she could concentrate for a few minutes without being interrupted.

Alyssa managed to sequester herself in the little-used estate room and was busily going over the latest estimates for labor costs when the door opened. Glancing up she saw Perkins hesitating in the doorway, scanning the room.

"I am over here, Perkins," she called out, "hiding. You must promise not to tell anyone I am here or I shall never finish my work."

"I naturally assume you are not including me in your instructions, madam," a deep, masculine voice bellowed across the room.

Alyssa almost dropped her pen when she recognized the duke's voice.

"Morgan," she whispered breathlessly. Her heart began to thump loudly. She rose from her chair, gripping the desk firmly to keep from racing across the room.

"Thank you, Perkins." Morgan dismissed the butler. "It appears you are taking your new job very seriously, Miss Carrington. I trust Mr. Walsh is not running you ragged?"

"Of course not," Alyssa answered, trying to keep her tone light. "However, it is a bit difficult getting anything accomplished when I am constantly interrupted."

"Are you enjoying your work?" Morgan pressed on, unable to stop himself. He had ridden six hours in a steady drizzle to see her and all he seemed capable of doing was making small talk.

"Yes, I enjoy my work," Alyssa replied, her eyes riveted on his lips. I want him to kiss me, she realized, nervously licking her lips. It is the middle of the afternoon, and all I can think about is being held in his arms and kissed.

"What?" she questioned, missing his inquiry. "I'm sorry, Your Grace, I did not hear your question."

"I was just admiring your dress, Miss Carrington," he said with a grin. "You look lovely."

"Thank you." Alyssa blushed.

"Have you missed me?" the duke asked in a silky voice.

"Oh, yes." The words slipped out naturally.

"Then come here and give me a proper greeting," he demanded in a sensual tone.

Alyssa's feet carried her swiftly to his side.

"Hello," he said simply, gathering her into his arms. He leaned down and kissed her full on the lips. "I've missed you."

His last words were uttered so softly Alyssa was not sure she heard correctly, but before she had a chance to think, Morgan was kissing her again. Alyssa relaxed, enjoying the feel of his arms around her and the gentle pressure of his lips. It felt glorious to be back in his arms.

Morgan felt his body respond immediately to her nearness, and he reveled in it. I have missed her, he admitted. But the house was too crowded with strangers, the risk of being interrupted too great.

"Go change," he whispered.

"What? What did you say?"

"Go change into your riding habit," he commanded. "Immediately. I want you to take me on a tour of the grounds."

"Now?" she asked, blinking her eyes in confusion. "You want to go for a ride now?"

"Meet me in the stables in twenty minutes," Morgan demanded. Giving her a final hug, he left the room.

Chapter Seven

Filled with self-loathing, Alyssa stood in her room, ripping off her pale blue morning dress. She had acted like a witless fool with the duke, rushing to his side like a trained cocker spaniel when he demanded a kiss. And the worst part was that she enjoyed it! The kiss of course, not the dictatorial manner he employed.

Now Morgan had insisted she join him for a ride and she again obeyed without protest. It was as though in his presence she lost the capacity to think and reason for herself. It was a maddening and perplexing occurrence Alyssa strongly felt must be corrected.

Huffing in annoyance, she searched the bottom of the wardrobe for her black leather riding boots. Locating the left boot, she was about to call for a maid when Lucy appeared.

"May I be of assistance, Lady Alyssa?" the young maid asked politely.

"Oh, Lucy, thank goodness you are here." Alyssa

sighed in relief. "I can't reach the buttons in the back of my blouse, nor can I find my other boot."

"Sit down," Lucy requested in her best lady's-maid voice. "I will attend you."

Deftly the younger girl closed the blouse, located the missing boot, and helped Alyssa finish dressing. Slightly calmer, Alyssa sat quietly as Lucy expertly brushed her hair, forming the copper tresses into a gentle upsweep. Lucy then carefully positioned the small velvet riding hat and secured it with several hairpins.

"All done," Lucy proclaimed with satisfaction. "The duke will be pleased."

Alyssa's eyes narrowed in suspicion. "Does everyone know the duke is at the manor?"

"Probably," Lucy admitted with a shrug. "Mrs. Stratton was out back talking to Ned when His Lordship arrived."

"I see," Alyssa replied with a wry smile. If Mrs. Stratton knew the duke was here, it was safe to assume everyone within the county would know by nightfall.

Entering the stables, slightly out of breath from rushing, Alyssa saw the duke standing outside the barn engaged in earnest conversation with Ned. The younger boy was holding tightly to the reins of a large gray gelding, and a pretty chestnut mare was tethered to the nearby post. Alyssa knew Tristan had been sending his horseflesh to the estate, but she had not yet seen these two particular horses.

"Lady Alyssa." Ned acknowledged her approach. "I've saddled your mount."

The stable boy led the gray gelding into the open yard, and Alyssa saw her sidesaddle was indeed on the horse. She walked up to the powerful beast and patted his nose affectionately.

"Aren't you a fine boy," she said in a gentle tone. "Where did you come from?"

"A small breeding farm in Kent," the duke answered, pleased Alyssa admired the animal. "He is yours."

"You bought him for me?" Alyssa's eyes widened in surprise as conflicting emotions swirled through her. She was genuinely pleased with the gift, but self-conscious about appearing weak and submissive with gratitude.

"He is a magnificent horse," she said finally, sounding defensive and touchy even to her own ears.

Her heart skipped a beat at the frosty look the duke sent her way, but he kept silent. Ignoring her rudeness, Morgan strode over to the chestnut mare, and vaulted unassisted onto the animal's back.

Impressed, but not wishing to appear so, Alyssa gracefully mounted the gray gelding with Ned's assistance.

"Please inform Mrs. Stratton the duke and I will be returning for luncheon later this afternoon," Alyssa told Ned as they rode out of the stableyard.

They rode together for several minutes in silence. Finally Morgan spoke.

"You're welcome."

"What?"

"I said you're welcome. For the horse. You were going to thank me for my gift, were you not?"

Embarrassed, Alyssa replied defensively, "I didn't ask you to buy me a horse." She knew she was behaving childishly, but seemed incapable of stopping herself.

"Don't you like the horse?"

"Of course, I like the horse," Alyssa snapped. "Anyone who has an ounce of sense would like the horse. He is a magnificent animal."

"Then what precisely is the problem?"

"Problem? There is no problem. Who said there was a problem?"

"My dear Miss Carrington," the duke responded, his eyes twinkling. "You are beginning to repeat yourself."

"And you, my dear duke, are beginning to annoy me." Tossing her head, Alyssa urged the gray on, deliberately distancing herself from Morgan.

He watched her race ahead of him, admiring the steady way she kept her seat on the horse. Her green velvet riding habit fit her snugly, accenting the generous curves of her body. Remembering his initial reason for wanting to ride with her, he spurred his horse after his prey.

Alyssa was forced to slow her pace, and he caught her where the rolling meadow met the woods. Morgan reached over and grasped her bridle, leading them both into the dense forest.

The ride had taken most of the anger out of Alyssa, and she chastised herself for acting so foolishly. She was behaving like a spoiled child and had probably succeeded in annoying him.

The duke brought the horses to a halt in a small clearing and dismounted. Alyssa scrambled down from her mount unassisted, somehow managing to land on her feet. She faced him squarely, uncertain of his mood.

"Would you care to explain what is wrong?" Morgan began in a patient voice.

"I . . . I . . ." Alyssa began lamely, totally at a loss for words. Absently crumbling a small leaf in her hands, she hastily blurted, "Thank you for my new horse. It was most unexpected, but exceedingly kind of you to buy him for me. I shall take great pleasure in riding him. I must also thank you for the extensive wardrobe you sent. The dresses are each magnificent, although perhaps a bit too numerous."

Morgan fixed her with an assessing glance. "Will you please tell me what has upset you, Alyssa?" he asked in an even tone, his hand resting lightly on her shoulder.

"I was so very glad to see you this morning," she said in a quiet voice, "until you started ordering me about. And . . . and . . . then you bought me that splendid horse."

"You don't like the horse?"

"No. I like the horse." She groaned with frustration. "I am very seldom given gifts, Morgan. Or orders. I suppose it will take time for me to become accustomed to it." She lifted her chin defiantly. "Then again, I may be unable to adjust."

Morgan's lips curved up in an indulgent smile. "Why do I get the distinct impression you are no longer referring to your new horse?"

"Because you are an intelligent man?"

Morgan gave a short laugh. "You have shown an amazing amount of independent spirit and sensibility during our brief acquaintance, Alyssa. I confess these are not attributes I usually seek in a female companion, but they are qualities I definitely admire in you."

Alyssa glanced at him with newfound respect. Her father had always mocked her abilities, and her neighbors had shunned her because of them. It was a refreshing change to meet someone who was not openly disapproving.

"I can only hope, Morgan, that your opinion does not drastically alter over time," she said, deliberately keeping her tone resolute and assertive.

He laughed loudly at that, a deep rumbling sound that began in his broad chest. "You have made your point, Alyssa. There is no need to belabor it."

Alyssa felt herself blush and she lowered her eyes. Morgan moved closer, gently brushing her cheek with his fingertips. When she lifted her head, he caught her face between his hands and bent down to capture her lips in a searing kiss.

Alyssa accepted his kiss, parting her mouth slightly so his tongue could slip inside. She felt the tremor of passion jolt her body as Morgan deepened the kiss, his hands reaching out seductively to cup her breasts.

Even through the thick material of her riding jacket, Alyssa could feel her nipples harden with passion, and she pressed her body intimately to his.

"Come, love," he coaxed, leading her away from the trees to the soft grass of a small, secluded clearing. "I've a grave hunger for you."

"Morgan," she protested quietly, "we are in the middle of the woods."

"Yes," he remarked huskily, removing his riding coat and loosening his cravat with each step. "And we are all alone. Isn't it marvelous?"

Alyssa could see Morgan's rippling muscles clearly through his white linen shirt, and her hand reached out to caress his arm.

"You are so very beautiful," she said in awe. The last time they were together in darkness, but today's afternoon light hid none of the duke's sculptured body.

He gave a small laugh. "Handsome, Alyssa," he corrected. "Men like to be told they are handsome."

She shook her head in disagreement. "You are beautiful, Morgan," she insisted.

She placed one palm on his shoulder, and he stood perfectly still as she ran her fingertips experimentally across his solid chest. Laying her palm flat for a moment she whispered, "I can feel your heart pounding."

"It beats for you, love," Morgan responded automatically, surprised to discover his words were indeed the truth.

Continuing her explorations, Alyssa's hand traveled across his flat stomach. Morgan sucked in his breath sharply, the anticipation almost unbearable. She did not disappoint him, and he gave a groan of pure pleasure as her hand slid below his waist and encircled his hard erection.

"It is so very large," Alyssa said in a solemn voice.

"It'll become even larger if you continue doing that, my love," he said raggedly.

"It makes me feel very odd touching you this way," she admitted. Tentatively, she caressed him, and felt him growing beneath her hand. "Tingly and breathless."

Morgan groaned at her innocent admission, nearly losing control. He suppressed a wild urge to throw her to the ground and take her. His hand reached down, closing over hers, and he pulled her arm up around his neck. She raised her other arm and then clasped herself tightly around his neck, pressing her body wantonly against him.

A quiver of pure delight speared his entire body, and Morgan knew he had to do something quickly before he lost all control. Pulling them both to the ground, he insistently pressed Alyssa onto her back.

"Now it is my turn, love," he told her. His hand reached down and lifted the skirt of her riding habit to her waist, exposing her lower body. He pulled at her underthings, searching feverishly for her bare flesh. Alyssa's eyes widened in shock as his hand slipped inside her pantaloons, lightly caressing the moist, silky curls at the top of her thighs.

Morgan kissed her deeply, his tongue delving into her mouth, his fingers moving in sensual rhythm across her most sensitive spot.

"You are already wet for me," he murmured, his breath hot in her ear. Alyssa clutched helplessly at his shoulders. Her skin felt hot, and every nerve in her body was on edge.

"Morgan, you must stop," she gasped.

"Hush, love," he whispered. Placing his hands beneath her firm buttocks, Morgan lifted her to his lips and kissed her intimately.

Alyssa cried out with shock and abruptly sat up. "My God, Morgan!" she screeched in horror. "Whatever are you doing?"

Morgan knew he was rushing her, but couldn't help himself. "Lie down, Alyssa," he commanded in a deep voice. "I am not going to hurt you."

Skeptical of his actions, Alyssa waited, not moving until he gently pressed her down on the grass. Alyssa felt the cool breeze on her flesh as Morgan opened her legs. She held her breath tightly as his head returned to the same sensitive spot. His tongue softly laved her and her hips jerked up in response. Alyssa arched her back, moving her body from side to side, quivering at the unfamiliar intimate stroking of his tongue.

Alyssa moaned. The pleasure was intense, almost painful, the feeling nearly unbearable. She whimpered as the stroking increased, mindlessly thrusting her hips forward to match the rhythm of his mouth. An unintelligible sound fell from her lips as the pressure peaked and Alyssa felt herself cross over the threshold of passion.

Breathing hard, Morgan continued to caress her gently with the palm of one hand while impatiently tugging at the stubborn fastenings of his breeches. Pulling himself free of his constricting clothes, Morgan gathered her in his arms and covered her with his heated body.

"I can't wait any longer," he told Alyssa in short, choppy breaths.

Hard and throbbing, Morgan's manhood slipped easily inside her. He felt her body stretch and open to accept him.

"Wrap your legs around me," he commanded hoarsely. She obeyed his command, and they moved in unison, locked together in an all-consuming passion. Alyssa could feel him thickening inside her, growing large with each deep thrust. Threading her fingers through his hair, she forcefully pulled Morgan's head to her lips and kissed him hungrily, just as his seed erupted inside of her. Panting hard, he collapsed atop her in total exhaustion, sated and fulfilled.

Alyssa stroked the back of Morgan's neck with a steady hand, enjoying the smooth feel of his dark hair. She could still feel his manhood deep inside her, and she squeezed her legs tightly around him.

"Am I too heavy for you?" Morgan asked in a sleepy voice.

"No, I am fine," Alyssa answered, wanting to hold on to the moment a bit longer. She closed her arms tightly around his back.

"The sky looks so blue." Alyssa sighed contentedly. "As much as I would adore spending the remainder of the day here, we had best think about returning to the manor. Mrs. Stratton has prepared luncheon for us."

"Mmmmm," Morgan uttered, gathering only enough energy to shift onto his back. His mind and body were far too complacent to consider moving. "I'm cold." He shivered slightly as a strong breeze blew.

"Well, if you buttoned your breeches, sir, you would stay much warmer," Alyssa said with a sly grin. When he made no move to do so himself, Alyssa tenaciously buttoned the pants.

She smoothed down her skirt and snuggled next to Morgan, deciding it wouldn't hurt to stay a while longer. It would afford them an opportunity to discuss their future together.

"What sort of plans have you made concerning our wedding?" she asked conversationally. When no answer was forthcoming, Alyssa repeated the question. More silence.

"Morgan?" Alyssa called his name softly. She raised

herself up on one elbow only to discover the duke was fast asleep. She made a feeble attempt to rouse him, but he looked so peaceful and content she concluded it wasn't worth the effort to wake him.

With a resigned smile she curled closer to his warmth. "I suppose Mrs. Stratton will have even more interesting news to gossip about after today," she muttered before closing her eyes.

Alyssa heard a distant voice calling. Her eyes opened instantly and she felt the panic rise in her throat when she noted the lateness of the hour. Morgan slept peacefully, sprawled out on the ground beside her, oblivious to the noise. She rose stiffly to her feet as the voice drew nearer.

"Morgan," she called out, searching the ground for her discarded riding hat and hairpins. "Morgan, wake up."

Concerned when the duke did not respond, Alyssa bent down and began shaking him.

"Morgan, you must wake up," she insisted loudly.

At her rough touch Morgan awoke, bolting to his feet.

"What is wrong?" he cried in alarm. "Is there danger?"

"Only of being discovered in our little trysting place," she answered with a laugh. Morgan looked so fierce, standing there ready to do battle, yet still not quite awake.

"I fear we both fell asleep, and were gone too long from the estate. I just heard someone calling. It must be Ned, sent out to find us."

"Ned?" Morgan questioned, running his hands through his disheveled hair in confusion. He shook his head roughly in an effort to clear his sleepy mind. "I guess Tris was right about my sound sleeping."

Quickly they readjusted their clothing and gathered

the few discarded pieces. "Let me help," Morgan offered as he saw Alyssa struggling with her hair.

Morgan twisted her long hair expertly and managed to secure both the hairpins and the hat. He does that better than I do, she thought with a twinge of dismay, not wanting to know why he was so deft with women's accessories. Brushing the leaves and grass from Alyssa's riding habit, Morgan declared they were presentable.

"We look none the worse for wear."

"Not quite," Alyssa disagreed, looking pointedly down at the duke's breeches.

He followed the line of her lovely green eyes to the front of his breeches. Grinning, he rebuttoned his misbuttoned pants.

"I, unlike yourself, am not that well acquainted with the clothing of the opposite sex," she told him primly as she untethered the horses.

"You'll soon learn, my pet," Morgan responded, helping her mount the gray gelding. Once they were mounted, Morgan led them carefully out of the woods.

As they emerged from the forest, Alyssa spotted Ned in the distance. Morgan flagged the boy down.

"The gray pulled a muscle in his leg. We were walking him back to the estate to prevent the muscle from stiffening," Morgan told the young boy smoothly.

Ned nodded his head in acceptance of the flimsy excuse. His knowing eyes did not miss Alyssa's breathless expression or slightly disheveled look. Still, it was not any of his business what other people did, and he was not one to gossip. Truth be told, he was happy to learn of the relationship between the duke and Lady Alyssa. Ned always thought she was a good and kind person, and he felt she deserved some happiness in her life.

"Shall I take the gray back to the stables for you,

Your Grace?" Ned offered in a neutral tone.

Morgan hesitated a moment, appearing to consider the lad's suggestion.

"I don't believe that will be necessary, Ned," he said. "You may ride on ahead. Lady Alyssa and I will follow at a slower pace."

Alyssa turned to Morgan after Ned obediently departed.

"Do you think he suspected anything?"

"Probably," Morgan grunted. "The boy is no fool, and you do look rather . . . um . . . satisfied."

Alyssa groaned. "I just hope he keeps his tongue. I don't fancy being the topic of conversation in every household in the county this evening."

"I don't think he will say anything. He seems like a sensitive lad."

Morgan insisted they ride at a sedate pace, intent on giving credence to the story Ned had been told.

"You spoke rather convincingly to Ned," Alyssa commented. "I'm not sure I liked how easily you lied."

Morgan regarded her intently for a few moments. "You would have preferred I told him the truth?"

"No, of course not. It is just that . . . well . . . you won't ever lie to me, will you, Morgan?" Alyssa asked in a serious tone.

"Never intentionally." He turned away from the somber look in her eyes and took in the passing landscape. "The land is well maintained through here," Morgan observed. "You have done a credible job of caring for the estate, Alyssa. Tristan will have a formidable task keeping up the high standards you have set."

Alyssa inclined her head, flattered by the compliment. "I hope Tristan won't resent all the hard work involved in running the estate. Of course, a competent bailiff can handle the more mundane tasks, but Tristan will be expected to listen to the concerns of the tenants and the problems of the laborers."

"Don't worry. Even though he is a younger son, Tristan was brought up knowing the responsibilities of a landowner."

"That doesn't sound like much fun. What was your childhood like?" she asked.

"Happy and carefree." Morgan sat back in his saddle, relaxed and comfortable. "My parents have been dead over ten years, yet I still miss them. They were very indulgent of their two sons. If not for the occasional discipline enforced by my grandfather, Tristan and I would have been insufferable brats.

"As the older brother, I was usually the leader of our escapades, but Tristan had his share of brilliant ideas. I remember one summer we decided to sail the ocean in search of pirate treasure. Since we needed a large sum of money to purchase a ship and hire a crew for our adventure, Tristan suggested we become highwaymen."

Alyssa grinned, eyeing Morgan with new interest. "Were you successful in your criminal endeavors?"

"No. All the inbred tenacity of two young boys is no match for a disgruntled coachman. After tooling hard for an entire day, we were unable to waylay a single coach."

Alyssa laughed. "Make-believe is such a marvelous childhood escape."

"If only real life were so simple," he mused.

Alyssa was surprised by the remark. Morgan had always struck her as a man who did what he wanted, not what was expected, and damn the consequences. She glanced over at him and he gave her a warm, friendly smile. Her heart thudded instantly and she felt a surging of hope. She could easily come to love this man. The thought of living with him and sharing a life together brought her a feeling of restless yearning.

Slightly embarrassed at the direction of her thoughts, Alyssa remained silent, and they soon arrived at the stableyard.

"Mrs. Stratton set up a late luncheon in the morning room, Lady Alyssa, since the workmen are repairing the dining room," Ned informed Morgan and Alyssa when they arrived.

"I will join you after I freshen up, Your Grace," Alyssa said brightly. "It will only take a few minutes."

Morgan shook his head reluctantly. "I deeply regret, Miss Carrington, I am unable to stay. I am expected in London this evening at Lady Chester's ball, and must leave immediately."

"Oh, I see," Alyssa replied in a small voice. "Will you be returning soon?"

"As soon as I can," he promised. Morgan bent his head and whispered into her ear, "I enjoyed our little outing this afternoon more than I can say. Shall you miss me when I am gone, love?"

"Not a bit," she lied, smiling up at him. "Have a safe journey."

Alyssa turned swiftly and walked back toward the house, for some perverse reason not wanting to stay and watch the duke leave. Once alone in her room, she removed her grass-soiled riding habit and gently laid it over the chair so it could be cleaned. She shivered slightly from the chill in the air as she stood in the middle of the room clad only in her chemise.

Seeking the warmth and comfort of her bed, she snuggled under the blankets and rested her head on the pillow. Her mind was filled with images of Morgan. She imagined him dressed for the ball tonight, ruggedly handsome in his black silk evening attire. She worried briefly why he had not suggested she accompany him to London; after all, they were engaged to be married. But Alyssa's common sense prevailed, reminding her that she was still in mourning for her father. It would hardly be a proper time to be introduced into society.

She suspected Morgan would inform her of their future plans once things were settled. He was far better versed in the matters of polite society than she. Still, Alyssa had every intention of discussing their wedding at length the next time they were together.

Hugging her pillow tightly against her chest, Alyssa closed her eyes. *I'll rest for a moment before I go eat.* Within minutes, she was fast asleep.

Morgan's thoughts were consumed with Alyssa as he tooled his matched chestnuts on the dusty road back to London. He truly regretted having to leave her, but it was necessary he attend a ball tonight given by Lady Chester in honor of Tristan and Caroline's engagement.

Besides the fact that he was the brother of the groom, it was also important to his mission for the government that he attend as many social functions as possible in hopes of flushing the Falcon out of his hiding place. So far, there had been no success in interesting the Falcon in the papers hidden at Ramsgate Castle or the duke's London home.

Morgan hoped for a lead in the case soon. Despite the assurances of Lord Castlereagh that the dowager duchess was not in any danger living at Ramsgate Castle, Morgan was worried about her safety. He would have a devil of a time convincing his grandmother to stay on in London after the party tonight. He doubted he would be able to keep her under his watchful eye much longer.

His relationship with Alyssa was a further, albeit far more pleasant, complication. He fully realized today there was no privacy to be had at Westgate Manor while the renovations were under way. He decided the best solution was to set Alyssa up in a place of her own as quickly as possible.

A house in London was out of the question. Alyssa was very proud of the work she was doing at Westgate Manor and Morgan knew she would not want to leave without being consulted. He laughed out loud, not believing he was willing to make so many concessions for a new mistress. But Alyssa was unlike any of his previous women, and she was entitled to special considerations.

Morgan's body tightened with excitement as he recalled their afternoon dalliance. Alyssa had clung to him with unbridled passion, fully matching his own ardor. She was an irresistible combination of innocence and sensuality, and he longed for the opportunity to explore this fascinating aspect of her character.

Yet beneath her self-reliance Morgan glimpsed a soft, vulnerable woman, who touched a small corner of his heart. He was starting to care for her beyond the need to satisfy his lust. What they needed was time together alone. That pleasant thought put a smile on his handsome face. Alyssa certainly would not bore him, with either her body or her mind.

Morgan flicked the reins and urged his team to a faster pace, anxious to reach London and conclude his business so he would be free to return. Return to Alyssa.

Chapter Eight

Morgan glided Caroline effortlessly around the crowded ballroom, his feet automatically following the rhythmic patterns of the dance. Lady Holland's ball was an unmitigated success, and everyone was having a marvelous time.

Except Morgan. It had been a long, tiring week for the duke, who had attended an inordinately large number of society functions in hopes of stirring the interest of the elusive Falcon. Thus far he had met with no success, and he knew if he did not learn anything soon, his usefulness to the War Ministry would end.

It was rare for the duke to attend so many parties of the season, and there was a great deal of speculation as to the reason for his sudden descent on the ton. Morgan again heard the rumors he was searching for a suitable bride, and the very thought made him shudder in distaste. The failure of his marriage had haunted him for years, and his mind had remained tortured until he made the firm decision never again o marry. He honestly couldn't say which he feared more, the French or a new wife.

As he and Caroline made the circuit around the vast ballroom, his eyes scanned the various faces, mentally recording those he saw, hoping he could somehow make some small connection that would lead him to the Falcon.

"Tristan and I have finally set a wedding date, Morgan," Caroline announced pleasantly.

"Mmmmm," the duke replied, too absorbed in his task of observing the other guests to pay much attention.

"Mother wanted to wait until the fall, but Tristan insisted he would wait only until early summer."

"How nice."

Caroline turned her head sharply to look up at Morgan and realized at once he was not paying the least bit of attention to her.

"I have decided that Tristan should wear a pink satin evening assemble," Caroline said in a droll tone. "Wouldn't he just look divine?"

"I'm sure," came the vague response.

"And I thought you might wear lavender satin, or perhaps even canary yellow and lavender stripes. I know that is a bit more extreme than your usual style of dress, but after all it is my wedding and I want everything to be just perfect."

"Yes, perfect."

"Wonderful," Caroline cried in a teasing tone. "I shall direct your tailor at Charing Cross to begin work on the suit immediately. Is that all right?"

"What? You want my tailor to make you a suit, Caroline? Whatever for?"

"Not for me, Morgan." Caroline laughed wickedly. "I want a suit made for you. To wear to my wedding."

Morgan turned his face down to hers and saw the twinkle in her eyes.

"Come now, Morgan," she pouted. "You have already agreed. You are not going to renege on your promise, are you?"

"No," he said slowly. "Of course you may have a suit made for me if you feel it is necessary."

"Ha!" Caroline exclaimed triumphantly. "You have just agreed to appear at my wedding attired in a yellow-and-lavender striped suit, Morgan."

"What?" he thundered, nearly colliding with another couple. "What did you say?"

"You heard me," she teased. "Honestly, Morgan, you should pay more attention to a woman when you make her a promise." She tapped her fan sharply on his shoulder. "I should hold you to that promise, to teach you a lesson."

Morgan laughed. "I guess you should. It is the very least I deserve for my rudeness. I haven't been a very attentive partner, Caroline." The duke executed an elegant bow. "Pray forgive me."

Caroline smiled charmingly. "Naturally I forgive you, Morgan."

The duke escorted Caroline off the dance floor, and they stood near the open French doors, catching a refreshing breeze.

"I wish I knew what holds your interest so intently," Caroline commented a few minutes later. Following Morgan's line of vision to a group of people on the far side of the room, she purred in a knowing tone, "It appears the lovely Mlle Madeline Duponce has caught your eye."

"Lovely?" Morgan responded, his eyes resting on the petite brunette. "I suppose there are some who might consider her attractive."

"There is no need to be coy with me, Morgan." Caroline grinned. "Madeline Duponce is one of the most sought-after women of the season. My poor brother Gilbert shall be crushed when he learns of your interest. I do believe he fancies himself in love with the darling French emigre. And how could he, the mere heir of a baron, compete with you, a wealthy and sophisticated duke?"

"You have an extremely vivid imagination, Caroline."

"Don't worry, Morgan. Your secret is safe with me."

The duke was about to correct her and tell her the field was clear for young Gilbert, but thought better of it. Perhaps it would be an intelligent notion to focus some attention on Mlle Duponce, Morgan decided. There were a number of French emigres whose loyalties were questioned by the War Ministry.

"Secret?" Tristan commented as he joined them. "Did I hear you say Morgan has a secret?"

"Morgan is smitten with Mlle Duponce," Caroline eagerly informed Tristan.

"So much for keeping secrets, Caroline," Morgan replied with a wry smile.

" 'Tis only Tristan," Caroline defended her actions. "If you can't trust your own brother, who can you trust?"

Morgan did not answer, his gaze still following Madeline Duponce.

"Oh dear," Caroline spoke suddenly. "Here comes my great-aunt Eudora. I haven't had a chance to speak with her all evening, and she wants to hear about the wedding. I know we were supposed to dance this set, but would you mind if I spend the time with her instead, Tristan?"

"Go on, love," Tristan replied affably. "I will stand here and look deflated."

Giving him a saucy look, she turned to intercept her great-aunt. As soon as they were alone, Tristan spoke to his older brother.

"It sounds as though Caroline has been matchmaking again. I sincerely hope she did not offend you,

Morgan. I know too well how you detest being paired with various women."

Morgan waved his hand. "Don't worry about it, Tris. Caroline was merely being observant. I was indeed staring at Mlle Duponce."

Tristan whistled in astonishment. "Well, if you have any intentions of paying court to Mlle Duponce, you will have a true challenge getting past her watchdog brother, Henri."

"Do you know Henri Duponce?" Morgan asked, suddenly alert to the coincidence.

"I've met him a few times. At Caroline's home, as I recall. I remember once teasing her about Henri having indecent designs on Priscilla. The truth is, it is Caroline's younger brother who pursues the lovely Mlle Duponce."

"And does she return his regard?"

"It is impossible to say. She certainly leads him on a merry chase, but I am told the French have a natural talent in that area. Caroline's father had apoplexy when he learned of Gilbert's interest. He has rather strong feelings about the French."

Morgan grinned, recalling Baron Grantham's rather spirited discussions of the war. "Yes, I remember. Have the Duponces ever been to Ramsgate Castle, Tris?"

Tristan considered the question for a few moments. "They attended our annual Christmas ball at the castle last year. It was such a crush, I imagine you never even saw them. They might have also been down to a house party or two last season, but I cannot recall for certain. You aren't really serious about this girl, are you, Morgan?" Tristan asked with a puzzled frown.

"I might be," Morgan replied mysteriously. "But not in the way you think, little brother. Excuse me, I am going to find out if Mlle Duponce has a partner for supper."

Morgan negotiated the crowded ballroom expertly, coming to rest at an ornate marble pillar near the group of young men surrounding Mlle Duponce. After observing her for several minutes, he could not help but admire what an accomplished flirt she was, bantering coy remarks with the suitors surrounding her, never favoring one in particular, yet encouraging them all.

A brief lull in the conversation afforded Morgan the opportunity to join the circle of admirers around Mlle Duponce. A quelling look from him sent several of the younger men scurrying quickly off, but a few of the stouthearted remained, including Caroline's brother Gilbert. It was young Gilbert whom Morgan addressed.

"Would you be so kind as to do the honors, Grantham," the duke said in a deep voice. "I have not yet been properly introduced to mademoiselle."

Gilbert's sullen expression revealed he would like nothing less, but he had little choice. Reluctantly the younger man complied with the duke's instructions.

"Mlle Duponce, may I present Morgan Ashton, the Duke of Gillingham," Gilbert said tonelessly.

"Mademoiselle," the duke responded in a silky voice. Lifting her hand for a kiss he added, "I am delighted to finally make your acquaintance."

Madeline Duponce flushed slightly at the duke's obvious interest in her, but remained regal and composed. Morgan's commanding presence made the other men beside her seem like mere boys.

"Your Grace," Madeline replied in a musical voice. "I am so pleased to meet you. Caroline has often spoken of Tristan's charming brother."

The duke favored her with a dazzling smile. "You flatter me, mademoiselle."

She returned his smile with one of her own, and Morgan was forced to admit she was a pretty girl. She was a small woman, barely reaching his shoulder. The low-cut neckline of her icy-blue satin gown accented her full-bosomed figure and set off her dark brown hair and eyes. As Morgan boldly appraised her, a sudden image of Alyssa's sweet smile flashed into his mind, but he ignored it as he continued to charm the young French girl. There was, however, no chance for further conversation, because Henri Duponce suddenly materialized at his sister's side.

"Are you ready for supper, Madeline?" Henri spoke to his sibling. "Lady Ogden has been kind enough to offer us a place at her table."

"How delightful," the duke piped in. "That is where I plan on sitting. May I?" He offered his arm to Madeline before either Gilbert or Henri could react. Confused, she looked from one man to the next, then shrugged her shoulders philosophically and accepted the duke's outstretched arm. Henri and Gilbert quickly took up their positions behind the pair and followed Madeline and the duke doggedly into the buffet hall.

Lady Ogden was immediately spotted by Gilbert at a large table in the corner of the dining hall.

"You will be joining us, Morgan?" Lady Ogden asked in a slightly puzzled tone as the small group settled in around the table.

"If you have no objection, Priscilla?" the duke replied.

"Of course not," she responded immediately. "I see you have made the acquaintance of Mlle Duponce. Have you also met her brother, Comte Henri Duponce?"

"I'm sure we have met at the gaming room at White's, have we not, sir?" Morgan lied in a challenging voice.

"Perhaps," Henri replied vaguely. He appeared to be even more annoyed with the attention Morgan was showering on his sister once he learned the duke's identity.

Madeline expertly covered the awkward silence with idle chatter, until everyone's attention shifted to the sumptuous meal Lady Holland had ordered for her guests. Instead of a long, elaborate formal meal, Lady Holland had planned a more informal late-night buffet. The buffet table fairly groaned under the profusion of food with a seemingly endless array of pheasant, roast, fowl, and fish entrees, numerous side dishes, vegetables, puddings, jellies, mousses, and finally the desserts of pastries, fruits and nuts, bonbons, and sweetmeats.

Elegantly garbed footmen in powdered white wigs moved swiftly from the buffet to the various tables strategically placed throughout the dining room, bringing food and wine to the guests. The room sparkled with the light from hundreds of small candles, as the fragrance of the elegant food blended with the sweet scent of the many fresh flower arrangements that decorated the tables.

Once everyone was comfortably seated at the table, Morgan directed the conversation toward Madeline.

"Tell me, Mlle Duponce, do you miss your native France a great deal?" Morgan asked in his most charming manner.

Madeline was briefly startled by his question, but answered readily enough.

"I regret to say, Your Grace, there is very little I remember about France. I was a young girl when my uncle managed to smuggle my brother Henri and myself out of Paris. We have never returned."

"And your parents, mademoiselle?"

"The guillotine, Your Grace," Henri answered for his sister in a curt tone. "They were not as fortunate as we were." Henri shot Morgan a quelling look.

"I am so very sorry," Morgan replied somberly, suspicious of Henri's tale. "I did not know."

"Ours is not an especially original story, Your Grace," Madeline spoke softly, trying to cover her brother's obvious hostility.

"But surely you hope someday to reclaim your lands and birthright," Morgan pressed on. "It is said that Napoleon is willing to assist in the restoration of the titles and property of many of those who fled during the revolution."

"We would not be so foolish as to trust the ranting of a madman, Your Grace," Henri said sharply. "We are staunch royalists, and would never consider lending our good name to the reign of the Corsican."

"You really must try the roasted venison, Morgan," Lady Ogden chimed in, attempting to change the volatile subject. "No one can compare with the culinary skills of Lady Holland's latest chef."

Morgan accepted her lead for the moment and allowed the conversation to drift onto the ordinary topics of food, the crush of people in attendance, and Gilbert's newest horses. He casually watched Henri Duponce throughout dinner, and came to the conclusion that there was more to the Frenchman than met the eye. Although appearing to participate in the dinner conversation, Morgan noted Henri kept a watchful eye on the guests around him. He was subtly on guard. Against who or what, Morgan could not be certain.

After dinner, the gentlemen excused themselves and entered the gaming rooms to indulge in a bit of whist and faro. Morgan was unable to seat himself at a table with Henri Duponce, and he quickly grew bored. Deciding he might have better luck with Madeline now that her brother was otherwise occupied, he went to seek out the French girl, but she was nowhere to be found.

"This is odd," he muttered to himself, circling the ballroom for a second time. He then spotted Gilbert's distinctive red hair near the open doorway. The younger man had a tight grip on Madeline's arm, and the two of them disappeared conspiratorially onto the balcony and out of sight.

Deciding he had probably tweaked Gilbert's nose enough for one evening, Morgan concluded it would be in very poor taste to follow the couple. After saying his farewells to first his brother and then his hostess, the duke left the party in far better spirits than when he had arrived.

He settled back in his carriage for the short ride back to his London residence, realizing how tired he felt. It had been a long week, but perhaps he had finally uncovered a clue. First thing in the morning, he would to go to the War Ministry and discover all he could about the Duponces. Afterward he could spend the remainder of the day visiting Westgate Manor. His secretary, Jason Cameron, recently completed all the arrangements for Alyssa's latest gift, and Morgan was anxious to present it to her. That rather pleasant thought brought a genuine smile to Morgan's lips.

The duke slammed the file down on the oak desk in frustration, cursing under his breath. He had spent the entire morning wading through endless files in the War Ministry and had been unable to come up with any pertinent information about the Duponces.

Their file was exceptionally brief. Henri and Madeline Duponce, two orphaned emigres who arrived in England 15 years ago with an uncle, Phillipe Lobeur, their mother's brother. Phillipe, deceased two years, apparently sent a vast amount of the family's fortune out of the country before he fled with his young niece and nephew. Subsequently, Henri and Madeline had led a comfortable life. They currently resided in London at a fashionable address on St. James Street, not far from where Morgan's own house was located. The Duponces also kept a small country home in Kent.

Having discovered nothing of interest in the Duponce file, Morgan began reading other files of French emigres, in hopes of perhaps making a connection to the Duponces that had been missed. His tireless search yielded nothing. In fact, there was nothing negative at all written about Henri or Madeline, whereas most of the other files listed something: a financial problem, some indiscretion of either a personal or business nature. The very absence of anything negative only enforced Morgan's belief that perhaps the Duponces were not as they appeared.

A discreet knock at the door pulled Morgan's attention away from the files for a moment.

"Enter," he commanded, not sure who it could be, since he had encountered no one, except the customary guards when entering the building early that morning.

"Good morning, Your Grace," Lord Castlereagh greeted Morgan. "I see you have been busy today."

"A wasted effort, I am afraid, Your Lordship." Morgan glared at the scattered files in disgust. "I have not been able to come up with one conclusive fact after sifting through all this material."

"Take heart," Lord Castlereagh sympathized. "We certainly don't expect the Falcon just to fall into our hands. I assume you have some sort of lead or you wouldn't be here."

"Well," Morgan hedged, not wanting to look like a fool, "I thought there might be some information about the Duponces, Henri and Madeline. Are you acquainted with them?"

"Duponce . . . Duponce." The foreign secretary absently rubbed his chin. "A brunette, isn't she, rather petite? And her brother, a tall, thin man who is very protective of her."

Given the foreign secretary's keen eye for a pretty woman, Morgan was not surprised Lord Castlereagh knew Madeline.

"I spent the better part of the morning reading their file. There is nothing here that even hints of scandal. It causes me to question why information about the Duponce family was collected."

Lord Castlereagh picked up the papers Morgan indicated and quickly read them.

"You have a point," Lord Castlereagh agreed. "On paper, they are exemplary. However, they must have garnered suspicion at one time or another."

"I agree," Morgan replied, glad to know that his suspicions might have some foundation. "I also discovered they have been to Ramsgate Castle in the past few months, perhaps more than once. I think these two warrant scrutiny."

"I'll assign two of my best men straightaway. Of course, it may prove nothing, but at this point it is the only lead we have."

"Is there any news about the information I planted in my home yet?" Morgan inquired.

"No," Lord Castlereagh admitted with disappointment. "Still, it has only been a few weeks. I have some additional information you can hide elsewhere, or perhaps even change the papers already hidden. I shall leave it to your discretion."

"Fine," Morgan answered. Taking the documents from Lord Castlereagh, he placed them in his breast coat pocket. "I expect to hear from you the moment anything of interest is uncovered about Henri and Madeline Duponce."

"I shall keep you informed," Lord Castlereagh promised with a smile. "I must make my excuses, Your Grace. The regent is expecting me for luncheon and I have a great deal of work to finish."

Morgan nodded his head in farewell and sat down at the desk. Knowing there was nothing left to do here, the duke decided it was the perfect time to set out for Westgate Manor. After all, it was nearly eleven o'clock.

Chapter Nine

"I have a surprise for you," Morgan said to Alyssa as he accepted the delicate porcelain teacup from her outstretched hand. There were no difficulties encountered on his journey from London. He had arrived at Westgate Manor in record time, interrupting Alyssa during her solitary tea.

"Not another gift," she exclaimed, still a bit thrown off balance by his sudden, unexpected arrival. "Truly, Your Grace, you must not continue buying gifts for me all the time."

"But I enjoy it."

"It makes me uncomfortable. I do believe I have received more gifts in the last few weeks than I have in my entire life. If you keep up at this pace, you will soon go bankrupt," she finished lamely, not wanting to appear ungrateful. She knew it appeared perfectly ridiculous to be objecting to beautiful and expensive gifts, yet she would have preferred the duke spend more time with her rather than give her trinkets. Or at the very least to be informed before he made an appearance at the manor.

"I daresay you will get used to my presents soon enough, my dear," he replied dryly. Pushing that less than appealing notion from his mind, Morgan instead concentrated on enjoying this rare moment alone with Alyssa.

She domestically arranged a plate of sandwiches for him and Morgan noted with a rakish eye that the scoop neckline of her new yellow muslin gown displayed her ample bosom to perfection. Her beautiful copper hair was pulled back in a loose upsweep, leaving her creamy neck open to his admiring gaze. He had an almost uncontrollable urge to lean forward and nuzzle her neck. He squirmed uncomfortably on the red brocade settee as the ache in his loins increased. The longer he looked at her, the more difficulty he had sitting still.

Alyssa realized he was staring at her, and she gave him a wary look. He was magnificently handsome in his fawn-colored buckskin riding pants that clung tightly to his powerful thighs. The brown jacket contrasted nicely with his white silk shirt, and as her gaze drifted to his ruggedly handsome face, Alyssa wondered how long it would be before he kissed her. And his kisses led to his touching her, pleasuring her, driving her wild. Distressed by where her undisciplined thoughts were leading her imagination, Alyssa unconsciously let out a small gasp.

"The tea was hot," she explained weakly at Morgan's questioning expression. For an instant Alyssa panicked, imagining Morgan moving closer, and knowing his touch would set her completely aflame, she moved skittishly to the back of her chair.

"The weather certainly has turned unseasonably warm, has it not?" she stated loudly, privately thinking she sounded like a complete idiot.

"Is anything wrong?" Morgan asked with a grin, suddenly realizing his nearness was making her uncomfortable.

"Of course not," she lied primly. "More tea, Your Grace?"

He shook his head no and grinned broadly at her again. Then he stood up.

"Come along, Alyssa. I have instructed Ned to hitch up the chestnuts. We are going for a drive."

Alyssa quickly rose to her feet to comply. For once she felt no spark of anger at Morgan's demanding tone. Anything was better than sitting here alone with him having these unladylike, sensual thoughts.

"Please allow me a moment to get my cloak and bonnet, Your Grace. I shall join you shortly."

Once comfortably settled in the open curricle, Alyssa tried unsuccessfully to relax and enjoy the ride. Sitting this close to Morgan made her taut with excitement. Alyssa was not paying much attention to her surroundings, being more interested in the duke than the passing countryside.

She was therefore surprised to discover they had reached their destination when Morgan turned the horses down a long gravel drive guarded by majestic cedar trees. At the end of the drive stood a dwelling resembling a small castle. It had two large drumtowers, with a tall narrow watchtower in the center, and was flanked on each corner with four square towers. The medieval formality of the gray stone structure was softened by the profusion of climbing ivy surrounding the entranceway.

"What a charming place," Alyssa exclaimed as they circled in front of the large oak double doors. The duke tossed the reins to the waiting footman and leaped out of the open curricle. Reaching up, he lifted Alyssa from the carriage. His arms tightened instinctively around her waist and he grasped her against his hard body, holding her close. Her heart skipped a beat as she gazed into his mischievous gray eyes.

"Are we expected?" she questioned, curious about whom they were going to meet. Alyssa nervously smoothed her dress, hoping she looked presentable. How like Morgan to not even warn her they were going visiting.

The young footman opened the front door and escorted them into the great hall. It was strangely quiet and Alyssa stole a look around as they waited.

Though not overly large, the great hall had vast, ornate plaster ceilings, giving the room an open and inviting look. The marble floor was a warm rose color, and the walls were painted a similar shade. Alyssa decided she liked the effect.

"Shall I show you about?" the duke inquired mysteriously.

"I don't understand, Your Grace," Alyssa said questioningly. "Does no one live here?"

"Not at present, but we shall soon remedy that. The key, Miss Carrington." The duke reached inside his breast coat pocket and produced a large brass key that he handed to Alyssa. "Most of the rooms are furnished, but I suspect you will want to make some changes. Do you like it?"

It took a few moments for Alyssa to grasp his meaning. "For me?" she squeaked in astonishment. "You have bought this house for me?"

"For us," he corrected softly. "I know how you value your self-reliance, so I am giving you ownership of the house. However, I plan to spend as much time here with you as possible. I wish I could return Westgate Manor to you, but Tristan and Caroline have fallen in love with the place. I had hoped this dwelling would prove an adequate substitute. You are not disappointed?"

"Disappointed?" she cried, still feeling stunned. "I am overwhelmed."

Alyssa knew the duke had numerous residences, and yet he had chosen a special place, remote and beautiful, just for them. The house represented more to Alyssa than an act of generosity. She felt that Morgan not only understood her need for identity and independence, but was obviously willing to indulge it. Her eyes filled with tears, and she quickly turned her head before the duke noticed.

"Thank you," she said simply, not sure what else she could say. "I shall always treasure this place, not because it is beautiful, which it is, but because you have chosen it for us."

"Come, let's explore the house," Morgan said, pleased she was happy and relieved that she did not resent the fact he had chosen a place for her in the country.

Previously, his mistresses were housed in London, where he paid their rent and living expenses while the liaison lasted. He had every expectation of this relationship enduring for a long time, but he was enough of a realist to know it would eventually end. Hopefully at a mutually agreed-upon time. In the meantime, they would have all the advantages of an intimate, loving relationship without the inconveniences and obligations of marriage.

Morgan knew it was extravagant to actually buy Alyssa this large house, but he felt it was important that she have some security. Along with the house, he would provide her with a substantial income.

They toured the house together after greeting the small staff. Alyssa's excitement and gratitude grew as they entered each room, and she exclaimed enthusiastically over the various objects in the house. She adored the Chinese curio with the lovely jade carvings, but thought the majority of the paintings were dreadful and must go. Each room held new delights, and it gave Morgan great pleasure to see her so happy.

"I think we should hang gold draperies in here, Your Grace," she decided as they examined the master suite. "With a matching satin coverlet, and a green Persian rug with brown and golden leaves. Do you like that idea?"

"My dear Miss Carrington, you certainly should know by this time I like anything you do in a bed-chamber." He grinned wickedly at her and shut the door firmly behind him. Alyssa felt her heart skip a beat as he began moving toward her.

"Your Grace," she protested when he took her in his arms. "Morgan, please, the servants!"

"The servants have the good sense to close their eyes to events that are of no consequence to them," he declared knowingly. His handsome face curved into a seductive smile, and he lowered his head to her lips. After her initial protest, Alyssa succumbed willingly to his kiss. Their intimacy was warm and consuming, and Alyssa shuddered with passion as Morgan whispered his erotic longings into her ear.

His hands could not stop touching her, stroking her, hugging her against him. He lifted her chin so she could look into his eyes and see his passion, his desire. Cupping her face gently between his two large hands, he placed a kiss on her forehead, and then on each cheek, moving down her lovely face until he reached her soft lips.

When their tongues met the hunger between them ignited, and the gentleness turned to urgency as their mutual passion flamed. Morgan pulled her closer to him, his tongue invading her willing mouth, demanding, probing, tasting her sweetness.

Every part of Alyssa's body was responding to his touch. Her soft moans as she arched her body against the hard proof of his arousal told him how wild he was making her feel.

He expertly guided her over to the large four-poster bed, trailing soft, wet kisses down the side of her neck. Morgan's hands reached out hungrily for her breasts. As he brushed his knuckles through the thin material of her bodice Alyssa sighed with pleasure and snuggled closer to his hard, throbbing manhood.

She kissed his throat, inhaling his intoxicating male scent, rejoicing in her nearness to him. It felt so good, so right to be held in his arms again; she savored every moment. She lifted her face to him and returned his kisses with a passion that sent his senses reeling.

"I've been away from you far too long, my love," he said breathlessly, his voice harsh with need. He was thrilled by her boldness, her obvious need for him.

Morgan fumbled with the tiny buttons at the back of her gown. Finally losing patience, he instead pushed the top of her gown down, exposing her breasts. His hands fondled the creamy white mounds while his tongue caressed first one nipple, then the other.

Alyssa moved her hips restlessly, rubbing against his swelled sex, trying to bring their bodies closer together. Her fingers went to the buttons of his shirt, and then she felt the crisp hairs of his bare chest and the hot moistness of his skin. Wantonly, she rubbed her hardened nipples against his naked chest.

"Oh, God," Morgan swore loudly, his breathing harsh and ragged. "I'm going to rip this gown right off you if you don't slow down, love."

Alyssa smiled shyly at his words, secretly thrilled she possessed the power to arouse his passions so intensely. She took a small step back and started undressing him.

Morgan stood still, allowing her to complete her task, enjoying this new facet of their lovemaking.

When he was completely naked, his manhood jutting out and throbbing, he whisked Alyssa around, making short work of the small buttons on her gown. Within moments she was undressed. Naked, they fell together on the bed in wild abandon.

Alyssa rolled onto her back and felt Morgan's finger slide inside her warmth as his tongue penetrated her mouth.

"God, you are so soft, so wet, so ready for me, love," he whispered, his fingers becoming more urgent as they stroked and parted her.

"I want you inside me," she moaned, frantically gripping his back.

He laughed joyously at her enthusiasm. "Then have your way with me, wench," he said, sprawling out on his back.

Alyssa looked perplexed for a moment. "I don't understand, Morgan."

He turned, grabbed Alyssa's hips with both hands, and swung her up in the air over him. Her bottom rested on his thighs, her legs on either side of his outstretched body.

"Oh my," she whispered, both shocked and thrilled. "Are you sure about this, Morgan?"

"Very sure, love," he drawled, his lips curling provocatively.

Following his instructions, she lifted herself up and, straddling him, slowly lowered herself until he was completely inside her. Morgan groaned, the hunger surging rampantly through his loins. He brought his hands up and stroked her breasts, thrusting against her.

She inhaled her breath sharply, and he immediately went still.

"Am I hurting you?"

"No," she replied in a raspy voice. "It feels wonderful."

That admission spurred him on, and his hand traveled down to her belly through the silky triangle of curls to find her moistness.

"You are so beautiful," he whispered in awe. Her copper hair was in wild disarray, her exquisite breasts rising and falling with breathless passion, her lovely face transfixed by the intensity of her emotions. He increased the pressure of his fingers between their bodies, and Alyssa began to move, rocking back against him in a primitive, sensual rhythm.

He was so deep inside her it drove him wild. Her muscles tightened around him, signaling the culmination of her pleasure. Morgan watched her face in wonder as Alyssa reached fulfillment. Her excitement triggered his own release, and he pushed himself higher inside her warmth, spilling his seed.

Afterward, as they both tried to calm their harsh breathing, Morgan pulled her down to his chest, holding her close to his racing heart. Alyssa's hair was a mass of tangles covering them both, and she brushed the silken tresses out of her eyes. She came to rest with her face against his neck, and, dazed with emotion, she revealed her heart.

"Oh, how I love you, Morgan."

The words slipped out so naturally, Alyssa didn't have time to consider what she was saying. Her body immediately tensed in anticipation of the duke's reaction. Yet silence greeted her declaration, and as it stretched on, Alyssa let out a long sigh. He must not have heard, she concluded with an odd mix of regret and relief. Loving Morgan was an emotional risk that left her with feelings of vulnerability and uncertainty. It was a situation best handled slowly.

"Am I crushing you?" Alyssa asked, needing to break the oppressive silence. Balancing herself up on her elbows, she relieved him of her weight. Her hair fell forward onto Morgan's face, and she reached over to gently brush it back from his damp brow. He opened his eyes and looked at her with such tenderness and softness that Alyssa felt a lump of emotion knot her throat. Quickly she rolled off him. If he continues to look at me like that I shall do something stupid, she decided. Like tell him I love him again.

Morgan did not like her moving off him so abruptly, and he immediately pulled Alyssa into his arms. Cradling her against the length of his body, he casually draped her leg over his thigh. After a few moments she began to relax, allowing the feelings of contentment to wash over her. She could see a large willow tree through the window on the far side of the room, and she watched lazily as a small bird tittered to and fro from branch to branch, calling its mate. Alyssa snuggled closer to Morgan, feeling sated and, perhaps for the first time in her life, safe. It was a glorious moment.

"It is time we thought about getting back, sweetheart." Morgan's voice shattered the companionable silence, bringing Alyssa sharply back to reality. "Mrs. Stratton will be wearing out the floorboards if we don't return before dark."

"And have another lovely bit of gossip to share with the rest of the county," Alyssa added with a small laugh. Naked, she jumped from the bed and began searching for her discarded chemise, fervently hoping that Morgan, in his earlier enthusiasm, had not ripped any of her clothing.

Alyssa sat on the edge of the bed rolling up her stockings while Morgan picked up his breeches. "When will we move in here, Morgan?"

"As soon as you feel the house is livable, my dear. It shouldn't take too long to make the house ready, provided you don't require extensive structural changes. No more than a few weeks, I imagine. Sooner, I hope, if this afternoon is any indication of how we will be spending our time here together."

A few weeks! If they were to occupy their new home in such a short time, Morgan must have already made all the wedding arrangements. Alyssa felt hurt that she had not been consulted, but honestly conceded she could have been very little help. She knew nothing of weddings, having never attended one herself.

"You have not planned an elaborate London ceremony, have you, Morgan?" she asked cautiously. "I was hoping we could have a very simple wedding ceremony, with only your family in attendance."

"Mmmmm," the duke muttered, his head under the bed as he retrieved his riding boots.

"Well, wouldn't you prefer it?" she pressed on. "I know that a large London gathering might be expected, but couldn't we beg off? After all, I am still supposed to be in mourning. I'm sure it would be acceptable."

"What would be acceptable?" Morgan questioned absently, searching among the bedcovers for his shirt.

"A simple, family ceremony."

"For what?"

"Our wedding."

"What!" Morgan's head jerked up in astonishment and he glared at Alyssa.

"All right," she countered quickly, taken aback by the look of fury on his face. "It was only a suggestion, Morgan. There is no need to get angry. We will do whatever you think is best." She turned her back to him and began pinning her hair, utilizing the large brass mirror that hung on the wall.

"My dear Miss Carrington, you will kindly explain to me what the devil you are talking about!" he yelled. He strode over to her, grabbed her arm, and swung her around to face him.

"Morgan, you are hurting my arm," she cried, frightened by the anger in his face and confused by his violent reaction. "I was merely expressing my desire for a simple wedding, rather than an elaborate London affair."

"You are speaking in riddles, my dear. I was not aware that we were getting married." He had lowered his voice, but Alyssa could still hear his scorn. Morgan released his iron grip on her arm and stood over her, looking menacingly down into her eyes.

"Not getting married?" she questioned, her confusion echoing in her voice. "Have you changed your mind?"

"It was never decided toward marriage in the first place," he declared in a deceptively calm voice.

"But . . . but that first time we were together," Alyssa stammered in a hoarse whisper. "Afterward, you . . . you said you wanted to take care of me. You . . . you offered me the protection of your name."

"Yes, I did. And you accepted," he answered slowly, a feeling of dread beginning to overtake him.

"I agreed to become your wife."

"You agreed to be my mistress," Morgan said softly, not understanding how there could have been such a colossal misinterpretation of his intentions.

"What!"

"My mistress," he repeated.

"Oh my God," she whispered in shock, so astonished she could barely speak. She sank down on a small chaise longue and tried to sort it all out. She could not.

Morgan stood by her and uncomfortably cleared his throat. Knowing he was only partly to blame did not entirely ease the guilt he felt. The duke reached out his hand to comfort Alyssa and she instantly came alive, jerking back as if he had struck her.

"Do not touch me," she hissed. "How dare you insult me by asking me to become your mistress?" Now that she had awakened from her trance, she was fighting

mad. Morgan thought he preferred her quiet brood-
ing.

Alyssa rose from her seat and paced the room like
a caged animal. "How could you be so cruel as to humiliate me in such a manner?" she railed at him.

Her righteous indignation struck a responsive
chord in Morgan, and he fought back.

"Don't you dare act the outraged virgin with me,
miss. As I recall, you came willingly to my bed," Morgan retorted, vainly trying to hold his temper.

Her eyes shot daggers at him and her face heated
with humiliation as she remembered her wanton behavior. "That was different, and you know it."

"How so?"

She refused to answer him. What was the point in
trying to explain it? It didn't matter. They were not
going to be married. She was a fool to have ever
thought they were. Alyssa shivered as a heavy coldness
centered in her chest. Her only thought was escape.

"I'm leaving," she stated in a flat tone. Only partially
dressed, carrying her shoes, cloak, and bonnet in her
arms, she fled from the room.

"Damnation," Morgan swore loudly. He sat on the
edge of the bed and struggled with his boots, listening
for the carriage. He was certain she would drive away
without him.

He was therefore surprised to step out into the fad-
ing afternoon sunlight and find Alyssa sitting stiffly in
the corner of the carriage. There was utter silence as
he entered the open coach and took up the reins. The
duke stared piercingly at Alyssa's lovely profile, willing
her to face him, but she stared stonily ahead.

Perhaps it would be best if they waited before discussing this gross misunderstanding, he decided.
Morgan allowed the silence to lengthen between
them, rapidly going over in his mind the arguments
he would present in his favor. He was not about to let

Alyssa go without a fight. It had been far too long since any woman had seriously engaged his interest.

He was prepared to offer her any material inducements she desired. Hell, he would even put the terms in writing. But marriage! Egad, the mere mention of the word made him break out in a cold sweat.

Compressing his lips in a tight line, Morgan flicked the reins and sent the chestnuts prancing down the drive.

Chapter Ten

Neither spoke a word.

Morgan finally broke the silence. "I am surprised you waited."

Alyssa merely huffed and tossed her head. She would have left in a heartbeat, had she the slightest notion of how to return to Westgate Manor.

"I can see that you are still upset by this entire misunderstanding," the duke tried again.

She favored him with a glare that could light a bonfire.

Misunderstanding! she inwardly fumed. He has made me the biggest fool in all of England, and he calls it a misunderstanding! I have given him my heart, as well as my body, and he has trampled it.

By the time they reached the drive to Westgate Manor very little of Alyssa's composure remained. All she wanted was to escape from Morgan and grieve in the privacy of her bedroom. Once alone, she could finally succumb to the tears that were threatening to choke the very breath from her.

Alyssa bolted from the carriage before it came to a complete halt, nearly breaking her neck as she jumped, startling both Morgan and young Ned, who stood waiting to take the curricle. As she raced for the door, she heard Morgan utter an explicit remark.

"Alyssa, wait," he commanded, and when she did not comply, he took off after her.

"Damn," she muttered under her breath. She could hear his heavy footsteps pursuing her and she ran faster. Alyssa managed to reach the entrance hall and she sprinted for the main staircase. Suddenly nothing seemed more important than reaching the safe sanctuary of her bedroom. She increased her speed desperately, taking the steps two at a time in an attempt to outdistance Morgan before he began the climb.

She shouldn't have bothered. Morgan caught up to her as she gained the landing and grabbed her forcefully by the arm, more roughly than he intended.

"That was a very stupid thing to do," he shouted, his frayed temper nearly done in. "We must talk about this, Alyssa."

"There is nothing to discuss, Your Grace," she spat at him. "Now let go of me this instant. I refuse to be manhandled by you any longer."

The vehemence in her voice enraged him. "I have had enough of this childish behavior. You will come downstairs to the library with me right now and discuss this in a calm and rational manner," he demanded.

"And if I refuse?"

"Then I will carry you downstairs, Alyssa, and lock you inside that room with me until we sort this mess out," he threatened.

Her eyes narrowed. His commanding attitude fueled her own anger. "I always knew you weren't a true gentleman."

Morgan smiled at her comment, amused by her insult. At least she was speaking to him.

Perkins met them outside the library doors. "Please see that we are not disturbed, Perkins," the duke said sternly, shutting the door in the astounded butler's face.

Alyssa walked slowly into the room. She heard the doors close and then the click of the lock. Morgan had locked them both inside the room. Summoning up the last of her pride, she began the attack.

"I won't be your whore."

"Good God, woman, is that what you think?" Morgan said, astonished at both her words and the infuriated way she spoke them.

"Am I wrong?" She stood with her legs braced apart and her hands on her hips, challenging him to disagree.

"I never thought of you as a whore, love." The sincerity and gentleness in his tone rattled her. "What we have shared is something rare and special. You affect me as no woman ever has. I don't want to lose you."

"Then we will be married," she whispered in a shaky voice.

Morgan frowned and shook his head. "Why do you insist on marriage?"

"Why do you refuse to consider it?" she countered.

"Marriage is too confining, too permanent a connection, Alyssa. I have been married and it was an abysmal failure, a rather unsavory and occasionally painful experience. I have wisely vowed to never marry again. Frankly, I do not believe I am suited to matrimony. We can have a far more satisfying relationship without marriage, and when by mutual agreement we decide to part, we can do so civilly, with no legal encumbrances. I will provide financially for you after we separate so you need never worry about money again. In many ways it is a far more advantageous arrangement."

Alyssa shook her head. He made it sound so simple. "What about society, Morgan? Will the members of the beau monde treat me with the same deference they would accord your wife? Would you dare walk into a crowded ballroom with your mistress on your arm? I'll own I know little of society, but even I know it would cause a great scandal."

Morgan grimaced. "I try to avoid most social gatherings, but I can take you to London and I will escort you to certain events. We can travel to the continent, Alyssa. Italy, Spain, Greece, France. This war won't last forever. I think we can be happy."

Alyssa closed her eyes for a few moments to gather her resolution. She was tempted, sorely tempted, but knew in her heart she must not yield. He spoke of ending their relations civilly, but she knew the humiliation would be unbearable when he grew tired of her and cast her aside. She would spare herself that pain at least.

"I cannot be your mistress, Morgan." There was sadness in her statement. She marched past him to the doors and began fumbling with the lock.

The pain in her voice tore at him. She was ending their relationship, he realized with astonishment and rising panic. Walking out of his life. Forever.

"So much for love," he threw out bitterly.

Alyssa froze, her back rigid. Slowly she turned around to face him. Her bruised heart twisted in her breast.

"How dare you speak to me of love?" she whispered, her face white with fury. "You first tell me what we shared is so rare, so special you cannot give it up. Yet you do not think it is worthy of marriage. Or is it me? Am I not worthy of the noble Duke of Gillingham?"

"Don't turn this back on me," Morgan snapped. "I've already explained about marriage. Tell me about love."

"All right, you insufferable cad! I love you. Yet I refuse to be your mistress. I refuse to become an outcast from society no matter what my heart says," she shouted, furious with him for making her admit her feelings, furious with herself for having them.

"Since when have you cared so much about society?" he questioned, strangely hurt to know that loving him was at the root of her great misery.

"Since you have decided to keep me apart from it," she replied. She looked at him, and her eyes filled with tears.

"All my life I have been excluded," she whispered, so low he had to move closer to hear her. Alyssa stared down at the carpet, her hands clasped tightly together. "My father could barely tolerate my presence. The local nobility never knew what to make of me, so they ignored me. My own people considered me one of the gentry, so they too kept their distance. I have never fit in anywhere, belonged anywhere." She shrugged her shoulders, then looked deeply into his silver-gray eyes.

"Loving you has been the most wondrous thing in my life, but I will not accept the path you choose for me, Morgan. You are right: I do not care about titles, or wealth, or position, or even society. Yet all of that is a part of your world and if I share your life, even for a brief time, I will not allow myself to be excluded from any part of it. I will not be cast on the outside again. Not even for you." Her tears, held in check for so long, fell freely now.

Morgan felt her pain deep within his soul, and knowing he was the cause of it made him angry. Angry with himself for not being able to give her what she wanted, what she so desperately needed.

"It was never my intention to hurt or insult you, Alyssa," Morgan said softly. "If you believe nothing else, you must believe that."

"I know," she replied honestly, blinking back her tears.

Reluctantly she met his gaze. Her heart constricted with anguish as she read the remorse on the duke's handsome face. If only his mind was not so firmly set against marriage. Alyssa quickly squashed the bud of hope blossoming within her heart. Fresh hope would only bring fresh pain.

"I would like to retire to my room, please." Alyssa bit her lip hard, fighting back the tears.

Morgan slowly unlocked the door, and Alyssa slipped out quietly, silent sobs shaking her shoulders as she ran from the room. Although he could no longer hear her cries, the sound of her pain echoed in his mind throughout the long, sleepless night.

The steady clanging of hammers grew louder in his ears. Slowly Morgan drifted to consciousness. He opened his eyes cautiously, only to shut them quickly against the brightness of the morning sun. The pounding in his head increased as the pain invaded his temples. Morgan gingerly shifted into a sitting position, but his vision blurred when he again opened his eyes. Resting his elbows upon his knees, he leaned forward, cupping his aching head in the palm of his hands. And still the pounding persisted.

The library was in a shambles, the floor littered with empty wine bottles, a testament to last night's indulgence. Morgan let out a loud groan of disgust. What a perfectly idiotic way to spend the night, he thought, drinking myself into oblivion. It certainly hasn't changed a damn thing. All I have to show for my excess is a cramped body from spending the night on a very uncomfortable settee and a monumental hangover.

A hesitant knock on the library doors brought his

head out of his hands. "Yes?" Morgan bellowed, furiously rubbing his temples.

"It is Mr. Henry Walsh, Your Grace. May I come in? The plasterers are here to work on the ceiling in the library."

Morgan was in the process of telling Mr. Walsh exactly what he could do with the plasterers when Perkins interrupted.

"Coffee, Your Grace," the dignified butler shouted to be heard over the tirade.

The shouting stopped. "Perkins? Is that you? Enter."

Perkins entered the room as bidden, neatly sidestepping an empty goblet thrown on the floor as he crossed the carpet. He made no mention of the deplorable condition he found both the room and Morgan in. He poured a large cup of coffee, handed it to the duke, and said, "I shall instruct Mr. Walsh to set the plasterers working somewhere else this morning, Your Grace. Then I shall bring you your breakfast."

"The hammering?" Morgan pleaded.

"I shall also tell Mr. Walsh to send the carpenters to the other side of the house."

After his third cup of coffee, Morgan began to feel a bit more human, although his mood remained foul. Perkins entered the room a second time, carrying a silver tray piled high with hot food. Morgan's stomach revolted at the smell, and he grimaced.

"Mrs. Stratton thought you might be hungry this morning, Your Grace," the butler said in a mild tone when he noted the look on Morgan's face. "After all, you did miss dinner last evening."

Determined that the butler not best him, Morgan took a tentative bite of toast. When he realized it was going to cooperate and stay in his stomach, he proceeded to cautiously finish it, and then progressed to the coddled eggs and sirloin.

As the duke ate his breakfast, Perkins silently began

to straighten the room. It seemed a very mundane household task for the elderly butler, but he performed it efficiently.

"I shall have Lucy clean these right away," Perkins said, holding up Morgan's rumpled jacket and neckcloth. "The rest of your clothing will be laundered while you are in your bath."

When Perkins held up the jacket, Morgan noticed a white envelope protruding from the inside breast pocket. The documents from Lord Castlereagh! He had completely forgotten about them.

"Just a minute, Perkins." Morgan removed the envelope from the jacket pocket. Now what do I do with it, he wondered, glancing down at his pocketless breeches. His eyes scanned the room quickly and came to rest on a large old-fashioned oak desk. It looked similar to one in his London town house. He recalled that desks of that style usually had a false bottom drawer.

"Whose desk is that?" Morgan asked the butler.

"No one's, Your Grace. I believe Mr. Walsh has decided to move it into the attic. It is not to be included among the new furnishings for this room."

"Perfect," the duke replied. As soon as he was alone he examined the desk and found the false bottom drawer on the lower left side. He slipped the documents inside. Granted, not a very original hiding place, he conceded, but it should be safe to store the documents. Morgan doubted he would be using them.

He pulled the bell cord to request more hot coffee, but when the butler did not appear, Morgan realized that the bell must be disconnected. Growing impatient, the duke slipped his boots on, hastily tucked his shirt in his breeches, and ventured out into the hall to bellow for a servant.

He spotted Alyssa before she was aware of him. She stood at the far end of the hallway talking quietly to

Ned. She was dressed in the same drab brown gown she had worn the very first time he had seen her. Even from that distance, he could see the deep circles under her eyes, the telltale signs of a sleepless night. She looked tired and vulnerable and beautiful.

After Ned left, Alyssa started walking down the hall. She stiffened noticeably when she saw him. Her eyes darted nervously around, and for a moment Morgan thought she would turn and run. But she held her ground.

Alyssa's heart raced strongly as she stood only a few feet from Morgan. His hair was rumpled, his face unshaven, his shirt collar opened, the white shirt unbuttoned halfway down his chest and hanging out on the left side of his breeches. He looked irresistible.

"Good morning," he said in a husky voice, uncertain of his reception.

She nodded her head slightly, not trusting her voice. They stood there, awkwardly staring at each other. I am going to start crying again, Alyssa realized suddenly with alarm, and turned quickly to escape him.

"Alyssa, stop," he implored, starting after her.

"Don't," she beseeched him as his hand clasped hers. She wrenched her fingers free. "Please, just leave me in peace."

Morgan winced at the agony he heard in her voice. "There are a few things we need to clarify, Alyssa." She lifted her head up, staring at him as though he had lost his wits.

"I do not wish to discuss this further with you, Your Grace," she said wearily. "We have already had our discussions. There is nothing left to be said."

"I beg to differ," he insisted as he guided her into the library and shut the door behind them. Alyssa allowed it, since she did not have the strength to fight him.

"First of all, I'd like to apologize for . . . for everything," he said lamely. He ran his hands through his hair in vexation, trying to gather his thoughts. This was proving more difficult than he imagined. Alyssa stood near the door, poised for flight, looking like a wounded doe.

The hurt and betrayal etched on her lovely face was too much for Morgan to bear. With a deep breath, he took the plunge.

"We shall be married as soon as I can produce a special license," the duke stated flatly.

The cold determination in his voice startled her. "I don't understand. Why have you suddenly changed your mind?"

Morgan's mouth formed a cynical smile. "It became rather clear to me last night, Alyssa. I have taken gross advantage of your vulnerability and innocence. Honor dictates I make amends."

Alyssa shook her head sadly. He must be feeling guilty. His words, meant to bring her joy, brought only deep remorse to her already bruised heart. She took a small breath to marshal her courage.

"We will never marry, Your Grace," she said tonelessly. "I could not endure our life together knowing you reluctantly shackled yourself to me in a moment of weakness. A none too sober moment of weakness, I suspect." Aimlessly she stroked the neck of an empty wine bottle resting on the desktop. "Someday you would come to hate me for forcing this unwanted marriage upon you. And that I could not bear."

For a split second he thought to argue his case, but caught himself. It was best to make a clean break of it now, he convinced himself. In the long run it would be best for both of them.

It was Alyssa who finally broke the long silence. Her voice was low as she spoke, but forceful.

"I have packed all the clothes you bought for me in the trunks they were delivered in. Ned will carry them down to the front hall. You may instruct Perkins where they should be shipped. The key to the house is locked inside the small jewel case, which is in the large green trunk. Ned will make the arrangements to send the gray gelding wherever you desire."

"Alyssa," the duke interrupted. "This is quite unnecessary. I purchased those things for you. I want you to have them, especially the house."

"I couldn't," she whispered hoarsely, remembering the blissful afternoon they had spent together at the lovely house. Was that only yesterday, she mused? It seemed a lifetime ago.

It hurt Morgan deeply that she would accept nothing from him. Yet the possibility existed she might have already unknowingly accepted the most precious gift any man could bestow upon a woman. And he wondered how in God's name he was going to broach that delicate subject with her.

"Alyssa, there are . . . um . . . consequences of the times we have spent together," he began carefully.

She looked at him in total bewilderment. He surmised she did not have the faintest idea what he was trying to say. So much for diplomacy, he decided. He was too tired and too hung over to be delicate.

"Oh, bloody hell," he swore. "When did you last have your monthly courses?"

Alyssa felt her face grow hot with embarrassment. She cast her eyes to the carpet, scarcely believing she heard his question correctly.

"For heaven's sake," she gasped, not knowing how he could possibly ask her such an intimate question. Or how she could possibly answer him. It was a subject she had discussed only one other time in her life, when she was 13 and Mavis had explained the miraculous changes her body was experiencing.

"Alyssa, our lovemaking could result in the creation of a child," Morgan pressed on. "Not having your monthly courses is a sign of pregnancy."

"I wasn't sure about that." Her crimson cheeks blanched white. "A child," she muttered, shaking her head to and fro. "How could I care for a child?"

"You must tell me at once if you are pregnant. Do you understand?"

"What will you do?"

Morgan sighed loudly and rubbed the back of his neck. "I will take care of you, Alyssa. You must trust me. I want your promise that you will write to me immediately. Send the letter to Ramsgate Castle or my London town house. Do you still have the addresses?"

She nodded. "You want me to write something that personal in a letter?"

He thought for a moment. "It is not necessary to write anything specific about the state of your health. Just send me a personal letter. I will understand your meaning. I have your promise, then?"

Alyssa agreed because it seemed so important to him. Naturally she had no idea what she would do if she did find herself in such a disgraceful predicament. Probably die of shame, for one thing.

Morgan let out a sigh of relief and sat down on the brocade settee, thankful that difficult task was completed. Absently he drank the last of his cold coffee, his eyes never leaving Alyssa's pale face. She looked to be in shock.

Alyssa became aware of his gaze and squirmed uncomfortably. "I also want a promise from you, Your Grace."

She could see that he was instantly on his guard.

"I would like to finish my job here at Westgate Manor. Mr. Walsh predicts the house will be ready for Tristan and Caroline to occupy by the end of the summer."

"I would not ask Tris to fire you, Alyssa," he interrupted, dismayed she would think him such a brute.

"I know," she said quietly. "But it will be very awkward having to see you. I want your promise that you will stay away from Westgate Manor until I leave."

Morgan's face remained expressionless, hiding the wound her simple request had inflicted on him.

"If that is what you wish."

"It is the only solution," she assured him, her heart breaking anew.

"Then so be it."

It was settled. There was nothing left to say.

Chapter Eleven

It was mid-May, nearly two months since Alyssa had last seen Morgan. The duke kept his promise and did not visit Westgate Manor, but Tristan, Caroline, and her sister, Priscilla, were there often conferring with Mr. Walsh on the renovations to the house. They always made a point of visiting with Alyssa during these trips and inadvertently kept her apprised of Morgan's activities.

Caroline would chatter enthusiastically about all the wonderful parties she and Tristan were attending in honor of their upcoming nuptials, and also about her new friend, the lovely Madeline Duponce. Caroline was convinced Mlle Duponce had captured the roving eye of the fickle duke, and Alyssa felt the familiar dull ache in her heart sharpen as Caroline described what a handsome pair they made. It became impossible for Alyssa to sit calmly by and listen to the endless round of social events the duke and his fair Madeline attended together without feeling physically ill, and she began avoiding Caroline.

Priscilla took an active interest in the manor's renovations, and Alyssa often sought refuge in her company. Alyssa never minded answering Priscilla's endless questions, and when she was unavailable to escort her about the estate, Priscilla always graciously explored on her own.

There were, however, more pressing problems for Alyssa to work out than the jealousy she felt over Morgan's latest conquest. As the days and weeks passed with still no sign of her monthly courses, Alyssa began to panic. It was almost beyond her realm of tolerance to entertain the possibility that she carried Morgan's child. It was her nerves, she decided. She was driving herself to distraction with worry. Fate would not be so cruel as to thrust an innocent babe upon a woman who was financially unprepared to raise a child.

The work at the manor house was progressing at a slower pace than Mr. Walsh predicted, and Alyssa was grateful. Keeping busy all day helped distract her mind, although her nights were often spent pacing her bedroom floor. As long as the renovations were under way Alyssa was assured of a position, and in her current state of upheaval her job represented the only stability in her life.

Tristan continued to come often to Westgate Manor, occasionally with Caroline, other times alone. Alyssa found solace in the company of Morgan's younger brother, and looked forward to his visits. He was an affable man, always in good spirits and blessed with a dry, rapier wit. Alyssa could always count on Tris to lighten her dour mood.

On this lovely spring morning the south garden beckoned Alyssa with its early roses in bloom. Taking an unaccustomed break from her work, she strolled among the flowers, marveling over the magical creations the new gardener's hard work had produced. She inhaled the sweet, heady fragrance of the perfect blossoms as she gathered a basket of cuttings for the vase in her bedchamber. The blooms still held morning dewdrops on their petals, moist and velvety to the touch. As Alyssa bent low to cut a flower from underneath the sprawling bush, she felt the blood rush from her face, making her feel light-headed and queasy. Yellow dots swam before her eyes, and then everything went black for a few seconds as she fell to the ground in a dead faint.

"Lady Alyssa!" Ned cried out in alarm when he saw her crumple to the ground. He rushed over to help. "Are you all right?"

Alyssa slowly opened her eyes. Colors swirled and blended until Ned's concerned features eventually became focused.

"I'm fine, Ned," she assured him shakily. Ned gently assisted Alyssa to her feet. "I must have lost my balance."

"Are you sure you aren't hurt?" Ned repeated, not convinced. "You look awfully pale. Let me help you inside so you can lie down."

Mr. Walsh met them as they came through the French doors. "My goodness, what has happened?" he exclaimed when he saw Ned with his arm around Alyssa, steadying her as she slowly walked into the room. "Have you injured yourself in some way, Lady Alyssa?"

"Goodness no, Mr. Walsh." Alyssa tried making light of the incident. "I was merely clumsy and fell. Ned was kind enough to help me. Thank you, Ned." She moved deliberately away from the lad and stood alone, clutching a mahogany end table to maintain her balance, vainly hoping they would believe her and leave. Alyssa felt the familiar nausea rise up in her throat, and prayed they would go before she disgraced herself by throwing up her meager breakfast. She closed her eyes and drew in deep breaths, trying to keep the nausea at bay.

"I'm getting Mavis," Ned declared, watching Alyssa with growing concern.

"It is not necessary, Ned," Alyssa protested, but he ignored her and left quickly. Mr. Walsh hesitantly assisted Alyssa to the settee and poured a goblet of water. He awkwardly fussed over her while they waited, and she thought she would scream over his unwanted attention. Her stomach pitched and rolled, and the effort it cost her to keep her upset stomach under control made her break out in a fine sweat.

They were both relieved when Mavis finally appeared. "Now what's all this about you falling down, my girl?" Mavis said in a blustery tone. "Ned said you fainted in the garden."

"I did no such thing," Alyssa insisted. "I just lost my balance. I don't know why everyone is making such a fuss." Alyssa stared up innocently at the small group of concerned faces surrounding her.

"I suspect you have been working her too hard, Mr. Walsh," Mavis decided, not liking the absence of color in Alyssa's face. The girl was white as a sheet.

Mr. Walsh sputtered. "I can assure you, I have not been overworking Lady Alyssa," he replied indignantly. He leaned down to observe her closely. "I do agree, however, she looks peaked. Perhaps it would be prudent for Lady Alyssa to rest today. I'm sure I can manage without her this afternoon."

Alyssa instantly opened her mouth to disagree, but the forceful protest in Mavis's eyes gave her pause. "Thank you, Mr. Walsh," Alyssa reluctantly replied. "I appreciate your concern. I shall see you in the morning."

"I hope you are feeling better soon," Mr. Walsh concluded before leaving the room.

"If you'll not be needing me for anything else, I'd

best be getting back to work," Ned chimed in. "Lord Tristan's new coach has arrived, and Hawkins needs my help cleaning it up." Alyssa was mildly annoyed that Ned ignored her nod of approval, but waited instead for Mavis's permission before he left.

Once they were alone, Alyssa could feel Mavis's sharp eyes on her.

"I'm fine, Mavis," Alyssa hastily assured her old nurse. "I don't know why everyone is making such a fuss."

"Well, you don't look fine."

"Thank you," Alyssa retorted wryly.

"I'll tell Mrs. Stratton to brew you some tea. It will help settle your stomach."

"How did you know my stomach was upset?" Alyssa stammered before she realized what she had revealed.

Mavis's eyes narrowed, and her lips compressed. "I think it's high time we had a talk, my girl. Isn't there something you want to tell me?"

"Oh, Mavis," Alyssa said, her eyes clouding with emotion. "It can't be true."

Mavis let out a long sigh, her nagging suspicions at last confirmed. "Just because you don't want it be true won't change things." She reached over and patted Alyssa's hand soothingly. "I daresay you aren't the first girl who's been surprised to discover she was carrying a babe," Mavis said.

"How will I ever take care of a child, Mavis?" Alyssa trembled, still trying to accept the reality of her condition.

"You're going to have help, that's for sure. I'll be with you, for one thing. And we will just see what the duke has to say about all this," Mavis concluded shrewdly.

Alyssa looked up at Mavis, admiring how nothing escaped the older woman's notice. "I cannot marry him, you know," she responded in a small voice. She sounded so forlorn, so unlike the strong, capable woman Mavis knew.

"You are going to tell him about the child, aren't you?" Mavis asked worriedly.

"Do I have a choice?"

"No," Mavis stated firmly.

"Then I shall tell him. I will write the letter this afternoon. The duke told me I was to contact him at Ramsgate Castle or in London if the need arose." Alyssa looked sheepishly down at her hands. "I hope you aren't too disappointed in me, Mavis."

"Of course not," the older woman said, hugging Alyssa tightly. Mavis had been sick with worry ever since Alyssa had, without emotion, informed her that she and the duke were not getting married. Whatever had broken the two of them up would have to be fixed, Mavis decided. There was an unborn child to consider. Mavis had complete faith the duke would do right by Alyssa, despite the younger girl's skepticism.

"Now enough weeping," Mavis said, feeling Alyssa's tears on her shoulder. "Everything will work out for the best. You'll see. Tell me, how have you been feeling?"

"Dreadful," Alyssa answered, grateful to finally be able to discuss all her symptoms. "I'm tired most of the time, and all I have to do is smell Mrs. Stratton's cooking and I feel nauseous."

Mavis nodded her head in understanding. "Your mother was the same way. Don't worry, it will pass."

Wordlessly she held out her snowy white handkerchief so Alyssa could dry her tears. They talked a while longer and calculated the baby would be born sometime before Christmas. By the time Mavis left her, sipping a weak cup of tea, Alyssa felt better. It was a relief to finally have the situation out in the open. She would contact the duke and a suitable solution would be found.

Alyssa spent the remainder of the day locked in her room at her writing table, trying to compose a letter to Morgan. She did not have the faintest idea what to say. Finally she wrote a brief note inquiring about his health and asking his advice on a suitable wedding gift for Tristan and Caroline. She copied the note twice on her best watermark stationery and sent one to Ramsgate Castle and one to the duke's London house in Grosvenor Square. Since she was not certain where the duke was in residence, Alyssa took no chances.

Alyssa boldly wrote *Personal* on the outside of both envelopes, hoping to snag Morgan's attention and cause him to come at once to Westgate Manor. In the end, she needn't have bothered. Her cautious efforts proved fruitless, because the duke never received either letter.

Henri Duponce enjoyed being a spy. He liked the excitement and the danger, and of course, the money. He was not like some, who spied because of loyalty or ideology. He spied because of the thrill it gave him.

The fact that spying was a treasonable offense, punishable by death, did not bother Henri. One had to be caught before one could be put to death, he reasoned, and Henri had no intention of being caught. Ever. He was much too clever for the dim-witted British authorities.

Obtaining information for the French was laughably easy. The so-called British nobility were entirely too well informed and too loose lipped for their own good. A few drinks, a few rounds of cards, and it was easy to discover who was currently working with sensitive information at the War Ministry.

Once a mark had been identified, it was a relatively simple task getting someone on the inside; the ton changed household servants as often as they changed clothes. After the informant located where the information was kept, the Falcon went to work. Even after all these months of working together, Henri was still in awe of the Falcon's talent. Cunning, ruthless, and light-fingered, the Falcon never failed to produce the documents. Although Henri had originally trained the spy, he admitted the Falcon's talents now rivaled his own.

Madeline Duponce entered the sitting room, interrupting Henri at his work. She was clad in a thin, transparent dressing gown, loosely belted at the waist. She crossed the room and came to rest at Henri's side, running her fingers gingerly through his hair. She rubbed her lithe body provocatively against him, trying to gain his attention. They had spent an exhausting hour in bed together, but her actions, coupled with the memories of himself thrusting deeply inside her willing body, made him harden again.

"Come back to bed, Henri." Madeline pouted, pushing her breasts forward tantalizingly. "I grow lonely for your company."

"You are an insatiable slut." He snorted with disgust. "You know I must copy this information and return it to the Falcon before six o'clock this evening. These documents must be returned to their owner before they are missed."

"But you have been in here for hours," Madeline whined. "Why is it taking so long?"

"I am using a new code," Henri admitted. "It is very complicated and requires my complete attention."

"A different code? Again? Why does the Falcon insist on changing codes constantly?"

"Because we have changed couriers and the Falcon does not wish to be placed in jeopardy if this man is caught. Very clever, no?"

Madeline made a face at him, showing her opinion of the matter.

"If I didn't know better, I would say you are jealous

of my admiration for the Falcon," Henri baited her.

"Ha," she retorted with a flip of her long brown hair. "What a ridiculous notion."

Madeline was not, as everyone thought, his blood sister. She was his accomplice and lover and was as possessive of him in private as he pretended to be of her in public. They had been two ragged urchins, barely surviving on the revolutionary streets of Paris, when Phillipe Lobeur had discovered them. He was fleeing the country and had been handsomely paid to bring his sister's two children with him. He did not properly care for the youngsters and they took ill and died. Phillipe was devastated by the loss, knowing he needed the children to obtain the guardianship necessary to access the vast Duponce fortune.

Since the true Duponce children were now dead, Phillipe picked up young Henri and Madeline from the streets, substituting them for his niece and nephew. When his sister and her husband were guillotined, Phillipe, guardian to the heirs, successfully gained control of the Duponce money banked outside of France. The trio settled in England and were promptly embraced by British society: the two young orphans and their "uncle," a noble emigre, who had managed to snatch his two young charges from the very jaws of death.

Appearances and manners were of paramount importance in society, and Phillipe made certain his wards possessed both. Phillipe was a ruthless, unscrupulous man, totally lacking in moral character, and he passed these traits on to Henri and Madeline. The pair learned their lessons well, and were endowed with a natural gift for deception that made them well suited for their current occupation.

"What are these?" Madeline questioned, sorting through the papers on Henri's desk. She held up two white envelopes from Westgate Manor.

"Oh, those," Henri said, dismissing them with a wave of his hand. "I picked them up by mistake. They are correspondence meant for the Duke of Gillingham. They were marked *Personal* and looked important. They are nothing. Some silly woman wants the duke to advise her on a wedding gift for Tristan and Caroline."

"Shall I put them in the pile to be returned with the other documents?"

"Don't bother. The seals have already been broken, and I don't want to waste the time it will take to repair them." Henri scribbled on his paper for a few more minutes, then put his writing quill down. "There. I have finally finished," he said with a satisfied sigh. "Now come over here and show me how much you really missed me."

Alyssa spent the time she waited for Morgan to respond to her letter in utter misery. Her nausea increased, becoming more unpredictable. She never knew when it would overtake her and she would have to race from the room, gagging and heaving. It made her life very difficult. She felt certain Mr. Walsh thought she must be seriously ill, when she had to stop him twice in the same day, both times in midsentence, to rush from the room and throw up her meal.

At Mavis's suggestion, Alyssa started carrying hard, dry biscuits in the pockets of her gown, nibbling on them the moment she felt the queasiness in her stomach. They helped a bit, and Alyssa was thankful Mavis possessed a considerable knowledge of what was best for expectant mothers. Alyssa came to rely heavily on her advice.

If Mrs. Stratton was curious about Alyssa's sudden demand for the unappetizing toasts, she made no comment. Alyssa was grateful the cook was too preoccupied with the remodeling of the kitchen to be concerned with anything else. The very last thing Alyssa needed was a lot of attention focused on her. Her nerves were frayed, and her pregnancy made her moods too unpredictable to stand up to any scrutiny.

The size of the work crew nearly doubled as Mr. Walsh, already behind schedule, became determined to complete the renovations on the house by the fall. The additional work load kept Alyssa occupied during the day, but at night her thoughts shifted. First to the tiny life growing inside her body and then to the infuriating man who planted it there.

Her thoughts shifted from joy to terror as she tried predicting Morgan's reaction to their unborn child. She would lie awake in her bed at night, fretfully wondering what arrangements Morgan would make for her and the baby.

She supposed he would set up some kind of living allowance for them. Maybe he would even offer to buy a house for them somewhere. She wouldn't object, as long as the residence was located someplace where no one knew her. Several years ago, Mrs. Stratton had told her of Lady Harmon's youngest daughter Anne, who had been ruined, according to reliable sources, by the very married Lord Albert Johnson.

Apparently Anne had been sent to Italy to have her baby and was never seen again. Alyssa knew, however, with Europe in such an upheaval, leaving the country was not a realistic alternative.

The thought of marriage often stole into her mind, but given Morgan's strong resistance to the institution, she held no romantic notions that he would insist she become his wife. Yet a tiny portion of her heart clung stubbornly to the notion that the duke would marry her out of genuine regard and affection rather than obligation. Deep within her heart, it was her most treasured fantasy.

Whatever the final solution, Alyssa knew she would

have to put her pride aside, remain calm, and accept what Morgan dictated. Despite their differences, she believed that Morgan would be generous and do anything within his considerable power to aid her and the child.

Paramount in her mind was the protection of this small life fluttering within her body that she at first feared, then resented, but now had grown to love. For the first time in her entire life there would be someone totally hers to love. She would shelter her child and protect him with her very life, making sure he never came to harm.

No matter where she eventually settled, Alyssa had every intention of passing herself off as a widow, hoping to ensure the baby would not carry the label of bastard. She shuddered at the thought of her innocent child being cruelly taunted by others and ostracized by society.

The scars from the pain of her own isolated childhood ran deep, and Alyssa was determined that her child grow up in a secure environment, never being allowed to feel shame over his origins or parents. It might not be possible to give this child his proper birthright, but he would grow up surrounded by all the love she could muster. This baby would always know how much she loved and wanted him and there would never be any doubt the child's needs would be placed above her own.

All the windows and the doors were open in an effort to allow the warm July breeze to circulate through the kitchen. It was Sunday, and Westgate Manor was strangely silent without the sawing and hammering. Alyssa sat quietly in her chair, taking tea with Perkins, Mrs. Stratton, Mavis, Ned, and Lucy. Everyone's attention was focused on Perkins as the butler read aloud from the *London Times* the glowing account of

Tristan and Caroline's wedding. Even though the paper was several weeks old, the splendid details of the glorious event were brought to life by the elegant prose, and the servants enjoyed sharing this intimate moment of their future employers' lives.

Despite her resolve to ignore the details, Alyssa listened along with the others, picturing the beautiful event in her mind. "The bride's dress, an enchanting creation of white silk and taffeta, was accented with delicate hand-stitched Brussels lace sewn into the neckline and sleeves. Tiny seed pearls decorated the bodice, and the bride carried a bouquet of orange blossoms."

Perkins paused a moment and took a sip of tea before continuing. "The vows were exchanged at St. George's in Hanover Square, with the prince regent himself in attendance. The groom's brother, Morgan Ashton, Duke of Gillingham, stood up with him and, likewise, the bride's sister, Lady Priscilla Ogden, supported her. The evasive duke was himself an object of interest in the choice of his wedding companion, one Madeline Duponce, sister to the Comte Henri Duponce. Speculation was rampant if another wedding would soon be occurring."

Alyssa nearly choked on her tea picturing Morgan with another woman as Perkins read that line. Alyssa left the kitchen abruptly, refusing to subject herself to any more pain. She stood alone at her bedroom window, wondering gloomily if Madeline was his mistress. As the tears fell freely down her face, Alyssa was momentarily distracted by the movement she felt in her belly. At first she was not certain what it was, the movement was so slight, but it happened a second time, and her tears fell harder. The baby had moved! It was so miraculous, and yet so frightening.

Alyssa cradled her belly protectively. I love you, little stranger, her heart cried. Even if your father cares nothing for us. Alyssa's tears started again as she thought of Morgan escorting Madeline Duponce to the wedding.

A knock at the door interrupted her tears.

"It's Mavis," the voice on the other side spoke. "I've come to see if you are all right."

Alyssa took a deep breath to compose herself. She wiped her eyes and let Mavis into the room. After closing the door, she turned to the older woman.

"Time is running short, Mavis," Alyssa said in a flat tone. "I have to start making some plans."

"Don't you think it would be best if you wait until the duke arrives?" Mavis asked tentatively.

Alyssa gave her a hard stare. "He is not coming, Mavis."

"Now you can't be sure about that," Mavis began.

"Stop it, Mavis," Alyssa interrupted. "It has been over six weeks since I sent those letters. I have heard nothing from him in all that time. 'Tis high time I faced the truth. The duke is finished with me."

"I feel certain you are wrong. You must write to him again."

"No!" Alyssa was vehement in her objection. "I refuse to humiliate myself further. You heard the newspaper report. The duke has found other, more pleasant things to occupy his time. I am on my own."

"You know that was just idle gossip in the newspaper," Mavis continued, still trying to convince Alyssa not to give up hope.

"I've already spent far too many sleepless nights trying to determine the duke's attitude toward becoming a father," Alyssa said sadly. "His silence has given me the answer."

"Oh my poor girl," Mavis said with genuine sympathy.

"I felt the baby move," Alyssa whispered softly in awe. She clasped Mavis's hands tightly in her own.

"There is no time for pity, Mavis. This child needs me: I am all that he has. For the sake of my baby, I must put away false hopes."

"What will we do?"

"First we must find a place to live. I intend to pass myself off as a widow, so we cannot settle too near Hampshire."

"What about money?" Mavis asked. "Will there be enough?"

"I have saved all my wages thus far. It isn't much, but it will help buy food for a while. How long do you think it will be before the babe begins to show?" Alyssa stood in front of the mirror, running her hands over her belly and critically examining her body. Her waist had thickened and her breasts were heavier, but so far her old, faded gowns still fit. She didn't think anyone noticed her body's physical changes, but if they had, she highly doubted pregnancy would be considered a possible explanation.

Mavis eyed her speculatively. "No more than another month or two before your belly begins to stick out," the old nurse predicted.

"Mr. Walsh will be leaving in three weeks' time. He expects the remainder of the work to be done under my supervision. If we stay until the renovations are complete, it will be the middle of September. Will my condition be obvious?"

Mavis shook her head. "Yes. I'm sure you'll be showing the babe by then."

Alyssa's shoulders sagged in defeat. "We need the extra time." She paced the room, thinking out loud. "I always inspect each day's work in the evening. If I wait until everyone has gone for the day before making my inspections, none of the workers will see me. Perkins can relay any problems I have uncovered to the appropriate workers the following morning. Mr. Walsh is leaving on holiday, and Lucy, Molly, and Hawkins will be visiting with their families. The servants won't return until Tristan and Caroline take up residence. Perkins will be here, and Ned of course, but somehow I will find the courage to tell them the truth about my condition."

"What about Mrs. Stratton?"

Alyssa groaned in frustration. "It will be embarrassing for Perkins and Ned to be told, but I know they will keep my secret. Mrs. Stratton has a deep regard for me, yet I fear her tongue would get the better of her good intentions. It is simply too risky taking her into my confidence."

"Now, wait just a minute," Mavis interrupted, warming to the plan. "Mrs. Stratton always talks about how much she wants to visit her cousin in Plymouth. If we can persuade her to leave within a few weeks, she won't return until Tristan and Caroline move in, and we shall be long gone."

"We would have additional time to find a place to live, and the extra weeks' salary will be most welcomed," Alyssa added.

"I have my pension from the duke, and we can stay in Cornwall with my sister Louise until we locate a cottage of our own to rent."

Alyssa had almost forgotten about Mavis's pension, so generously provided by the duke. How could he be so kind to a woman he hardly knew, and yet abandon his unborn child? His bastard child, she reminded herself sharply.

"Do you think we could do it?" Mavis asked.

"The only problem I foresee is Tristan and Caroline," Alyssa concluded. "Tristan's last letter stated they are not even considering a move to Westgate Manor until Christmas. The house won't be ready before the new season starts, and Caroline plans to be in London attending all the social gatherings. I'm sure he will be busy with her and not able to visit here as

Adrienne Basso

often. I can write him more frequently about the workmen's progress, and when Tris does come, I shall be indisposed."

"Don't you think he will become suspicious?"

"Perhaps. If he does, we will leave. I only pray he is too interested in his new bride to care much about me or this house."

"Then it is settled," Mavis concluded with a sigh.

"Yes," Alyssa agreed slowly, her mind still occupied with the problem of money. She thought about all the extra furniture nearly overflowing in the attic. "I have some ideas about how we can raise a bit of extra money before we leave."

"Well, that's enough planning for now," Mavis admonished, not liking how tired Alyssa looked. "You lie down and take a nice long nap. I'll wake you when dinner is ready."

Alyssa was about to protest before realizing how drained she felt. Now, more than ever, it was important she take care of herself. There was a lot to be done. September would arrive all too soon and she needed to be prepared to leave Westgate Manor. Forever.

Chapter Twelve

Tristan strolled into the duke's study, seating himself in front of the desk where Morgan was working. He made himself comfortable in the leather chair, and then casually propped his feet up on the desktop.

"Caroline wants to know if there will be room in your coach for us tonight. Grandmother has begged off from the evening's festivities, and Caroline insists you and Madeline will need a chaperon to the opera."

Morgan gave Tristan a disgruntled stare. "And just how does Caroline know I am taking Madeline to the opera this evening?"

Tristan stretched his arms up over his head and yawned. "They both attended Lady Jersey's little soiree this afternoon. Although it would hardly take a genius to know you will be escorting Madeline. You have been practically glued to that woman's side for the past few months."

Morgan's ears detected the hint of sarcasm in Tristan's voice.

"You don't approve, little brother?" Morgan asked, with a raised eyebrow.

"Don't get your dander up, Morgan," Tristan remarked. "I was merely making an observation. But since you have asked my opinion, well, it's not exactly that I don't approve, I simply don't understand the attraction."

"You don't think Madeline Duponce is attractive?" Morgan smiled, a rare occurrence these days. "I never thought the day would come when you wouldn't appreciate a beautiful woman. Has marriage changed you so much, Tris?"

Tristan shrugged. "Oh, I suppose Madeline is pretty enough," he admitted. "God knows, my new brother-in-law, Gilbert, is still smitten with her, despite your monopolizing the fair mademoiselle's company. But for all the time you spend with her, you don't seem very happy, Morgan. I had always hoped if you finally settled on another woman it would bring you joy."

"I have not settled on Madeline Duponce," Morgan corrected his brother. "Let's just say she amuses me for the moment." Morgan was impressed with Tristan's accurate perception of the situation, and he hoped it was not obvious to others. He truly had grown tired of the French woman's company over the last few months, but it was vital to his mission for the War Ministry that Morgan stay as close as possible to Madeline Duponce and her brother Henri.

Morgan reached over to the sideboard and grabbed two glasses. He poured out a generous portion of port for both himself and his brother. Handing Tristan the glass, he neatly changed the subject.

"Tell me, when are you moving into that mausoleum of a house I gifted you with? I thought it was going to be ready in August."

"So did I," Tristan answered with a laugh, accepting the fact Morgan did not wish to discuss Madeline. He was still concerned about his brother, but he didn't press it. He knew if Morgan wanted to confide in him he would do so when he was ready and not before. "The work on the house certainly has taken a damn long time thus far, and it is far from being finished. My admiration for Grandmother has increased a hundredfold these last few months. How she ever put up with Grandfather renovating Ramsgate Castle for twenty years is beyond comprehension. And they lived there for long periods while the work was done. It must have been maddening."

Morgan laughingly agreed. "No wonder it is her coat of arms that is etched in stone above the main entrance."

"We still retain hopes of taking up residence in Westgate Manor sometime before Christmas. Caroline wants to wait until everything is perfect before we move," Tristan continued. "Although many people have already retired to their country houses, there is still enough social activity to keep Caroline content living in town." His handsome face darkened with a frown. "I hope we are not becoming a nuisance, Morgan. We can always go stay with Caroline's family if you want your privacy back." The woeful expression on Tristan's face told Morgan how little that idea appealed to him.

"Don't be ridiculous, Tris. This is as much your home as it is mine. Truth be told, I am glad for the company, as is Grandmother. You know how much she enjoys being with Caroline."

"I promise to be out of your hair fairly soon. Mr. Walsh has already left Westgate Manor and Lady Alyssa is overseeing the final work."

Morgan felt his heart lurch at the mention of Alyssa's name. A day seldom passed that he did not think about her. At first he had tried to convince himself that the need he felt for her was merely physical, but no other woman had sparked his interest, either in or out of bed.

He told himself the feeling would pass with time, but time moved very slowly. He missed Alyssa's animated conversation and her spirited attitude toward life. At times he was actually disappointed she had not written to inform him she was carrying his child. It was a selfish, almost cruel thought, but it would have provided him a legitimate excuse for reentering her life.

"How is Miss Carrington faring these days?" Morgan inquired in a casual voice.

"I wish I knew," Tris answered, taking a sip of the excellent wine. "The last few times I have called at Westgate she has been indisposed. If I didn't know better, I would say Miss Carrington was avoiding me."

Morgan scoffed at the idea. That certainly did not sound like the Alyssa he knew. She never ran from anyone. Except him.

"I very much doubt that," Morgan said in a knowledgeable tone.

"Yes, well, you are probably right. Most likely she has fallen victim to my deadly charms and after finding herself hopelessly in love with me, cannot face me since I am now a married man, forever beyond her reach."

"I do not find that amusing, Tristan."

"For God's sake, Morgan, calm down. I was only jesting." Tristan was surprised at the dark scowl on Morgan's face. He looked positively menacing.

Morgan ran his fingers through his hair and took a deep breath. "Sorry, Tris. I'm afraid I've been a bit touchy lately."

This was interesting, Tristan decided, alert to Morgan's possessive attitude toward Alyssa Carrington. He tried testing Morgan further.

"You know, I often wondered why Lady Alyssa

never married. She is a most pleasant person, intelligent, charming, amusing. Properly gowned, she would be quite stunning." He eyed Morgan carefully, not at all disappointed with his brother's reaction.

"She is very beautiful," Morgan whispered, an almost dreamlike expression crossing his features as he remembered the first time he had seen Alyssa naked. She had been so lovely, so open, so giving of herself. Morgan admitted to himself how much he missed her, especially after spending so much time in the company of Madeline Duponce, who was vain, selfish, and demanding.

Morgan became aware of Tristan's scrutiny and immediately put his guard up. "With the unusual way she was raised, I imagine there weren't many opportunities for Miss Carrington to meet eligible men."

"Yes, I'm sure you are right," Tristan agreed, not missing a detail of the wistful expression in Morgan's voice and eyes when he spoke of Alyssa Carrington. However, he was willing to let the matter drop. For now. Tristan had every intention of finding out how the prim Miss Carrington was able to so deeply affect his stoic brother. It was a mystery that demanded to be solved.

The large grandfather clock in the hall struck six o'clock. "I'm sorry to cut you short," Morgan apologized to Tristan, relieved to have an excuse to end their discussion. "I have a meeting to attend at six-thirty and I don't want to be late. I will be ready to leave for the theater tonight at eight o'clock, if you and Caroline decide you want to join me." With a brief nod of farewell to his brother, Morgan hurriedly left the study.

Morgan sat across from Lord Castlereagh carefully reviewing the latest dispatches. The information he had left in both his London house and at Ramsgate

Castle had slowly made its way into French hands. Although his private beach at Ramsgate Castle was seldom used anymore by the French couriers, any information the duke was given by the War Ministry had been discovered and passed on to the French. The Falcon was doing a very thorough job.

Morgan had been led on a merry chase all summer and was frustrated by the fact that he was no closer to revealing the Falcon's identity than when he first began. He was convinced that Henri Duponce was spying for the French, and it was also likely his sister Madeline was involved, which was why Morgan kept in close contact with the pair. He was also fairly certain that Henri was not the Falcon, merely an accomplice. So far neither the duke nor the agents assigned to the mission had been able to catch the spies in the act, or produce anything but circumstantial evidence.

"This is a brief list of the latest stolen information that was to be sent across the Channel," Lord Castlereagh began without ceremony. "We managed to intercept the courier on his way to France this time, but it took a while to decipher the code. I believe the majority of the information came from you. Can you verify it?"

Morgan nodded his head after he finished reading the dispatches. "These were in my London house," he said, reading the first page and tossing it on the desk in disgust. "The other two were in my study at Ramsgate Castle. One of which was locked in a very intricate hiding place, I might add. They certainly have me well covered. No piece of information I have hidden has gone undetected."

"And the fourth?" Lord Castlereagh questioned, handing Morgan a final paper.

"The fourth?" Morgan echoed, a puzzled expression on his face. He read the paper carefully.

"I realize that page contains information older than

the others, but we had a devil of a time breaking the code. Don't you recognize it?"

"I do," Morgan said slowly, realization beginning to dawn. "These particular papers were never in either of my homes, Lord Castlereagh."

"Where exactly were they kept?"

"In a place I thought they would be safe," Morgan said, a genuine smile etching his handsome face. The information he held in his hands had been hidden in an old desk in the library at Westgate Manor. He had not laid eyes on it since it was placed there nearly five months ago. "I believe, Lord Castlereagh, this is the break we have been waiting for. It seems the Falcon has finally made a mistake. And one that shall cost him dearly."

"Tris . . . Tristan," Morgan bellowed loudly. He stood outside Tristan and Caroline's closed bedroom door, pounding continuously. "Tris, I must see you right away. Meet me in my study in five minutes," he commanded, walking away before his brother had a chance to argue.

"Merciful heavens, Morgan," the dowager duchess scolded her grandson, stepping into the hall to see what all the commotion was about. "Why are you standing there shouting like a fishmonger?"

"Sorry, madam," Morgan apologized with grin. "I was trying to get Tristan to come out of his bedchamber. It is imperative that I speak with him immediately."

"I do believe that Tristan is busy, Morgan. He and Caroline are . . . are . . . resting before their evening out tonight," the duchess announced.

"Resting, ha," Morgan drawled. "Tristan and Caroline are always 'resting.' Morning, noon, and night they are 'resting.' I know they are newly married, but I have something of grave importance to discuss with

Tris. I promise I shall not detain him long. Then he can return to his 'resting.' " Morgan gave the duchess a roguish grin. "Why Grandmother, I do believe you are blushing."

"I most certainly am not," the dowager duchess replied in her most regal tone. Her cheeks flushed, and the duke's grin broadened. "You are just impossible at times, Morgan."

Morgan went over and gave the dowager duchess a kiss on her cheek. He was feeling better than he had in months, delighted over the turn of events his meeting with Lord Castlereagh had produced. He needed information that only Tristan could provide, and was unwilling to wait another minute to question his brother. "Do tell them to hurry, Grandmother. If Tristan isn't out of there in ten minutes, I shall be forced to go in after him."

"You will do no such thing," the duchess replied in a shocked voice, the twinkle in her eye betraying her true feelings. "Now run along, Morgan. I am sure your brother will attend you as soon as possible." She shoved him, none too gently, toward the staircase.

A rather disgruntled Tristan appeared in Morgan's study 20 minutes later. He had not bothered to finish dressing and wore no neckcloth or coat, only a cambric shirt with the collar open, breeches, and boots. He was clearly displeased with his brother's untimely interruption.

"What the devil is so important it could not wait until this evening, Morgan?" Tristan demanded the minute he walked into the room.

"Calm down, Tris," Morgan spoke quietly. "I apologize for disturbing you, but it is very important. To start with, I must know the whereabouts of Henry Walsh. I need to contact him immediately." Morgan grinned. "And by the way, your breeches are unbuttoned."

Tristan gave his brother a chilling stare, and then calmly fastened his partially buttoned pants. "You did interrupt me in the middle of something rather pressing, Morgan," he told him. "I doubt Caroline will ever forgive you."

"I am sure she will endeavor to try," Morgan interjected smoothly. He continued with his requests, ignoring his brother's scowl. "I will also need a complete list of all the workmen you employed at Westgate Manor. Also the suppliers. I realize you will not have everything that I require, which is the reason I must speak with Mr. Walsh. I know you must have some records; I want to see all of them straightaway. I also need to know who visited the house with you and Caroline. Basically I want a list of anyone who has stepped foot on the grounds of Westgate Manor in the last five months."

Morgan looked at his brother expectantly. Tristan stared back, perplexed. "Morgan, you are not making the least bit of sense. Even if I can produce this information for you, which I doubt, what in the world are you going to do with it?"

Morgan thought for a moment. He could not fabricate a plausible lie, and debated telling his brother the truth. Ultimately Morgan decided it would be safer for all concerned if no one knew about his search. Even though it was possible the Falcon was somehow connected to Tristan, the duke decided it was best not to enlighten his brother. "Never mind why I need these documents. Can you produce them?"

"Morgan," Tristan said in an exasperated voice, drumming his fingers on the desk, "what is this all about?"

"Just trust me, Tris," Morgan interrupted, still refusing to tell his brother the reasons for his bizarre request.

"All right." Tristan threw up his hands in vexation.

"I'll do the best I can. I should warn you I will be unable to contact Henry Walsh. He is visiting his family somewhere in Ireland and will not return to England until the end of the month. I have a few of the papers you require, but the majority of the bills and work orders are kept at Westgate Manor. The person you really need to speak with is Alyssa Carrington. She handles all the paperwork, as well as the hiring of the work crews."

"What?"

Now it was Tristan's turn to make his brother uncomfortable. "You know Lady Alyssa has directed the renovations. If I remember correctly, you were the one who recommended her for the job in the first place."

Morgan merely grunted.

"It certainly was an excellent suggestion, Morgan. She has done a superb job. She has very competently managed the budget and neatly kept all the records."

Morgan rose from his chair and paced the room. Now was not the proper time to see Alyssa. His feelings toward her were still too uncertain, his mind too confused. Besides, he had promised to stay away. "Can't you send a messenger and request the documents?" he suggested. "Or perhaps you could go yourself?" He looked at Tristan hopefully.

Tristan smiled at his older brother, enjoying his discomfort. He was pleased to see his theory about Alyssa Carrington had merit. "No, I can't Morgan. I'm not exactly sure what you are looking for. Now, if you care to enlighten me . . ." Tristan's voice trailed off.

"I'll go," Morgan muttered, glaring at his brother. He felt restless and strangely excited.

"Fine. Is there anything else?" Tristan asked, sauntering over to the doors.

"No," Morgan replied. "I shall leave for Westgate tomorrow morning at first light. Thank you, Tris."

*   *   *

Morgan arrived at Westgate Manor just after noon the following day. As he guided his stallion down the gravel drive, he almost didn't recognize the place. The brickwork had been carefully washed and all the loose bricks securely mortared. Fresh paint covered all the wood, and the broken windowpanes had been replaced. New shrubbery lined the drive, and the well-manicured lawn looked healthy and green. Everything looked fresh, clean, and inviting.

He dismounted and stood in front of the large oak doors with their new shining brass fixtures. " 'Tis oddly comforting to discover some things don't change," Morgan muttered to himself as he waited, in vain, for someone to come for his horse. He thought about shouting for Ned or Perkins, but instead walked the horse around back to the stables.

Morgan found no one in the stables, so he unsaddled the horse, gave him some fresh water and grain, and tethered him in an unoccupied stall. Then he proceeded to the kitchen entrance, certain he would find Mrs. Stratton there, busy simmering something on the stove.

Morgan surprised Perkins. The butler was sitting alone at the table finishing the last of his luncheon. "Your Grace!" Perkins sputtered in astonishment when Morgan stepped into the cozy room.

"Good day, Perkins." Morgan spoke casually, acting as though he had seen the butler yesterday instead of five months ago. "Isn't anyone at home?"

The butler took a moment to consider the question before answering. "All the servants were given leave to visit with their families before Lord Tristan returns. Only Ned, Mavis, and myself are attending the house."

"And Lady Alyssa?"

"Indisposed," Perkins answered automatically. It was his stock answer to those few individuals who

195

called on Alyssa. In actuality, Alyssa was in the south garden with Mavis gathering fresh vegetables for dinner. He strongly doubted she would want to see the duke, especially given her present condition.

Morgan's eyes narrowed at the butler's statement. It seemed as though Tristan was not exaggerating when he commented that Alyssa was avoiding him.

"No matter," Morgan replied briskly. "I will see her after I have finished my other business. You may tell her that, if you wish."

Without further comment Morgan left the bewildered butler, heading for the library to locate the desk where he had hidden the documents. As he opened the door, Morgan paused a moment to verify he had entered the correct room. Nothing was the same, from the new red velvet drapes to the intricately patterned oriental rugs. He scanned the room quickly, admiring the new decor, then looked again. There was no desk.

He was about to bellow for Perkins when the butler appeared at his side.

"Can I be of assistance, Your Grace?"

"Yes, Perkins," Morgan replied. "Where is the library desk that sat under that window?" Morgan pointed to a bay window in the center of the room, then glanced around a third time, trying to get his bearings. "This is the library, isn't it?"

"Yes, Your Grace. It is the library. The new furnishings were put in place last month."

"Of course," Morgan interrupted, suddenly remembering. "And the old furnishings were to be stored in the attic. Can you show me where?"

Silently Perkins led Morgan to the top-floor storage room. Morgan spent the next twenty minutes walking through the maze of neatly stacked furniture while Perkins looked on expressionlessly. Several times, the duke banged his head on the low eaves, cursing loudly each time. After an additional ten minutes of fruitless searching, Morgan's patience was wearing thin. He was getting a headache and getting angry.

"It is not here, Perkins," Morgan finally concluded. "Is this the only place the old furniture is stored?"

"I believe so, Your Grace."

"Perhaps the desk was moved to another room?"

"I couldn't say for sure, Your Grace," Perkins answered, knowing very well what had happened to the desk.

Morgan's lips compressed in a thin line. Perkins returned his hard stare with a blank look, but Morgan could tell the butler was lying.

"I feel certain Lady Alyssa will know what has become of the desk. Tell her I shall await her in the front salon."

Morgan saw the flash of panic in the butler's eyes before he replied, "I have told you, Your Grace. Lady Alyssa is indisposed and not receiving visitors."

"Oh, but she will see me, Perkins," Morgan said in a low, hard voice. "Even if I have to drag her out of her bedchamber."

The butler could not mistake Morgan's determination. Morgan turned and left the attic room, Perkins at his heels. The duke paused briefly in the middle of the second floor hallway, contemplating the closed bedroom doors.

"Which one is hers, Perkins?"

"She is not in her bedchamber, Your Grace."

The muscle in the side of Morgan's jaw flexed as he fought to keep his temper under control.

"Where is she, Perkins?" Morgan ground out.

Perkins debated his options for a few moments. His loyalty to Alyssa was unbending, even though he no longer worked for her. The old butler was deeply moved when she had confided her embarrassing condition to him, and he vowed to aid her in any way possible. Yet as he looked at the stubborn determination on the duke's face, he knew nothing on earth would keep this man from seeing Alyssa.

"She is in the south garden with Mavis, Your Grace," Perkins whispered. "Go out through the drawing room doors and follow the hill down past the rose garden; then turn to your right."

As Morgan strode outside in the mild fall air, his anger decreased with each step. There was no reason why this had to be an unpleasant meeting, he decided. He would make it as brief as possible. He would simply state his business, obtain the information he needed, including the whereabouts of that goddamn desk, and be on his way.

He followed Perkins's directions, descending the hill and quickly passing the rose garden. He knew he was getting close when he heard Alyssa's voice, although he could not understand her words. Then suddenly he saw her at the bottom of the hill, standing on the edge of the vegetable patch.

Her back was toward him, and the first thing he noticed was her unbound hair. It hung freely down to her waist, waves of luscious copper delight. She continued chatting with Mavis as she reached down to pick some greens. She casually placed the basket she carried down next to her and, after filling it, turned sideways to lift her small harvest.

As she turned her profile to him, a small gust of wind blew, molding her loose-fitting dress against her body. Morgan stumbled, almost falling flat on his face when he saw her swollen body and the truth that it revealed.

Several long minutes elapsed as he stood there, paralyzed by the sight of her heavily burdened with child. His child. He was shocked. He could feel the tenseness claim his body as a myriad of questions raced through his mind.

All these months and she had never contacted him. A wave of possessiveness washed over him as his eyes remained riveted to her belly. His child grew there. He stood perfectly still, awed by the hope and promise of the life that grew within her body. A life that he helped create that would have forever been denied to him if fate had not intervened and brought him here today.

What a fool he had been! She had promised to write to him if there was to be a child, and he had trusted her to do so. And now he discovered she had betrayed that trust. His mind reeled with disgust as he walked toward her.

Alyssa heard someone approaching and she turned, fully expecting to see Ned or Perkins. She saw Morgan and froze, then blinked several times, not believing her eyes. There had been so many countless nights she had dreamed of seeing him again, she wasn't quite sure he was real. Then he moved closer to her and spoke.

"Good afternoon, Miss Carrington," he said in a harsh, cold voice.

Chapter Thirteen

Alyssa stood unmoving as Morgan advanced. The blood slowly receded from her face, and she continued staring at him in disbelief.

After all these long months of waiting and hoping that he would come, it was nearly impossible to accept his sudden appearance. The duke spoke to her, but she did not comprehend his words. Her brain slowly accepted what her eyes confirmed, and she feasted on the sight of him.

Alyssa could see the tension in his wide shoulders, feel the anger radiating from his smoldering gray eyes. He was as proud and arrogant and startingly handsome as she remembered. The endless, sleepless nights she had endured insisting to herself that she no longer cared for him were washed away in a single moment. Looking into his silver-gray eyes, the eyes that had haunted her dreams from the first time she beheld them, Alyssa knew deep within her heart she had never ceased loving Morgan.

He stopped directly in front of her. He did not look

at her face, but held his gaze downcast, seemingly against his will, to her bulging belly. Her own eyes followed his and came to rest also on her large stomach.

They continued to stare at her belly, each waiting for the other to speak. The mounting tension frazzled her nerves and Alyssa backed away. She moved her basket up slightly, shielding herself and her unborn child from the duke's intense gaze. The gesture infuriated him.

"Is it mine?" he asked curtly, through his teeth. He knew of course it was his child, but the pain and anger ripping through his gut compelled his ruthless tongue. His brain filled with accusations, his heart cold with mistrust, Morgan struck out at her, needing to hurt her as she had wounded him by her selfish act of keeping the existence of his child a secret.

Alyssa's face whitened, and her eyes blazed with emotion. "How dare you?" she choked furiously. Her eyes filled with tears, the pain of his words crushing her fragile heart. Humiliation and anger collided inside Alyssa, and she drew back her hand, slapping him across the cheek with all her strength. Then she broke into anguished sobs.

Morgan rubbed his abused face absently, caught off guard by her response, yet not completely surprised by Alyssa's violent reaction. He had deliberately provoked her anger. Morgan's fury lessened as her anguished cries penetrated his haze. He listened to the raw emotion in her sobs and felt her pain. Instinctively he reached out to offer comfort.

"Don't touch me," she hissed, her breath coming in sobbing pants. She resisted the embrace, twisting and turning to escape his arms, but he would not be deterred.

"Let me," he whispered hoarsely, pulling her against his broad chest gently but firmly.

Too weary to fight, she ceased her struggles, but held herself rigid beneath his embrace. He softly caressed her hair and back, soothing the stiffness from her body, trying to ease the ache he had created in her heart. Gradually she relaxed, grudgingly accepting the comfort he offered.

Eventually Alyssa's sobbing ceased. Morgan reached inside his pocket and handed her a snowy white linen handkerchief. She accepted the cloth and stepped away from him, blowing her nose loudly in a most unladylike manner. Her actions brought a brief smile to Morgan's lips. She did not return the handkerchief, placing it inside the pocket of her gown.

He stood close to Alyssa, so close he could smell her fresh scent. She wore a plain pink muslin gown with a high ruffled neck, elbow-length sleeves, and no waist. Her height and natural thinness emphasized the size of the burden she carried. His hand hovered over her belly uncertainly, longing to caress the living roundness, but not sure if she would allow him to touch her again.

"May we sit down?" Alyssa requested, finally breaking the silence. She was physically and emotionally drained. "I find I tire easily these days."

The duke was instantly solicitous of her, his gaze drawn again to her womb where his child lay. As they walked the short distance to the large bench nestled beneath the oak trees, Alyssa noticed Mavis was no longer in the garden, and she felt glad. She fervently prayed her old nurse had left before witnessing the disgraceful behavior of both herself and the duke.

"When?" he asked simply when they both were seated.

She understood. "The baby will be born sometime in December, before Christmas, I think."

"Does anyone else know?"

"Only Mavis, Perkins, and Ned. And now you, of course."

"Why in the hell didn't you tell me? I cannot believe you would keep something this important from me."

Alyssa heard the fury he tried to suppress—but could not—in his voice. She did not understand. How did he not know about the baby? She had written to him exactly as he instructed.

"Why should my baby be of any concern to you?" she asked bleakly. "You have just rather blatantly questioned the paternity of my child."

Morgan glared at her. "It is my child," he stated firmly. "Why have you not told me?"

"I wrote to you," she said softly. "Twice." His possessive declaration proclaiming the child as his own sent a warm rush of emotions to her bruised heart.

"Where did you send the letters?"

"One to your house at Grovesner Square in London, the other to Ramsgate Castle."

"I never received them," he stated flatly, not sure he believed her, but unable to come up with a single legitimate reason why she would be lying.

"Oh," she replied, uncertain if he was being truthful. Yet judging from Morgan's shocked reaction, Alyssa knew he had not known she was pregnant.

"What are you planning to do? Where will you go?" he asked plainly.

"Mavis and I will travel to Cornwall. Her sister, Louise, has kindly agreed to take us in for my lying-in. After the baby is born we hope to settle there, if I can find work."

"How will you support yourself?"

"When I am strong enough, I will get a job. Mavis's pension will pay the rent, and I hope to earn enough for us to eat."

He closed his eyes, trying to blot out the picture of her struggling to survive on her own with a bastard child to care for. It would never happen. Not while he had a breath left in him.

Morgan gave a deep sigh. He looked at Alyssa closely and saw the deep strain around her eyes, the paleness of her face. She could not endure any more of this emotional upheaval. They would discuss her situation later. No, not discuss, he corrected himself. He had already decided the course of action he would take, and nothing would deter him from it. They would be married, of course. Immediately.

Morgan was not entirely convinced Alyssa had not deliberately hidden her condition. He was concerned she might refuse to marry him. After all, she already rejected his proposal once. Her future plans, obviously given a great deal of thought, did not include him. Morgan knew he must take total charge of the situation or he ran the risk of losing both her and his child.

Alyssa searched his handsome features boldly, trying to discover his true emotions. He had listened without comment to her plans for their child, leaving her no clue to his true feelings. Was he happy about the baby? Did he want to be a part of the child's life? All Alyssa knew with certainty was that Morgan was a man who took his responsibilities seriously. Any moment now he would probably offer his financial assistance. Alyssa did not think she could bear the humiliation. She tried to distract his thoughts.

"If you did not travel to the manor to discuss my child, why are you here?"

It was the perfect opening to change the subject and give Morgan the time he needed to plot his next move. He quickly seized it. "I have come on business that requires your assistance. Will you accompany me to the house?"

She agreed, and they walked in strained silence back to the manor and entered the newly decorated library. Alyssa deliberately avoided the large over-stuffed chairs she had difficulty getting up from, perching herself instead on a dainty gold chair with elegantly carved legs. She looked decidedly uncomfortable.

Morgan chose not to sit, but stood by the windows, facing her, his arms crossed over his chest. He wasn't sure where to begin. The important mission that brought him to Westgate Manor seemed insignificant compared to the personal drama his life had now become.

"You told me you needed my assistance?" Alyssa prodded, hoping this discussion would not take too long.

"Yes," Morgan said slowly, trying to gather his thoughts. "I need to see your work papers on the renovations. I must have a list of all the men who have made repairs on the house, as well as those men who delivered the supplies."

"Is there a problem?" she asked, bewildered by his strange request. "I thought Tristan was pleased with the way I have handled the work thus far."

"There is no problem, I assure you," the duke replied. "My request has nothing to do with your work."

"I keep my files in the estate room. I shall get them straightaway." Before he had a chance to comment, Alyssa had risen from the chair and was out the door.

She returned several minutes later and handed Morgan three large folders. "This is the payroll file, which lists each workman by name and occupation. This second file holds all the furniture deliveries; you will notice that not everything has been received yet. The third file names all the companies that provided raw materials: lumber, plaster, brick, and so forth. Is that everything?"

"Yes, this is precisely the information I require," he said, admiring the neatly written lists in her crisp, bold script. "There is one other matter, Alyssa. Do you know what happened to the old oak desk that was in here?"

"Desk?" she replied innocently, her heart racing. Why would he ask her about the desk? Alyssa could scarcely believe he had noticed it was missing. "All the old furniture was moved to an attic storage room."

"I have already checked the attic," Morgan responded. "The desk is not there."

"The desk is not there?" she parroted.

"No."

"How odd." Alyssa furrowed her brow, making a great show of trying to remember. "I am afraid I don't know where else to look for the desk," she finally replied, lowering her gaze.

She was a terrible liar. For a mere instant Morgan wondered if a connection could possibly exist between Alyssa and the Falcon. He quickly discarded the notion as ridiculous. Yet Alyssa looked so worried.

"Is there something you are not telling me, Alyssa?" Morgan asked softly.

Alyssa heard the slight edge to his voice, and unconsciously began wringing her hands.

"Why is the desk so important?" she inquired, still not quite able to look him in the eye when she spoke.

Morgan frowned. "You know where the desk is, Alyssa." It was a statement, not a question.

"It is . . . it is not here," she confessed, her cheeks flushing with humiliation.

"Where is it?"

"I sold it."

"You sold it," he repeated, perplexed. "Why would you do that?"

She shrugged her shoulders. "I needed the money."

She waited expectantly for him to chastise her. Alyssa had a sudden flash of memory back to Miss Ryan, a former governess, who was always catching her at some wrongdoing. *Think carefully before you act, Alyssa,* Miss Ryan would say in her nasal voice, *because your past misdeeds will always come back to haunt you.* Alyssa glanced ruefully down at her large belly, then up at Morgan's scowling face, and conceded Miss Ryan had been a very smart woman indeed.

"Who bought the desk?"

"Mr. Hopkins," she replied in a voice filled with remorse. "He owns a small shop in the village. He often helped me sell items from the manor to raise money to pay Lord Carrington's gambling debts."

"Of course that was when you owned the manor," Morgan commented dryly. "Does Mr. Hopkins still have the desk?"

"I presume so, unless he has found a buyer."

This did create a problem. The desk had left the manor house, which meant anyone could have discovered the documents hidden there and sold them. Even Alyssa. She had just admitted she was desperate enough for money to sell old furniture that didn't even belong to her. Morgan's lips compressed as he pondered this latest twist.

When the Falcon struck, the documents the spy wanted always remained hidden in their original location; presumably so the owner wouldn't know the security had been breached. Morgan theorized the Falcon either copied the documents on the spot, or if there wasn't sufficient time, stole them, but always returned them later.

If the Falcon or one of his underlings had discovered these papers, they should be hidden in the false bottom drawer of the old desk. If they were not there, Morgan must assume someone else had taken the papers and, realizing the potential profit, sold them. If that were the case, it was merely a strange coincidence Lord Castlereagh's agents had uncovered the information. No connection between the Falcon and Westgate Manor would exist. It was imperative Morgan locate the desk as quickly as possible. Alyssa must bring him to Mr. Hopkins's shop at once.

"Get your things," the duke commanded. "We are going to pay Mr. Hopkins a visit."

Alyssa made a small sound of distress. Her heart filled with terror at the very idea of venturing into town.

"Morgan, please," she pleaded, glancing down at her expanded waistline. "I cannot go into the village."

"I would not ask this of you unless it was vitally important, Alyssa," Morgan said.

Her green eyes searched his features solemnly. His expression was open and direct.

"I will go with you."

Alyssa regretted the words the moment they were spoken, but she did not refute them. She was responsible for the missing desk and felt obligated to help Morgan retrieve it. Perhaps if she was very careful and very lucky, she would not meet anyone she knew.

Morgan went searching for Ned while Alyssa trudged upstairs to fetch her cloak and bonnet. As soon as Ned was found, Morgan instructed him to hitch up Tristan's new phaeton and bring it around front. The weather was warm, and the open carriage would be more comfortable for the ride to the village.

Morgan waited impatiently at the bottom of the long staircase for Alyssa. She took a very long time. He stood there fidgeting, rocking back and forth on his feet, and disciplining himself not to go charging up the stairs.

Morgan heaved a sigh of relief when she finally appeared on the second-story landing. Gracefully she descended the staircase, stopping directly in front of him. She was covered from head to toe in a long, loose black evening cloak; an obvious attempt to shield her bulk from curious eyes. She wore a wide-brimmed bonnet that almost obscured her face entirely, and clutched a small leather reticule in her hands.

"Are you ready?" he asked.

Alyssa nodded, not trusting her voice, and allowed him to guide her out the front door. She instinctively dug in her heels as she stood before the shiny new phaeton, but at Morgan's gentle touch she moved forward. The duke sat next to her and accepted the reins from Ned. He glanced over at Alyssa. There was a hint of tension in the way she held her shoulders and a faraway look in her eyes as she stared out the side of the carriage.

The half-hour ride to the village was accomplished in complete silence. Alyssa held her breath as they entered the main street and drove down the lane at a sedate pace. Morgan was acting as if they were taking a leisurely afternoon ride through Hyde Park, and Alyssa wanted to scream at him to move faster.

"Where is Mr. Hopkins's establishment?" Morgan asked.

"Down at the end of this block, on the left," Alyssa replied quickly, her anxiety evident in each word she spoke.

It was a Thursday afternoon, and the street was not very crowded. Alyssa was grateful the carriage attracted little attention as they pulled up on the opposite side of the street, across from the small shop. She let out a tremendous sigh of relief when she saw Mr. Hopkins's establishment was empty. She waited impatiently for Morgan to hitch up the horses and assist her from the carriage, her eyes darting nervously up and down the street. The last thing she wanted was to be noticed.

Once her feet were firmly on the ground, Alyssa lowered her head and sprinted to the shop. The tinkling of the small bell on the door was a sweet sound of victory for Alyssa. She had succeeded in entering the shop without being seen.

"Most impressive, my dear," Morgan whispered in her ear.

Alyssa jumped at the sound, and then looked around worriedly to see if anyone else had followed Morgan into the shop. She was vastly relieved to discover they were alone.

"May we please get this unpleasant business taken care of as quickly as possible?" she snapped.

He grinned, and Alyssa itched to throw her reticule at him. He looked so handsome, so devilish, as if he were enjoying her agitation. Didn't he realize how nervous she was? Didn't he understand how truly mortified she would be if she encountered anyone she knew?

Mr. Hopkins came out of the back room. "Good afternoon," he called out to them. "How may I help you?"

Mr. Hopkins was a good-natured man, a shrewd but honest businessman. His small shop was cluttered with a variety of knickknacks and furnishings of various sizes and quality. He was a large man, and his impressive bulk only emphasized the clutter in his establishment. He was also hopelessly nearsighted without his spectacles, which he was constantly misplacing. He did not have them on now. Alyssa moved forward to greet him.

"Good day, Mr. Hopkins," she said in a breathless voice, not believing her luck when she noticed his missing glasses.

"Lady Alyssa." The shopkeeper's face lit up with delight as he recognized her voice and fuzzy features. He had many successful business dealings with Alyssa over the years, and always liked the dignified girl. "What a nice surprise. What can I do for you on this fine afternoon?"

"I've come about some of the furnishings from the manor," she explained.

"Oh, fine," Mr. Hopkins answered. "Tell Ned to bring the cart around back, and I'll help him unload."

Alyssa blushed to the roots of her hair. Stealing a glance over at Morgan, she fully expected the duke to be furious, but instead he was smiling charmingly. He appeared to be enjoying himself immensely. Alyssa suppressed a strong urge to throw something at him.

"No . . . no, Mr. Hopkins," she corrected the shopkeeper. "I haven't brought anything to sell. Actually, I've come to buy something back."

"Buy back, you say?" Mr. Hopkins queried, scratching his head, not certain he heard right. The gentry were an odd lot, for sure, but Lady Alyssa had always struck him as a levelheaded person.

"That will not be necessary," Morgan interrupted in a firm voice. "I only wish to examine the desk. That is, if you have no objections, Mr. Hopkins?"

Mr. Hopkins raised his chin and squinted toward Morgan's voice, noticing him for the first time.

"Don't mind at all," he said. "If you'll wait a minute, I'll get my spectacles, Your Lordship, and then I can help you find whatever it is you're looking for." Mr. Hopkins shuffled away, muttering to himself about the queer ways of some folks.

"No!" Alyssa shouted in panic. "Please don't trouble yourself, Mr. Hopkins. I can assist the duke in locating the item."

She turned around and confronted Morgan. "You dragged me all the way out here just so you could look at that damn desk?"

"Are you still going to help me find it?" he questioned with a maddening grin.

Alyssa took a deep breath and forced herself to remain calm. "Certainly," she replied sweetly.

Without too much difficulty, they located the desk

in the corner of the shop. Alyssa watched, dumbstruck, as Morgan removed a drawer from the desk, opened the false bottom, and took out a large white envelope.

Morgan was very pleased with the look of total bewilderment on her face. It was obvious she had no idea the documents were there. Any nagging doubts he had about Alyssa's connection to the Falcon were immediately dispelled.

"I don't suppose you are going to tell me what is in that envelope?" she asked.

"No."

"Or how it came to be there?"

"No," he stated firmly. "Now, if you will just give me a moment, I want to thank Mr. Hopkins for his assistance."

Alyssa stood by the door, gritting her teeth as she waited for Morgan. She was keeping a tight grip on her control, even though she wanted desperately to throttle the duke. What was taking him so long? All she could concentrate on was racing back to the carriage unseen. She had only taken the great risk of entering the village to make amends for selling the furniture.

Naturally Alyssa knew she had no right to sell the furniture, but she reasoned Tristan and Caroline would neither notice nor care. Her need of funds had simply been greater than her conscience. She felt ashamed of her actions and intended to return the small sum of money to Morgan, hoping the matter would be forgotten.

Finally Morgan finished his conversation, and Alyssa noticed Mr. Hopkins pocketing several coins. Alyssa loudly called out her farewell to the shopkeeper from a safe distance. Checking both sides of the street carefully to confirm it was free of pedestrians, Alyssa began her mad dash toward the waiting carriage.

Morgan caught her before she bolted. Grabbing her arm firmly, he started across the street with her. Alyssa was focused so intently on reaching the safe obscurity of the phaeton, she failed to notice Morgan considerably slowing their pace. She tugged insistently on his arm, and when he didn't move she was forced to raise her head.

She glanced at him briefly, turning her head to follow the duke's line of vision down the nearly deserted block. Alyssa's heart lurched and her eyes widened with fear. Heading straight for them was the biggest gossip in the entire county, Lady Jane Roberts, and her oldest daughter Cecille.

Chapter Fourteen

Alyssa felt her mouth go dry as she tried to speak.

"For God's sake, Morgan," she pleaded. "Hurry up."

"They have already seen us, Alyssa. Our only chance is to brazen it out."

"Oh, lord." Alyssa swallowed convulsively, trying to dislodge the lump that had settled firmly in her throat.

"Who are they?" Morgan inquired casually.

His calm attitude served only to heighten Alyssa's anxiety, and her hands twisted the material of her cloak.

"The older woman is Lady Roberts; the younger girl is her daughter Cecille. I met them several years ago at a market fair. Lady Roberts is easily the biggest gossip in the county."

"I thought that honor belonged to Mrs. Stratton."

Alyssa groaned. "This is not funny, Morgan. You know I cannot meet them. Please, we must leave," Alyssa whispered frantically.

Morgan patted her hand reassuringly and remained

rooted to the spot. Within seconds the two women had reached them.

Alyssa gasped out loud as Lady Roberts and Cecille stood a scant six feet away from her and Morgan. With her free hand, Alyssa clutched the front of her large cloak, trying to conceal her body. Morgan tightened his grip on her arm.

Maybe we can remain unnoticed, Alyssa prayed, hoping for a tiny miracle. Turning her head she focused her complete attention on the large display of silk and satin fabrics in the window of the mercantile shop, pointedly ignoring the women. Just when Alyssa was almost convinced her ploy had succeeded, Morgan spoke.

"Good afternoon, ladies," he began conversationally. He elegantly removed his hat and bowed slightly to the two women. "I don't believe I have had the pleasure of making your acquaintance. Would you do the honors, my dear?"

Alyssa wanted to kill him. She stared at his handsome profile, stunned by his audacity. There was an ominous silence and Alyssa's face went white.

"Lady Roberts, Cecille, may I present His Grace, the Duke of Gillingham," Alyssa said icily.

Lady Roberts's face was a mask of uncertainty. Alyssa could tell by her startled expression that Lady Roberts was very much aware of Alyssa's condition, and would have preferred to ignore them. Yet she could not openly snub the introduction of a duke.

In the end, Lady Roberts opted to pretend everything was as it should be, and hesitated only a moment before acknowledging the introduction. Cecille, blissfully unaware of the volatile situation, made a pretty curtsy and stared at the duke with a flirtatious eye. She was obviously impressed with his handsome person as well as his lofty title. Cecille gave a small giggle at the duke's comment, fluttering her pale eyelashes at him. Alyssa felt nauseous.

The three others exchanged a few minutes of stilted conversation while Alyssa waited stoically by Morgan's side, barely breathing, never blinking, and staring blankly ahead.

After what seemed like an eternity to Alyssa, the conversation ended. Lady Roberts and her daughter made their good-byes; Lady Roberts pointedly excluded Alyssa. Not until the pair reached the end of the block did Morgan finally release Alyssa's arm.

Alyssa stared at him for some time, her emotions in turmoil. He returned her gaze steadily. Alyssa felt a coldness radiating from deep within her soul and she gathered her cloak closely, her arms curving instinctively in a protective gesture around her womb. Moving blindly, she walked to the carriage, somehow getting inside without the duke's assistance. A few moments later she sensed Morgan's presence, and the phaeton moved down the street.

Alyssa felt the cold, dull ache invade her heart. Biting her lip, she tried to suppress her emotions but failed. Disbelief, shame, and despair washed over her. Her eyes glistened with tears. Finally she succumbed to her overwrought emotions, bent her head, and cried.

Alyssa was too caught up in her despair to notice the carriage had stopped.

"Please don't cry, Alyssa." Morgan spoke loudly to be heard over her weeping.

The sound of his voice jarred her out of her misery, and her tears began to lessen as anger became the dominant emotion.

"Why did you speak to them? They were almost past us. They would have strolled by without uttering a word if you hadn't opened your mouth!" she accused.

"Lady Roberts and her daughter had already seen us. It seemed cowardly to ignore them."

"Cowardly? Have you completely lost your wits? Do you know what it has been like for me these last few months? I have made myself a virtual prisoner at the manor in an effort to keep my unborn child safe from the prying eyes of the Lady Robertses of this world."

"Alyssa, please, sweetheart, don't upset yourself so much," the duke begged. He reached over and gently wiped her tears. His caring gesture only enraged her further.

"Get away from me," she wailed, slapping his hands. "I cannot tolerate your touch."

"Alyssa, stop this. You must calm yourself."

"No, I will not calm myself," Alyssa spat out defiantly. "Did you see the expression on Lady Roberts's face? She was appalled. It will be all over the county by nightfall. How she and her precious daughter met the rakish Duke of Gillingham in town today. With his pregnant whore, Alyssa Carrington."

Morgan flinched visibly at her bitter words, but allowed Alyssa to continue to vent her anger without interruption.

"I don't care about the humiliation to myself. Truly. I know what I am, what I have become. I am a fallen woman, no longer acceptable in polite society. But my baby deserves better. I have gone to such great lengths to protect my child, our child. And then, in one instant, you have destroyed it all by standing in the middle of the street and practically announcing to the biggest gossip in the county that I carry your bastard. A blacker heart doesn't exist in the devil himself, Morgan."

The duke was horrified. He never imagined his actions would bring her such suffering. "If you would just calm down and listen to me," he begged, fear etched in his voice.

She heard the fear he could not keep out of his voice, and it gave her pause. She looked into his bleak eyes and felt her fury start to crumble. Their gazes held for several long, silent moments.

"Forgive me, my sweet," he whispered in a ragged voice.

Fresh tears shimmered in Alyssa's wide, distraught green eyes. "I thought to pass myself off as a widow in Cornwall." She gave a hollow laugh, then spoke softly. "I realize how naive that sounds. It will be impossible to spend the rest of my life continually worrying someone will discover my child is in truth a bastard. That is the price, I suppose, for trying to live a lie."

Her pain and vulnerability tugged at his heart. Guilt engulfed him, for he knew he was responsible.

"My God, Alyssa," Morgan whispered, his voice choked with emotion. "How you must despise me."

"I only wish that I could," she answered, her voice so low he had to strain to hear her words.

Morgan reached out, gently embracing her. Inexplicably she allowed it, and after a time rested her head on his strong shoulder, giving in to her complete exhaustion.

Loath to let her go, Morgan shifted his weight slightly and picked up the reins firmly. Still holding Alyssa in his arms, he slowly continued the journey back to the manor, never once relinquishing his strong grip.

Alyssa was nearly asleep when they arrived at Westgate. Drowsily, she straightened herself as Morgan climbed out of the carriage. Before she even had a chance to realize what was happening, he lifted her down from the phaeton. Walking past an openmouthed Ned, Morgan carried her into the house.

Once they were in the hall, Alyssa struggled to stand on her own.

"Morgan, please release me," she protested. "I weigh far too much for you to be carrying me about."

"I believe you have just insulted my manhood, Miss Carrington," Morgan answered her with a wink. He cradled her closer against him, and she shyly burrowed her head into his neck, enjoying far too much the feel of his strong arms around her.

Morgan paused for a moment at the bottom of the staircase to speak with Perkins, and then proceeded up the long flight of stairs, carrying Alyssa every step. He entered her bedchamber, fumbling a bit with the doorknob, and placed her ever so gently on the bed.

She struggled to sit up in the soft bed, her large girth making her clumsy. Chuckling at her awkward efforts, Morgan reached out to help. She eyed his outstretched arm warily, not at all pleased with his obvious enjoyment over her predicament. She wished she could accomplish the task on her own, and knowing she could not only added to her annoyance.

Suppressing an almost irresistible urge to stick her tongue out at him, Alyssa grudgingly accepted his assistance. Morgan let out an exaggerated groan as he hoisted her into a sitting position.

"That's not funny, Morgan," she snapped. "I'd like to see how nimble you were if you carried this extra weight."

"I'm sorry, love," he answered, trying to keep the amusement out of his voice. "It's just that you so resembled an overstuffed duck, wings flapping wildly, when you tried sitting up by yourself."

"A duck . . . a duck," she sputtered. "What . . . what a perfectly nasty thing to say."

He unfastened her cloak and placed it on a chair near the door.

"You are right, of course," he said, trying to sound contrite. "Truthfully you looked more like a goose."

Alyssa groaned loudly and threw herself back, lying flat on the bed. "I'm sure I look more like a cow," she murmured bleakly.

Morgan was quickly at her side. He clasped her chin and forced her eyes to meet his. Her green eyes loomed large in her pale face, and he was instantly sorry for his teasing.

"I've always thought you were a beautiful woman, Alyssa," he said in a husky voice. "But I have never seen you look more lovely than you do at this moment."

His hand reached down, hesitating for a split second before stroking the swell of her belly where his child was growing. His eyes widened in shock at the hardness of her stomach; he didn't know it would feel so solid.

Embarrassment flamed as Alyssa felt his hands trembling slightly while he explored the living roundness. She moved her hand over his, trying to pull him away.

"Don't," he protested, his voice a hoarse whisper. "Alyssa, please let me touch our babe."

She kept her hand over his, but the gentle pleading in his voice stopped her from pushing his hand away. Suddenly the baby moved, strongly kicking out against the hands that had awakened him, almost as if in greeting.

"Good God," Morgan said, startled by the movement. "Does that happen often?" He pressed his hand against her, waiting for another kick.

Alyssa shrugged her shoulders, her eyes moist with unshed tears at the wonder and excitement in Morgan's voice. She could almost believe he loved the child she carried.

Alyssa shifted stiffly, and Morgan reluctantly released his hold. He assisted her into a sitting position for a second time and propped several large pillows behind her back, trying to make her as comfortable as possible.

"We must talk, Alyssa," he said, regarding her solemnly.

She nodded her head in agreement. "We really shouldn't be alone together in my bedchamber, Morgan. Perhaps it would be best if we went downstairs?"

Morgan laughed at her ridiculous statement. "It is a little late to be worrying about proprieties, isn't it, Miss Carrington?"

She grinned in response and rubbed her forehead. "Yes, well, I suppose I am being a bit stuffy."

"A bit," he agreed with a heart-wrenching smile.

She loved it when he smiled. It made him look younger and less serious. She looked at his disheveled hair and intense gray eyes and sighed. She wondered if their child would favor him, secretly hoping it would.

Morgan sat next to her and held her hand firmly. Alyssa enjoyed the warm feel of his skin, the strength of his fingers.

"I first want to explain about my appalling behavior today," he said firmly.

Alyssa winced at the memory, but did not protest. She strongly doubted a logical explanation existed, but she wanted to be fair. She waited expectantly.

Morgan squirmed a bit under her open gaze. Now that he had her undivided attention, he wasn't sure where to begin. Especially since his actions had caused such great misery.

"I needed you to take me to the desk at Mr. Hopkins's shop," he began.

"To retrieve the white envelope," she interjected. "That you haven't told me anything about."

Morgan grimaced at her. "That I will not tell you about."

He began nervously pacing the room.

"I admit I did not do all that I could to avoid meeting Lady Roberts this afternoon. But I was desperate to

221

make you see how much you need me, Alyssa. I want to marry you and take care of you. I want our child born at Ramsgate Castle. Yet I feared you would not allow it."

She stared at him in confusion. "I don't understand, Morgan."

"Alyssa." He rubbed his hand along his jaw, then looked to the ceiling. Keeping his eyes there, he muttered softly, "I cannot allow you to push me out of your life."

"You are serious," she said, amazement and wonder etched in her voice. "You want us to marry? Truly? Yet you have vowed never to marry again."

Morgan lowered his eyes and looked pointedly at her stomach.

"You deliberately wanted Lady Roberts to see us together to make sure I would marry you," she repeated, wanting to be certain she understood.

"Yes."

She shook her head and began laughing. "Didn't it ever occur to you it might be best to ask me first, before you resorted to such high-handed tactics?"

"You have refused my proposal in the past, Alyssa," he challenged, "and demanded that I not see you again."

"You should have asked me, Morgan," Alyssa said quietly.

The duke closed his eyes and drew a deep breath. "Will you do me the great honor of becoming my wife, Alyssa?"

Alyssa felt a cold panic rise up unexpectedly and struggled for common sense. "I am grateful you want to be part of our child's life, Morgan. Yet I fear you might come to regret this decision to marry me. I could not bear it if you began resenting me and my child."

He gazed powerfully into her brilliant green eyes

and felt a surge of tenderness toward her. "There are many aspects of marriage I find distasteful, but one thing I know with certainty. I could never resent you, nor our child."

"I will marry you, Morgan," she said faintly, her emotions swirling. Alyssa nestled back among the pillows, trying to still her pounding heart. She waited expectantly for his kiss, but instead of embracing her, the duke reached out and covered her with a soft blanket.

"I want you to get some rest," he said. "I'll send Mavis to wake you in a couple of hours." After flashing her a brilliant smile, he was gone from the room.

Alyssa was positive she wouldn't be able to sleep a wink after all the tumultuous events of the afternoon, but within a few minutes she dozed off.

Alyssa came awake with a start when Mavis entered the room a few hours later. She sat up quickly, feeling light-headed and disoriented. Darkness had fallen, and Mavis was busy lighting the lamps, filling the room with a soft glow.

"I had the most incredible dream, Mavis," Alyssa said drowsily, shaking her head back and forth. But one look at Mavis's excited face revealed it had not been a dream after all.

"I'm getting married," Alyssa stated in a voice filled with awe.

"That you are, my girl," Mavis answered, the excitement and pleasure evident in her voice. "And about high time you got around to it, I'd say."

Mavis headed straight for the dressing table and poured fresh water into a large china basin. She produced a cake of rose-scented soap and a clean towel. Then she turned to Alyssa expectantly. "Well, hurry up, my girl. No need to dawdle. You don't want to keep the groom waiting, do you?"

"What? We are getting married now? Tonight?" Alyssa sputtered. "But what about the banns? And the license? And the minister?"

"His Grace has taken care of everything," Mavis said with a wave of her hand. She spoke of Morgan as if they were old friends. "All we are missing is the bride."

Still dazed, Alyssa walked over to the dressing table and let Mavis help her out of her gown. She remained quiet while the older woman fussed over her toilette, arranging Alyssa's hair several times before it was done to her satisfaction.

"And now for the dress," Mavis said, her old eyes gleaming. She rushed over to the oak armoire and reverently removed a lovely pale rose dress Alyssa had never seen before. The material was a lightweight crepe, which perfectly suited the waistless style of the gown. The neckline was square, demurely low cut, with an elegant white lace insert. The sleeves were long and tight fitting, with the shoulders puffed and the same beautiful white lace adorning the cuffs. A matching rose-colored satin ribbon was attached beneath the bodice to be tied under the breasts. Alyssa thought it was a most charming dress.

"Where did this gown come from?"

"Do you like it?" Mavis asked worriedly. "I picked it out myself. There wasn't very much time, and not much of a selection, but I thought it was pretty."

"You bought this dress for me?"

"I picked it out," Mavis corrected her. "The duke bought it for you. Are you pleased?"

"I couldn't have chosen better myself, Mavis," Alyssa answered honestly. "But where did you get it?"

"In the village," Mavis replied. "I went to the fancy dress shop all the fine ladies of wealth and privilege patronize. The duke sent me on my errand the moment you agreed to the wedding. He told me to buy whatever I thought you needed, and spare no expense.

I went in Lord Tristan's new carriage, I did. Ned drove me."

Alyssa grinned at the pride in Mavis's voice. She wasn't sure what her old nurse had enjoyed most, buying the dress in the snobbish shop or riding in the new phaeton.

Nervously Alyssa allowed Mavis to put the lovely dress on her, heaving a sigh of relief when they saw how well the gown fit. Alyssa examined her reflection critically and was pleased. The gown complemented her coloring, and her nervous excitement brought a natural sparkle to her eyes and a flush to her cheekbones. One last adjustment to the profusion of curls on her head and she was ready.

Morgan was waiting at the bottom of the stairs, and she was glad for his comforting presence. She noticed the flare of appreciation in his eyes at her appearance, and it gave her courage. When she reached the last step, Morgan handed her a simple bouquet of white and pink roses, gaily tied together with long white satin ribbons. It was the perfect finishing touch. She looked like any other radiant bride, except for her rounded belly.

"Are you ready?" he asked in a deep voice.

She nodded slightly. Even though Morgan was dressed in the same sapphire-blue coat and buff-colored breeches he had worn earlier, he looked so handsome her pulse quickened. Alyssa could tell his shirt and cravat had been freshly pressed, and his black Hessian boots showed evidence of new polish.

They entered the drawing room together, and Alyssa gasped with delight at the magical transformation. Candlelight softly bathed the room, and the intoxicating scent of fresh flowers was everywhere. A large fire blazed in the hearth, adding its warmth, with the cheerful crackling of the logs breaking the silence. Alyssa felt relieved to discover the room relatively empty of people. Besides Mavis, who had already begun sniffling, were Perkins, Ned, and two unknown gentlemen. Morgan introduced the first man as Mr. Potts, a magistrate, who had been kind enough to procure the special license needed. The other gentlemen was the minister, Rev. Harrow, who would perform the wedding ceremony. Both men resided in Winchester, twenty miles to the north, which accounted for Alyssa's ignorance of their identities.

If these two rather imposing gentlemen were shocked by the bride's condition they gave no indication. Alyssa assumed Morgan had been sensitive enough to inform them beforehand of the situation. She was very grateful to him for saving her the embarrassment of having the ceremony performed by someone she knew. She doubted she would possess the audacity to face Rev. Jameson with her belly protruding and repeat her wedding vows.

The actual ceremony was very brief. Morgan and Alyssa stood together in front of the minister, with Perkins, Ned, and Mavis gathered close around. Mr. Potts stood a bit off to the side, not wanting to intrude on this intimate moment.

Alyssa listened intently to Morgan's strong voice as he firmly spoke the traditional promises, and made a silent vow never to give him cause to regret this marriage. The heavy gold band felt warm on her skin as Morgan slipped it onto her finger. She looked down at the sparkling diamonds and sapphires with amazement.

"You may kiss the bride," Rev. Harrow said, and Morgan was very pleased when Alyssa turned around to meet his embrace. He kissed her lips softly and then caressed her cheek.

Mavis sniffled loudly. Alyssa smiled and turned to accept her old nurse's congratulations. She hugged Perkins and Ned, and shook hands with Mr. Potts and

Rev. Harrow. At a nod from the duke, Perkins popped open a bottle of champagne and everyone drank a toast to the health of the bride and groom.

After emptying a second bottle, the well-wishers discreetly withdrew leaving Morgan and Alyssa alone.

Chapter Fifteen

"I don't know how you managed all this in a few short hours," Alyssa remarked breathlessly. She felt strangely shy and nervous being alone with her new husband. "It was most kind of you to make the arrangements with Mr. Potts and Rev. Harrow. Thank you."

"It took a bit of doing," Morgan explained in an off-hand manner. "I was lucky to find Mr. Potts and Rev. Harrow so accommodating. I decided it would be easier if we had someone from another county handle all the arrangements." The duke's husky voice filled with humor. "I must confess I didn't relish the idea of dragging you off to Gretna Green."

"Yes, I have heard Scotland can be cold this time of year. I was surprised, however, to notice one guest was markedly absent. Was Lady Roberts busy this evening?"

He turned to her sharply, but relaxed when he saw her smile. "Yes, she had a previous engagement." He grinned, understanding this was Alyssa's way of telling him he was forgiven for this afternoon's fiasco. "I imagine Lady Roberts will be singing a different tune the next time she meets the Duchess of Gillingham."

"I believe she will," Alyssa mused, looking again at her exquisite wedding band. It was funny how this single piece of jewelry had miraculously changed her from a social disgrace to an acceptable member of society.

"More wine?" Morgan offered, opening another bottle of champagne.

Alyssa's stomach grumbled loudly. "Truthfully, I would prefer something to eat," she replied bluntly.

Morgan smiled fondly. "Perkins should be bringing in our wedding supper shortly. Shall I ring for him?"

"Don't bother," Alyssa answered. "The bell cord is not connected. The workmen are scheduled to fix it early next week. It has been incorrectly installed once already, and I intend to inspect the work personally this time."

Morgan frowned at her words. "I am afraid that won't be possible, madam" he explained. "I plan on leaving for Ramsgate Castle tomorrow morning, and naturally you shall accompany me."

Alyssa was distracted from commenting by the arrival of Perkins. She remained silent while the butler and Ned arranged the elegant meal on a small table cozily positioned in front of the fire.

Alyssa took one look at the mouth-watering array of food and sent Perkins a questioning glance. With Mrs. Stratton away visiting her sister for the past few months, the reduced staff had been eating a limited fare. The fragrant cream of oyster soup, poached filet of fish, ham with brandied peaches, carrot pudding, and plums jellied in Chablis wine were far beyond the culinary talents of Mavis.

"We had some assistance from the Rose and Thistle Tavern, Your Grace," Perkins explained.

"Everything looks splendid," Morgan complimented the butler. "Thank you, Perkins, we shall serve ourselves."

The moment the door shut, Alyssa spoke.

"I cannot possibly be ready to leave here by tomorrow morning, Morgan," she stated in a firm voice.

He raised an eyebrow. "Come and have some dinner, madam," he commanded, ignoring her outburst.

Alyssa stared hard at him for several moments, but sat in the chair he held out for her without commenting further. Morgan settled comfortably in the matching leather wing-back chair and took a long sip of his champagne, his eyes never leaving hers.

Alyssa quickly grew tired of glaring at him as her stomach rumbled. Heaving a sigh of exasperation, she opened the lid on the porcelain tureen and ladled out the hot soup, serving her husband first.

"I have responsibilities here, Morgan. I cannot just suddenly leave," Alyssa said, tasting her soup.

"Your responsibilities are to me, madam," he insisted. "Tristan will simply have to find someone else to supervise the completion of the renovations at the manor."

"Naturally, Tristan will hire a new person, Morgan," Alyssa agreed. "I did not mean to imply I intended working for any great length of time."

"How long?"

"I . . . I am not sure," she hedged. "Another week perhaps, maybe two."

"No," he stated emphatically.

"I beg your pardon?" she replied, her voice rising in volume.

"I said no, madam. We shall leave for Ramsgate Castle in the morning. Perkins or Ned can manage until Tristan hires someone." He gave her a charming smile. "Do try the ham, my dear. It is quite delicious."

Alyssa felt her stubbornness rising. She slowly let

out her breath. Morgan watched her struggling to keep her temper under control and felt mildly disappointed when she succeeded.

"You are being most unreasonable," she replied through her teeth. "And exceptionally bossy."

"One of my more charming qualities, don't you think?"

His sly grin did not escape her notice. "You, sir, are enjoying this entire conversation far too much for my liking," Alyssa commented, biting into her ham.

"Perhaps," he said lightly, finishing his champagne. "But if I correctly recall, less than one hour ago you vowed to obey me. Do you intend to keep that promise, my dear?"

"Of course," Alyssa stated vehemently, trying her best to look sincere. "As long as it suits me."

Morgan chuckled, pleased to see her independent spirit emerging again.

"We really must leave early tomorrow morning, my dear," he said in an apologetic tone. "I have pressing business that cannot wait. If you insist, however, you may join me at a later date."

Smugly Morgan refilled his wineglass, feeling certain she would reject his offer.

"Thank you, Morgan," Alyssa replied calmly. "It is very considerate of you to give me the option. I shall let you know my decision in the morning."

Feeling neatly outmaneuvered, Morgan picked up his wine goblet, thought better of it, and returned it to the table without drinking. Better to keep a clear head, he decided ruefully.

"I don't suppose you would care to explain the nature of this important matter that makes our departure tomorrow morning necessary?" Alyssa ventured.

"I have pressing business," Morgan replied vaguely. "More plums?"

"No, thank you," she answered. "I have a fair knowledge of business, Morgan. Perhaps I can be of some assistance?"

"Not on this particular matter, my dear," he insisted firmly. "Although it would be a help if you answered a few questions concerning the renovations of the manor house."

"What do you wish to know?"

Morgan sat up eagerly. Interviewing Alyssa might lead to a valuable clue. "Did you hire each man on the work crews or did Mr. Walsh do the employing?"

Alyssa took a moment to remember. "I engaged the majority of the work crews. A few of the specialty craftsmen were brought in by Mr. Walsh, especially the plasterers and the artist who painted the wall mural in the dining room and on the second story."

"Where did you find the men you hired?"

"All were from the village or the neighboring farms."

"Were there any strangers among them? Men that you did not personally know?"

Alyssa considered his question thoughtfully for several minutes. "I don't believe so. I will have to check the payroll, but I'm fairly certain all the workmen I hired were from this county."

"What about the craftsmen Mr. Walsh hired? Were these men known by him?"

"I'm not sure. I do know he worked with the painter before. They mentioned a ceiling mural in Lord Thomasville's chapel that was painted last winter. I'm also fairly certain two of the plasterers worked on other jobs with Mr. Walsh prior to coming to the manor. I don't know about the others." Alyssa sighed heavily. "If you explained precisely what you are attempting to discover, I might provide you with more pertinent information, Morgan."

The duke weighed his decision carefully before speaking. "I placed the envelope you saw me recover from the old desk the last time I was at Westgate

Manor in early spring. Since that time, I have reason to believe someone discovered the envelope, read the contents, and sold the rather sensitive information inside. Do you have any suspicions who that individual might be?"

"No," she admitted, feeling totally puzzled. What could possibly be inside the envelope that someone would want to buy? Alyssa tipped her head coyly to one side. "You realize, of course, I understand less now than before your explanation."

"I am sorry," he answered solemnly. "I don't mean to be so bloody mysterious. You must believe me when I say it is safer if you don't know the whole truth."

Alyssa became alarmed at his serious tone. "You are not in danger, are you, Morgan?" she said in a voice laced with fear.

"No," he reassured her, touched by her concern. "It would help, however, if I could determine which individuals had access to the desk."

"Anyone on the estate could have easily come to the library and searched the room. Would someone have been sent here specifically looking for these papers?"

"It is possible," Morgan replied, impressed with her quick grasp of the situation. "My theory is that someone stumbled upon the papers by accident, but was knowledgeable enough about the information to realize its value."

"What exactly was inside the envelope, Morgan?" Alyssa joked. "A treasure map?" At his answering frown, Alyssa became more serious. "I can verify the workmen I hired were locals, known by me personally. The only strangers working at the manor were the men engaged by Mr. Walsh. Only he can vouch for their character. There wasn't anyone else here, unless you suspect Tristan and Caroline."

"Anything is possible," Morgan retorted grimly.

"Not Tristan," Alyssa whispered in horror.

"No, of course not Tris," Morgan hastened to assure her. "Caroline did, however, bring countless numbers of her friends and family to the manor. Can you recall if a Comte Henri Duponce or Madeline Duponce visited?"

Alyssa stiffened visibly at the questions, instantly recognizing the Duponce name. "I never met either of them, but Caroline and Priscilla seldom bothered me during their visits unless they had a specific question. Generally I was too busy. Mr. Walsh always spent time entertaining them. The one person I distinctly remember Mr. Walsh mentioning was Caroline's younger brother, Gilbert. Mr. Walsh thought he was an exceptionally enlightened individual."

Morgan merely nodded at her answer, trying to digest the information. "If you will excuse me, my dear, I must spend a few moments reviewing the folders you gave me earlier today."

"Now?" Alyssa's green eyes darkened with astonishment. True, they were hardly a typical bride and groom, but it was their wedding night.

"Yes, now," he answered. "You go off to bed. I'll join you in a little while."

Alyssa was hurt, but did not want to appear waspish, so she left Morgan to his privacy. She entered her bedchamber, feeling in a bit of a temper, and sat down at the dressing table. Quickly she undid her upswept hairstyle, vigorously shaking out her hair. She reached automatically for her brush, but could not find it on the table. As she examined the room closely, she saw none of her personal items were in the room.

Alyssa left the bedchamber in search of Mavis.

"Oh, there you are," Mavis said, suddenly entering the hallway. "I thought you might have gone to your old room by mistake."

"I don't understand, Mavis."

"Tonight you will be sleeping in the master suite, Your Grace."

"Oh," Alyssa squeaked softly. A sharp quiver of delight speared her heart. Morgan always slept in the master suite.

"Come along now, Your Grace, you don't want to keep your husband waiting."

Alyssa rolled her eyes. "Merciful heavens, Mavis, stop calling me Your Grace. Just because I have married a duke does not mean I'm going to start putting on airs. I'm still the same woman I was yesterday." She looked down at her rounded belly. "Perhaps a bit more respectable than yesterday, but the same woman nonetheless."

Mavis merely huffed. "The duke has asked me to assist you with your evening toilette, Your Grace," Mavis insisted defiantly.

Alyssa threw her arms up in frustration and followed Mavis down the hall, grumbling all the way about how bossy everybody seemed to be today. Her sour mood diminished, however, upon entering the bedchamber and spying the large bathtub set before a roaring fire. Alyssa squealed with delight and cast Mavis a grateful glance. Maybe life as a duchess wouldn't be so bad after all.

Alyssa remained quiet as Mavis helped her remove her gown, pretty new lace-trimmed chemise, and lightweight petticoats. Alyssa sat on a low chair while Mavis untied her slippers and helped unroll her silk stockings. With Mavis's assistance, Alyssa carefully sank into the tub, relaxing her tired muscles in the soothing warm water. Mavis bustled about the room, putting away her clothes.

"We need to get you a proper lady's maid," Mavis grunted. "I'm too old for this."

"Ha." Alyssa snorted. "You are enjoying every minute and you know it. Besides, I'm sure the duke will assign someone to attend me when we arrive at Ramsgate Castle." Alyssa sat up suddenly, sloshing water out of the tub onto the hardwood floor. "Mavis, you are going to accompany me to Ramsgate Castle, aren't you?"

"I'd like to see anyone try to stop me," Mavis retorted. "You need someone to look after you and that baby."

"Thank goodness." Alyssa sighed with relief. She didn't think she was ready to face her new life as a duchess without the unfailing support of Mavis, not to mention coping with the unknown mysteries of childbirth.

When Alyssa was finished with her bath, Mavis lent a strong arm to steady her as she climbed out of the tub. Mavis quickly wrapped Alyssa in a large bath towel, and when she was dry, slipped on her nightgown.

"Are you sure about this nightdress, Mavis?" Alyssa questioned, buttoning the sleeves. " 'Tis a bit revealing." The new nightgown, chosen by Mavis, was an ethereal garment, made of soft, transparent silk. The heart-shaped neckline exposed most of Alyssa's shoulders and quite a bit of her breasts. The sleeves were long and billowing and gathered tightly at her wrists with small buttons. Alyssa felt half naked in the garment.

"Why, you look lovely, my girl," Mavis insisted.

"I am hardly a blushing young virgin, Mavis," Alyssa commented dryly, thrusting out her belly. "And it isn't necessary for me to look seductive for my husband. After all, it probably wouldn't be wise to . . . to . . . I mean it probably isn't safe if we . . . um . . ." Alyssa stammered, focusing her eyes intently on the rug.

"Consummate your marriage?" Mavis finished in a no-nonsense tone. "I spoke with the midwife when I was in the village this afternoon. She told me it would be fine. That is, as long as you are careful, and not too . . . um . . . rough." Now it was Mavis's turn to blush.

That rather embarrassing but important bit of advice given, Mavis left the room. Alyssa did not want to climb into the large four-poster bed alone. Instead she settled down in a big overstuffed chair in front of the fire to wait for Morgan. Growing bored, she scanned the room for something to occupy her time and discovered a worn volume of Shakespeare sonnets on the nightstand. Returning to her outpost on the chair, she covered her legs with a warm quilt and began reading the book.

Morgan discovered her there several hours later, fast asleep. The fire was nearly out, but the soft glow of the embers illuminated her pale skin and coppery hair. He crossed to the other side of the room and began undressing. Naked, he shrugged into the burgundy velvet robe left by the bed. He stood quietly for several minutes watching Alyssa as she slept, admiring her delicate beauty.

His wife. Difficult to believe. He had promised to never again domesticate himself, and yet it had happened. This marriage, Morgan vowed, would not be like his first. Remembering with painful clarity his wedding night with Valerie, Morgan shuddered. It had taken almost an hour to persuade her to make love. He had exercised great restraint, but Valerie was horrified by the entire act, weeping copious tears and refusing to speak to him.

Morgan tried for months afterward to woo Valerie into his bed, to establish a relationship with his wife, but she remained rigid and unyielding. She suffered his advances, physical and emotional, with a martyr-like attitude, blaming him for her fear and lack of response. He never understood her. She was like two different women, pleasant and charming in front of others, cold and distant when they were alone together. Defeated, Morgan eventually ceased trying to be a husband.

Alyssa stirred in her sleep, focusing Morgan's attention back to the present. True, Alyssa was a very different person from Valerie, and he smiled when he thought of their lovemaking. No problem in that quarter. But there was much more to marriage than sex, and this marriage was certainly off to a rocky start. He wondered if they would be able to overcome their differences and rectify their misunderstandings. He certainly intended to try.

Alyssa came awake suddenly, startled to find Morgan staring at her.

"Are you finished?" she asked in a sleepy voice. Alyssa yawned lazily and rolled the stiffness from her neck. "Did you find what you were looking for?"

"In a way," he answered. "Come to bed now, Alyssa. It is very late."

Morgan reached out his arm to help her rise, giving a sharp intake of breath when he saw her stand. Her nightgown had slipped off one shoulder completely, making her look slightly rumpled and very desirable. He jerked his gaze away, appalled at the sharp twist of desire burning in his loins. Here was a woman nearly six months gone with his child and he was already hard and throbbing at the thought of bedding her.

But Morgan hesitated. Having no experience with expectant females left him clueless in gauging Alyssa's feelings. Would she welcome his advances? Was it safe? Could he harm her or the child? Morgan highly doubted Alyssa would know the answer and he didn't want to create a sexual situation that might be unfulfilling for either of them.

Disciplining himself to ignore his base desires, Morgan gingerly assisted Alyssa into the bed. Shrugging off his robe, he quickly slipped between the sheets.

He realized his mistake the instant his bare leg touched her naked thigh. Alyssa's nightgown was bunched up about her waist, and Morgan groaned aloud when he realized she was naked underneath. Rapidly he removed his leg. It didn't help. He could still feel the heat from her warm body. She smelled like fresh roses, and he longed to reach over and pull her into his arms.

Morgan rolled onto his back, shifting his position and moving as close to the edge of the bed as possible. He silently thanked Tristan for purchasing such an enormous bed. If he put enough distance between himself and Alyssa, Morgan reasoned, he would be able to control himself. He might even be able to sleep for a few hours.

They lay in tense silence for several long moments. Alyssa waited expectantly for Morgan to turn and gather her in his arms. When she realized he wasn't going to, she turned toward him and came up on her side, balancing herself on her elbow.

It was nearly impossible to see his face in the dim light, but Alyssa could hear his ragged breathing, and felt the waves of tension emanating from his stiff body.

"Morgan?" she asked softly.

She heard his quick intake of breath. "Yes," he answered sharply.

Now that she had his attention, Alyssa was in a quandary, unsure how to proceed. "I . . . I've decided to accompany you to Ramsgate Castle tomorrow morning," she said lamely.

Morgan smiled into the darkness. "I'm glad," he remarked, knowing a scene could be avoided in the morning because he had never had any intention of leaving the manor without his bride. Alyssa sighed softly and squirmed closer.

Taking a deep breath, Morgan tried to concentrate

on the green velvet bed hangings faintly visible in the semidarkness. Methodically he counted the swags of trim in an effort to focus his mind on something, anything, besides his lovely, half-naked wife.

"Morgan?"

"What?" he snapped.

"I'm cold," Alyssa lied, hoping he would take the hint. She desperately wanted to be held in his arms.

"I'll get another blanket," he volunteered quickly. Morgan rose from the bed and walked to the chair by the fireplace. He retrieved the quilt Alyssa had left there, but on his way back to the bed he stumbled in the darkness, banging his shin on the edge of the large satinwood bed frame.

Alyssa sat up abruptly, listening to Morgan's loud colorful swearing. "Morgan? What happened? Are you hurt?"

"I am fine," he replied, gritting his teeth. The pain in his leg successfully cleared his mind of visions of seduction. "Is there anything else you require while I am up, madam? A piece of fruit, a sip of wine, a drink of water, perhaps?"

"No, nothing else," she replied softly.

He practically threw the blanket at her before yanking the covers back and falling into the bed. He again took a strategic position on the far side of the bed, his leg throbbing with pain.

"Good night, madam," he said.

"Good night," she echoed hastily. She waited for several minutes, gathering her courage before she spoke again. "Morgan?"

"Go to sleep," he growled, dipping his shoulder and presenting his back to Alyssa. He made a great show of noisily puffing his pillows before burrowing down and pulling the coverlet up to his chin.

His dismissive gesture effectively silenced her. Grimly she arranged the extra quilt over herself. Imitating his actions, she rolled to her side, reluctantly shifting her body so her back was toward him. She felt the tears rise up in her throat, but swallowed them. She refused to cry, refused to admit how hurt she was by his coldness. He is just tired, Alyssa reasoned. He needs time to adjust to our married state. Eventually Alyssa managed to convince herself their marriage was not a colossal mistake. Exhaustion overcame anxiety and she fell asleep.

Morgan lay awake long into the night, listening to her deep, steady breathing. He wished he hadn't been so curt, but it was unavoidable. It was impossible for Morgan to hold and caress Alyssa without making love to her, and Morgan felt frustrated by his ignorance. He didn't know if it was safe in her pregnant condition and he would take no risks with her or the child. He decided Alyssa would be examined by the family physician as soon as he could be summoned to Ramsgate Castle. The first question the duke would ask the good doctor was the state of his wife's health. And the next would be about marital relations.

Chapter Sixteen

Morgan came awake slowly, the dream still fresh in his subconscious. His hand gently caressed smooth, soft skin. His body felt hot, his manhood swollen. He pushed his hips against the smooth softness, thrusting rhythmically. He heard a moan of pleasure and thought, for an instant, the noise came from his own throat, but he heard the sound again, louder this time, and it brought him completely awake.

Alyssa was sprawled over him, her arms entwined around his neck. The erect nipples on her full, creamy breasts touched his chest sensuously through the silky fabric of her nightdress. The nightgown was bunched about her waist, and she was gloriously naked beneath it. Her legs were slightly parted, and his hand was between her thighs. Morgan thought he would explode with wanting as her hips moved instinctively against his exploring fingers. Passion engulfed him and his fingers slipped deeper inside her warmth.

She moaned again, arching herself against him. Morgan reached over to cup her full breasts with his other hand, moving her onto her back. He ran his hand caressingly down her soft body, but stopped abruptly when he encountered the swelled mound of her belly. He sat up suddenly, removing his hands from her flesh, guiltily rearranging her nightclothes.

Morgan concentrated on slowing his ragged breathing while Alyssa mumbled in her sleep and snuggled closer to him.

"No more of that, my girl," he said hoarsely, deliberately distancing himself. He straightened the bedcovers, tucking the blankets firmly around his sleeping wife. "I must wait until I know it is safe for you and our babe."

After Morgan was certain Alyssa was sleeping soundly, he left the bed, relieved to see dawn fast approaching. He donned his robe and crossed the room to the cold hearth. He lit a satisfactory blaze before seating himself in the same overstuffed chair Alyssa had occupied the previous evening. Distracted, he picked up the book of Shakespeare sonnets.

After rereading the same line three times, he gave up the attempt.

Resting his head against the soft, cushioned back, he fell asleep.

When Alyssa woke several hours later, she was alone in the room. She looked automatically toward the empty side of the bed, searching for confirmation that Morgan had indeed shared the large bed for the night. The indentation of his head was visible on the pillow, and Alyssa ran her hand caressingly over the spot. Vague, sensual feelings entered her body and she shook her head sharply, chasing away the most erotic dream. Morgan touching her, caressing her. Her sexual daydreaming was abruptly interrupted by a loud knock on the bedchamber door.

"Oh good, you're awake," Mavis said with a smile, answering Alyssa's bid to enter. The older woman set a small breakfast tray with warm toast, fresh fruit, and a steaming pot of hot chocolate on the bedside table next to Alyssa. "The duke told me I was not to awaken you, but it was getting late, and I thought you might need my help." Mavis gave Alyssa a sly smile. "Of course the duke said you needed your rest. I imagine you didn't get much sleep last night."

Alyssa blushed hotly, wanting very much to throw the covers over her head and hide. If only Mavis knew the truth.

"Did the duke say what time we are leaving this morning?" Alyssa inquired, biting into the toast Mavis had brought.

"No. He said it wasn't a long journey, and he hoped to leave before noon, if possible. I believe he was waiting until you were up. Very considerate of him, don't you agree?"

"Mmmmmm . . . that certainly describes my husband accurately," Alyssa responded sarcastically. She brushed the crumbs from her meager breakfast off her hands and set the empty tray on the coverlet next to her. "Come and show me what wonderful new traveling costume you picked out for me, Mavis. We don't want to keep the good duke waiting, now do we?"

An hour later, Alyssa strolled into the morning room, interrupting Morgan at his breakfast. The small dining table was scattered with papers from the folders she had given him yesterday, and he was intently studying each page as he absently chewed his food. Alyssa cleared her throat loudly to gain his attention.

Morgan stood up instantly, pleased to note his lovely bride was dressed for traveling. Lack of sleep had left him in no mood to argue with Alyssa if she had changed her mind about leaving with him today.

"Good morning," he said courteously, holding out the chair on his right. "Have you breakfasted yet?"

"Mavis brought me some toast," Alyssa answered, looking with longing at the remains of his hearty meal.

Morgan smiled at her expression, quickly gathered the papers up from the table, and rang for Perkins.

"The duchess is ready for her breakfast now, Perkins. And please bring in another fresh pot of coffee," Morgan instructed the butler.

Alyssa sat quietly at the table, her eyes downcast. Morgan noticed she nervously twisted her wedding ring around on her finger. "Did you sleep well?" she blurted out.

Morgan raised an eyebrow in question over her sudden outburst. No, Alyssa, he wanted to tell her, I did not sleep well. My body was hard and throbbing and aching for release. Instead, he politely lied. "Very well. And you, my dear?"

"Just fine," Alyssa responded, her voice trailing off. Except for a most erotic dream, she mentally added.

They were relieved of the burden of further strained conversation by the arrival of Perkins with a large tray full of steaming hot food. Alyssa concentrated on consuming every last bite of the marvelous breakfast, while Morgan watched in amazed silence as she devoured the meal. She glanced up as she finished the last of her eggs and caught his eye. Embarrassed, she slowly lowered her fork.

"I guess I was hungrier than I thought," she said, her cheeks reddening.

Morgan grinned broadly. "Do you want me to have Perkins bring you another plate?"

She paused for a moment before answering, knowing he was teasing her. "That depends," Alyssa responded thoughtfully. "How long do you think it will be before we can have luncheon?"

Morgan chuckled. "I shall tell Mavis to pack an enormously large basket of treats so you may indulge yourself on the drive whenever the mood strikes."

"That would be delightful." She eyed him shyly. "When do you wish to depart?"

Morgan shrugged his shoulders. "Anytime you are ready. I shall tell Perkins to have Ned hitch up the phaeton."

"We are taking Tristan's new carriage with us?"

"Merely borrowing," Morgan corrected. "I shall have one of my servants return it tomorrow. It is the only carriage here, and I think it is preferable to having you mounted on horseback for the entire journey."

"But what about Mavis? There is only room in the phaeton for the two of us."

"I shall send a coach to bring Mavis and the remainder of your belongings to Ramsgate Castle tomorrow. I've already told Mavis about these arrangements."

"I see," Alyssa responded slowly. She rose from her chair and stood by the large bay window, looking out onto the lawn. "Is there anything else?"

"Well, I did instruct Mavis to pack a small overnight satchel for you. There is very little space in the phaeton for luggage."

Morgan watched her rigid back, knowing she was upset and not certain as to the cause. "Is something wrong, Alyssa?"

She turned around to face him. "No . . . not exactly. I have always been the one who makes all the decisions, all the arrangements. I am unaccustomed to someone else giving the orders."

"You are my wife now, Alyssa. It is my responsibility to see to your welfare," Morgan stated firmly. "And that of our child."

His responsibility. It was the most depressing thing Alyssa could imagine. She felt the tears well up in her eyes and turned away from him again. It was hardly a secret why they had married, yet hearing him state it so plainly hurt, especially after his distant behavior last night in their bedchamber.

"I shall be ready to leave shortly," she said, walking sedately past him, moving steadily toward the door. She hoped desperately he would reach out and stop her, longing for some degree of physical contact between them, but he did not.

Morgan resisted the impulse to hold her, not certain if his gesture would further upset her. He was puzzled by her attitude, which was nothing new, but he did not want to unwittingly cause her additional grief.

Alyssa stood in the large entrance hall, flanked by Mavis and Perkins. She bid a hasty good-bye to Mavis, and then faced Perkins. She spoke to the butler for a long time before reaching out and hugging him tightly. Morgan glanced away, feeling like a voyeur witnessing this intimate moment. He realized for the first time how difficult it must be for Alyssa to be separated from the only people she cared about.

"Ready?" she asked in a breathless voice. They all walked out into the bright sunlight. Morgan assisted Alyssa into the carriage, and then turned to take her satchel from Perkins. The butler looked him squarely in the eyes.

"You'll take proper care of her, Your Grace." It was a statement, not a question.

"I will, Perkins," Morgan promised solemnly. He climbed into the carriage as Alyssa made her farewells to Ned. With a final wave to the small group, Morgan and Alyssa departed.

"We will come to visit Tristan and Caroline often," Morgan remarked kindly. "You shall have many opportunities to see Perkins and the others again."

"I know." Alyssa sniffled. "Please forgive my foolishness. Perkins has always been very special to me." She gave a small laugh and wiped her eyes. "When I was a young girl, I used to lie in my bed at night wishing Perkins were my father. A little odd, don't you agree, for the daughter of the viscount to long to be the child of the butler?"

Alyssa paused a moment as the deeply buried childhood feelings of vulnerability and abandonment surfaced. "Perkins always tried to make me feel special—wanted. I shall never forget him for his kindness," she whispered.

Morgan reached over and squeezed her hand reassuringly, marveling over how she had emerged from such a neglected childhood to become a fine, determined woman.

They remained quiet for the majority of the journey to Portsmouth, with only an occasional comment about the fine weather. Morgan drove at a sedate pace, in no hurry, and the gentle rocking motion of the finely sprung carriage made Alyssa sleepy. She dozed fitfully, and was awakened when Morgan announced they had reached the grounds of Ramsgate.

Alyssa caught her breath as she looked through the tall oak trees and saw the castle. Its huge stone walls glistened in the autumn sun, and the ornately decorated Gothic spires disappeared majestically into the sky. As they drove down the gravel drive, Alyssa felt her heart beat faster with each turn of the wheel. She was not sure she was ready for this. The castle was enormous, stretching on endlessly. Alyssa felt overwhelmed.

Morgan pulled up in front of the elegant Ionic portico at the front entrance of the castle, and Alyssa craned her neck heavenward to gain a full view of the medallion crest of a lion's head carved in stone above the doorway.

"My grandmother's family coat of arms," Morgan told her. "Tristan and I have long suspected it was her reward for putting up with my grandfather."

Alyssa had only a moment to mumble an unintelligible remark before three footmen, splendidly garbed in crimson and gold livery, raced down the steps to assist them out of the carriage. They were quickly followed by a stout, formally garbed man who Morgan introduced as Burke, butler of the castle.

"I am honored, Your Grace," Burke said ceremonially, bowing to Alyssa in welcome. "We were all very pleased when the duke sent word he was bringing the new duchess here to Ramsgate."

Alyssa smiled in greeting, uncertain what to do. Was it proper etiquette for a duchess to shake the hand of one's butler when meeting him for the first time? She didn't have much time to dwell on that problem, because Morgan clasped her elbow and was propelling her through the large, ornate doors and into the gigantic entrance hall.

Alyssa swallowed hard when she saw the reception awaiting her. Double rows of servants lined the hall, crisply attired in various uniforms that proclaimed their positions within the household. They were standing in an almost military fashion, their expressions blank, yet all eyes were turned expectantly toward her.

"I should like to introduce select members of the staff," Burke began, but he halted in midsentence when he got his first full-figured look at Alyssa and realized her pregnant condition. She was impressed with the way he regained his composure, stumbling only slightly as he introduced the housekeeper, Mrs. Keenly.

Alyssa took hold of Mrs. Keenly's hand, graciously greeting the older woman. "I should like to meet all of the staff please, Mrs. Keenly," Alyssa requested with as much dignity as she could muster. To hell with proper etiquette, Alyssa recklessly decided. She would give the staff enough gossip to keep them buzzing for a week.

It took almost an hour for Alyssa to greet each of the servants, and Morgan watched with growing admiration as they were captivated by her quiet dignity. By the time she finished, Alyssa had succeeded in impressing them all. Morgan felt very proud.

"The dowager duchess awaits you in the sitting room, Your Grace," Burke whispered to Morgan when Alyssa began her long walk back toward her husband.

"Very good, Burke. We shall join her directly."

Alyssa smiled triumphantly at Morgan as she reached his side. She felt as though she had just survived a baptism of fire.

"Come along, my dear," Morgan requested. "There is someone else I want you to meet." He squashed the momentary pang of guilt he felt as Alyssa trustingly complied. He knocked briefly on the sitting room doors to announce their presence before entering.

Alyssa walked into the room blissfully unaware of who awaited them, still reeling from her encounter with the staff. She stopped short when she saw a small, very dignified elderly lady seated on the settee. Morgan left Alyssa's side, crossed the room, and bent down to kiss the woman's cheek. Alyssa clearly saw the love Morgan held for this person reflected in his handsome face, and she realized at once the woman must be his grandmother. Alyssa felt a momentary rush of panic, and she brought her hands instinctively down in front of her waist, uncertain of her reception.

All too soon Morgan returned to Alyssa's side. Tugging her by the hand, he brought her forward to be presented to the duchess. Alyssa felt her cheeks flush hotly and wondered what sort of impression she, and her protruding belly, were making on this extremely dignified lady.

"My dear," the dowager duchess said softly. She

stood up and clasped Alyssa's hand firmly. "How delightful to finally meet you."

Alyssa was relieved to see the kindness in the older woman's eyes as she tactfully looked up into Alyssa's face, instead of down to her expanded waistline. Alyssa made an awkward curtsy, but the dowager duchess pulled her upright.

"No need for such formality, Alyssa," the dowager duchess insisted. "We are family. Come, you must sit down and rest. I am sure that you are weary from your journey."

Alyssa was relieved to hear no censure in the older woman's voice and relaxed a bit, although she was still nervous. She did not know the dowager duchess was in residence at the castle. Alyssa sat down on the settee, startled when Morgan sat unusually close beside her. The dowager duchess sat in a small gold-leaf chair on Morgan's right.

They were prevented from making additional conversation by the arrival of Burke and several footmen bringing in tea. Alyssa's stomach rumbled at the sight of the delicious food, and Morgan chuckled. "Better bring in another tray of pastries, Burke. The new duchess has a voracious appetite."

Alyssa stared at Morgan in mortification. "Well, no thanks to you, sir, I am eating for two," she hissed at him, low enough so the servants would not overhear. But the dowager duchess caught Alyssa's words and she discreetly coughed behind her hand to conceal her smile.

"Morgan, you mustn't tease your wife so," the dowager duchess admonished, secretly delighted at his behavior. She could feel the tension between her grandson and his pretty new wife, but there was something else there, just below the surface. The dowager duchess felt a spark of hope for the success of this very unconventional marriage.

She had been more than a little shocked to receive an urgent note from Morgan informing her of his hasty marriage, his pregnant bride, and requesting she travel to Ramsgate Castle at once. She had many unanswered questions for her grandson, but she fully intended to form her own opinion about his new bride.

"Would you do the honors, Alyssa?" the dowager duchess requested, inclining her head toward the tea service. "I take mine with cream and one spoon of sugar."

Alyssa nodded, moving closer to the heavy silver tea service the footman had placed on the elegant mahogany tea table. Her hand trembled slightly as she handed the dowager duchess a brimming cup of tea. She next poured a cup for Morgan and lastly one for herself. The dowager duchess was pleased to note Alyssa prepared Morgan's tea exactly as he preferred it, without asking, and then took the initiative to fill a plate of food for her husband.

"Morgan tells me you are a Carrington, my dear," the dowager duchess commented. "I knew your grandparents and both your mother and father."

Alyssa's teacup rattled at the mention of her family. "Oh, really," she replied, dreading what might come next.

"Yes," the dowager duchess continued. "I thought your mother was a charming woman."

"I never knew my mother," Alyssa explained, relieved that the dowager duchess had not mentioned her father. "She died when I was very young."

"Yes, I know. How is your father faring these days?"

Morgan interrupted before Alyssa had a chance to respond. "Alyssa has only recently come out of mourning for the viscount, Grandmother. He passed on this spring. I do believe I mentioned this to you," Morgan finished pointedly. He glared at his grandmother.

She smiled back at him, very pleased at his protective attitude. "Perhaps you did, Morgan. I must have forgotten. Well, at my age, what can you expect?"

Morgan snorted at that remark. What was his grandmother up to? She knew Alyssa's family history completely, probably better than he did. And she never forgot things. He gave her a warning scowl that seemed to bring her tremendous delight.

Alyssa watched the exchange between the two with growing fascination, glad that she was no longer the focus of attention. She was not at all offended by the dowager duchess's questions. She was, in fact, pleasantly surprised at the congenial way the dowager duchess was treating her, especially under these circumstances.

"I am pleased Morgan decided you should come to Ramsgate Castle," the dowager duchess remarked. "It has always been one of my favorite residences." The dowager duchess paused for a moment, as if a thought had suddenly occurred to her. "I hope you will not mind my being here, Alyssa?"

"Oh, no, Your Grace," Alyssa hastily countered. "Truth be told, I shall be most grateful for your company."

The dowager duchess nodded in approval over Alyssa's sincere response. Despite the rather bizarre circumstances of their marriage, the dowager duchess found herself pleased with Morgan's choice. He just might be able to make a go of it this time, she thought.

"Do have another crescent sandwich, Alyssa," the dowager duchess insisted. "And try some of Cook's marvelous scones. I promise if my grandson makes another uncalled-for comment about your eating habits, I shall kick him in the shins."

Alyssa chuckled softly, turning her eyes to the duke. He gave her an engaging smile, and she felt her heart turn wildly in her breast. "Thank you," she whispered, her eyes locked on Morgan's handsome face as she took another scone. Suddenly flustered, she looked away.

"You really must go upstairs and rest, my dear," Morgan said after Alyssa finished eating her pastry. "I am sure you must be tired."

"I quite agree," the dowager duchess immediately chimed in. "You do look weary. I shall instruct Burke to serve dinner in your rooms tonight. Newlyweds do need their privacy. Morgan shall escort you to your chambers."

They all rose in unison. The dowager duchess turned to Alyssa and gave her a small hug. "I am thrilled that Morgan has made such a wise choice in his bride. I wish you much happiness, Alyssa."

Alyssa returned the hug and felt tears sting the back of her eyes at the dowager duchess's kindness. She felt immensely grateful to have discovered an ally in this woman. Given time, they might become true friends. Alyssa held on tightly to the arm Morgan offered her, and they left the drawing room.

"This is probably the largest staircase I have ever seen," Alyssa commented as they mounted the wide circular stairs. Generations of ancestors, their portraits encased in plaster frames, watched their every step. When they finally reached the landing, gold sconces lit the hallway, and the oak flooring was carpeted with a thick oriental runner.

They made several twisting turns before reaching their final destination. Alyssa turned to the duke jokingly. "I shall need a map to find my way around."

"I suppose these vast hallways do resemble a maze," he agreed. Finally Morgan stopped and opened the door to Alyssa's new bedchamber. "Here are your rooms. I hope you find them satisfactory."

The bedchamber was vast, with a separate sitting area and large sets of windows on two walls. The predominant color of decoration was green, from the intricate tapestry wall hanging to the thick, green-patterned Aubusson carpet. The bed was an enormous affair, decorated with Spitalfield silks and ostrich-feather plumes. The furniture was dainty and feminine but extremely ornate, with gold-leaf trim. Alyssa could not imagine the dowager duchess selecting all the frilly accompaniments, and decided Morgan's first wife must have decorated the suite.

"The room is very . . ." Alyssa searched in vain for a polite adjective.

"Overdone?" Morgan supplied, walking into the room and lightly fingering the silken bed trimmings. He had forgotten how elaborate Valerie's tastes had been. If memory served him correctly, he had only entered this bedchamber twice.

Alyssa ventured a tentative smile, wondering if there would be any objection to her making some changes. She glanced speculatively up at the enormous feathers adorning the top of the bed, hoping she would be able to sleep under them.

"You must refurnish the room to suit you, Alyssa," Morgan said. He turned the handle on the door of the adjoining bedchamber slowly, speculating if it was still locked. It wasn't, and he strode into his own rooms, Alyssa following close on his heels. "And these, of course, are my rooms," he added unnecessarily.

Alyssa looked around curiously, immediately preferring the rich appointments of Morgan's chamber to her own. The room was decidedly masculine, with heavy, dark furniture, spartan decoration, and drapes in shades of tan and gold decorating the windows and bed. The room was warm and inviting. Morgan pulled the bell cord, and his valet, Dickinson, immediately materialized.

"Has Mrs. Keenly assigned a lady's maid to the duchess?" Morgan asked his stiff-necked servant.

"I do believe Mrs. Keenly has chosen Janet, Your Grace. If that meets with your approval, my lady?" Both men turned to stare at Alyssa.

"I am sure she is very capable," Alyssa answered, vaguely remembering being introduced to her new maid.

"Very good, Your Grace. I shall have Janet summoned. She will attend you at once." The valet gave a low bow and soundlessly left the room.

Alyssa stood inside Morgan's bedchamber for a few moments longer until she felt his eyes upon her.

"I shall wait for Janet in the other chamber," she stammered, feeling as though she were intruding.

Morgan watched the various expressions flit over her face and wondered what she was thinking. She grabbed on to the connecting door and he spoke. "You may close the door on your way out. By the way, there is a very sturdy lock on it." He wasn't sure why he had made such a remark. Either to inform her or remind himself.

She was startled by his comment and did not know how to respond. "Will you be joining me for dinner?" Alyssa asked, deciding to ignore his mention of the lock.

"Yes," he replied in an even voice. "I have some pressing business I must attend to, but it should be concluded by this evening. If there is a change in my plans, I shall inform you."

"Very good. I shall see you later then."

Chapter Seventeen

Alyssa slept fitfully, coming awake suddenly, her mind disoriented by her dreams. She sat up in the enormous bed and glanced about. The window curtains were closed, but the light from the dying fire illuminated a portion of the room, casting unreal shadows. She heard a noise and held her breath, waiting for something, anything, to emerge from the shadows. When nothing happened she let out her breath slowly, chiding herself for being so fanciful.

She squirmed back under the covers and gazed up at the dark ceiling, her ears straining for sounds. A sharp crashing noise followed by a muffled curse brought her attention to the closed door that connected her chamber to the duke's. Alyssa leaned forward in the great bed and squinted her eyes. She could see a faint beam of light emerging from under the door. Morgan was in his room. Awake.

He had sent his regrets for dinner, and she was disappointed but not surprised by his absence. He had been formal and distant ever since their arrival at

Ramsgate Castle, and she got the distinct impression he preferred his solitude to her company.

Another loud crashing sound brought her out of the bed, and before giving a thought to her actions, Alyssa opened the connecting door. Her eyes searched the dim, candlelit room until she found the duke. He was sprawled in a chair near the fireplace. A small wooden table lay broken on the floor next to one of his boots.

He had removed his coat and neckcloth and was dressed in a white shirt, black pantaloons, and one boot. The shirt was open at the collar, and Alyssa could see the small curls in the fine mat of dark hair just below his throat. She took a step toward him, and his head jerked up. For several moments he simply stared at her, and then he growled, "What the hell are you doing in here?"

Alyssa sucked in her breath and stared at him wide-eyed. "I heard a noise," she explained in a breathless voice. "I saw the light beneath your door and came to investigate. Forgive me for disturbing you, Your Grace." She turned to leave, but stopped when she felt his hand gently touch her shoulder.

"I . . . I knocked over that damn table trying to take off my boots," he said, his voice slightly slurred. She could detect the faint aroma of brandy on his breath and realized that he had been drinking. She paused a moment, wondering what she should do. They simultaneously looked down at his feet.

"Isn't Dickinson here to assist you?"

"I sent him to bed hours ago," Morgan drawled. "However, since you are awake, will you kindly lend a hand, my dear?" He hobbled back to his chair and threw himself into it. Giving a loud sigh, he ran his hand through his disheveled hair and thrust out his booted foot expectantly.

"Yes, of course," Alyssa replied, following him. She looked down at the boot in bewilderment, not having the foggiest notion how to proceed.

She bent over, facing him, and gave the boot a sharp tug. It didn't budge. She tried again, with the same result. Alyssa glanced up at Morgan and saw his eyes were fastened on her face. He gave her a lopsided grin, and her heart thudded. "Grip the heel, madam" he instructed softly.

She did as he bid and was finally able to loosen the boot, but was still unable to remove it. She dropped his foot suddenly in frustration, straightened up, and rested her hands on her hips. "Now what," she challenged, her face flushed by her exertions.

Morgan took a long sip of brandy, and then sat upright in the chair. "Turn around and straddle my foot. That's right. Now grab hold of the heel, tightly . . . tightly, and pull as hard as you can."

Alyssa let out an indignant shriek as she felt his other foot push against her buttocks, but she held on to the boot. Miraculously, she retained her balance as it gave way, and she yanked it off his leg. She turned, waving the Hessian triumphantly, before dropping it on the floor beside its mate.

"You would make an excellent valet, my dear," he said with a husky note in his voice as he stood up. "I must tell Dickinson that, the next time he annoys me."

They laughed together softly, but Morgan abruptly stopped when he took full measure of Alyssa's appearance. Her hair was hanging loosely down her back, her cheeks were flushed, and her eyes were sparkling with humor. Her nightgown, though a modest cotton garment with a high, ruffled neckline, was nearly transparent when she stood before the fire. Her unself-conscious beauty charmed him, and for a moment he forgot her pregnant state and leaned forward to kiss her.

Alyssa saw the hot gleam in Morgan's eye and gratefully moved closer. How she had longed for his embrace! Alyssa felt his hand tentatively stroke her cheek, and then his lips claimed hers in a gentle kiss. His mouth grew more demanding, and she returned his kiss without restraint, parting her lips, inviting his probing tongue. Her arms slipped around his broad shoulders as she arched her body closer to his, deepening their kiss.

Morgan lovingly stroked her hair as he placed gentle kisses on her cheeks and throat, and then buried his face in the hollow between her neck and shoulders. As he began kissing Alyssa's breasts through the cotton nightgown, her breathless moan of desire brought him to his senses.

Morgan felt his desire for her twist in his groin, but he gently disengaged himself from their ardent embrace. He took a moment to steady his ragged breathing. "You should be in bed, madam," he said gruffly.

"Oh yes, Morgan," she readily agreed, rejoicing in the feel of his hard, strong body. Alyssa moved away from him, toward his impressive bed in the center of the room, her fingers busily unfastening the numerous tiny buttons down the front of her nightgown as she walked.

"Your own bed, madam." His voice sounded cold and hard to her ears, and she turned to face him. She stared at him for one long frozen moment and shivered. Her hand clutched the front of her nightgown closed as she waited in restless anticipation for him to reach out for her, praying she had mistaken his meaning.

When his words finally sank in, Alyssa blushed violently, her eyes dropping to the carpet. His taut rejection wounded her heart and paralyzed her tongue. Trembling, she practically ran from the room, desperate to leave him before her tears started falling. She slammed the door connecting their chambers and leaned back against it, her body vibrating with shame and fury.

Never had she experienced such humiliation. Morgan's curt rejection stunned her, creating a deep void, an emptiness inside her. Alyssa felt her dreams for a loving marriage crumbling as the hot, salty tears coursed down her face. Fumbling in the darkness she found the key in the latch and turned it, locking the door.

Morgan heard the click of the lock and felt a sharp pang of regret shoot through his chest. Furious, he turned and kicked his boots, knocking them across the room. He reached automatically for the half-empty decanter of brandy, but stopped before pouring the amber liquid into his glass. This would not have happened if he were completely sober. Alyssa had been so responsive, so passionate, almost beyond temptation, yet his weakness brought them both suffering.

Morgan sat in his chair, staring moodily at the dying embers in the fireplace. This marriage was off to an even more dismal start than the first. A rather sobering thought indeed. Morgan felt frustrated and sad, and then became angry, determined Alyssa would not slip away from him. Somehow he would find a way to gain her trust.

Morgan hoped to begin anew with Alyssa the next morning, but an urgent summons from Lord Castlereagh demanded he return to London immediately. There was no chance for a private good-bye with his wife, as she was breakfasting with his grandmother in the morning room when he made his announcement.

Alyssa's face remained cool and remote, but inwardly she felt relieved. Perhaps if they put some time and distance between them, the horrible pain inside her would ease.

"What do you mean, you are off to London today,

Morgan?" the dowager duchess said in annoyance. "You have only just arrived."

"It cannot be helped, Grandmother," Morgan replied in a neutral tone. He gave her a quelling look, and she understood he wished to be alone with his wife. The dowager duchess rose to quit the room, but Alyssa turned, her eyes flashing with such fear and panic that the older woman immediately sat back down in her chair.

Morgan's eyes narrowed in anger at their sudden display of solidarity, his face set in harsh lines. It annoyed him that his grandmother felt the need to protect his wife, almost as much as it bothered him that his wife felt she needed protection. Casting them both a glacial stare, the duke strode from the room without another word.

"Morgan is certainly in a foul mood this morning," the dowager duchess commented as soon as they were alone. Her keen eyes flickered speculatively at Alyssa, noticing the younger woman unconsciously twisted and untwisted her linen napkin. "I'm sure he is just distressed at having to leave you so abruptly, my dear."

Alyssa looked at the dowager duchess in utter amazement, and then shocked them both by bursting into tears.

"Forgive me," Alyssa sniffled, trying to cease her wrenching sobs. "I'm usually not such a watering pot. I feel very tired and my emotions are overset. I'm afraid I didn't get much sleep last night."

With a commanding wave of her hand, the dowager duchess cleared the room of servants. "There is no need for apologies, my dear," the dowager duchess responded with sincere sympathy. "I imagine you have had a rather rough go of it these last few days."

Alyssa gave her a wry smile, emphasizing how much of an understatement that comment was. "It has been difficult," she admitted softly. "And it only continues to get worse, I fear."

"Then we must change this unacceptable situation." The dowager duchess spoke with such conviction, Alyssa felt a tiny flicker of hope bud within her heart.

"Is it possible?" Alyssa questioned, battling to keep that hope alive.

"Naturally. After all, 'tis obvious my grandson is in love with you."

Alyssa's head whipped up at that preposterous statement. "I believe you are very much mistaken," she responded incredulously.

The dowager duchess smiled wryly. "The same way I am mistaken that you care for him?"

Alyssa's expression of disbelief changed into one of horror. "I had no idea my feelings were so conspicuous."

"They aren't," the dowager duchess informed her. "I was merely acting on a theory where your feelings were concerned." She patted Alyssa's hand reassuringly. "It makes me very happy to know you love him, Alyssa. Morgan is a man much in need of a woman's love."

Alyssa shook her head, certain the dowager was wrong about the duke's feelings. "Morgan has never made any pretense about the reasons for our marriage. He is an honorable man. For him, there was no other choice."

"Nonsense," the dowager duchess vehemently disagreed. "Of course he is a man of honor, but he would not have married solely for the sake of the child. I have watched my grandson closely through the years and there is nothing on this earth that can induce Morgan to act against his will. He might have persuaded himself the child was the basis for marrying you, but there is more to it. I am positive."

"Whatever his reasons, he surely has regrets now.

He can barely stand the sight of me," Alyssa confessed, the feelings of pain and emptiness returning to torment her.

"Tell me why," the dowager duchess requested softly. And because she asked with such kindness and compassion, Alyssa did. She started at the beginning when she had first met Morgan at Westgate Manor, and spoke of the dreadful misunderstanding about becoming his mistress, and his shock at discovering her pregnancy. Alyssa held nothing back, pouring her heart out, reliving every glorious and atrocious moment.

When Alyssa at last finished her long discourse, she felt oddly at peace with herself. She peeked over at the dowager duchess sitting silently next to her, suddenly nervous as to the older woman's reaction.

To Alyssa's total astonishment, the dowager duchess favored her with a genuine smile. "This is even better than I had hoped for."

"Pardon me?"

"Don't you understand, Alyssa? You have just described a most explosive and tempestuous relationship. Morgan is anything but indifferent toward you. Given time, he will come to understand his true feelings." Another warm smile brightened the dowager's face. "Finish eating your breakfast so we can begin making plans. There is much to do, and I am uncertain how long Morgan will be away. I suspect he won't want to be gone from your side very long."

The next few days passed quickly for Alyssa. She spent nearly every moment of her day listening to and learning from the dowager duchess on subjects as varied as the proper way to organize a dinner party for sixty to the best approach to enticing a wayward husband.

Significant physical changes were also made. Alyssa's suite of rooms were completely remodeled, effectively removing all traces of Valerie. Next, a complete wardrobe of new dresses was ordered, and even though they were by necessity waistless, the dowager duchess chose both fabrics and colors that flattered Alyssa.

Mavis arrived, and Alyssa was bolstered by her calming presence. Mrs. Glyndon, the dowager duchess's companion, appeared at Ramsgate Castle the following day. Alyssa thought she was a kindly woman, even though she blushed furiously and stammered nervously when first introduced to the duke's pregnant bride.

The most difficult encounter came on the third day, however, when Tristan, Caroline, and Priscilla made a sudden, unannounced appearance. Alyssa, the dowager duchess, and Mrs. Glyndon were enjoying an early afternoon tea when Burke announced the couple.

Caroline bounded into the room, beautifully garbed in a red velvet traveling costume that highlighted her fair coloring. "Grandmother," she exclaimed, embracing the dowager duchess. "How wonderful to see you again."

"Slow down, love," Tristan drawled, following his exuberant wife into the drawing room. "It has only been a few days since Grandmother left London." He bent down, gently kissing the dowager duchess on the cheek.

"I have missed her company very much," Caroline retorted. She turned expectantly toward Alyssa, addressing her remarks directly to her. "We ran into Morgan last night at Lady Harrowby's ball, and he told us the most shocking tale."

"Did he now?" Alyssa replied sweetly, bracing herself for what was to come.

"Yes," Caroline continued, faltering a bit under the

dark warning scowl Tristan was casting in her direction. "He told us he was married. To you, Miss Carrington." She said the last sentence in a voice of total disbelief.

"Why else would I be here at Ramsgate Castle, Caroline?" Alyssa replied.

Fresh amazement swam in Caroline's eyes and she looked to her husband for support.

"My hearty congratulations, Alyssa," Tristan said smoothly, breaking the heavy tension. "I always knew my brother had innate good taste. You will make a splendid duchess." He reached down to embrace Alyssa, but stopped short when he saw her swollen belly.

Alyssa met his eyes steadily, almost daring him to make a comment. Tris smiled broadly at her, and then winked mischievously. "Well done, my dear," he whispered in her ear.

Alyssa flushed, but returned his smile, greatly relieved at his ready acceptance.

"Aren't you going to congratulate the new duchess, Caroline?" the dowager duchess asked in a brisk tone.

"Of course," Caroline hastily agreed, rushing over to Alyssa. Her jaw dropped open as she beheld Alyssa's pregnant condition, but she wisely made no comment. Briefly she hugged Alyssa and then scurried back to Tristan's side.

Priscilla embraced Alyssa also. "I wish you great happiness," she said, taking Alyssa's hand and bending to kiss her cheek. It was unclear from Priscilla's expression what she thought of Alyssa's impending motherhood.

After everyone was seated, the dowager duchess rang for Burke to bring more tea.

Alyssa racked her brain for a subject to break the awkward silence. "Tell me, Caroline," she inquired pleasantly, "how is your friend Mr. Brummell faring these days?"

"Not well, I am sorry to report," Caroline answered, grateful for the opportunity to make amends for her earlier rudeness. "I am afraid Beau was involved in a perfectly dreadful incident with the regent this past July."

"Really?"

"Yes," Caroline said, perking up immediately. "Beau and several of his cohorts, Lord Alvanley, Sir Henry Mildmay, and Henry Pierrepoint, I believe, all won a great deal of money gambling at Waitier's. They decided to celebrate their good fortune by giving a ball at the Argyle Rooms. The regent was no longer on speaking terms with either Beau or Mildmay, but the four dandies decided it would be bad form not to invite the regent." Caroline paused a moment to catch her breath before continuing with her narrative.

"When the regent arrived, the four hosts were naturally standing in the front of the room, receiving their guests. The regent greeted only Alvanley and Pierrepoint, deliberately ignoring the other two."

"Oh my," interjected Mrs. Glyndon.

"Well, that is when Beau sprang into action," Caroline stated dramatically. " 'Alvanley,' cried Beau, in a clear, loud voice. 'Who is your fat friend?' "

Mrs. Glyndon gasped in horror. "Did he actually call the regent fat?"

"He most certainly did," Caroline confirmed. "Truthfully, there could be nothing else said that would have infuriated the regent more. His vanity is so easily wounded, and he is particularly sensitive about his bulk."

"We have certainly heard enough about Brummell and his endless quarrels with the regent, Caroline," Priscilla said.

The dowager duchess nodded her head in agreement. "Why didn't Morgan come with you today, Tristan? Did he tell you when he would be returning to Ramsgate?"

"I expect Morgan to arrive by the end of the day," Tristan replied. "He was meeting with our architect, Mr. Walsh, sometime this morning. After that, I believe, his business will be concluded. Oh, by the way, he sent this message for you, Alyssa." Tristan reached inside his coat pocket and handed Alyssa an envelope.

"Thank you, Tristan."

"If you ladies will excuse us, Caroline and I need to clean up after our dusty ride." Tristan stood and stretched his long legs. "Burke will show you to your room, Priscilla, whenever you wish. We shall see you all later this evening. Come along, my dear."

After they had gone, Mrs. Glyndon and Priscilla also left. Alyssa sat alone with the dowager duchess, rubbing her fingers along the edge of the letter Tristan had given her.

"Go ahead and open it," the dowager duchess admonished, making no comment as Alyssa quickly scanned the note.

"Morgan writes he will return to the castle as soon as his business is concluded."

"That is all?"

"Yes. Oh, and he did inquire as to my health," Alyssa replied bleakly. "Why do you think he went to Lady Harrowby's ball last night?"

"I really don't know, but I'm sure he had a good reason."

"Do you think Madeline Duponce was there?" Alyssa tried to sound casual, but failed miserably.

The dowager duchess sighed heavily.

"As I have stated on more than one occasion, I honestly don't believe Madeline Duponce is Morgan's mistress," the dowager duchess said emphatically, answering Alyssa's unasked question. "But you know the only way you will ever discover the truth, don't you, Alyssa?"

"I must ask him myself," she replied, not forgetting all that she had been taught about marital relationships from the duchess. "Did you ever face such a dilemma?" Alyssa inquired.

The dowager duchess leaned back in her chair thoughtfully. "My husband, Richard, was a very handsome, exciting man. Morgan favors him in looks, but in personality he was very much like Tris, charming and quick-witted. There were numerous women in society, some who even claimed to be my friends, who chased after Richard. He never indulged in any affairs with members of the ton, but there was an incident with an opera singer."

"What did you do?"

The dowager duchess gave a small laugh. "I cried a lot at first. And then I got angry. Very angry. I confronted Richard, demanding that he give up his ladybird. A rather foolish and naive move on my part. It was then, as it is now, an acceptable practice for married men to keep mistresses. And certainly not a wife's prerogative to object. Some wives, I've discovered, are actually grateful to have their husbands' attention focused elsewhere."

"What happened?"

"Richard left. He moved into our London town house and informed me I was not allowed to visit unless invited. Eventually he came back. Bringing lots of gifts and expensive jewelry. I was still hurting, and yet I felt glad he returned. That was the only time he strayed in thirty-five years of marriage."

"You must have loved him very much," Alyssa whispered.

"I did. I do." The dowager duchess shrugged her shoulders and wiped the dampness from her eyes. "I still miss him, even though he has been gone almost seven years."

Alyssa reached over and hugged her tightly. It felt good to be the one offering comfort for a change. Just then Burke opened the drawing room doors and announced in a clear voice, "The duke has asked me to inform you he shall be joining you momentarily."

"I will only stay to greet him," the dowager duchess insisted as she saw the look of apprehension cross Alyssa's face.

Morgan hesitated a mere heartbeat before sauntering into the room, his masculine presence dominating his surroundings. He eyed the two women warily, unsure of his reception. "Welcome back, Morgan," the dowager duchess said in a neutral tone. "Tristan was just explaining your business would be concluding this morning. I trust everything was completed to your satisfaction?"

"Yes, Grandmother," he answered, not missing the censure in her tone. She is still angry with me for leaving, he decided, and then dismissed the thought from his mind. He turned his complete attention toward his wife, who sat with her eyes downcast, stubbornly avoiding his gaze.

"Burke informed me Tristan, Caroline, and Priscilla have arrived. I am sorry I was not here to greet them. I had hoped to leave London sooner, but I was delayed at the last minute," Morgan said, his silver-gray eyes never leaving Alyssa's tense frame.

Alyssa took a deep breath and looked up at him. Her stare was direct and unwavering, and he smiled with relief at the reinstatement of her strong will.

The dowager duchess noticed it also, and she interpreted it as her cue to leave them alone. "Now that Tris and Caroline are here, we shall have a small celebration at dinner this evening to formally welcome Alyssa into the family," the dowager duchess announced before shutting the door firmly behind her.

Grinning, the dowager duchess strolled leisurely down the hall, her destination the kitchens at back of the house. She wanted to confer with Cook as soon as possible, so a truly spectacular meal could be prepared for tonight. She had just passed the wide circular staircase in the main entrance hall when a loud commotion halted her steps.

The dowager duchess pivoted around and saw Alyssa racing down the hallway, her skirts billowing out behind her. Morgan appeared almost immediately, shouting angrily at his wife to stop. The dowager duchess reacted quickly, placing herself directly in Morgan's path, giving Alyssa the extra time she needed to make good her escape.

"Now what has gone wrong?" the dowager duchess exclaimed in exasperation, her accusing tone letting the duke know instantly where she placed the blame.

Morgan gritted his teeth in frustration, biting back the scathing retort that sprang to his lips. "How the hell should I know?" he shouted. "We were having a perfectly normal conversation when I foolishly decided to give my new wife a bridal gift. She took one look at it, threw it in my face, and ran from the room in tears."

"What exactly was this gift, Morgan?" the dowager duchess inquired suspiciously.

"An emerald-and-diamond necklace," he explained, the anger still in his voice. "Why?"

"Come back to the drawing room, Morgan," the dowager duchess said coaxingly. "I think it is time we had a little chat."

Chapter Eighteen

Alyssa reached the sanctuary of her bedchamber and slammed the door shut. She paused a moment to calm her breathing, furiously wiping the tears from her face with the back of her hand. Her reaction had been dramatic and overstated, but the minute Morgan pulled the slender velvet box from his breast coat pocket, she felt her control slipping. Her thoughts were consumed by the notion that Morgan's grandfather had brought gifts of jewelry for his wife to make amends for marital infidelity. One brief glance at the sparkling emerald-and-diamond necklace and Alyssa had felt enraged. Without giving any thought to the consequences, she had flung the necklace at Morgan and bolted from the room.

Alyssa knew she had overreacted, but regrets would solve nothing. Rubbing her temples vigorously, she rang for her maid and requested a bath. She needed time to gather her thoughts before confronting the duke again. If only she could soak some sense into her head.

Enjoying her privacy, Alyssa sank into the hot suds. Relaxing in the comforting warmth, she tried to formulate a plausible excuse for her earlier behavior and compose a sincere apology for her bewildered husband. Gliding the soap aimlessly across the water she sighed with dismay. *Will it always be like this between us?* The tension, the distrust, the bitterness. Being a controlled and reasonable woman had always been a point of pride to Alyssa, but as of late, it seemed any contact she had with Morgan sent her emotions into chaos.

Alyssa let out a shaky breath and shifted her position. She attempted to step out from the slippery tub, but quickly realized she could not balance herself without assistance.

Alyssa called out loudly for Janet, unsure if the maid could hear her cries for help. Alyssa folded her arms over her chest to ward off the chill and waited as the water grew colder. She yelled again, tossing her head back in frustration when her cries went unanswered.

The duke walked slowly to his bedchamber after a very frank and enlightening conversation with his grandmother and heard Alyssa's cry for help. He entered her rooms and discovered his wife reclining in her bathwater.

"Oh, Janet, thank goodness you've come," Alyssa exclaimed as she heard the door open. She gave a small laugh. "I need your assistance. I'm afraid my considerable size makes it impossible to get out of this tub. I am convinced I shall turn into a wrinkled prune if I don't leave this water soon."

Morgan smiled at her predicament and strode over to the tub. Kneeling behind it, out of Alyssa's field of vision, he reached over her shoulder and grabbed the sponge floating lazily in the lavender-scented water.

Alyssa reacted sharply when she saw Morgan's masculine arm dip into the water, and tried to twist around to view him, but the tub was too narrow. "I've already finished with my bath," she whispered brokenly as Morgan brought the sponge up and began to gently wash her.

He ignored her protest and continued with his explorations. The sponge became an erotic, torturous tool as it softly caressed her shoulders and breasts and then disappeared into the murky water to her touch her calves and the insides of her thighs. Alyssa shivered in response, the cooling water and his tender hands awakening her dormant longings.

"You're getting cold," Morgan breathed into her ear. He stood up and lifted her out of the tub, water cascading down her glistening skin. Carefully he wrapped her in a warm towel.

Alyssa stared at him mutely, stubbornly resisting the impulse to throw her arms around his neck. Tenderly Morgan reached out to her and began to dry her damp body. When he reached her swelled belly, she turned suddenly away from him, but not before he caught the look of alarm that crossed her face.

"Alyssa, are you all right? Are you in any pain?"

"No, no, I'm fine. It's just that I . . . I understand all too well the aversion you have for my bulky shape," she whispered, shielding herself from his view.

"My God," Morgan swore. "Is that what you think?" He turned Alyssa around toward him and, cupping her face between his large hands, drew her face close to his. Their lips met tenderly in a kiss filled with loneliness and longing. "I think you are a very beautiful woman. So warm, so passionate, so giving. I have avoided intimate contact because I did not trust myself to contain my desire."

"You've done an excellent job of remaining celibate so far," she whispered. "We haven't even consummated our marriage."

"Forgive me," he said. He leaned over and brushed

back the hair from her neck with his fingers, languorously kissing her neck and throat. "I never meant to neglect you, love. I didn't know until Grandmother informed me it would be safe for you and the babe if I bedded you."

"Why didn't you ask me?" she demanded as his lips moved lower down her throat.

"I didn't think you would know the answer." Morgan sighed. "It is all right, isn't it?"

"Oh, yes," she encouraged him. Morgan raised his head, and their eyes locked. He touched her cheek with his fingertips, his eyes brilliant with desire and tenderness. Morgan lifted Alyssa into his arms and swiftly carried her to the bed.

The air bristled with the excitement sparking between them as their hunger for each other, so long denied, took control. Morgan loomed over her as she stretched back on the bed, his mouth covering hers searingly, his tongue probing her sweetness. Alyssa felt the familiar ache building as his hands stroked her breasts, and his fingers lightly teased her nipples. Her breasts felt full and eager, and she arched her back against his warm touch.

Her towel fell open, and she lay before him, naked. She looked flushed and alluring. Morgan's strong hands delicately stroked her hips, and she shuddered as she felt his rigid member pressing against her. Her hands moved across the wide expanse of his chest, dropping lower down his taut body, and she quickly undid the buttons of his breeches. Boldly she reached inside his pants, her fingers enfolding his manhood, which was already swollen and hard.

Her touch was like fire. Morgan groaned loudly as Alyssa continued to stroke him, her fingers feather light as she traced along his length. His member grew even larger under her loving attention, and Morgan thrust hypnotically.

Overwhelming desire consumed him, and Morgan almost choked himself in his haste to untie the knot of his cravat.

"Here, let me help you," Alyssa said with a small laugh. She knelt up on the bed and removed his coat and shirt, pausing a moment to run her fingers through the warm pelt of dark hair on his chest. Sensuously she rubbed herself against his massive chest, her swollen breasts and rigid nipples aching with desire.

"Morgan?"

"Yes, love." His voice cracked slightly.

"How the hell are we going to get your damn boots off?" she whispered playfully in his ear. Laughing, Morgan wrapped his arms around her waist and pulled her tightly against his hard body, capturing her mouth in a fierce kiss. Leaving her breathless, he sat on the edge of the bed, quickly removing his boots, breeches, and underthings.

Naked, he joined her on the bed, his handsome features clearly betraying his ravenous hunger. Morgan kissed her lightly along the cheek, throat, and shoulders, progressing down to the luscious swell of her full breasts. Her breathing was ragged, and Alyssa could hear the sound of her own heart beating wildly in her ears as his head dipped lower, his warm breath grazing the softness of her inner thighs.

Gently his fingers parted her thighs, and his tongue curled across the sensitive bud of her desire. She quivered at his touch, her hips moving restlessly as the ecstasy built, consuming her with excitement.

"Oh, Morgan," she whispered, reveling in the powerful surge of desire his wondrous touch ignited.

She rolled her hips forward, the torrent of sensations breaking within her as his tongue laved her moist, aching flesh.

He rose up on his elbows, wrapping his arms

around her, his thighs insistently pushing her legs apart. He eased himself inside her warmth and moistness. Her eyes widened and she gasped. "Morgan," she said in a strained voice.

"Am I hurting you?" Morgan asked with concern.

"No . . . no. You're just so large."

He groaned at her candid remark and felt his arousal grow. "You do it then, love," he whispered in her ear.

She looked up into his face, intoxicated by his silver-gray eyes and the barely contained desire within them. Tentatively her legs rose up and clasped around his waist. Slowly she thrust herself up upon his swollen manhood.

"You are remarkable," Morgan managed to get out.

Gradually she built up the rhythm with long, lazy strokes that left them both breathless at the sweet torment. With each penetration, Morgan felt himself slipping further and further out of control as he drove himself deep inside her.

His hand slid down between them, delving into the warm, moist curls until he found her, and he skillfully brought her to a second climax as he reached his own release.

Morgan loomed above her, his breath choppy, wanting to hold her close, but not wanting to burden her with his weight. His manhood was still swollen, nestled inside her body.

He gazed affectionately down at Alyssa. Her eyes were closed, her lips slightly parted, her breathing soft. She looked so peaceful, so contented. He shifted his weight off her and rolled onto his back pulling her up against his side.

She curled up around him, swinging her arm across his chest and wrapping one leg over his thigh. Morgan reached over and pulled up the satin coverlet to keep them warm. He heard her deep sigh and felt terribly arrogant at her obvious satisfaction.

And then her calm, clear voice broke the silence. "Is Madeline Duponce your mistress, Morgan?"

Alyssa immediately felt the change in his body as he stiffened in shock. His hand squeezed her arm tightly as though he were fighting to remain calm.

"Grandmother explained about my grandfather's opera singer," he answered, ignoring her question entirely. "And your violent distaste for expensive jewelry."

She cleared her throat nervously. "Yes, well, I am sorry about the necklace," she said. "I do realize I over-reacted. But I still want to know about Madeline Duponce."

"No," he stated in a flat tone.

She pulled out of his arms, sitting upright so she could view his expression. "No." she repeated, her voice rising. "No, you will not tell me, or no, she is not your mistress?"

"The latter," Morgan drawled.

"Oh," Alyssa responded, lowering her voice considerably. She waited a moment and then once again leaned back in her husband's arms. He welcomed her eagerly.

"Was she ever? Your mistress, I mean," Alyssa pressed on.

He looked up at the rose-colored silk bed trimmings.

"Madeline Duponce is not at present, nor has she ever been, my mistress. I have never bedded the woman; in fact, I have never even kissed her. Truth be told, I don't even like her very much. I have not kept a mistress for quite a long time. The last woman I approached with the notion gave me a rather severe dressing down and told me she never wanted to see me again."

Alyssa winced at the memory of that encounter.

"She sounds like a very intelligent woman," Alyssa ventured lightly.

"In the past I always greatly admired her intellect. As of late, I am not as certain of her capacity for rational thought and behavior," Morgan replied.

"Why did you buy me that necklace?"

"Fool that I am, I thought my bride would appreciate a wedding gift," he said in a sour tone.

"It was lovely," Alyssa whispered, genuinely sorry for her earlier actions.

"How could you tell?" he commented wryly. "You hurled it at me so quickly, I doubt you had time to see it."

"But it flashed so brilliantly in the sunlight," she quipped. "It must be magnificent. And knowing you, it is probably very expensive."

"It was," Morgan said with an exaggerated sigh. "Now I don't know what I shall do with it."

Alyssa punched him on the chest playfully. "You shall give that lovely necklace to your wife, sir."

Morgan grabbed her arms and lifted her up to his face, their noses touching. She saw the flash of humor in his eyes, and then the mocking scowl. "Pray tell, my love, just what exactly has my wife done to deserve such a rich prize?"

Alyssa forced herself to look contrite. "I suppose, my husband, I shall have to earn my reward," she remarked, placing a hungry, demanding kiss on his lips. Morgan laughed, savoring the feel of her lips and tongue, his passions beginning to stir again.

"If you continue kissing me, my dear," he teased, "I will have to purchase more than a mere necklace for you."

Alyssa smiled provocatively at him, rubbing her breasts tantalizingly against his chest.

"Sweetheart, wait," he requested, as his manhood stiffened. "I don't want to start something we cannot properly finish. Are you sure this is all right?"

"It is very all right, Morgan," she whispered.

"We shall be late for dinner," he protested half-heartedly. "Grandmother is planning a special dinner to properly welcome you into the family."

"Since I am the guest of honor, they cannot begin without us," Alyssa reasoned, lowering her head to his stomach.

"It would be most impolite," Morgan agreed in a hoarse voice as Alyssa pressed kisses down his stomach and then on his thighs. "To start without us, I mean."

"Yes, it would be most impolite. The dowager duchess would never be that rude, would she, Morgan?"

"No." Morgan groaned. Alyssa slowly lowered her head between his thighs. He could only tolerate a few minutes of her torture before pulling her up on top of him. "I do believe we shall be very late to dinner, my love," he told her, kissing her hungrily.

"I do hope so, Morgan," she whispered, returning his kisses with equal enthusiasm. "I certainly do hope so."

Caroline paced the floor by the large bay window in her bedchamber, attempting unsuccessfully to contain her distress. Tristan sat in a comfortable chair by the roaring fire, book in hand, casually observing his wife as she marched.

"Sit down, Caroline," he admonished. "I believe you are starting to wear a hole in the carpet."

"I do not find that the least bit amusing, Tristan," she said, her blue eyes flashing. "How can you sit there so calmly? Don't you realize what has happened?"

Tristan slowly lowered his book and stared at her. "I am not sure I understand what you are referring to. Would you care to enlighten me, my dear?"

Caroline threw her arms up in agitation. "For God's

sake, Tristan, stop being so obtuse. You know perfectly well I am referring to Alyssa. Your brother's new wife. The latest Duchess of Gillingham. Who looks as though she is about to birth the new heir to the dukedom at any moment."

"I fail to see how Alyssa's condition directly affects you," he commented dryly.

She narrowed her eyes at him. "Stop toying with me, Tristan. We both know you are next in line to inherit the dukedom. All that has now changed. Morgan has a new wife who will obviously be producing the next heir anytime. I simply cannot believe Morgan has done this to us!"

Tristan snapped the book shut in anger over her last remark. "What are you babbling about, Caroline?"

Caroline hesitated a moment, then continued with her tirade. "Morgan always said he would never again marry. He has formally named you his heir. Even on our wedding day he remarked he fully expected me to carry on the Ashton line and produce the next duke. I always assumed you would eventually inherit the title."

"Obviously your assumptions were incorrect," Tristan said strongly, his voice still laced with anger.

"It is not fair!"

"I had no idea you were such a snob," Tristan said lightly, his face void of emotion. "I fear you have made a grave mistake in your choice of husband, Caroline. If you had your heart set on becoming a duchess, you should have set your sights higher than a mere second son."

His words stopped her dead in her tracks. Caroline glanced over at her husband. She could tell by the very blankness of his expression he was wounded by her thoughtless remarks. Remorseful, she rushed over to Tristan's chair and knelt at his feet.

"Oh, Tris," she whispered, clutching at the sleeve of

his coat. "I did not mean to distress you. Morgan's sudden marriage has been a great shock."

"I am sorry I cannot give you what you so greatly desire, my dear."

Caroline felt the tears gather in her eyes. "No, Tris, I am the one who should apologize. For being such a fool. The title isn't important, truly. Without your love, I honestly don't believe I could survive. Please tell me I am forgiven," she pleaded.

Tristan lifted her into his lap, and she snuggled against his broad chest. "Of course I forgive you, Caroline," he said softly. "I regret you allowed your emotions to become overset. Still, you were gravely mistaken believing you would someday become the Duchess of Gillingham."

"But Morgan said—" she began, but stopped when Tristan glared at her.

"I don't care what Morgan said," he interjected, becoming annoyed again. "Despite what my brother may have led you to believe, I have always known he would once again marry when the time was right. We should wish him joy now that he has finally found the proper woman."

"My goodness, Tris, I cannot believe you don't feel any resentment toward your brother. Morgan gets everything, merely because he is the firstborn son. My father was a younger son and has had to struggle financially for most of his life. I always resented my uncle for inheriting the lion's share of the wealth."

"My situation is entirely different, Caroline. I have substantial properties from both my grandmother and mother, not to mention an allowance and a significant share in a vast majority of Morgan's business ventures."

"Oh," Caroline answered in a small voice. She was completely unaware of their financial situation. Tristan had always been very casual about spending money, and there always seemed to be plenty of it. Who or where it came from was never an issue. "Are you telling me that we are . . . are well off?"

"Extremely," Tristan answered dryly. The muscles in his jaw cramped. "Apparently I have misjudged you, Caroline. You are not really a snob. In truth, you are a fortune hunter."

"Hummph," Caroline huffed with a toss of her blond curls. "Forgive me for being pleased to learn of our financial security."

He gave her a small hug. "I suppose we ought to have discussed this sooner." He kissed her temples soothingly, and she relaxed against him.

"Does this mean we are very rich, Tristan?" Caroline turned her head up, gazing at him with sparkling eyes.

Tristan wrinkled his nose at her. "Perhaps," he responded cagily. "This does not mean, however, you have my permission to start spending money like the regent, Caroline."

Caroline gave a small laugh. "I understand, Tris. It is a great relief knowing we have financial security. When I think of my poor sister Priscilla, I shudder. Lord Ogden's lands were entailed, and since there were no children born from her marriage, Priscilla received nothing from her husband's estate or family. It was dreadful and she was very hurt and angry. Now Priscilla depends solely on my father for her keep, and you know how tightfisted he can be."

"You need never worry about that happening to you, Caroline," Tristan said seriously. "There is more than enough money for you to be well provided for if something ever happened to me."

Caroline felt a lump rise in her throat at the thought of losing Tristan. She didn't know how she would possibly cope. How could she face each morning without her beloved Tris?

"I have been acting like a complete ninny over this

entire incident," she said, her blue eyes darkening with distress.

"I know it must be difficult for you to comprehend my feelings in this matter, but I truly don't resent my brother for being firstborn. Morgan has always been kind and generous. He has watched over and tried to protect me most of my life. In order for me to succeed the title, Morgan must die without issue. Surely you can understand, Caroline, 'tis far too high a price to pay."

"I understand," she said softly, sincerity replacing the distress in her lovely face. "I, too, care for Morgan. I promise I shall work very hard at making Alyssa feel welcome in our family. For Morgan's sake. And yours."

"Thank you. I know Morgan will appreciate your efforts. I suspect their sudden marriage will prove a difficult adjustment for both of them." Tristan patted her hand affectionately. "Do cheer up, Caroline. This baby might be a girl. Then if you and I have a son, he could inherit the title."

Caroline's face lit up at the thought, but she frowned, wondering if Tristan was mocking her. "It wouldn't be disloyal to hope that Alyssa's baby is a girl, would it, Tris?"

"A healthy, normal baby girl?"

"Naturally."

He gave her a heart-melting smile. "I don't see why not. It can be our little secret." Enfolding his young wife in a passionate embrace, Tristan amply demonstrated his forgiveness.

The dowager duchess beamed with delight as she sat in regal splendor at the head of the large mahogany dining table. Morgan sat to her right and Tristan to her left, and seated closely beside them were their respective wives. The dowager occupied the position at the head of the table, and Priscilla sat at the opposite end.

Both couples arrived sheepishly late for dinner, but the dowager duchess was not upset, especially in the case of Morgan and Alyssa. Morgan seemed far more relaxed than he had been in months, and Alyssa fairly glowed, the sparkle in her deep green eyes as brilliant as the stunning emerald-and-diamond necklace she proudly wore around her neck. As always, Tris and Caroline mainly had eyes for each other, but the dowager was pleased to note Caroline's subtle attempt to compensate Alyssa for her rude behavior earlier. Time and again, Caroline addressed her comments and questions to Alyssa, deliberately steering the conversation toward topics that would specifically include Alyssa's participation.

Yes, the dowager duchess was very pleased indeed with her two handsome grandsons and their lovely wives. Ceremonially, she lifted her wineglass, and pushing back her chair noisily, rose to her feet.

"Children," she said in a firm voice. "I should like to propose a toast." She waited while everyone stood up, glasses in hand. "To the new Duchess of Gillingham. And the duke. Long life, good health, and great happiness."

"To the duke and his bride," Priscilla said merrily.

"Hear, hear," Tristan chimed in loudly, drinking down his wine.

"And to my beloved Tristan and dear Caroline," the dowager duchess continued. "A lifetime of love and happiness."

"Tris and Caroline," Morgan echoed with a smile, his goblet raised high. "And to you, Grandmother. For your endless love, devotion, and above all, great wisdom."

The dowager duchess felt the tears well in her eyes as they all faced her with glasses raised, genuine affection evident in each face. I am truly blessed, she concluded. Pray God it will last for a very long time.

Chapter Nineteen

In the following weeks, Alyssa gradually adjusted to her new role as duchess. Ramsgate Castle was already run with great efficiency under the combined guidance of Burke and Mrs. Keenly, and Alyssa saw no need to intervene when it was obviously unnecessary. The dowager duchess remained at the castle, and both Morgan and Alyssa were happy she elected to stay rather than accept Tristan and Caroline's invitation to return to London with them for the remainder of the season.

Alyssa felt her relationship with Morgan was progressing, even though they were a far cry from achieving the honesty and trust she knew was vital to maintaining a lifelong involvement. Alyssa held her love for Morgan deep within her heart, allowing it to surface on those occasions when circumstances were simply too emotional for it to be contained. Morgan's feelings for her remained a mystery, yet she knew he cared for her, and Alyssa secretly harbored the hope he would someday come to love her.

For now, Alyssa was content to concentrate her efforts on the coming birth of her child. To that end, she sat in the drawing room on this chilly morning in late November, carefully embroidering neat, tiny stitches on a small garment for the baby. Caroline, recently arrived with Tristan the evening before for a short visit, sat with her.

"Your stitches are perfectly uniform," Caroline remarked, gently fingering the small garment. "I doubt I possess the patience to produce such exquisite stitches."

"I share your amazement for my handiwork," Alyssa responded, holding the tiny garment aloft. "Being in confinement produces a sudden interest in the most unusual activities."

Caroline cast a sympathetic gaze at her sister-in-law. "The endless waiting must be maddening."

"It is," Alyssa readily agreed. "The only thing keeping me sane is knowing it will soon be over." She patted her large belly gently. "And it is for a very good cause."

"What good cause?" Morgan inquired casually, entering the drawing room. His eyes immediately rested on Alyssa as if he could tell merely at a glance how his wife was faring this morning. Her color was high, but her face looked fatigued, and he detected faint circles under her eyes. He wondered if she had had difficulty sleeping last night.

"Did you sleep all right?" he asked solicitously.

"Fine," Alyssa lied, deliberately avoiding his eyes.

"You should have called me," Morgan admonished, bending down to kiss his wife on the forehead. He knew she had been lying by the way she scrupulously avoided eye contact with him. "I would have sat with you."

"There was no reason to disturb you," Alyssa stated quietly. She took a deep breath to steady her nerves.

287

Her fingers nimbly pushed the thin needle through the fine fabric as the tension in the room subtly built.

"Caroline, where is your wayward husband this morning?" Morgan inquired, needing to divert the restless energy building inside him. "Tristan expressed an interest in accompanying me to Charter Oaks this afternoon. Lord Edmunds has a champion mare he might be willing to part with if I can tempt him with the right price."

"Tristan is working in the estate room with your secretary, Mr. Cameron," Caroline responded. "I'd be happy to remind him of your afternoon outing." She hurried out of the room before Morgan had a chance to reply, closing the door behind her.

Alyssa rose awkwardly from her chair and stretched out the aching muscles of her back. Morgan appeared instantly at her side and reached down, his strong fingers massaging her lower back. Alyssa groaned in appreciation and arched her spine, the tension in her sore muscles lessening.

"That feels wonderful." She moaned. "I'm not sure why I feel all twisted in knots this morning."

"It is because you didn't get enough rest last night, madam," Morgan scolded. "You should have called me."

"You should have come of your own accord," she whispered.

Morgan sighed heavily, knowing she was right. He should have gone into her bedchamber last night to check on her. The door connecting their bedchambers had been closed last night, and for the past several weeks after Baron Welles, the family physician, firmly instructed Morgan to sleep in his own bed. Morgan understood physical intimacy with his beautiful wife was impossible, but he certainly possessed enough self-discipline to offer the comfort of a strong embrace without becoming a sexual animal.

So why didn't he enter Alyssa's bedchamber last evening when he heard her restlessly tossing and turning in her bed? Because he was a coward, he admitted to himself in disgust. Because somehow, some way, his beautiful, dignified, unique wife had wormed her way solidly through his defenses and into his heart. And he felt completely unequipped to cope with these feelings. Fear of failure caused him to act like any other coward. Morgan kept a reasonable distance.

Alyssa abandoned her embroidery and rose to her feet. She met his eyes, and the distress he saw there propelled him forward. Morgan stretched his arms around Alyssa, pulling her against his chest, her back toward him. Her temple grazed his lips, and he kissed her there gently before bending his head to nuzzle her neck. "I'm sorry," he said breathlessly in her ear, so faintly she was uncertain she understood his words correctly.

She leaned back, enjoying the feel of his strong arms around her. Reaching up she stroked his fingers, clasped together across her swollen belly.

"I love you, Morgan," she confessed quietly.

He tightened his grip on her stomach. "I'm glad."

She knew better than to hope for any other response, but for once it didn't seem to bother her as much.

"Have you made any other plans for today besides fleecing Lord Edmunds?" she inquired casually, breaking the intense emotion crackling between them.

"Ha," Morgan guffawed. "You, madam, are obviously unaware of how truly tightfisted Lord Edmunds can be. 'Tis not merely sound business practice, but a matter of honor besting him in a deal, especially when purchasing an animal from his stables."

"Well if Tristan accompanies you, I pity Lord Edmunds. One of you is bad enough, but the combined strength of two is quite unbeatable. The poor man won't know what's hit him."

Morgan smiled, basking in her praise. "I suppose Tris and I do present a formidable team. Tell me, what are your plans today?"

Alyssa walked over to the long windows and gazed hungrily out at the brilliant autumn sunshine. "First I thought I would start my day with a ride through the south meadow, followed by a brisk walk about the gardens, and spend the remainder of the afternoon shopping in the village."

"I know it has been difficult being so limited in your activities," Morgan began in a condescending voice.

"You do not have the slightest notion of how it has been for me, sir," she interrupted, not liking his tone.

That gave him pause. "You are right, Alyssa," he conceded. "I don't know. But I'd be pleased to take a stroll in the garden with you now, if you feel up to the task." He amended his statement when he saw her face light up. "A short walk. And be sure to dress warmly."

"Naturally," she retorted, ringing for Burke to summon her maid to fetch her woolen cloak and bonnet.

"Oh, and by the way, Baron Welles will be joining us for dinner this evening," Morgan informed Alyssa as he assisted her into her pelisse.

Alyssa's shoulders sagged. "Morgan, is it really necessary for the good doctor to dine with us every other evening?"

"I thought you liked Baron Welles," the duke said, deflecting her question. He prudently decided now was not the appropriate time to inform her he had already made arrangements for the physician to move into Ramsgate Castle a few weeks before the baby was due to arrive.

"I like Baron Welles very much," Alyssa countered. "It does, however, make me rather nervous having a doctor intently studying my every move. I am only having a baby, Morgan. It is not as though I were gravely ill."

"I find Baron Welles's presence has a calming effect on me," Morgan declared. "I know we will all appreciate his assistance when the time comes."

"Yes, yes, of course," Alyssa grudgingly agreed. "I shall tell Cook to prepare the apple tarts the baron so enjoys. Now, may we please go on our walk before you think of some ridiculous reason why we cannot go out today?"

The stabbing pain woke Alyssa from a sound sleep. Groaning loudly she tried sitting up, but another pain struck. Glancing at the ornate porcelain-and-gold clock on the mantel, she noted it was two o'clock. After her invigorating walk with Morgan she had returned to the drawing room. Feeling too tired to make the long climb to her bedchamber, Alyssa stretched out on the couch for a few minutes.

I must have fallen asleep, she reasoned. Firmly gripping the edge of the settee, she managed a sitting position, wondering if Morgan and Tristan had left for Charter Oaks. Another sharp pain hit her, and realization began to dawn. Was it possible? Could the baby be coming?

Alyssa sat silently, fighting the increasing pain and sudden nausea, when Tristan walked in unexpectedly.

"Oh, good, you're awake," he said pleasantly. "Business prevented me from accompanying Morgan this afternoon, and I hoped we could have lunch together. When I came earlier, you were asleep. Gentleman that I am, I decided to battle my hunger and wait for you. I shall tell Burke to have luncheon served immediately. My God, Alyssa, what is wrong?" Tristan's voice became ragged as he saw her pale face and convulsing body.

"It's the baby, Tris," Alyssa ground out when she caught her breath. "I'm having the baby." She clutched her arms around her belly, cradling the pain.

"Now? You are having the baby now?" His eyes widened in shock. "But that is impossible. It is too early."

"I know, Tris," she said, her eyes betraying her fear. "Something must be wrong."

"Nothing is wrong, Alyssa," he replied soothingly, angry at himself for distressing her with his thoughtless remarks. "The baby has simply decided now is the proper time to be born." He rushed over and yanked insistently on the bell cord for Burke. Tristan was excessively relieved when the butler readily answered his call.

"It is the duchess, Burke," Tristan told the butler calmly. "Her labor has started. Kindly fetch my grandmother." Alyssa moaned softly. "At once," Tristan added.

Burke cast a concerned eye toward Alyssa, who sat perched on the edge of the settee, rocking slightly to and fro. "The dowager duchess is out visiting with the vicar this afternoon, my lord."

Tristan ran his fingers nervously through his hair. "That's right. I forgot. Caroline is with her also. All right, then call Mrs. Glyndon." Tristan was of the opinion his grandmother's companion could be a bit flighty at times, but he desperately needed a woman's assistance. Mrs. Glyndon would have to suffice.

"Mrs. Glyndon accompanied the dowager duchess," Burke replied.

Tristan's shoulders slumped. Don't panic, he insisted to himself. Alyssa needs you to remain calm. "Have Mavis sent in here immediately, Burke," Tristan said decisively.

"Mavis and Mrs. Keenly have gone to the village to do the weekly shopping," Burke announced, his downcast eyes betraying his unhappiness with the answer he was forced to give.

"Bloody hell! Are there any goddamn women left in this castle?" Tristan practically shouted at Burke.

"Tristan, for heaven's sake, stop yelling at poor Burke. It is not his fault." Alyssa would have found the whole situation extremely amusing if a rather strong contraction had not gripped her precisely at that moment.

"I am sorry, Burke," Tristan apologized. "Please call Janet." Alyssa's maid was young, but at this point he had little choice. Janet should be able to prepare the bedchamber properly and assist Alyssa with her clothing.

Burke looked miserably at Tristan. "Janet has gone into the village with Mavis and Mrs. Keenly," the butler blurted out.

Tristan was biting his lower lip, trying not to break into nervous laughter. This is utterly ludicrous, he thought. A loud moan from Alyssa sent him into action. His military training came rushing to the forefront, and he barked out his commands.

"Send footmen out immediately with urgent messages for the duke, Baron Welles, the dowager duchess, and Mavis. Instruct everyone to return to the castle at once. I will stay with the duchess until someone arrives."

"Very good, my lord," Burke replied, rushing out to follow Tristan's orders.

Tristan walked back to the settee and looked down confused at Alyssa. "What can I do to help you, Alyssa?" he asked softly.

"I don't know, Tris," she admitted, her breathing shallow. "Perhaps I should go upstairs?"

"Yes, an excellent idea," Tristan quickly responded, pleased they had a plan of action. "Grab on to my arm firmly. I shall help you stand."

Alyssa took a deep breath and, gripping the arm Tristan held out to her, pulled herself upright. He immediately placed his other arm around her waist to steady her and they began to walk slowly across the room together.

"Tris!" Alyssa suddenly called out in alarm. She glanced down at the floor and then up into his eyes. "Something strange is happening." She looked at him with pure terror in her eyes, and he stared in amazement at a small puddle on the Aubusson carpet at her feet.

Alyssa continued gazing at Tristan's face, refusing to look down at the floor again.

"Is it blood?" he finally whispered.

"No . . . no, I don't think so," she answered, trying to rack her memory for some information—any information—about birth. "I think the water sack around the baby has broken."

Tristan took a deep breath. Was this normal? Or was something horribly wrong?

No longer able to stand the suspense, Alyssa cast her frightened eyes downward, crying out in dismay when she saw the rug. "Oh, my God."

"What? What is it, Alyssa?" Tristan yelled frantically. "Is the baby coming?"

"I've ruined the rug," she whined.

"Goddamn it, Alyssa," Tristan yelled. "Don't scare me like that. To hell with the damn rug."

"There is no need to shout, Tris," Alyssa responded, breathing in short spurts as she felt another contraction beginning. "I am standing right next to you."

"Sorry." He held on to her tightly when the contraction gripped her, and then grinned sheepishly. "We are a rather pathetic pair, aren't we?"

Alyssa giggled as the pain eased a bit. "We are indeed, Tris."

"At this rate your child will be born on the staircase," Tristan advised. Without hesitation he scooped Alyssa up into his arms and exited the room.

"Are you sure you can make that long climb, Tris?" Alyssa asked when they stopped at the bottom of the staircase.

"Are you challenging my masculine abilities?" he teased, shifting her expertly in his arms and easily climbing the winding staircase. "Are you feeling any better?" he asked when they reached the second-floor landing.

"Like I could go dancing," she said flippantly just before another sharp pain attacked her. Tristan turned the handle on her bedchamber door, kicking it open with his booted foot.

"You have a very pretty room," Tristan said, trying to distract her from the pain.

"Wait, Tris," Alyssa said when she realized he was about to place her on the bed. "I want to go into Morgan's bedchamber. I want our child to be born in his bed."

"Splendid idea," Tristan agreed, gladly complying with her wishes.

He sat her gingerly on the edge of the mattress and rang for a servant. Dickinson appeared, his eyes widening in horror when he beheld Alyssa clutching the bedpost, breathing noisily.

"Summon two maids to assist the duchess with her clothes and prepare the room," Tristan commanded Morgan's valet.

When the maids arrived, Alyssa was able to give them instructions. Tristan waited outside, restlessly pacing the hallway while the mattress was stripped and clean linens were placed on the bed. With the help of the two maids Alyssa changed into a clean, dry nightgown. One of the maids brushed and braided Alyssa's hair. Propped up with pillows, Alyssa was sitting nervously in the middle of the huge bed when Tristan returned.

"You look infinitely better," he remarked, still concerned about her paleness. He fervently wished Morgan would return.

The two maids remained on the fringes of the bedchamber, acting as chaperons. Tristan knew it was highly improper for him to be in the bedroom with Alyssa, yet he was reluctant to depart.

Alyssa could see his indecision. "Don't leave me, Tris," she pleaded softly, her eyes wide.

"No," he assured her. "I will stay until Morgan arrives."

Time dragged slowly as they waited together, the pains coming at infrequent intervals, some sharp, others not nearly as intense. Tristan rambled on with stories about his childhood and various pranks he and Morgan had pulled as youths. Anything to keep Alyssa's thoughts distracted from the ordeal she was experiencing. She was grateful for his comforting presence, holding tightly to his firm hands when the contractions intensified.

Morgan literally burst into the entrance hall several hours later, having ridden from Charter Oaks in a record two hours' time. He was dusty and sweaty and nearly frantic with worry for Alyssa.

"Where is my wife?" he barked at Burke as the butler tried to assist him out of his greatcoat. Morgan slapped away the butler's hands impatiently and ripped the garment off himself, spewing buttons on the marble floor.

"Where is my wife?" he repeated, his face tensing with worry.

"Upstairs, Your Grace," the butler began, but Morgan did not stay to listen to any additional information. He took the stairs two at a time and had gained the landing before Burke stooped down to pick up the duke's recklessly discarded greatcoat.

Morgan flung open the door to Alyssa's bedchamber, his heart skipping a beat when he saw the empty bed. He bellowed loudly for Burke and then Dickinson as he rushed into the hallway, muttering profanities as he strode.

"Morgan," Tristan called out. "We're in here."

Morgan stopped in the middle of the hallway, turning toward his bedchamber door in total bewilderment.

"Tris?"

"In here, Morgan."

"What the hell are you doing in here?" Morgan shouted, yanking open the door. "And would you please tell me where my wife is?"

"I am right here, Morgan," Alyssa responded from her position in the bed.

He took one look at her pale, tense face and let out the breath he was holding. He strode quickly across the room and drew her into his arms.

"How are you, love?" he whispered, lightly stroking her silky hair. "I came as quickly as I could."

"The baby is coming, Morgan," she blurted, feeling the sobs choke her throat. As he held her tightly in his arms, the control she had been exerting on herself slipped, and she succumbed to her fears. "It is too soon, Morgan," she whispered.

Morgan held her against his broad chest, looking over the top of her head at his brother. "Where is Baron Welles?" Morgan asked, his expression grim.

"Burke sent a footman to summon the good doctor several hours ago. I am sure he will arrive shortly."

Just then Mavis entered the room, clucking and fussing, with Mrs. Keenly on her heels. "Well, my girl, seems as though we have an impatient babe waiting to be born," Mavis said, crossing over to the bed. Alyssa moved back, disengaging herself from Morgan's tight embrace so she could see her old nurse. He allowed it, but his hands still rested comfortingly on Alyssa's shoulders.

"Mavis." Alyssa sighed with relief. "Thank goodness you are here." The older woman smiled reassuringly at her, reaching a gnarled hand to brush away the few loose tendrils of hair on Alyssa's forehead.

"Why is this room so crowded?" Mavis announced in a brisk tone. Burke and Dickinson hovered in the doorway while the maids exchanged glances with Mrs. Keenly, and Tristan's color heightened. The distinct sound of shuffling feet could be heard. "Are you staying?" Mavis addressed her question directly to Morgan.

"Yes," he answered quickly. "I'll clear everyone else out." The room emptied before Morgan had a chance to voice his command. Only Tristan remained.

"Good luck," Tristan said to Alyssa, squeezing her hand in farewell.

"Thank you, Tris," she replied with a small grin. "I am so grateful you were with me today. I could not have managed without your help."

"Send Baron Welles up as soon as he arrives, Tris," Morgan told his brother. With a final smile of encouragement, Tristan left the room.

Alyssa leaned back against the pillows, sighing heavily. Mavis filled a basin with cool water and wet a clean cloth. She walked around to the opposite side of the bed, since Morgan refused to relinquish his position, and wiped Alyssa's face.

"Is the pain very bad?" Mavis asked.

Alyssa chewed her lower lip, her eyes darting to Morgan's tense face. "No," she responded evasively.

"Try to get some rest," Mavis advised. "You'll need your strength later."

Alyssa looked up at the two beloved faces and sighed. How can I possibly rest when I feel like my body is being twisted in a vise grip? she wondered.

"Can't we give her something for the pain?" Morgan questioned Mavis, his eyes alert to the way Alyssa gritted her teeth when the next contraction began.

"No," Mavis answered. "Usually nothing is given to ease the pain of childbirth. Perhaps the doctor will have something, but don't count on it."

"I'll be fine, Morgan," Alyssa contended as the pain faded. "Are you sure you want to stay? I've heard birthing can be a messy sight."

"I want to stay," Morgan insisted in a voice that clearly illustrated his determination.

"I shall be glad of your comforting presence, Morgan," Alyssa whispered gratefully.

Chapter Twenty

Alyssa labored all through the long night. Morgan remained at her side throughout, offering his support and what little comfort he could. He had never felt so helpless in his entire life as he watched her struggling desperately to give birth to their child.

Toward morning Alyssa slept fitfully, and Baron Welles was finally able to convince Morgan to leave her side for a few moments to eat something. Morgan reluctantly agreed, but he refused to leave the room. He sat broodingly at a small table in the corner of the bedchamber eating methodically, not tasting the food, his bleak eyes riveted on the bed where his young wife dozed.

Alyssa's color was gone, her hair damp with perspiration. She had grown progressively weaker, the strong contractions sapping her strength. Baron Welles anxiously touched her brow, alarmed at the warmth he felt. His skilled hands traveled down to Alyssa's abdomen, gently examining her. He gave a deep sigh and closed his eyes.

Mavis stood across from the physician, her lips moving in silent prayer. She was frightened. Alyssa had been laboring for so long with very little progress.

"You have to do something," Mavis whispered to the baron. "She cannot continue like this for much longer."

"I know," the baron reluctantly agreed. "I'll talk to the duke."

Morgan became alert as the physician approached him. "What is wrong?" Morgan demanded before the baron had a chance to speak.

"The child is not in the proper position for birthing," Baron Welles explained. "Often, when this occurs, the baby turns on its own. I was hoping that would happen in this case. It has not."

"What can you do?"

Baron Welles cleared his throat. "Not very much, I am afraid, Morgan. I can try to save one of them." The baron sighed heavily. "You would have to decide which one."

"My wife or my child?" Morgan responded with anger, the pain crushing his heart. "You expect me to choose one over the other?"

"There is another alternative," Mavis insisted, moving closer to the two men. "Tell him."

"I could try turning the baby myself," Baron Welles admitted. "If I can move the infant into the correct position, the duchess might be able to deliver the child."

"Have you ever done this before?" Morgan inquired, grasping the slim hope the doctor offered.

"No," Baron Welles confessed. "I must tell you, Morgan, the risks are great. I could do more harm than good."

Morgan turned his head away, staring blindly into the roaring fire. "Mavis?" he questioned hoarsely.

"It's their only chance, Your Grace," Mavis readily

answered. "You see how weak she has become. If we wait much longer, she will not be able to help at all. You must let the doctor try."

"All right," Morgan agreed, his calm voice masking his inner turmoil.

"You will have to hold her down, Morgan," Baron Welles instructed. The doctor washed his hands in clear, warm water, and nervously pulled back the sheet covering Alyssa's body. At the doctors' nod, Morgan leaned over his sleeping wife and grabbed her wrists. He raised them over her head, anchoring her arms securely. Then he whispered softly to her.

"Alyssa. Sweetheart, can you hear me?"

Alyssa's eyelids fluttered open, her head turning toward the familiar voice. "Morgan," she croaked, licking her dry, parched lips. "Is it over yet? Is our baby here?"

He winced at the weakness in her voice, but would not allow his concern to show on his face. "Almost here, Alyssa," he said in a soothing tone. "The babe needs a bit of help. Try to stay calm, sweetheart. Baron Welles is going to do what he can."

"All right," she answered in a trusting voice. And then the room filled with Alyssa's piercing screams as the baron attempted to move the child.

"Morgan," she screamed, her body writhing in agony, the stabbing pains shooting through her body. "What is he doing to me? Stop him, I beg of you. Please, you must make him stop!"

Baron Welles worked as quickly as he could, trying to ignore Alyssa's agonizing cries. Morgan felt the stinging tears in his eyes as Alyssa continued pleading with him to end her torment. Her beautiful eyes were glazed with pain as she bucked and writhed against the unbearable torture.

Morgan was preparing to yell at the doctor to stop when Baron Welles cried out in triumph. "I think I've done it," he exclaimed. Wiping the beads of perspiration off his brow with his sleeve, he lifted his head.

Alyssa slumped in Morgan's arms, her body limp and lifeless. "Alyssa!" Morgan shouted with fear. Mavis reached out her hand to steady the duke.

"She has only fainted, Your Grace," Mavis declared. "Let her rest a few moments before we revive her."

Alyssa regained consciousness on her own, a strong contraction gripping her exhausted body. "You must try to bear down," Baron Welles instructed. "The babe is in the correct position and should be able to pass through the birth canal."

Alyssa did as she was told, her hands crushing Morgan's as she panted and pushed. Suddenly everything happened very quickly, and with a final strong push the child slipped from Alyssa's body. The room echoed with the indignant cries of a howling infant.

As he listened to the hearty bellows of the tiny babe Morgan knew he had never heard a more beautiful sound in his entire life.

"It's a girl," Baron Welles cried with excitement, carefully severing the cord. He handed the baby into Mavis's waiting arms.

"A girl," Morgan repeated, dumbfounded. He lifted Alyssa into his arms, holding her close against his heart. It was finally over. The baby had been safely delivered. And Alyssa had survived. Morgan offered a silent prayer of thanks for the lives of his wife and daughter.

"I don't believe it," Alyssa murmured weakly. "Is she all right?"

Morgan looked down at his wife, his face splitting in an ear-to-ear grin. "Her voice certainly works very well," he said.

"She is perfect," Mavis pronounced, placing the freshly washed baby in Alyssa's arms.

"Oh my," Alyssa whispered, her voice choking with

emotion as she viewed her daughter for the first time. Morgan gathered them both closely in the circle of his arms, his happiness overflowing.

"She is so very tiny," Morgan remarked, carefully touching the infant's brow.

"You're not disappointed, are you, Morgan?" Alyssa asked worriedly.

Morgan looked down at his wife, shocked. "Disappointed?"

"That she isn't a boy?"

"Good God, no," he replied honestly.

Mavis took the baby out of Alyssa's arms and thrust the infant toward Morgan. "Here," Mavis said, handing the duke his daughter. "You look after her for a moment while I take care of Lady Alyssa."

Morgan gingerly accepted the baby, rigidly cradling her in his arms. "Is this right?" Morgan questioned Baron Welles, his uncertainty clearly visible on his face.

"Fine," the doctor replied with a smile. "Hold her a bit closer to your body, Morgan. And be sure to support her neck and head."

Ever so gently Morgan inched the baby close to his chest. He watched with total amazement as she snuggled contentedly against him and yawned daintily. A loud knocking at the door distracted him, and when he saw both Mavis and Baron Welles were busy attending Alyssa, he barked out loudly, "Come in."

The baby visibly jumped at the sudden, booming noise, but did not cry. Instead she slowly opened her eyes and gazed up inquisitively into her father's handsome face. At that moment, Morgan fell in love with his tiny daughter.

"I'm sorry to intrude," the dowager duchess began hesitantly, entering the room. "We have been so worried, and I thought I heard . . . oh, Morgan!" The dowager duchess stared in wonder at her grandson as he proudly held his child.

"Grandmother, come in," Morgan called. "You too, Tris, Caroline. There is someone I want you all to meet."

Morgan swaggered up to the trio to display the baby.

"So precious," the dowager duchess cooed. She reached out and softly stroked the infant's head.

"Well, what is it, Morgan?" Tristan asked. "A boy or a girl?"

"A girl, of course. Can't you tell, Tris?" Morgan responded with a superior air.

Caroline and Tristan exchanged a secretive smile. "Congratulations, Morgan," Caroline said softly. "How is Alyssa?"

"Resting comfortably." An exhilarated Baron Welles joined the group. "She is exhausted from the ordeal, but not in any danger. There is no longer any sign of fever, thank God, but I shall keep a close watch on her for the next few days."

"Let me hold the baby, Morgan," the dowager duchess commanded. Reluctantly Morgan handed over the infant, and he was very pleased to note she fussed when leaving her father's arms.

"She is a perfect angel," the dowager duchess announced. "I do believe she has your chin, Morgan. And my nose. Yes, definitely my nose."

"She is splendid, Morgan," Tristan piped in. "You must go downstairs and announce the good news to the staff, Morgan. Burke and Mrs. Keenly have been frantic with worry all night."

Morgan nodded in agreement and went over to the bed to see Alyssa. He bent down and kissed her gently on the brow. "Try to get some rest, love," he whispered. "I'll come back to see you later."

The dowager duchess seated herself in a comfortable chair near the fire, declining the invitation to accompany the others. She preferred the company of her great-granddaughter. She gazed at the babe with true adoration, refusing to place the infant in her cradle until she had been properly rocked to sleep. Only then did she quit the room.

"Have you thought about a name for our little girl yet?" Morgan asked Alyssa. He removed the heavy tray with the remains of her evening meal from the bed and sat on the coverlet.

"I was thinking we could call her Katherine," Alyssa responded, glancing toward the cradle where the infant lay sleeping peacefully.

"Katherine," Morgan said with a grin. "You know of course that is Grandmother's given name."

"Yes. Do you think she will be pleased?"

"She will be insufferable," Morgan exclaimed. "You see how she already dotes on the infant. I can't imagine how much more she will spoil the child if she is her namesake."

"Good. I like the notion of someone spoiling my daughter," Alyssa stated firmly. "We shall name her Katherine. And her second name will be Eleanor, for my mother."

And thus on a bright chilly morning in December, three weeks after her birth, Katherine Eleanor Ashton was christened in the private chapel at Ramsgate Castle. Tristan and Caroline proudly stood as godparents for the infant. The dowager duchess insisted on holding her namesake for the majority of the brief ceremony. Alyssa was forced to laugh at Morgan when he grumbled about it later that evening.

"You hover over Katherine so protectively, Morgan." Alyssa laughed softly as she nursed her daughter. "How ever will you manage when she is a grown woman, with suitors coming to call?"

"Good God," Morgan swore, blanching visibly at the notion. "Eager young bucks calling on our daughter. Do you want to give me premature gray hair?"

Alyssa laughed louder, enjoying Morgan's obvious distress. "Gives you a different perspective on women now, doesn't it, Your Grace?"

"Yes, I suppose it does," he agreed with a spectacular smile. Morgan watched his wife as she suckled the baby, his controlled expression revealing none of the emotional turmoil within.

The love he felt for Alyssa had grown over the weeks; at times the emotion nearly overpowered him. But he was frustrated. He had finally given his heart boldly away, yet poised on the verge of revealing his love, he felt simultaneously afraid and exultant. Morgan knew Alyssa believed he married her for the sake of their child. Since he obviously doted on his new daughter, he feared Alyssa would misinterpret his declaration of love. Morgan wanted no misunderstanding of the depth and intensity of the love he felt for his wife. And so he waited, fearful and apprehensive, for the appropriate moment to tell her.

"Have you been making any progress with the Christmas celebrations?" Morgan asked, expertly taking the half-sleeping baby from Alyssa's arms. He propped his daughter up on his shoulder and paced quietly as she digested her meal.

Alyssa observed them with amazement. Her tall, arrogant, powerfully built, impeccably groomed duke was gently stroking the infant's back. Katherine let out a very loud belch, and her parents smiled indulgently. Morgan transferred the baby to the elegant cradle, tucking the blankets carefully around her tiny form. Then he turned to his wife.

Alyssa had not yet fastened her gown, and he clearly saw the creamy round globes of her lovely breasts. He felt himself harden almost immediately, and clasped his hands together tightly in front of him, trying to get his randy behavior under control.

Morgan cleared his throat and asked again about the Christmas festivities.

"Your grandmother has been explaining some of the various traditions of the castle to me, and she is assisting with all the arrangements," Alyssa replied.

"Good. You are not overworking yourself, are you, Alyssa? Baron Welles has told me it will take several weeks before you are fully recovered from Katherine's birth."

"I am making an excellent recovery. Baron Welles remarked upon it this morning, as a matter of fact. He also said I will be perfectly fine in just a few short weeks," she said pointedly.

It took Morgan a few moments to absorb the meaning of her statement, and he delighted at Alyssa's fierce blush when he leered at her.

"Perhaps short weeks for Baron Welles, my dear," Morgan whispered with fierce passion, "but a lifetime for me."

He reached out suddenly, pulling her intimately against him. Morgan lowered his head to claim her lips with his own. His kiss was tender and giving, but Alyssa could feel the control he was exerting over himself.

The familiar quickening excitement claimed Alyssa as she touched her tongue to his and locked her arms around his neck. Provocatively, she moved her body against his, and she heard him groan loudly as his hands slid caressingly down her waist and hips.

"If you continue kissing me with such fervor, I shall disregard all the good doctor's advice," Morgan said hoarsely.

"I'm sorry," Alyssa replied in a husky voice, her eyes smiling when they met his.

"I doubt that, madam" Morgan responded dryly. He

disengaged himself from their embrace and kissed her chastely on the forehead.

"An overly large stack of boring correspondence awaits me in my study," Morgan said, effectively shifting the subject. "I shall join you for tea later this afternoon, if you promise to rest now."

"All right, Morgan," Alyssa answered, surprising her husband with her ready compliance. She grinned wickedly at him. "After all, you have just amply demonstrated it is in my own best interest if I have a rapid recovery."

The duke's infectious laughter could be heard echoing down the hall as he left his wife's bedchamber.

Christmas day dawned bright and fair. After morning services, held in the chapel at Ramsgate Castle and attended by both the family and members of the staff, everyone gathered together in the ballroom. Alyssa, under the dowager duchess's guidance, had turned the room into a Christmas fair to which all the servants and tenant families were invited.

The ballroom was festively decorated with seasonal greenery and brightly colored ribbons, and lit with numerous red, green, and white candles. There were lots of gaily wrapped presents piled up on the large table, and several sideboards were filled with delectable food. There was a wide variety of culinary delights to suit all tastes, but the undisputed centerpiece of the table was an elaborate Yorkshire Christmas pie. Mrs. Keenly explained proudly to Alyssa how she had personally supervised the creation of this masterpiece, the recipe for which required stuffing a pigeon inside a partridge, the partridge inside a chicken, the chicken inside a goose, and finally the goose inside a turkey. It was all then baked in a pastry case made from a bushel of flour and ten pounds of butter.

Mrs. Keenly was also very pleased with the dessert

table that boasted a pyramid of glass salvers piled with containers of jellies, ice creams, custards, syllabubs, and candied fruits, various tarts, sweetmeats, pies, and cakes.

After everyone had eaten their fill, the gifts were distributed by the family members. Alyssa stood next to Morgan, along with Caroline, Tristan, and the dowager duchess, as they handed out small gifts to everyone attending the party. The good feelings and laughter echoed through the enormous room as the musicians played and the dancing began.

Morgan discreetly signaled this was the family's cue to leave so the celebration could continue without them. Alyssa climbed the wide circular staircase with Caroline, and they whispered together, confirming the safe delivery of Morgan's Christmas present. Alyssa happily anticipated the yuletide supper and intimate family gift exchange planned for later in the evening.

"I do believe this is the most enjoyable Christmas I have ever spent," Caroline exclaimed. "I often heard of the elaborate Christmas celebrations given at Ramsgate Castle, but never before attended one."

Alyssa nodded her head in agreement. "It is quite a remarkable day. Grandmother said the German custom of giving Christmas gifts was first introduced and popularized by her friend, the Duchess of York."

Caroline and Alyssa parted in the hallway, and Alyssa entered her bedchamber, Morgan on her heels. She instructed Mavis, who was sitting with the baby, to go down to the ballroom and join in the celebration. Alyssa assumed Mavis's vacated chair, rocking her daughter's cradle contently, her green eyes never leaving the baby's perfect cherubic features. It was uncanny how much the child resembled Morgan, from her silver-gray eyes to her strong little chin. Alyssa was debating whether to wake the infant to feed her, when

Morgan reached down and scooped up his sleeping daughter.

"I must admit, Alyssa," he stated in a firm voice, "our child grows more beautiful with each passing day."

"Naturally that is your opinion, Morgan." Alyssa laughed. "Katherine looks exactly like you."

She took the now squirming infant from her father and settled back in a comfortable chair in front of the roaring fire to nurse her. The room was soon filled with the noisy sounds of the baby as she gulped down her meal.

"She isn't very dainty, is she?" Morgan said with a smile.

"She does have a tendency to rush her meals," Alyssa agreed.

After the baby burped, Alyssa handed her back to Morgan. Katherine's nurse was enjoying the Christmas festivities with the rest of the staff, and Alyssa knew Morgan would not object to caring for his daughter.

"I need to rest before dinner. Please lay Katherine in the cradle when she falls asleep. I will hear her if she needs me."

Morgan nodded in understanding. "I shall instruct Dickinson to send Janet to help you dress for dinner later this evening."

Alyssa stared back uncertainly at her reflection in the long, narrow mirror. She was pleased to note her figure had returned to its normal slimness, except for a fullness in her breasts that served to emphasize her womanly charms. Her gown, specially made in London for this evening, was a far more elaborate style than she normally wore. The rich white Chinese crepe was smooth and flat in the skirt front, with a pleated back extending to a short train. The skirt itself had five ruffles of eyelet, mounted with embroidered bands of rich gold. The bodice of the dress was also embroidered in gold, gathered under the bust, with small set-in short sleeves, slightly off the shoulder, that showed a lovely expanse of smooth white skin. Long white kid gloves reaching her elbows, and soft, white, flat-heeled slippers on her feet completed the ensemble.

Frowning, Alyssa stepped back farther from the mirror. In addition to selecting her frilly dress, Janet had spent the past hour creating an ornate hairdo. Alyssa's glorious red hair was brushed sleek, drawn up to the crown of her head, and braided into numerous separate strands which were arranged into standing loops with wire and high-backed combs to hold them erect. Fresh flowers from the castle hothouse were generously intertwined.

"You look magnificent," Janet announced. "His Grace won't be able to keep his eyes off you tonight."

Alyssa forced a small smile. "I don't doubt for a moment the duke will notice me," she said ironically. "Thank you, Janet, for all your hard work."

After the maid left, Alyssa continued staring at herself, trying to decide whether or not she liked her new image. Morgan abruptly entered the room. She drew a deep breath and faced him, hoping for a positive response.

"Good evening," he said, his eyes betraying his startled reaction to her ensemble. "Are you ready to go downstairs?"

"You don't like it," Alyssa said in a disappointed voice.

"What do you mean, I don't like it? The new dress is lovely. You are as beautiful as always, my dear."

"You know, Morgan, I never have liked the way you can lie so readily," Alyssa snapped. She walked to her dressing table and picked up her comb, then hesitated, her arms wavering. What can I possibly do to fix this? she wondered dismally.

"It isn't all that bad," Morgan ventured. She met his eyes in the mirror and gave him a chilling stare. "All right, Alyssa. It looks as if birds are nesting on your head. Satisfied?"

She broke into nervous giggles at his rather accurate description. "Don't just stand there, Morgan," she admonished. "Help me get this stuff off my head."

He complied with good nature, first removing the flowers and then the combs. Alyssa carefully unbraided the various strands, pulling her hair free of the wires. Finally free of all the paraphernalia, she shook her head, tossing her curls.

"That feels infinitely better," she concluded. "I'm not sure how I would have carried all that extra weight on my head throughout the evening."

Morgan took the brush out of her hand and began stroking the luxurious tresses. "This is how I prefer your hair, my dear," he whispered in her ear. He ran his fingers caressingly through her curls, and their eyes met again in the mirror.

The amusement was gone from Morgan's eyes as he gazed at Alyssa's bared shoulders hungrily. He pulled her back against his hard, aroused body, allowing himself to feel the sweet agony, his lips caressing the exposed skin.

"Is there enough time?" Alyssa whispered, a gruff edge to her voice.

"What?" he stammered, sure he had misunderstood her meaning.

She turned around in his arms and faced him. "I asked you if there was enough time," she repeated, raining small kisses down his cheek.

"Are you sure you are well enough?"

Alyssa could feel the tensing of all his muscles as she nuzzled her mouth against his neck. "I do have

this painful ache," she murmured provocatively,
bringing his hand down to the juncture between her
legs. "Right here."

Morgan's eyes met hers, and he laughed with
delight. "You are in luck, madam. I believe I have the
very cure for what ails you."

Chapter Twenty-one

Alyssa reached up and untied the intricate knot of Morgan's cravat, her eyes never leaving his. Her teasing fingers opened the collar of his shirt and slid caressingly through the fine mat of hair on his chest. He groaned loudly, his hands automatically reaching for the hooks at the back of her gown.

Slowly, tantalizingly, they undressed each other, their eyes locked together. When they were both finally naked, Morgan swung Alyssa up in his arms and placed her on the bed. She could feel the cool, smooth silkiness of the satin coverlet against her bare bottom as Morgan settled himself over her body.

"You are so beautiful, my love," he whispered in a husky voice, lowering his head to kiss her.

Alyssa returned his kiss eagerly. She allowed long-dormant sensations to claim her, making her body tingle and yearn for him. His hands slid between her thighs, searching, probing, until they found her inner warmth and moistness. She writhed against his hand as he fondled her, her breath coming in short gasps.

Morgan tried to hold back, wanting to prolong the pleasure for both of them, but Alyssa would not allow it. She reached out and grabbed his rigid manhood, pulling him toward her, opening her legs in sensual invitation. She was so hot, so wet, so on fire; his control snapped. He placed his hands beneath her buttocks and lifted her to receive him. He plunged deep inside her, and she welcomed his entry, locking her legs firmly around his waist and pulling him even deeper into her body.

"Alyssa," he cried out. "You are so incredibly tight, I can barely stand it." He claimed her mouth in a hot kiss, his weight pressing down on her as he thrust fiercely inside.

Alyssa lifted her hips to meet him, her arms around his back, holding him tightly. She was lost in the sensations coursing through her body. When Morgan felt her nearing her release, he could no longer contain his excitement and spilled his seed inside her just as she reached fulfillment.

Afterward they lay together, Morgan gently caressing Alyssa's cheek. He was propped up on one elbow, looking tenderly down at her. His heart swelled with a peace and contentment he had never known before.

"I do love you," Morgan stated in a clear, strong voice.

Alyssa stiffened slightly at his words and then smiled shyly at him. Tears of happiness gathered in her eyes. "I have long suspected you might, but I must confess, 'tis marvelous to hear the words."

"I realize I have been behaving like a perfect idiot, but love is not an emotion I can easily admit." He gazed into her eyes and Alyssa saw the vulnerability and yearning in them.

"Have you loved me for a long time?" she asked, holding his arm tightly.

"Probably," he responded, glad he had finally been

able to admit his true feelings for Alyssa, yet not entirely comfortable with his declaration. Morgan flashed her a brilliant smile and delicately traced the outline of her naked back. "We had best rise and get dressed. I imagine everyone is wondering what has become of us."

Reluctantly they arose from the bed, and after much tender kissing and caressing, started to get dressed. Morgan had a much easier task of fastening Alyssa's gown than she did of tying his neckcloth. After several false starts, Morgan finally pronounced them presentable, although he hoped Dickinson wouldn't see him. His stodgy valet would be mortified if he saw the shambles the duke's cravat was in.

Alyssa and Morgan stood together holding hands for a moment outside the drawing room doors. She squeezed his hand affectionately. As the duke swung open the door, she whispered softly, "I love you, Morgan."

Beaming, they entered the room, their slightly disheveled appearance and thoroughly happy expressions bringing a smile of glee to the dowager duchess's face.

Presents were exchanged, and Morgan cast his wife a puzzled glance when he held aloft her gift of a leather bridle.

"Thank you, my dear," he said politely. Alyssa laughed at his confusion.

"There is a second part to your gift, Morgan," she teased. "But I am afraid the missing piece is hardly fit company for the drawing room. You will find her tethered in the stables."

"And might I add, big brother, Lord Edmunds informed me your wife drives an even harder bargain than you do," Tris exclaimed with a laugh.

"You bought the mare from Lord Edmunds?" Morgan exclaimed when he realized what they were laughing about. "The horse I was attempting to purchase the day Katherine was born?"

"The very same." Alyssa giggled, delighted with her surprise. "Tris told me how much you admired the animal, and since I was responsible for dragging you away from Charter Oaks before you completed the transaction, I felt it was the very least I could do. The gift is also from your daughter."

"Thank you, Alyssa," Morgan said, crossing the room to embrace his wife. " 'Tis a wonderful present. And now you must open my gift." He handed Alyssa a small, gaily wrapped box.

Excited, she tore open the packaging, stiffening slightly when she saw the jewel box. Hesitantly, she lifted the lid, gasping loudly as she beheld the box's contents: teardrop shaped emerald-and-diamond earrings matching her bridal necklace rested on a puffy satin lining, surrounded by a noble tiara of diamonds. Centered in the crown of the tiara shone the largest emerald Alyssa had ever seen.

"My goodness," Caroline exclaimed, her eyes widening when she saw the magnificent gems. "Those jewels are fit for a queen, Alyssa."

"Do you like it, sweetheart?" Morgan inquired, an anxious note in his voice.

"I am truly overwhelmed," Alyssa responded. "I have never before seen anything like these jewels."

"Very impressive," Tristan agreed. Reaching behind the settee, Tristan picked up a large, unwrapped box sporting a lopsided red bow. "Your turn, Caroline," he said, handing his wife the package.

Absently Caroline began untying the ribbon, her eyes still riveted to the sparkling gems Alyssa held so delicately in her hands. Inside Caroline's box was another box, and inside that a third box. Caroline smiled indulgently at Tris, wondering what sort of a prank he was playing on her. Finally she pulled out a jewelry case not unlike Alyssa's. With trembling hands she opened the case, giving a short shriek of excitement as she saw the contents.

"Why, it is just like mine," Alyssa announced when Caroline lifted her tiara out of the box. "Except there are sapphires in place of the emeralds."

Caroline swallowed hard, the tears gathering in her eyes. Tris sat on the arm of the settee and leaned over to kiss his wife.

"Still think you married the wrong brother?" he teased, nibbling on her ear.

"Oh, Tristan," she said in a tearful voice. "Whatever shall I do with you?"

Tris folded his arms across his chest. "Why, you must give me my present," he demanded.

"That I will do when we are alone," Caroline whispered, handing him a short, square box. He tore through the wrappings like a child and was obviously very pleased with the rare jade horse statue inside.

"Come, let's adjourn to the dinner table," the dowager duchess requested. She lovingly fingered the delicate gold locket around her neck, her Christmas gift from Morgan and Alyssa. Inside the locket was a small painted likeness of Katherine. "I instructed Burke to set the food on the sideboard so we may serve ourselves. I wanted the servants to continue their celebration in the ballroom."

As they feasted on oyster and lobster pies, roast beef with piccadilly sauce, rissole potatoes, and Brussels sprouts with walnuts, the conversation centered on the events of the day. Alyssa was serving the plum pudding with brandied hard sauce when Tristan mentioned the annual winter ball held at Ramsgate Castle.

"Will you host the winter ball at the castle this year?" Tristan asked his brother.

Morgan leaned back in his chair. "I hadn't really

given it much thought, Tris." He stroked his chin in a reflective manner. "It would provide an excellent opportunity to introduce Alyssa into society, but I'm not certain she is up to the task."

"I am feeling perfectly fit, Morgan," Alyssa protested, giving him a saucy wink. He grinned back at her.

"Oh, do say you will consider it, Alyssa," Caroline chimed in. She sat up importantly in her chair. "You know Tristan proposed to me at last year's winter ball."

"Must have indulged in too much wine," Tristan grimaced mockingly. "Ouch," he exclaimed, as Caroline punched his arm. "That hurt!"

"Serves you right for teasing Caroline," the dowager duchess stated firmly. "It would be delightful having the ball this season. But only if you feel well enough, Alyssa. Caroline and I will naturally offer whatever assistance you need."

"I really am fine," Alyssa insisted, a bit daunted by the prospect of meeting so many strange people. She looked over at Morgan and saw the love in his eyes. Her confidence soared. "I think we should definitely host the ball. I promise to work very hard to ensure it will be a charming affair."

"Good. It is settled," the dowager duchess concluded. "We shall begin compiling the guest list tomorrow afternoon."

The next morning Morgan and his secretary, Jason Cameron, were working on estate business when Burke announced an unexpected visitor.

"Lord Castlereagh," Morgan exclaimed in surprise when the foreign minister entered the room. "I was unaware you were in Portsmouth."

"We are visiting with Lady Castlereagh's family in Southampton," Lord Castlereagh began. "I received some very distressing news this morning and thought it imperative you be informed at once." The foreign minister glanced pointedly at Jason Cameron, and the secretary, understanding his meaning, left the two men alone. "The two agents assigned to follow the Duponces have disappeared."

"Disappeared?" Morgan repeated.

"The operatives failed to report at the prearranged destination. Currently I have agents scouring the countryside, but we are unable to locate them." Lord Castlereagh sighed heavily. "There is more, I am afraid. Recently uncovered evidence suggests a member of your family is connected to the Falcon's activities."

"What!" Morgan shouted, instantly springing to his feet.

Lord Castlereagh rubbed his hands together nervously but continued with his report. "The evidence is quite damning. Perhaps you can explain to me how your brother, a second son and recently resigned army officer, is such a wealthy man?"

"My brother has come by his money honorably," Morgan answered in a chilling tone. "If you collected the proper intelligence on him, you would know the truth. I refuse to tolerate any slurs upon Tristan's character." Morgan paced the room anxiously, his mind racing. "When we first started this entire venture, I was the implicated spy. It is obvious the Falcon has simply shifted the evidence to Tristan."

"The case against your brother is much stronger," Lord Castlereagh insisted. "He has had both access and opportunity to ferret out the information we planted. Money can be a strong motivation to even the most loyal of men."

"You do not know what you are saying," Morgan declared strongly. "I refuse to listen to any more of this nonsense without viewing this so-called evidence myself."

"Unfortunately that is impossible," Lord Castlereagh reported. "The operatives who have vanished were those gathering the evidence. The documents are now missing along with the men."

"Enough!" Morgan shouted, slamming his fist down on the desk. "I have followed your instructions for the past few months with no results. 'Tis high time I took charge. From this point on we do things my way, Lord Castlereagh."

"What exactly do you propose?"

"Our annual winter ball at Ramsgate Castle will take place in a few weeks. I intend to set a trap that will capture the Falcon and end this fiasco once and for all," Morgan declared in a voice filled with determination.

"I shall lend whatever assistance you require," Lord Castlereagh interjected.

"Good. I shall contact you after I have formulated my plans. You will need to provide the juicy bait for our trap. I trust you and Lady Castlereagh will be in attendance that evening?"

"Yes," Lord Castlereagh answered with a small grin. "We will most certainly be at the ball. I have a strong suspicion it will prove to be a most memorable evening."

"How are the arrangements for the ball coming, my dear?" Morgan said to Alyssa when he discovered her hunched over her writing desk later that afternoon.

"I am not entirely sure," Alyssa confessed, holding up several pieces of paper. "I finally decided to work in my bedchamber, away from Grandmother, Caroline, and Mrs. Glyndon. 'Tis nearly impossible trying to concentrate on details while the three of them constantly reminisce about previous triumphs at other balls."

"What are you working on now?" Morgan inquired sympathetically.

"The menu," she answered. "I have given up trying to determine the quantity of food required. I've never fed three hundred people at one time. I shall list the various foods I want served and leave it to Mrs. Keenly to sort out the rest."

"What about the guest list?"

"Which one?" Alyssa asked, shuffling through her papers again. "Grandmother has given me two separate lists. Those who will be issued an invitation to the ball, and those who will also be spending the night." Alyssa handed Morgan a stack of papers.

He read through the lists, making several notations. "Tell Grandmother and Burke to assign the bedchambers. I will instruct Jason to assist Mrs. Glyndon in addressing all the invitations. And put Caroline in charge of the decorations. Anything else?"

Alyssa sighed with relief. "That is an excellent start. I must confess, I never realized it would be so complicated."

"You are sure it is not too much?"

"No, I don't think so," Alyssa replied. She remained silent for several moments, and then said brightly, "You know, this will be my very first ball, Morgan."

He looked startled for a second, and then pulled Alyssa to her feet. He put his arms around her waist and squeezed her against him. "I shall be deeply honored to escort you, my lady."

She kissed his neck and snuggled against him. "I just want you to be proud of me, Morgan," she whispered, a slight edge of doubt in her voice.

"I have always been proud of you, love," he told her firmly, clasping her more tightly to him.

He felt her move her head against his shoulder, and

then she stiffened noticeably in his arms. He looked down, his eyes following her line of vision to the papers on the desk.

"Would you care to explain to me, Your Grace," Alyssa said as she struggled to escape his arms, "why you have added Madeline Duponce and her brother, Henri, to the guest list?"

Morgan refused to release her, holding her tighter, lightly stroking her back, and trying to formulate his response.

"I am waiting," Alyssa remarked coldly.

"They attended the ball last year," Morgan said, his voice vague. This time he allowed Alyssa to remove herself from his arms. She stood back from him and tilted her chin defiantly.

"Not good enough," she stated succinctly. "You must know I created this year's list starting with those guests invited last year. Obviously I removed the Duponces."

"They must attend," Morgan said in a flat tone.

Alyssa's eyes widened, but she did not back down. "I see they are also invited to spend the night. Why?"

"They must attend," Morgan repeated, refusing to meet his wife's eyes.

"No," Alyssa blurted out, folding her arms across her chest.

Morgan turned to her with a chilling stare, disapproval marring his handsome features. "I am the master of this house, madam. You will do as I say."

Alyssa did not draw back, refusing to be intimidated. "I am not your servant, sir. I am your wife. And mistress of this house. I refuse to have that woman in my home unless you can provide a reasonable explanation for it."

Morgan's expression of severity changed to one of resignation as he accepted defeat. Alyssa was correct. She did have the right to know his reasons.

"Sit down, Alyssa," Morgan instructed. "I have much to tell you." He began his tale with his first meeting with Lord Castlereagh and ended with his plans to trap the Falcon on the night of the ball.

Alyssa said nothing while Morgan spoke, her mind absorbing all the incredible details. "You don't actually believe Tristan is involved in any of this?" Alyssa asked when Morgan had finished.

He shook his head. "Of course not."

"Will it be safe here at Ramsgate? For Katherine? And Grandmother?"

"Yes. I have already added several extra guards, and plan on increasing their numbers on the night of the ball."

"I must confess, Morgan, I find it all very . . ."

"Unbelievable?" he supplied. "I share your feelings, my dear."

"Are you sure that neither of the Duponces is the Falcon?"

"I am not completely certain, but I do believe they are merely accomplices. It is impossible for them to have removed all the various papers I planted. They simply did not have the opportunity."

"What about the servants?"

"No," Morgan insisted. "Again there was not access to both my residences, not to mention the papers at Westgate Manor."

Alyssa sat up sharply, understanding dawning. "So that's what those important papers in the library desk were. French spies at Westgate," she mused, shaking her head. "I suppose we owe the Falcon a debt of gratitude."

"How on earth did you reach that bizarre conclusion, madam?"

"If you did not have to search for the hidden documents in the old desk, you never would have returned to Westgate Manor. In a way, the Falcon is responsible for our marriage."

Morgan gave a snort of laughter. "I shall be sure to inform him of that interesting fact when we finally meet."

"Are you sure your plan will work?" Alyssa asked, realizing Morgan had left unanswered her question about the Falcon's identity. Clearly he had a suspect in mind.

"I have great faith in this trap. The bait I will leave will be too irresistible for the Falcon to ignore. Besides, if my suspicions are correct, the Falcon will already be here at the castle. It will merely be a case of catching him in the act."

Alyssa met his eyes squarely, her expression grave. "Whom do you suspect, Morgan?"

"Gilbert Grantham, Caroline's brother," he responded heavily. "I hate to brand any man traitor, but I know how enamored Gilbert is with Madeline Duponce. Men have been known to do foolish things in the name of love."

"My God," Alyssa said, her voice low. "Poor Caroline and Priscilla. They speak so fondly of their brother."

"I have yet to prove my theory. And there is one other possibility, although it is almost too ridiculous to entertain," he muttered to himself. Gathering Alyssa into his arms Morgan stated firmly, "You are not to worry about this, Alyssa. I will take care of everything."

"I trust you, Morgan," she replied quietly. "If there is anything I can do to help you . . . ?"

"No," Morgan insisted, his voice stern. "I will not have you exposed to any danger. You must promise me that you will not interfere."

"I will do as you request, Morgan," Alyssa said, avoiding his eyes. She had no intention of staying out of things if she saw Morgan in trouble. "But you will be careful, won't you?"

"Of course," he answered automatically. He leaned down and began kissing her. "I think you have been working too hard on this party, love."

"Oh, do you now?" Alyssa laughed throatily. Morgan tenderly nibbled her ear.

"As your husband I would be remiss in my duties if I did not insist you put the preparations for the ball aside for a time," Morgan said. Running his fingers lightly down her waist and over her hips he sighed. "I believe a bit of bed rest is in order."

"If you join me in the bed, Your Grace," she teased, "I shall never get any rest."

"Afterward, my love. Afterward."

Chapter Twenty-two

Three weeks later Alyssa stood next to Morgan, her face expressionless, as she was introduced to Caroline's family. The Granthams arrived at Ramsgate Castle early on the morning of the ball, accompanied by Tristan and Caroline. Lady Grantham, a small, stout woman, gushed endlessly over Alyssa, congratulating her on both her marriage and the birth of Katherine, while Baron Grantham, Caroline's father, merely grumbled his salutation and began an earnest conversation with Morgan about horses.

Priscilla greeted Alyssa as if they were old friends, and then introduced her brother, Gilbert. Alyssa forced a friendly smile, trying to picture the pleasant young man as a notorious French spy. She could not.

Alyssa excused herself from the group to attend to the many last-minute entertaining details. The dowager duchess immediately offered her assistance and they left the drawing room together.

"I thought I would scream like a madwoman if I had to listen to any more of Lady Grantham's mindless chatter," the dowager duchess exclaimed. "Thank goodness you rescued me."

Alyssa smiled fondly at the dowager duchess. "You might change your opinion and decide to run screaming from me," Alyssa informed the dowager with a laugh. "I intend to put you to work."

"Fine," the older woman readily agreed. "I will do anything you wish, and gladly, as long as I don't have to entertain the Granthams."

"We shall assign Tristan the task of amusing his in-laws," Alyssa decided. "I'll also ask him and Caroline to greet any other early arriving guests so I won't be constantly interrupted today. Will you please check the music selections so I can give the musicians their final instructions later this evening?"

Alyssa sorted through the various papers on her writing table, handing the dowager duchess the list of musical selections. "Anything else?" the dowager duchess inquired as she began reading the paper.

Alyssa paused a moment before answering. "I cannot think of anything, yet I know I will have dozens of questions the minute you leave."

"Don't worry so much, Alyssa," the dowager duchess insisted. She reached out and patted the younger woman's shoulder. I know everything will be perfect tonight. If you have further need of me I shall be in the nursery with Katherine." She leaned over and gave Alyssa a small kiss on the cheek for encouragement before leaving the room.

The remainder of the day passed in a blur for Alyssa as she constantly checked and rechecked all the arrangements. She knew she was being overbearing when Burke suggested for the third time she needed to rest before the ball and, finally taking his hint, she retreated to her bedchamber.

While Alyssa was waiting for the tub to be filled for

her bath, Morgan walked into the room carrying a plate of food.

"I brought you a light respite," Morgan explained, munching on a handful of grapes. "I strongly suspect you have been far too busy to eat a proper meal."

"Thank you, Morgan," Alyssa said gratefully, biting into a hunk of cheddar cheese. "I have been busy and too on edge today to eat very much." They ate the food in companionable silence, watching the two young footmen fill Alyssa's bathtub with hot water.

"I'll assist the duchess with her bath, Janet," Morgan told the maid who was hovering expectantly near the waiting bathwater.

Alyssa gave Morgan a stern look. "It will take me hours to complete my bath if you help me, Morgan," she told her grinning husband. "Today of all days I do not have time to dawdle."

Morgan feigned a wounded expression and popped the last piece of dried fruit into his mouth. "I was under the impression you appreciated my talents as a lady's maid, madam."

"Oh, Morgan." Alyssa sighed. "Please stop. I am far too nervous to cope with your teasing." She turned her back to him. "Now help me off with my dress before the water grows cold."

He deliberately waited until she was comfortably settled in the tub before making his next statement. "The Duponces have arrived."

"Have they?" Alyssa responded in high voice. She played fitfully with the chunk of lavender-scented soap. "I assume they are comfortably settled in their rooms?"

"I suppose," Morgan answered with indifference. "I had Burke show them to their chambers. I made certain they are sleeping in a separate wing from the Granthams. It will make it more challenging for them to remain in contact with the Falcon."

Alyssa shook her head. "I still find this all very difficult to believe," she said. "Are you sure about all of this? Gilbert seems to be a decent sort of man."

"Men are not often what they appear to be, Alyssa," he responded lightly.

"Neither are women," she muttered under her breath, and then flashed him a winning smile. "Please send Janet in to help me wash my hair, Morgan. It is getting late and I need time to get ready for this evening so I can properly dazzle our guests."

"I am the only one you need to impress, love," he said in a quiet voice. "And you have already done that to perfection."

She felt her waning confidence soar at his remark. "Thank you, Morgan," she whispered. She put her arms around his neck and pulled him down for a kiss. She gave him a sweet, gentle kiss, but Morgan demanded more. He could feel her breasts rubbing enticingly against his chest, dampening his shirt, and it aroused his passions. He thrust his tongue forcefully into her mouth, giving her a hot, hard kiss.

Alyssa finally broke away from him, her breath raspy, grateful she was sitting down because her knees felt weak with desire. Morgan's smoldering gaze caught and held her deep green eyes. Slowly, tantalizingly, he stood on his feet and began taking off his clothes. Alyssa finally found her voice after he had thrown his shirt on the floor and was making short work of his boots.

"Morgan, please," she murmured, not certain if she was pleading with him to cease or hurry. Naked, his taut, muscular body hardened with desire, he reached down into the tub and scooped her out of the water. Alyssa clung to his neck as he whispered words of erotic longing in her ear. He placed her slippery, wet body on the thick rug before the fireplace, his hands stroking her hips and thighs, igniting her desires to a fever pitch. He teased her with his hands and tongue until she arched herself against him, pleading silently with him to release her from the burning agony.

Morgan positioned himself above her and thrust into her in one powerful motion, and she welcomed him, tightening her muscles as the climax immediately claimed her. He continued to pump against her, seeking his own fulfillment, and she wantonly encouraged him, stroking his back, biting his shoulder, whispering the titillating words of lovemaking he had taught her, until he found his own release.

Morgan collapsed on top of her, exhausted but totally contented. He felt Alyssa shiver and realized she was still wet from her bath. He reluctantly left her, pulling down the warm towel on the rack in front of the fire to dry her.

"You realize, of course, my hair is as tangled as a rat's nest," she said with mild reproach in her voice.

"I think you look utterly charming, my dear," he answered, grinning. "And totally sated."

"Stop looking so smug, Morgan," she continued in the same tone. "I shall have to take another bath, and since my water is now cold, fresh water will have to be heated. It will most likely delay your washing."

Morgan smiled at her. "But I already instructed Dickinson to see to my bathwater. I suspect the servants are filling a tub in my chamber as we speak."

"Perfect. Clearly the only fair solution to this dilemma is my joining you in your bath, Your Grace," Alyssa declared, standing up and adjusting her towel.

Morgan leered at her, a seductive grin on his handsome face. "You are such a practical woman, Alyssa. I do believe it is one of the reasons I love you so much."

Comte Henri Duponce opened the door soundlessly and slipped quietly into the bedchamber, effectively startling its occupant.

"God's blood," a voice from the shadows muttered. "What the hell are you doing in here?"

"I need to finalize the instructions for our plans this evening," Henri explained. "That is unless you have changed your mind, Falcon?"

"You should have waited for me to contact you, idiot," the Falcon hissed. "What if someone had seen you come into my bedchamber?"

Henri shrugged his shoulders. "No one did," he replied. He strolled casually across the room and draped himself in a chair before the fire. "You should not be so concerned about your reputation, cheri."

The Falcon whirled on Henri, resisting the impulse to strike him. "I have not come this far, my dear Comte Duponce, to be compromised by the likes of you. This mission is far too important to risk having our secrets uncovered by your carelessness."

Henri smiled lazily at the Falcon. "You realize, of course, the duke could be setting a trap for us."

The Falcon gave Henri a bland stare. "Naturally I have considered the possibility. In fact I do believe I shall be disappointed if Morgan does not attempt to catch us this evening. I know the duke thinks he is very clever, but he has been unsuccessful in all of his previous attempts at discovering my identity. Besides, the prize he dangles before us is too great to neglect."

"Yes," Henri agreed, rubbing his hands together greedily. "I imagine Wellington's specifications for a spring campaign will bring a large price."

"You must exercise great caution tonight," the Falcon insisted. "If by some chance we are discovered, we must make good our escape."

"Have all the arrangements been made?" Henri asked.

"Yes," the Falcon responded. "There will be a boat waiting for us on the beach if it becomes necessary. I expect Madeline to act her part perfectly tonight. It is imperative she keep Morgan occupied tonight. I still do not think he suspects I am a spy, but he will have his guard up."

"Don't worry about Madeline," Henri said. "She knows very well how to pique a man's interest. But what about the new duchess? Will she not demand her husband's attention?"

"The duchess will be too busy playing hostess to concern herself with her husband. She might become jealous of Madeline's monopolizing Morgan's time, but Alyssa will not make a scene. It is not in her nature."

"You seem very certain," Henri said lightly.

"I am," the Falcon insisted in a commanding tone. "But it is a smart idea for you to keep a watch on the duchess. I will hold you responsible if she tries to interfere." Henri nodded in understanding. "Now get out of here. And for God's sake, make sure no one sees you."

A noticeable hush descended over the crush of guests in the enormous ballroom as Morgan led Alyssa out to the middle of the dance floor. She had finally succeeded in conquering her nerves as the last of the introductions to her numerous guests ended. Yet as every eye in the crowded room turned toward them, Alyssa felt her insides begin to churn.

Morgan, regally composed and arrogant, looked down at his radiant wife possessively. She had greeted their guests with elegance and dignity, but as she stood with him now, he could feel her nervousness. He took her into his arms and waited. Alyssa gripped Morgan's hand tightly and placed her hand upon his shoulder, precisely the way he had instructed. She kept her gaze focused intently on the gold buttons of his black evening jacket, mentally reviewing the steps of the dance as she waited for the music to begin.

The silence continued. She raised her head and looked up into Morgan's eyes, the tranquil expression on her face revealing none of her inner panic. "Why aren't the musicians playing?" she whispered frantically.

A smile tugged at Morgan's lips, and he met her gaze with mischief in his eyes. "They are waiting for my signal, love."

Alyssa wanted to throttle him, but she dared not express her exasperation with so many people watching their slightest movement. "Morgan, will you please give your signal before I faint from nerves?" she said through her teeth, her mouth frozen in an unreal smile.

"Have patience, madam," Morgan retorted. "I want to savor this moment as I am held here, spellbound by my stunningly beautiful wife."

Alyssa seriously contemplated kicking him in the shin at that moment, but as she read the sincere admiration in his eyes, her ire, along with her nerves, melted. Taking a deep breath, she dazzled him with a brilliant smile and announced, "I am ready now, Morgan."

He pulled her even closer, and then the music started and they were moving and twirling around the room. Alyssa heard several audible gasps, but she could not be sure if it was because of how scandalously close Morgan held her, or because they had opened the ball with a waltz.

It was the dowager duchess's suggestion that the dancing begin with the controversial waltz: she insisted it would be a clever idea to give the gossips something juicy to focus their disapproval on, instead of commenting on Morgan's very sudden marriage and Katherine's almost immediate birth after that marriage.

Alyssa was glad she had agreed. While she had never

been formally taught the many intricate steps of the more traditional dances, the steps of the waltz were fairly simple to master. She glided effortlessly along the floor, thoroughly enjoying the feel of being held in Morgan's arms. He danced, as he did most things, with unconscious grace and style, and she was content to merely follow his expert lead.

"Have I told you, love," he whispered delicately in her ear, "how truly splendid you look this evening?"

Alyssa blushed faintly under his praise. She knew the simple white silk gown she wore emphasized her willowy height and brilliantly showcased her magnificent jewels. She wore the entire emerald-and-diamond ensemble tonight—necklace, earrings, and tiara—not caring if it was a bit extreme. Morgan had given her these jewels with love, and she treasured them far beyond their considerable monetary value.

"I am pleased to inform you I am actually enjoying myself this evening," she admitted shyly.

He smiled lovingly down at her. "So am I," he said. "But I am afraid our delight will come to an end along with our dance."

Alyssa frowned, knowing he spoke the truth. Morgan had warned her repeatedly this afternoon he would spend a large part of the ball in the company of Madeline Duponce.

"You will be careful, Morgan," Alyssa requested, wide-eyed with concern, as the strains of the waltz came to an end.

"Of course," he said. "Try to relax and enjoy yourself. If we are lucky, this whole thing will be over very quickly. And successfully."

After escorting Alyssa off the dance floor, Morgan brought her to a corner of the room where Tristan and the dowager duchess chatted with a small group of guests. The duke bowed low, formally kissing his wife's hand in farewell. "Keep a close eye on her, Tris,' Morgan instructed his younger brother, and then he disappeared into the crowd.

Chapter Twenty-three

Morgan is only playing a part, Alyssa reminded herself as Madeline let out another throaty laugh. When Alyssa had first been introduced to Mlle Duponce, she felt proud of her display of only mild curiosity upon finally meeting her nemesis, and inwardly chided herself for ever being so irrationally jealous of the tiny French woman. As the evening progressed, however, Alyssa was having difficulty keeping up her nonchalant air and the pretense that all was normal. Each flirtatious gesture Madeline bestowed on the seemingly mesmerized Morgan set Alyssa's teeth on edge.

To make matters worse, Comte Henri Duponce had attached himself to her side in the absence of Morgan's attention, and Alyssa was annoyed by his persistent company. She found his manner bold and unappealing, his flippant remarks offensive. After several unsuccessful attempts at removing herself from the comte, she gratefully spotted Baron Welles on the far side of the crowded room. Alyssa hastily excused herself and strode purposefully toward him, temporarily losing the comte in the process.

After speaking briefly with the baron she scanned the room, noticing Morgan and Madeline leaving the ballroom together. Gilbert was nowhere to be seen, but Alyssa noted with alarm that Henri immediately followed his sister and the duke. Alyssa also joined in the chase, and she observed Henri entering the duke's private study.

Alyssa panicked for a moment, fearful Morgan might be in some sort of danger. She stood in front of the study door for several minutes, debating her course of action. She listened intently, pressing her ear against the hardwood door, yet she heard nothing. Bracing herself for a confrontation of some kind, Alyssa unceremoniously yanked the door open.

Henri had his back toward her and was obviously searching the deserted room.

"Is something amiss?" Alyssa inquired in a steady voice. Her eyes scanned the room in confusion, searching for Morgan and Madeline. She could have sworn she saw them enter the room.

Alyssa's voice startled Henri and he jumped, turning quickly at the sound to determine the source.

"Your Grace," Henri said with obvious relief in his voice. "I didn't hear you come in."

"Are you looking for something?"

"Not precisely," Henri answered evasively. "Have you seen my sister, Madeline, or your husband recently? I thought I saw them come in here."

"The last time I saw your sister she was dancing with Gilbert Grantham," Alyssa lied boldly. "I'm sure she is with him."

Henri gave her a cold stare. "You must be mistaken. The duke has hardly let Madeline out of his sight all

338

evening. I know I saw them come in here. Where could they have gone?"

"If they did enter the study, which I doubt, they have obviously departed," Alyssa replied sweetly, her eyes flashing angrily at his attempt to humiliate her by mentioning Morgan's attentive behavior to another woman. "I am sure we will be able to locate them in the ballroom. Would you escort me back, please?" As much as she disliked Henri's company, she preferred he be with her rather than harassing Morgan.

Defeated, Henri began to leave with Alyssa, but before closing the door behind him he gave the room another hard glance.

"Look, that door is ajar," Henri cried, his finger pointing toward the door. "They must have gone outside."

"In this cold?" Alyssa questioned unbelievingly. "I am certain you are mistaken, Comte. The wind must have blown the door open."

"Well, I intend to find out," he told her, heading for the open door.

Alyssa hesitated a fraction of a second before following. "If you insist on pursuing this, Comte, then I will accompany you."

"As you wish," Henri replied with an indifferent air.

He hurried out into the cold, misty night with Alyssa close on his heels. They followed the garden path that ran the length of the house, their way eerily illuminated by the full moon. Their feet made a crunching sound on the gravel as they walked silently along at a brisk pace.

"There doesn't appear to be anyone out here," Alyssa said after a few minutes. "Let's return to the ballroom before we are missed." Alyssa was beginning to doubt the wisdom of her actions as the cold wind cut through the thin material of her gown, and she realized dismally how very alone she was with this dangerous man.

"Wait. I think I heard something," Henri cried.

They both paused and listened intently.

"I didn't hear anything," Alyssa insisted nervously. "I am sure the duke and Mlle Duponce are not outside in this frigid cold. I am returning to the house before I freeze. You may do as you please, Comte Duponce." Alyssa turned and walked away from Henri, determined to put as much distance between them as she could.

A loud crash halted her steps. "What was that?" Alyssa questioned automatically.

"It sounded as though it came from up there." Henri pointed to a window on the second floor of the west wing. He saw the sudden flash of fear in Alyssa's eyes. Moving quickly next to her, he menacingly grabbed hold of her wrist. "I think, Duchess, you know far more about Madeline and myself than you should."

"I do not have the slightest idea what you are referring to, Comte Duponce," Alyssa replied in her most regal imitation of the dowager duchess. "Remove your hands this instant."

For a split second, Alyssa thought she had succeeded with her bluff, but the comte narrowed his eyes at her in anger. "There must be a side entrance," he decided, his eyes searching the length of the castle. "Show me."

Realizing there was no other alternative, Alyssa reluctantly complied. When they reached the entrance, Henri pulled her through the side door and into the house. They walked down the deserted hall to the back staircase, Henri's grip on Alyssa tightening with each step.

The hallway lamps were lit, but because of the party there were no servants in this section of the house. Alyssa paused momentarily at the bottom of the steps, but Henri tugged insistently on her arm. With a sigh, she gathered up her silk skirts and hastened up the staircase, her heart pounding with fear at what she might discover.

They paused when they reached the second-floor landing, barely breathing as they listened for further clues.

"I think the noise came from that door," Henri declared, indicating the first room on his left.

"That is the estate room," Alyssa told him, worrying it might be where Morgan had hidden the documents he wanted the Falcon to steal.

Walking to the doorway, Henri slowly turned the latch. Throwing open the door suddenly, he thrust Alyssa inside the room ahead of him. She faltered a bit but regained her balance and quickly scanned the room.

"Morgan," she cried, rushing across the thick carpet toward the duke. He lay slumped on the floor, apparently alone in the room. "What happened? Morgan, are you hurt?" She pulled him up from the floor into a sitting position. He shook his head groggily, his face pale.

"Alyssa?" he questioned, blinking his eyes rapidly. Morgan gingerly rubbed the back of his head, wincing slightly as he touched a tender lump on his scalp. "Someone must have struck me from behind. How on earth did you find me? Are you alone?"

"Comte Duponce is with me," she answered in a warning tone. She moved to the side so Morgan could see Henri, who stood by the door.

Henri hesitated only a moment before striding into the room. He reached down, roughly pulling Alyssa away from her husband.

"I hate to interrupt such a charming little domestic scene, but I have business to attend to. Such a pity you have become involved, Duchess. Now I shall have to kill you, along with your husband."

"Leave her out of this, Duponce," Morgan said dangerously, standing on his feet.

"I am afraid she is already in it, Your Grace. We cannot possibly make good our escape if she informs the authorities. The risk is too great."

Alyssa struggled furiously against Henri's hold, successfully breaking away from him. Morgan took advantage of the momentary diversion to lunge for the rapiers hung over the fireplace. He managed to grasp one, but as he dislodged it, the second sword also fell from the wall. Henri quickly retrieved it.

He gave Morgan a sly grin. "I knew you would not go to your death without a fight. It shall give me great pleasure to cut you to ribbons while your lovely wife watches," Henri cried, lunging toward Morgan.

As the contest began, Alyssa retreated to a corner of the room, her eyes darting about for a means of escape. She watched breathlessly as the swords flashed back and forth, the meeting of steel against steel ringing through the room. Each clanging noise vibrated through her, and she stood transfixed, watching the men circle each other, testing for weakness, determining each other's measure.

Facing each other, their physical differences were instantly apparent. Morgan was taller and had a larger, more powerful frame than the willowy Henri. Alyssa hoped Morgan's obvious strength would give him the advantage, but even her untrained eye could discern Henri was an expert swordsman, graceful and swift. Helplessly she watched them battle, the swords seeming to move with a life of their own, blurring in a quick flurry of movement.

In minutes both men were tiring and panting for breath as sweat lined their brows. She watched them lock together again and again, their arms straining, faces grimacing, muscles rippling. Continually, Henri took the offensive and Morgan somehow managed to parry, but Alyssa could see Morgan was beginning to slow down. She knew the blow he had suffered to his head had dazed him, and he wasn't at full strength.

The taunting comments streaming from Henri's foul mouth set her nerves on edge, but they were answered only by an occasional grunt from Morgan. Alyssa wondered how long they could continue the fight with the same intensity, as they chased each other about the room, grim concentration and determination etched in their faces.

Suddenly Morgan tripped over a fallen chair. He stumbled back, losing his footing and dropping his guard. Henri pressed the advantage, thrusting mightily forward, his blade finding its mark in Morgan's right shoulder. Morgan rolled quickly out of the path of the sword before Henri could strike a second time. Miraculously Morgan regained his balance, resuming a ready stance.

"Tiring so quickly, Your Grace?" Henri taunted as they continued their battle.

Terrified, Alyssa watched the small stain of blood on Morgan's shoulder spread rapidly at each thrust of his sword. She saw the white lines around his mouth, his face tightening in pain. She knew he could not fight much longer with such a strategically inflicted wound. Frantically her eyes darted about the room, coming to rest on Morgan's desk. She remembered him telling her that, as a precaution, he often kept a pistol hidden in the drawer of his desk. Keeping a watchful eye on the dueling men, she inched her way over to the desk and pulled open a drawer. Nothing. Frowning with distress she continued her unobtrusive search of the desk drawers, her eyes never leaving Morgan and Henri.

She sighed with grateful relief when she at last discovered the weapon. Slowly she grasped the handle of the long pistol, gripping it tightly, her fingers sweating. Unseen, she pulled it from the drawer and held it hidden at her side, out of sight in the folds of her gown. Swallowing hard, she eased back the hammer, praying the gun was loaded, and waited with mounting dread for the moment she feared would eventually come.

Even though Henri too seemed to be tiring, he continued to mount an aggressive attack. Then Henri stumbled slightly, his movements momentarily clumsy, and Morgan's thrust caught the edge of Henri's sword. With a powerful flick of the wrist, Morgan sent the weapon flying across the room, effectively disarming his adversary. Alyssa let out a tremendous sigh of relief, but her joy was premature; she saw Henri reach inside his coat and withdraw a small pistol. Instinctively knowing he would show no mercy, Alyssa acted swiftly.

Automatically she swung the pistol up and steadying the weapon with both hands, fired, praying her shot would hit the right man. There was a deafening noise and an almost blinding flash of light and smoke. Henri turned toward Alyssa, his face a mixture of surprise and confusion, as he crumpled to the floor in a heap. His gun flew out of his grasp as he hit the ground.

Alyssa watched him in horror, her eyes wide with disbelief. She staggered back, dropping the pistol to the floor as if it were burning her hands, and brought her palms up over her ears to stop the constant ringing.

"Good lord, I've killed him," she whispered, Henri's shocked expression as he fell haunting her mind. Her knees buckled and she leaned back against the wall, sinking to the floor. She turned frightened eyes to Morgan, and he quickly reached her side, his strong arms encircling her and raising her to her feet.

"Christ," Morgan swore loudly. "Alyssa, are you all right?"

"My God, Morgan," Alyssa cried, her voice choked with emotion as she held on to him tightly, seeking comfort in his crushing embrace. "He was going to shoot you. I had to try to stop him. But I truly did not mean to . . . to . . ."

Morgan kissed her gently. He stroked her hair and tried to soothe her. "Alyssa, love, don't upset yourself. You haven't killed anyone."

"What!" she shouted in disbelief. She pulled back from the security of Morgan's arms to look again at Henri's inert form. "He is not moving, Morgan."

"True," Morgan confirmed with a rascal's grin, relief spreading through his aching body. "But he is breathing." He hugged Alyssa tightly against him, thankful they were both still alive. "I must admit, madam, you never fail to astound me. I never knew what an excellent shot you were."

Alyssa stiffened in his arms, almost afraid to reveal the truth. "Actually, Morgan, I have never fired a pistol before in my life."

"Bloody hell!" Morgan cried in amazement. "Your shot might have gone anywhere. It could have even hit me instead."

"A risk I was forced to take," she told him philosophically. "I suppose it was a miracle my bullet did find the right mark."

"Unfortunately I recall all too well a time when you might have preferred your shot to strike me," Morgan retorted, lifting her chin.

"Probably," she admitted, tears forming in her eyes as she realized for the first time the dire consequences her actions could have had.

"I love you, Alyssa," Morgan said solemnly. He placed a soft kiss on her cheek.

"I love you too, Morgan," she responded. She sighed

deeply and closed her eyes, trying to regain command of the whole nightmare of events. "What shall we do with Henri?"

"I know of several willing officials here tonight who will gladly take him off our hands." Morgan grimaced with pain as he tried to move his bleeding shoulder.

"You're wounded, Morgan," Alyssa exclaimed when she saw his expression. "It is still bleeding. Come and sit down while I find someone to help us."

"Stop fussing, Alyssa," Morgan replied. He continued to protest, but he sank gratefully down in the chair she provided for him, suddenly feeling lightheaded from the loss of blood.

"I shall go and fetch Baron Welles at once," she decided. "Will you be all right until I return?"

"I am fine," he told her in a quiet voice. "I strongly doubt he will be going anywhere." Morgan inclined his head toward the unconscious comte.

Alyssa reached down and tenderly pushed back the stray lock of dark hair from Morgan's forehead, worried by his pale color and obviously diminishing strength. "I'll be back in a few moments," she told him. She quickly ran from the room. He heard her light footsteps grow faint as she raced down the stairway.

Finally succumbing to exhaustion, Morgan leaned his head back against the wall and drew a deep breath. His mind was in a confused state as he tried to piece together the evening's events. He had left the ballroom with Madeline after observing Gilbert entering his private study. At Madeline's insistence they had entered the room together to investigate. Morgan suspected a trap, but instead had caught Gilbert leaving the room through the French doors. He had given chase, but was struck on the head from behind before catching up with Gilbert. The next thing Morgan remembered was Alyssa's concerned face as she shook him awake in the estate room. He had no recollection of how he had come to be there in the first place.

A sudden commotion at the door interrupted his thoughts. Alyssa came rushing through the door with Baron Welles, Tristan, and several footmen trailing close behind.

"Carry him to his bedchamber," Morgan ordered the servants, pointing to Henri. "And post a guard out front. Baron Welles will attend to him shortly."

"I swear, good brother"—Tristan chuckled as he supervised Henri's removal from the room—"you will go to any lengths to avoid attending a ball."

"Let me examine your wound, Your Grace," Baron Welles demanded, placing a basin of warm water and a roll of bandages on the table beside Morgan's chair.

"Allow me," Tristan said. He pulled out a blade and cut away the blood-soaked evening coat and fine linen shirt surrounding the wound. It was an angry red gash, but the wound was clean and not too deep. The blood barely flowed.

"There doesn't appear to be much damage," Baron Welles reported. He quickly and expertly bandaged the shoulder. "I'm sure it will cause you a bit of stiffness for a few days, but you will recover." Baron Welles addressed his last comments to the worried Alyssa.

"Thank you," Morgan said to the doctor, gingerly moving his arm and testing its strength. "Tristan, I need your help."

"Of course." Tristan responded immediately to the urgency in Morgan's tone. Before Morgan had an opportunity to voice his commands, Burke entered the room in obvious distress.

"You must come quickly, Your Grace," Burke said to the duke. "There is a loud commotion on the beach."

"Morgan, wait," Alyssa cried as the duke bounded out of the room. "You'll catch your death in the cold night air." Her warning went unheeded. She huffed in annoyance, but followed resolutely behind Tristan and Morgan.

Flaming torches of fire cast an unreal illumination on the scene at the beach. Upon their arrival, Morgan quickly received a report from one of his security men.

"We surprised the trio before they had a chance to reach their boat," the man informed him. "They refused to come with us, and we were afraid to rush them. We await your orders, Your Grace."

The events near the shore appeared to be at a stalemate. Several of Morgan's security men had formed a semicircle a fair distance away from three cloaked figures who stood on the enormous gray rocks that edged the beach. The three were poised on the edge of one of the steep cliffs, away from the winding path that led to the sand below, effectively trapped.

"What is going on here?" a voice behind them cried. Alyssa shrieked loudly as she turned around and faced Gilbert Grantham.

Tristan placed a reassuring arm on Alyssa's shoulder. "It is only Gilbert, Alyssa," he said in a calm voice.

At his words, Morgan turned sharply and faced Gilbert. "I'll be damned," the duke muttered in amazement. Gilbert ignored the rather unorthodox greeting and called out to the trio on the cliff, recognizing Madeline's cloaked figure.

"Madeline, are you hurt?"

"No," came the reply. "Tell these men to back away, Gilbert. We want no trouble."

"Gilbert, go find Tristan," a second voice cried out in distress.

"Caroline?" Tris exclaimed in wonder, squinting in the darkness. Morgan and Alyssa exchanged worried looks.

"Let her go, Priscilla," Morgan shouted. "There is no means of escape. It is over."

"So you are still alive, Morgan," Priscilla screeched. "I must assume, then, that Henri is dead. What a pity."

At her words, Madeline screamed with grief and nearly fell to the dirt. "Stand up straight, you fool," Priscilla commanded. "Your idiot lover might be dead, but I have no intention of sharing his fate. Not when our escape lies only a few feet away."

Sobbing, Madeline regained her balance and took the pistol Priscilla handed her. She turned it on Caroline.

"Priscilla, there is nothing more to be gained by this," Morgan shouted. At his signal, the men moved closer to the women.

"Stop them, Morgan," Priscilla shouted when she saw the men advancing. "Stop them now or Caroline dies."

"Good God," Tristan swore. "What the devil is going on? Did Priscilla just say she was going to kill her sister?"

"Morgan," Caroline cried out in fear. "Please, you must do what Priscilla asks."

"No," Morgan responded sternly, but he held his hand up, effectively halting the further advance of his security men. "I have not tracked the Falcon this far to have her escape."

"Ha," Priscilla laughed hauntingly. "Don't act so smug, Morgan. You did not discover my true identity until this very moment. I'm sure you thought Gilbert or even your dear brother Tristan was the culprit."

"You are right of course, Priscilla," Morgan responded. He turned and whispered to Tristan. "I'll try to distract her. If you can reach the beach, do you think you can scale the rocks on the side of the cliff and disarm her?"

"Yes," Tristan replied. "Even though I don't have the damnedest idea what is going on."

"I will accompany you," Gilbert interjected, and at

Morgan's nod of approval the two men began to make their way to the path on the far side leading to the sandy beach below.

Morgan again turned his attention to the women. "You have been far too clever for me, Priscilla," he yelled. "That is why I know you are intelligent enough to realize you are captured. Surrender now, before someone else gets hurt."

"Never," she exclaimed with passion. "We both know I am as good as dead if I surrender to the authorities. Spying is, after all, a treasonable offense. I have nothing to lose and everything to gain. Now move these men out of my way at once."

Morgan signaled the men to drop back, hoping Tristan and Gilbert had reached the shore and were at this moment scaling the rocks. Seeing that Morgan was at a loss for words, Alyssa spoke up.

"Lady Ogden, please," she said beseechingly. "It is fruitless to continue."

When Priscilla opened her mouth to reply, Tristan leapt up from behind the cliff and knocked her to the ground. Gilbert swiftly followed him, and the waiting men on the ridge rushed the women. In a moment it was all over.

Madeline began sobbing and cursing loudly in French while Priscilla remained silent, her body defiantly rigid as she was led away by two men. Caroline collapsed with relief against Tristan, clinging tightly to him, while Gilbert awkwardly patted her arm, trying to offer his sister whatever comfort he could.

Alyssa shivered as the wind swirled, her arms numb from the cold. She tugged on Morgan's sleeve and he put his arm around her, suddenly feeling the biting wind. "Come, love," he whispered. "The Falcon is finally unmasked. Let us return to the house before we freeze."

Chapter Twenty-four

Alyssa sat in a chair before the fireplace in Morgan's bedchamber, wrapped in a soft quilt. Absently she sipped the mulled wine Mavis had prepared for her, wondering if she would ever feel warm again. Off in the distance she heard a clock chime, and she decided if Morgan did not appear soon she would go and fetch him herself, despite the late hour.

The door opened and Alyssa raised her head expectantly, but it was only Dickinson. "Aren't they finished yet?" she questioned Morgan's valet as he walked over to the heavy mahogany armoire and began methodically rearranging Morgan's clothes.

"The duke is still in conference with several government officials," Dickinson explained. "And Mrs. Keenly has just completed serving a second late-night buffet. It appears the guests do not wish the ball to end."

Alyssa smiled at the censure in Dickinson's voice when he spoke of the party. "I suppose I haven't been a very congenial hostess, have I, Dickinson?"

"No, Your Grace," he answered. "But fortunately I don't believe the guests have noticed."

Alyssa's response was interrupted by Morgan's sudden entrance.

"At last," she exclaimed, jumping up from her perch. The quilt fell to the ground and she ran to Morgan, her silk nightgown glimmering in the firelight.

"Brandy, Dickinson," Morgan instructed his valet in a tired voice. He gathered Alyssa into his arms and held her tight. "I am exhausted."

"How is your shoulder?" Alyssa asked with concern. "I promised Baron Welles I would change the bandage and put this bascilicum powder on it. He also gave me some laudanum if you need it. Are you in pain?"

Morgan's shoulder felt on fire, but he preferred not to drug himself until he had spoken to Alyssa. "I'll take some laudanum before we go to sleep tonight," he told her.

"Come lie down on the bed and let me tend your wound, Morgan," Alyssa coaxed.

Morgan allowed Alyssa to help him off with his coat. Underneath, he still wore his ripped and bloody shirt. She removed that also, and then gently cleaned and rewrapped the wound. She left his side to rummage through his dresser drawer, finally finding what she sought. She returned just as he was taking off his breeches. He reached out automatically for the garment she handed him, thinking it was his dressing gown. Amused, he held up the garment for inspection.

"What is this?"

"A nightshirt," Alyssa responded in a firm voice. "Now hurry up and put it on before you catch cold."

"But I never wear . . ." Morgan began protesting, but he stopped when he saw her determined face. He donned the garment, too tired to argue.

Morgan sat up comfortably in the bed and patted the empty place beside him. Alyssa scrambled up next to him and snuggled close. Dickinson entered the room with Morgan's brandy, his face expressionless.

"Do you require anything further, Your Grace?"

"Not tonight, Dickinson," Morgan answered.

"Oh, Dickinson," Alyssa called out as the valet reached the bedchamber door. "Please remind Baron Welles to pay a visit to the duke tomorrow morning to check on his condition. I want to be certain his wound is healing properly."

"Yes, Your Grace," Dickinson replied in a bland voice. Then he shut the door firmly behind him.

"I do believe Dickinson is beginning to like me, Morgan," Alyssa said brightly. "Don't you agree?"

Morgan laughed, stopping abruptly at the slice of pain tearing through his shoulder. Alyssa lightly touched his arm. "Please let me pour you some laudanum, Morgan."

"In a moment," he agreed. He downed his brandy and settled back against the pillows. "I know you are curious about what has transpired in my study tonight. If I drink that stuff, I know I will be too lightheaded to make much sense."

"Well, if you feel up to it," Alyssa commented, her curiosity eating away at her. "Is Priscilla really the notorious Falcon?"

"She is indeed." Morgan snorted. "She certainly had everyone fooled, myself included."

"What could have possibly possessed her to do such a horrendous thing?" Alyssa could not keep the amazement out of her voice.

"Money," Morgan stated simply. "It appears she was furious with Lord Ogden's family for cutting her off, and hated having to depend on her tightfisted father for her keep. She met Henri Duponce shortly after her husband's death and was recruited by him to spy for the French. She became so adept she was soon directing the operations."

Alyssa shook her head with disbelief. "How could she become a traitor to her own country, Morgan?"

"Priscilla's conception of loyalty is nonexistent, Alyssa. She discovered a hidden talent within herself and decided to exploit it. She had absolutely no conscience concerning who was injured in the process. Even members of her own family."

"Is that why she falsely implicated Gilbert?" Alyssa asked.

"When the couriers were first discovered to be using the beach here at Ramsgate, she tried to implicate me. When that failed, she turned the evidence on Tristan and Gilbert." Morgan ran his fingers through his hair.

"Was Gilbert ever involved?"

Morgan gave a small grunt of laughter. "It seems Gilbert discovered the evidence implicating me and decided to investigate the matter on his own. It turns out he was never really interested in Madeline Duponce, but merely using her to obtain information."

"Were you able to determine who discovered the papers at Westgate Manor?"

"Priscilla found them. That was how she knew I was persuing the Falcon. She sold the information anyway, knowing it was genuine. Then she decided to plant evidence against Tris and Gilbert in an effort to throw me off her trail."

"But what happened tonight, Morgan? I saw you leave the ball with Madeline, and then you disappeared. How did you end up in the estate room?"

"I saw Gilbert enter my private study. Since I was still under the false impression he was the Falcon, I followed him. I had been glued to Madeline's side all evening, so naturally she came with me. We saw Gilbert leave through the French doors as we entered, and I gave chase, but was hit from behind before I could catch up to him."

"Who hit you?" Alyssa questioned.

"Madeline." Morgan grinned sheepishly. "Gilbert, who was merely going outside for some fresh air, reentered the house without seeing me. Then Priscilla came outside in search of Madeline. She had already successfully retrieved the information I planted and decided it was time to make her escape. The two women dragged me back into the house and left me for Henri to finish off. And he probably would have succeeded if my independent wife had not thankfully decided to intervene."

Alyssa shivered at the memory of the vicious sword fight and held Morgan closer, grateful he had survived with only a shoulder wound. "How did Caroline get involved?"

"Innocently, it appears. Caroline noticed Priscilla and Madeline heading down toward the shore and followed them, thinking something was wrong. She caught up to them just before my men tried to apprehend the women. Priscilla decided to try to use her sister as a shield so she could escape. A small boat was anchored offshore waiting to take Priscilla, Madeline, and Henri away. Presumably to France."

"What will happen to them now?" Alyssa whispered.

"Henri and Madeline know a great deal about the workings of the French intelligence system. If they can provide enough useful information to the War Ministry, their lives may be spared for a time. After that . . ." Morgan's voice trailed off.

"Oh, Morgan," Alyssa whispered, the horror evident in her voice.

"They will be given a fair trial," he insisted. "Several operatives have been killed, not to mention the damage done to our troops by the military information that was sold. Someone must be held accountable."

"And Priscilla?"

"Baron Grantham is a very influential man. He was successful in dissuading Lord Castlereagh from putting his daughter on trial." Morgan sighed heavily. "I have also promised Tristan I will try to persuade the ministry to deport Priscilla to America once the war has ended. Even though a deportation sentence is extremely harsh, at least her life will be spared."

Alyssa shuddered. Although Priscilla's crime was reprehensible, Alyssa could not stomach the idea of having her put to death for it.

"How is Caroline taking all of this?"

"She is truly devastated. Tristan said they would return to Westgate Manor in the morning. He hopes spending time alone together will help her recovery."

"Speaking of recovery," Alyssa prompted. "You had better get some rest yourself." She got up from the bed and poured a substantial dose of laudanum in a glass of water for Morgan. "Drink it," she instructed. "I want to go and check on Katherine. Mavis is sitting with her tonight. I'll be back in a little while."

When Alyssa returned later, Morgan was fast asleep. She watched him as he slept, lightly stroking her fingertips over his jaw. She remembered with fearful clarity how close she had come to losing him tonight, and her eyes filled with tears. Shaking her head, she chased the horror from her mind and slipped between the sheets. She cuddled close to Morgan's warmth, resting her head against his uninjured arm. In minutes she too was sleeping.

The next morning, Alyssa bid good-bye to a tearful Caroline and an uncharacteristically subdued Tristan.

"Promise you will write," Alyssa instructed as she stood alone in the hall with Tristan while Caroline waited in the carriage. "I want you both to return to visit us as soon as Caroline is ready."

"We will," Tristan agreed. "It will take a bit of time for Caroline to accept everything. I believe she is still in shock."

Alyssa felt a lump rise in her throat at his solemn, concerned expression. "I am so sorry, Tris."

"Don't worry, Alyssa. Caroline and I will be fine. Truthfully, I am more concerned about you. Your endurance will be sorely tested in the next few days taking care of my brother. I was with him this morning during Baron Welles's examination. The doctor has prescribed complete bed rest for the next five days. Morgan was most displeased with the idea."

"I can cope with my obstinate duke," she responded. Stepping forward Alyssa opened her arms for Tristan's affectionate hug of farewell. "Godspeed, Tris," she whispered.

Alyssa stood on the front stone steps for a few moments, watching the carriage disappear down the long drive. When the carriage was gone from view she went in search of Mrs. Keenly to compliment the housekeeper on making last night's ball an outstanding success.

Alyssa spent the remainder of the morning bidding her guests farewell, the dowager duchess standing supportively by her side, boldly lying to anyone who inquired about the whereabouts of her two grandsons. Alyssa could tell by the strain in the older woman's eyes she was fully aware of everything that had occurred, but was putting on a marvelous front. Alyssa was fairly amazed that a society that so prized juicy gossip had thus far learned nothing of the tumultuous events of the previous evening. She hoped for Caroline's sake it would remain unknown for a while longer.

After the last of the guests had finally been packed off, the two women went together to check on Morgan. They discovered him propped up in bed, baby Katherine leaning comfortably against his muscular thigh. Morgan was calmly reading a newspaper while the baby chewed furiously on a teething ring. Mavis sat in a nearby chair, keeping an eye on both of them.

"It is about time, madam," Morgan said in a mocking tone. "Our poor child must be starving. She has been gnawing on that ring for the past half hour."

Alyssa merely smiled at her husband and picked up the gurgling baby. As she retreated to a warm corner of the room to nurse her daughter, the dowager duchess sat near the bed, engaging her grandson in earnest conversation.

Katherine's loud belch broke the gentle calm of the room, and the dowager duchess broke off in midsentence to smile at the baby's hearty appetite.

"Now that Katherine is finished, I will accompany her to the nursery," the dowager duchess declared. She rose majestically from her chair and took the baby from Alyssa. Mavis followed them out of the room, clucking something about the proper way to carry a baby.

Alyssa turned her grinning face to Morgan. "You realize, of course, it is just a matter of time before they come to blows over Katherine."

"I am putting my money on Mavis," Morgan declared. "You should have seen the vile stuff she brought for my breakfast this morning. Called it gruel. She refused to bring me a proper meal, insisting I needed to regain my strength."

"How was it?" Alyssa inquired casually, not doubting for a moment Mavis had managed to get her obstinate husband to eat every bite of the porridge.

"Not too bad," Morgan admitted. He scowled suddenly, his face intently studying Alyssa's as she approached the bed. "I'm not going soft, am I? First letting you make me wear this ridiculous nightshirt, next allowing an old woman to bully me into eating invalid food."

"No, Morgan," Alyssa assured him gently, kicking off her shoes and joining him on the bed. "You are merely exercising good judgment in allowing those

358

who love you to care for you properly."

He frowned for a moment, considering her words. "It makes me feel weak, Alyssa. And a bit vulnerable. I don't like it."

"Good lord, Morgan," Alyssa admonished. "You are recovering from a stab wound. The very least we can do is fuss over you for a while." She scowled back at him, then decided to change the subject. "What was Grandmother lecturing you about so enthusiastically?"

He grimaced, remembering the conversation. "She was singing your praises, as usual. And telling me I don't appreciate my wife enough."

Alyssa leaned back against the pillows and crossed her arms over her chest. "Grandmother does have a valid point," she remarked flippantly.

"I know," Morgan agreed, turning on his side to face her. "I haven't appreciated you enough, Alyssa. Or, God help me, shown you how happy I am that you and Katherine are a part of my life." He grinned mockingly. "I suppose my brush with death should change my attitude."

"Will it?"

"A bit," he replied seriously. "After all, Alyssa, you did save my life."

"As you did mine, Morgan, the day you walked into Westgate Manor," she said with all sincerity.

"I know I have hardly been a model husband—" he began, but Alyssa cut him off.

"Our marriage began on a dismal note, Morgan; there is no disputing that fact. But I feel we have made great improvements in our relationship over the past few months. Don't you agree?"

"Yes, I suppose," he answered. "I so want to do everything in my power to make you happy, Alyssa."

Alyssa felt the tears gathering in her eyes at his humble expression. "Do you love me, Morgan?"

"I do," he said in a husky voice. "More than I ever dreamed I could love another human being."

"Then it is enough," she told him simply. "As long as you continue to love me, nothing can ruin our happiness."

He looked deeply into her sea-green eyes and saw her love reflected back at him. He reached over and pulled her head toward him for a soft, inviting kiss.

"You must be very careful not to reinjure your shoulder." Alyssa laughed throatily as he began pulling the pins from her hair. "I am sure Baron Welles would not approve of this, Morgan." Desire darkened her eyes when she looked into his beloved, handsome face.

"Then you know what we must do, my love?" Morgan whispered, pressing lazy kisses on her neck.

"What?" Her voice was barely a whisper.

"We must not inform him," Morgan stated firmly. He pulled her tightly against his chest and proceeded to make sweet, gentle love to his wife.